HEIRESS

APPARENTLY

HEIRESS
APPARENTLY

DIANA MA

AMULET BOOKS · NEW YORK

Images are used courtesy of the following: Jacket and page ii, *center image*, Mercedes deBellard; *center image skyline*, photograph by Xuanyu Han (Getty/1057591360); *bottom left*, JayKay57 (Getty/157473098). Page iii, *clockwise from top left*: *Portrait of a seated woman*, *Portrait of a Chinese aristocrat of Canton*, both courtesy Musee des Arts Asiatiques-Guimet, © RMN-Grand Palais/Art Resource, New York; Mercedes deBellard; Qianlong; Yongzheng (courtesy of the Metropolitan Museum of Art).

Cataloging-in-Publication Data has been applied for and may be obtained from the Library of Congress.

ISBN 978-1-4197-4996-4

Text copyright © 2020 Diana Ma
Illustration by Mercedes DeBellard
Lettering by Jen Wang
Book design by Hana Anouk Nakamura

Printed and bound in U.S.A.
10 9 8 7 6 5 4 3 2 1

ABRAMS The Art of Books
195 Broadway, New York, NY 10007
abramsbooks.com

To my parents, Ma Ching Shu and Ma Chao Chang,
for sharing your stories with me

I'm breaking two cardinal rules tonight. One—never date a competitor for an acting role. Two—never go on a first date that involves competitive sports. So, why am I bowling on a first date with a guy I met in the audition waiting room for a toothpaste commercial?

The answer is simple. Two days ago, Ken Wang strolled into the audition waiting room—seriously channeling that scene in *Always Be My Maybe* when Keanu Reeves walks into the restaurant. Slow-motion coolness, hair swinging, music, and everything.

That's why all my rules flew out of my head.

I wasn't the only one staring, but I was the one Ken approached that day—maybe because I was the only other Asian there. But that's not why he asked me out ten minutes later. *That* had more to do with the intense sparks firing off between us as we talked. So, in a moment of weak-kneed, breathless infatuation, I agreed to go bowling with him.

Now I'm wearing rented bowling shoes that smell like a decaying corpse and doing neck rolls to warm up. Because I'm incredibly competitive. It's why I *have* those two rules about dating and competition in the first place.

Ken flashes me a slow smile that shows off his gleaming white teeth as he prepares to let his ball fly. *With a smile like that, he's going to get the part.* It doesn't even bother me that I'm up for the same role. That's how crushed out I am.

"Strike!" he yells in triumph over the clash of bowling pins. "Might as well give up now, Gemma."

My eyes narrow. I may have lost out on a toothpaste commercial to a guy with the world's most perfect teeth and the kind of smile that makes me shiver down to my toes, but I'm not going to concede defeat in a game of bowling. "You think I'm going to let you win on our first date?" I fake punch him on the shoulder to give myself an excuse to touch him. "It sets a bad precedent."

Ken smiles at me again, and a spurt of pure pleasure rushes through me. *Is it possible to get addicted to a smile?* My stomach flutters madly as I walk over to the rack of bowling balls to make my selection. Not that there's much to choose from. All the balls are scuffed and scratched with the shine beaten out of them, and half of them look like they're a game away from retirement.

It's a Sunday night, and only a few other lanes besides ours are occupied. Bowled Over Alley has seen better days for sure. The lighting is dim, and although smoking is banned in LA, decades of smoke have already seeped into the walls and carpet, making everything gray and dingy. I kind of love that this is where Ken brought me for our first date. He's being himself and not trying to impress me, and I like that.

I heft up a twelve-pound ball that might've been neon pink at one point. It's hard to tell. Regardless of the color, the weight of the ball feels nice and solid in my hands.

"Sure you can handle that?" Ken points to my twelve-pounder.

"Ask me again after I've kicked your ass," I say sweetly. *Maybe I should go easy on the smack talk.* Paul, my ex-boyfriend from high school, used to complain about how competitive I can get.

"I think it's *your* ass that's going to get kicked." Ken's eyebrows lift, making his face wickedly suggestive. "But don't worry. I'll go easy on you."

He's so freaking sexy that the retort on the tip of my tongue almost flies right out of my head. *Almost*. But I just can't let Ken get in a dig like that without a response, no matter how distracted I am by the slow heat simmering in my body. "Contrary to popular belief, size really *doesn't* matter, so when—not *if*—you lose, don't blame it on my balls being bigger than yours." Was that too much? Paul had hated it whenever I said anything even slightly risqué. *It's not like you*, he used to say. Which just goes to show you that he didn't know me at all. Big surprise—Paul and I lasted only three months.

"Ouch!" Ken dramatically clasps a hand to his chest as his eyes light up. "Damn, girl. You give as good as you get."

Grinning like crazy, I soak up Ken's admiration. Maybe bowling on a first date isn't such a bad idea. And maybe I should quit worrying about silly dating rules and be myself. It's just that I don't have much of a dating track record, and I don't want to blow it with Ken. The three months with Paul was my one and only relationship. Guys at my mostly white suburban high school had a certain vision of me—as an innocent, goody-two-shoes Asian girl. And white guys like Paul who were actually into that kind of thing were always disappointed by me. But now that I've left high school and the state of Illinois behind, I hope things will be different.

"I don't want you to get the wrong impression about me." I plunk my ball into the ball return rack. "So I should let you know that I play to win."

"Yeah, I can tell." Ken looks me over slowly. As if he likes what he sees.

Electricity tingles through me. I get the feeling that things *are* going to be different. That I didn't make a mistake in moving to LA after graduating from high school a few weeks ago. For one thing, there wasn't *anyone* as cool as Ken back in Lake Forest, Illinois. So, if it weren't for the smell of ancient smoke and the residue of a thousand previous feet in my shoes—I'd think I was in a dream.

Over the next half hour, Ken and I do more flirting and accidentally, on purpose, bumping into each other. Still, when it's my turn to bowl, I tune out Ken's friendly heckling and snap my attention back to the game. Like I said, I'm competitive.

When Ken takes his turn, we switch roles. I try to distract him with wisecracks, but he stares down the lane with laser focus. Apparently, we're both competitive.

I end up winning by a hair. "And let the gloating commence!" I announce gleefully.

A shadow flits over Ken's face, and anxiety licks at my stomach. Oh no. Please don't let him be like Paul, who never could stand to lose. I'm competitive, but one thing I'm *not* is a sore loser. Good-natured ribbing is part of the fun, but some guys don't seem to think so. Not when they've lost.

On the fly, I convert my fist pump in the air to a shrug. "Beginner's luck." Instantly, I hate myself for doing it. That's how I was with Paul, always worrying about his ego. It's one of the reasons I broke up with him. I swore to myself that I'd never get into another relationship like that.

The shadow disappears from Ken's face. "You won fair and square, so no false modesty, OK?" He opens a can of soda and hands it to me.

Relieved, I accept the soda, and we sit down together on the black vinyl bench. "My friends back home accuse me of being too competitive," I admit. "They've collectively banned me from Monopoly."

Ken laughs. "I'm competitive too. It comes from having Chinese parents." He starts mimicking his parents. "You got a 99 percent on that test? How did everyone else do? Anyone get a 100 percent?"

"Right? I got an A-minus one time, and my mom made me talk to my English teacher about it." To be fair, Mom only did that once, and it was because she thought I deserved better.

"Well, what did you expect?" he teases. "You *did* get the 'Asian D' after all!"

I start cracking up, and it feels *so* good. I never laugh about this kind of thing with my white friends, who wouldn't get the joke. But with Ken, we're sharing an inside joke instead of being the butt of a joke.

"Strict parents, huh?" Ken asks.

"No," I admit. "They pushed me hard to do my best in school, and I had a curfew, but that's about it."

He raises his eyebrows. "So your parents are OK with you coming to LA to be an actress?"

I laugh. "Not exactly." They were less than thrilled that I deferred my college admission to UCLA to pursue my dream. "I mean, they didn't rage or threaten. It was much worse than that." I drop my voice to a theatrical whisper. "They were *disappointed.*"

We talk about our parents a bit more, and then Ken scoots a quarter of an inch closer to me. My shoulders tense in excitement. *Is he going to kiss me?* Instead, he asks, "Hey, do you want to go get some food?"

I swallow my disappointment and tell myself that it's a *good* thing that he actually wants to hang out and get to know me instead of trying to shove his tongue down my throat.

We leave the bowling alley and go to the diner next door, and Ken tells me about driving an Uber and being a gripper on the set of a low-budget rom-com, although what he really wants is what we all want—to be an actor full-time. I consider telling him about the callback I just got for a role I *really* want, but I don't want to jinx my chances, so I keep it to myself for now. Instead, we talk about our chances at getting the part for the toothpaste commercial. "You've got this," I tell him.

"I'm sure you were great in your audition, Gemma." He sounds totally sincere, like he wants this role for me as much as he does for himself.

"I have to admit that I had a hard time making toothpaste seem exciting." My voice turns sultry. "Now in cool mint *and* hot cinnamon."

Ken laughs. "If you said the lines like that, then I'm sure you got the part!" He comes around the table and slides into my side of the booth so that we're almost hip to hip. "Let me try." Staring into my eyes, he says, all low and gravelly, "Toothpaste fresh enough for those special close-up encounters."

My throat feels very dry suddenly. Ken puts his hand on the back of my head, making the hairs on my neck stand on end, and then he slowly pulls me toward him. He kisses my cheek, and one side of his mouth quirks up at my involuntary sigh. Then his lips meet mine.

Our kiss is slow and sweet—everything a first-date kiss should be. Then my brain goes into overdrive. *He really knows what he's doing. Has he kissed a lot of people? Where should I put my hands? Am I kissing him back too hard . . . or not hard enough?* A. Hot. Guy. Is. Kissing. Me. *Shut up, brain, and let me have this.*

Ken pulls back just as I'm finally getting into the kiss, my insides melting into goo. Disappointed, I promise myself that next time I'll let myself enjoy kissing Ken. *If* there's a next time, that is.

"So, can I see you again?" he asks with another ultra-sexy smile.

It's a wonder I don't puddle to the floor in relief. And even more of a wonder that I sound almost chill when I reply, "Sure."

CHAPTER TWO

A few weeks later, I'm the *happiest* girl on the planet. Like pinch-me-I'm-dreaming happy. Ken and I are actually together, and he's driving us somewhere to celebrate his getting the toothpaste commercial job. I don't mention that I also got a second callback for that role I'm trying to land. In fact, I haven't told anyone. As awesome as it is to make it to the third and last round of auditions—getting this role is still a long shot, so I'm trying not to get my hopes up.

The car is heading west, but Ken won't tell me where we're going. "It's a surprise."

I *love* how spontaneous and fun he is. His chiseled features and rocking body don't hurt either.

Twenty minutes later, we're at the beach. I jump out almost before Ken can park. "This is perfect! I mean, I love Lake Michigan back home, but an *ocean* beach is just so . . ." I stretch out my arms to take in the pale gold sand and white-capped waves rolling into the horizon under the burning sun. "Glorious!"

Smiling, Ken comes around the car toward me. "Glad you like it."

For the next couple of hours, it's like we're in one of those Asian music videos. The kind that comes on the screen as background in karaoke rooms, no matter what song you've chosen. I'm not talking about the part where the girl is wandering sadly in the rain. I'm talking about the flashback scene when she's frolicking on the beach in a flowing white dress with the boy of her dreams.

Before I know it, we're standing in the frothy surf, holding hands with the sky a sublime splash of oranges and pinks overhead. If someone else had described this moment to me . . . I'd be making merciless fun of how cheesy it was. But I'm here with the most beautiful guy in the world, and he's gazing into my eyes, and it's not cheesy at all.

"I don't want to see anyone else but you, Gemma," he says.

Joy melts my bones. "Me neither." I can't believe that of all the girls Ken could be dating—he wants to see *me* exclusively.

He smiles at my fervent agreement. "So, I guess you're my girlfriend now."

"And you're my boyfriend!" It's way too late to play it cool.

Ken kisses me just as the sun is setting over the ocean. And it's perfect.

I'm in a fantastic mood when Ken drops me off at my apartment in downtown LA. I have a boyfriend! *And* he's cute and übercool! Now all I need is to land a part to pay this month's rent and my happiness will be complete.

My role as an extra in a low-budget play adaptation of *The Wizard of Oz* has just ended, and although I'm not sad to give up playing a Munchkin (at five foot four, I'm not *that* short), I wish I knew where my next paycheck was coming from. It's depressing how quickly the savings from working at my mom's museum are disappearing. Maybe I should take an overnight shift at UPS like Glory or work as a waitress like Camille. All of us are trying to make it as actresses, but of the three of us living in this tiny two-bedroom apartment, I'm the only one who doesn't have a steady part-time job.

Luckily, I pay the lowest rent since I'm willing to sleep on the living room pullout couch.

My foot sinks into the squishy part of the carpet at the entrance like it's being sucked into a wet bog. I swear there's something moving under the carpet. The rest of the apartment isn't much better, with its cracked plaster walls and furniture my roommates got from a downtown LA "Buy Nothing" Facebook group, but I'm still grateful to have this place.

It's unusual for both of my roommates to be home at the same time I am, but when I walk inside, there they are. Camille is sprawled on the couch, going over lines. She was lucky enough to land a bit part in a play recently. Glory is sitting cross-legged on the uneven carpet, looking at casting calls on her phone, since she's between jobs. I knew Glory from acting in a few plays together in Chicago. She's a few years older than I am, but we bonded immediately and kept in touch when she moved to LA last year. Glory was the first person I called when I decided to move to LA, and she generously let me crash at her apartment. And when my Craigslist search for a permanent place came up short, Glory even more generously let me move in with her and Camille.

I shudder when I think about how I could have ended up rooming with some of the others I interviewed with. Like the girl who kept telling me LA was different from "where I come from." I'd told her that I'm from a suburb of Chicago, and she replied, "Oh, I mean where you *really* come from."

"How was your date with Ken?" Glory asks, putting down her phone and stretching her arms overhead. Glory would never ask where I'm *really* from. In fact, she gets the even more cringey "*What are you?*" on a regular basis. She's part Japanese, part Samoan, part white, and all big swoon-worthy muscled tallness with a sexy deep voice and acid humor. Everyone I know has at least a little crush on her. Me included.

"It was awesome!" That doesn't even cover it. Ken is the coolest guy I've ever met, and I still can't believe he's my boyfriend.

"Where was this surprise destination?" Camille's eyes are bright with interest. With her blond beauty queen looks, she'll probably be the first of us to hit it big, but she's so nice that I can't even resent her for it.

Glory grabs some snacks from the kitchen while I settle down on the couch next to Camille at their demand to tell them everything.

I give them a recap of my date, and pretty soon we're laughing and swapping stories about other dates. Camille tells us about a guy who, at the end of an agonizing date, asked her to rate him on a scale from one to ten.

Glory claims that she can't remember ever having a truly bad date.

Camille and I groan and pelt her with chips.

"Fine!" she says, covering her head against the barrage of chips. "I do have epically bad breakups if that counts!"

Camille and I look at each other. "Oh, it counts all right," I say as Camille nods vigorously. "Example, please!"

Glory tells us about dating a roommate who turned stalkerish after the breakup. "The worst thing was that because she was my roommate, I still had to live with her. One day I went into her room because I couldn't find my favorite hoodie and thought that maybe she'd taken it. I didn't find the hoodie . . . but I found a plastic zip-lock bag of my own hair on her dresser. Apparently, my ex-girlfriend had been going around the apartment, secretly collecting my hair!"

"That's so creepy!" Camille says.

I have to agree. "Glory, your ex-girlfriend was white, right?"

Glory nods. "Yup."

I roll my eyes. "I do not understand white people's obsession with Asian women's hair." I looked worriedly at Camille. "No offense."

"None taken," she replies calmly. "On behalf of my people, I apologize."

We concede that Glory wins hands down for worst breakup.

"I've lost too many roommates by getting involved with them," Glory says darkly. "That's why none of us are hooking up with each other."

Camille has a slightly wistful look on her face. I get it. On a sexuality scale, I'm mostly straight with definitely not-straight leanings, and Camille is probably the same. For me, that just means "I'm into guys, but girls like Glory get me all hot and bothered too." After all, I'm not dead. Not when it comes to Glory.

I don't have a lot of dates under my belt, and nothing in the same league as my roommates' stories, but I do my best. I tell them about my parents' friend's doctor's cousin's son—which was just enough degrees of separation for me to agree to show him around when he came on a visit from Taiwan. Everyone pretended that it hadn't been a setup, but I knew better.

"I'm not trying to perpetuate any nerdy Asian guy stereotypes," I warn my roommates, "but this guy just happens to be nerdy and Asian." I don't want Camille to think that all Asian guys are nerds.

Glory snickers because she knows this is a disclaimer that sometimes has to be made in mixed company.

Camille nods. "Of course." This girl's earnestness is seriously winning my heart.

"The date was fine," I say. "No sparks, but he was a nice enough guy. Then, at the end, he tells me he brought me some presents. He opens up his backpack. . . ." I pause for dramatic effect and take a sip of water. "And then he starts pulling out, one by one, the kind of tacky souvenirs your parents might bring you back from a trip . . . when you were eight." To be honest, I wouldn't know. My parents hardly took trips without me and certainly not abroad to places like Taiwan.

Glory is laughing so hard that there are tears in her eyes.

"Like what?" Camille's eyes are round in fascination.

"Like a key chain with a plastic heart and a cheesy saying in English. I think it was something along the lines of *Two hearts make one love*." I hold up a hand when Glory snorts water out with her laughter. "Wait for it."

Camille is practically bouncing on the couch. "Tell us," she demands.

"A music box. With figurines of Snow White and all seven dwarves on top."

"Oh, please tell me it played 'Someday My Prince Will Come,'" Glory begs.

"Of course it did," I say. "He played it for me and then gazed at me with puppy dog eyes through the entire song. *So* awkward."

Glory is on the floor now, and Camille is gasping through her laughter.

"The best thing was my mom's reaction."

Mom had sifted through the brightly colored cheap plastic on my bed and then said, "All the way from Taiwan? Why bai fei qian on this?"

Laughing at the memory, I say, "She didn't get why he would waste his money on cheap trinkets. She thought he should've brought me pineapple cakes from Taiwan instead."

Mom loves her sweets. She's always asking her best friend, who's also Chinese, to bring back pineapple cakes from Taiwan. One time, I asked her why she's never gone to Taiwan or China. She replied with something vague, but I knew that she was hiding something.

Once Camille catches her breath, she asks, "Is Taiwan part of China? Is that where your parents are from?" These are the kind of

"Where are you from" questions that I don't mind. Camille's not asking because my Asianness makes me foreign in her eyes—she's just a new friend who genuinely wants to get to know me. But the answer to her question about Taiwan is complicated. Ever since the losing side of the Chinese Communist revolution fled to Taiwan in the late forties, mainland China considers Taiwan to be a part of the mainland. Taiwan disagrees. My dad would say that's an oversimplification, but I can't explain geopolitics the way he can.

"Taiwan is a separate country from China," I say simply. "My parents aren't from Taiwan. They're from China." Then I change the subject. It's because I know the next inevitable question. And it's not an offensive one. It's just one that I can't easily answer. *Have you ever been to China?*

The answer is no. But the *why* is anything but easy to answer. My parents have not only never been back to China themselves—but they've forbidden me to go myself.

And I have no idea why.

CHAPTER THREE

I take a seat in a hard plastic chair in the audition waiting room and surreptitiously check out the competition sitting across from me. For the first audition, the room was packed, and for the first callback, it was about half-full. But for this second callback, there are only two other women—both Asian. One has a pretty, round face, and the other has an elegant beauty. If the director is looking for cute, the first one will be picked; if it's glamorous that they want, then it will be the second one. *Where does that leave me?* With my hair in a ponytail and minimal makeup, I'd describe my vibe as more "girl-next-door," except Asians don't get to be "girl-next-door." We're either exotically cute or exotically glam.

I smooth out the sheet of paper that the receptionist gave me when I checked in, hoping I have a shot at this role. *Sonia Li, ex-girlfriend.* That's it. I guess it's going to be a cold read again. The last two times were a cold read too—a scene with Sonia in a fight with her ex-boyfriend Ryan.

Quickly, I review everything I know about *Butterfly*, the film I'm auditioning for. *Butterfly* is a midbudget movie slated for nationwide release and put out by a smallish but reputable studio. It's also a remake of *M. Butterfly*, and from what I know of the play and the nineties film adaptation, I'm guessing the Sonia Li character is the updated version of the minor character Helga, the wife who's eventually discarded. In both David Henry Hwang's play and the original film version, Helga is white, but I guess she's Asian in this remake.

The only other female character I can think of is another minor one—Comrade Chin—but she's supposed to be an older woman. I glance at the other two women, and they both seem to be around my age. Probably not auditioning for Comrade Chin, then.

I swallow hard and then go get a cup of water from the dispenser. The other two women track my movements. The round-faced one blushes when she catches my eye and looks back down at her own paper—not that staring at the one line will help her much in the audition. Even though that's exactly what I'll probably do too.

The other woman smiles at me with cool confidence. Her sheet of paper is nowhere to be seen. "Callback for the Sonia Li role?" She tosses her long hair over her shoulder, and it spreads like ink on her crisp white blouse. "I'm Vivienne."

"Um, yeah. The Sonia Li role. I'm Gemma." I drink the water in one long gulp and accidentally dribble some onto my shirt. Great. All my competition has to do is introduce herself and I turn into a nervous klutz. Carefully, I sit back down in my chair.

The blushing woman looks up and introduces herself as Julie.

Vivienne leans forward and says confidentially, "I'd love to get this role. Working with Eilene Deng would be a dream come true."

My jaw drops. Eilene Deng is my idol! I've seen everything she's ever been in, even the single awful season of her failed sitcom. "You're kidding," I breathe reverently.

"What part is she playing?" Julie asks, eyes round.

Vivienne laughs. "Oh, she's not acting in this film. She's directing."

I frown, excitement dampened by the suspicion that Vivienne's messing with us. "At the first audition, the casting director said the director is Jake Tyler." Jake has been in the movie industry for years, and he has a reputation for having a short temper and demanding standards.

"Yes, that's right," Vivienne confirms. "But Eilene was brought on as co-director."

Ah. It actually does make sense for the studio to hire an Asian co-director since the main director is white. "How do you know this?" I ask.

"Oh, you know how it is." Vivienne waves an airy hand. "One of my mom's businesses is a Vietnamese fusion restaurant that Eilene loves, and Eilene let something drop about co-directing this film during an event the restaurant catered."

No, I don't know how it is. My mom is an art director at a museum, and my dad is a political science professor, so we're solidly middle class, but that doesn't mean I occupy the stratosphere that Vivienne seems to. I mean, come on—she's on a first-name basis with Eilene Deng, and an upscale fusion restaurant is *one* of her mom's businesses? Still, there's nothing mean-spirited about Vivienne's gossip, so I ask, "Do you know anything else about the film?"

Her eyes hood over. "No, not really."

I don't blame her for being evasive. After all, we're here to compete for a role, not make friends.

"Julie Chu," the receptionist calls out. "You're up."

Julie stands up nervously, and Vivienne and I both wish her luck. We fall silent as Julie goes into the audition room, and Vivienne puts on earbuds to listen to something on her phone. It's a smart move—straining to hear what's going on in the audition room through the thin walls is never a good idea, so I put on my own earbuds.

Thirty minutes later, Julie comes out. She gives us a brave smile, but I can tell it didn't go as well as she'd hoped. I feel bad for her but also hopeful for my own chances. I take out my earbuds, hoping I'll be called next.

Soon afterward, the receptionist calls out Vivienne's name, stumbling over the pronunciation of Vivienne's last name, saying something like "Na-goo-yen" instead of pronouncing "Nguyen" as a one-syllable word without a hard *g* or *y*.

Vivienne whispers to me, "Nguyen is the most common Vietnamese last name, but white people just can't seem to get it right."

I smile. She's my competition, but I can't help but like her.

Vivienne is in there for longer than Julie, and when she comes back out to the waiting room, she's beaming. I take out my earbuds in time to hear her cheery "Good luck!" loud and clear. She leaves the waiting room with a spring in her step. This is definitely *not* a good sign for me.

Left alone in the waiting room, I'm about to put my earbuds back in when I catch a murmur of voices from the other side of the walls. Uh-oh. I really should put those earbuds in. My fingers hover indecisively near my ears. *No good has ever come of eavesdropping in an audition waiting room.* But I let the earbuds fall to my lap in a messy heap of white cords.

"What does it matter?" a male voice says in response to something I don't catch.

"Isn't that why I'm here—to tell you what matters?" a woman's voice replies.

"Beautiful and poised—she's perfect!" He's obviously talking about Vivienne. My stomach drops.

The woman's voice is too quiet for me to hear her reply.

The man is easy to hear; he sounds almost angry. "You're sure this is the hill you want to die on?"

"We'll see," the woman says. "We've got one more possibility."

"Why bother? I already know which one I want!"

At that moment, the receptionist calls out from her desk, "Gemma Huang, they're ready for you."

I stand, and my knees wobble. *Why bother, indeed?* Why should I even go in if the director has already made up his mind to cast

Vivienne? I take a deep breath and tell myself that I didn't come all this way just to give up before I even get into the audition room. With my heart thudding wildly, I open the door and step into the room.

Like the first two times, there's a cameraperson ready to film the audition scene. Sitting behind a long table are two good-looking, middle-aged people—a white man and an Asian woman. The man must be Jake Tyler, the director. But I have eyes only for the woman.

Eilene Deng. There's no mistaking that fine-boned face and sardonic arch of black eyebrows for anyone else.

My hands grow hot, and my voice shrivels up in my throat. *It's really her.* I guess I didn't actually believe Vivienne when she said that Eilene Deng would be co-directing the movie. Because I'm getting light-headed from the shock of coming face-to-face with my idol. A voice in my head starts babbling excitedly. *I'm a huge fan! You were the best thing in* Danger Hospital*—it's too bad the show was canceled after just one season! Oh my god, I can't believe I'm meeting Eilene Deng!!* Blinking in starstruck awe, I give myself a mental shake. *Get it together, Gemma.* Eilene Deng does not want some crazed fan gushing over her.

Eilene holds out my lines for the cold read with a friendly smile, but Jake doesn't even look at me. I take the scene from Eilene, hoping she doesn't notice how damp my fingers are. Quickly, I scan the scene. Sonia's dashing away from Ryan after a fight. He's running after her in the rain. It seems that this takes place right after the scene I read the last two times.

"Let's do the first take without the cameras, OK?" Eilene says.

"OK," I say, jittery with anxiety.

Jake delivers Ryan's first lines. "Sonia, wait. You must be soaked to the bone." The stage directions say that Ryan takes off his raincoat and wraps it protectively around Sonia, who shivers and nestles into his embrace. "My little butterfly, I know you're not mine to worry about anymore, but I'll always look after you." *Seriously? Who says stuff like that? And why isn't Sonia throwing the raincoat back in his face?*

Frustration pounds through all my pulse points as I try to get into character. "And who's going to look after you, Ryan?" I'm supposed to say this wistfully, but it comes out flat. "When I was yours, I would have gone to the ends of the earth for you." *Gah.* This dialogue is actually getting *worse.*

Jake says his next lines like he's half-asleep.

Sweat beads on my upper lip. The stage directions tell me that Sonia is starting to get flirtatious, batting her eyes at Ryan, but it seems silly for Sonia to be batting her eyes, so I skip this direction. *I bet Vivienne pulled off the eye-batting perfectly.* "Careful, Ryan. You might be getting more than you bargained for." My voice is so stilted that I might as well be reading an IKEA instructional manual instead of coming on to my ex-boyfriend.

Eilene interrupts me. "What do you think of your character, Gemma?"

"Excuse me?" I blink at her in confusion. It must be really bad for Eilene to interrupt me just a few lines in. My knees weaken in panic.

"Can we just get on with this?" A petulant frown mars Jake's sculpted good looks.

Eilene ignores him and patiently repeats her question.

I feel as if I'm back in high school, having just been sent to the principal's office to answer for some mysterious offense. Not that I'd ever been sent to the principal's office, but I still have anxiety dreams about it. "Sonia seems a little . . ." My voice trails off because there's no good way to finish the sentence. ". . . unrealistic?" I finish weakly.

Jake snorts.

"Unrealistic how?" Eilene encourages me.

"Um." My tongue feels like it's swathed in itchy wool—it would be crazy to point out to a director that the character they're casting for is a stereotype. "Well, it's just that one minute she's all doormat-y . . . and the next . . . she's like, uh, seducing him?" Eilene actually seems to be listening, so I keep going. "I mean, if I were Sonia, I'd be angry that my ex-boyfriend is being sleazy and posses-sive. I wouldn't be desperately trying to get him back. I'd be—well, I'd be trying to keep my last meal down."

Eilene laughs, but Jake doesn't. He looks like he wants to be anywhere but here.

My chin lifts. "But I'd also make damn sure he knows what he's missing."

Jake's unfocused gaze snaps back to me.

Eilene's mouth curves up in a smile. "Bu cuo."

"What did you say?" Jake asks Eilene, sounding a fraction less bored.

"I said she's not wrong," she replies calmly.

That *is* what "bu cuo" literally means in Chinese, but in common usage, it means "not bad," with a strong implication of praise that's lost in translation. Chinese parents get a bad rap for being stingy with praise, but really, a measured Chinese "bu cuo" is worth a hun-dred casual American "very good"s. And that's what is causing hope to light up in me like a small, burning star.

Eilene turns to me. "Let's take it again from the top. OK with you, Gemma?"

"Sure," I squeak, terrified that I'm going to screw up all over again. How am I going to play Sonia convincingly?

Jake shrugs and picks up his lines. As he starts up again, calling Sonia his "little butterfly," a scene from *M. Butterfly* pops into my head—probably because I know the play frontward and backward by now. One of the characters says that it takes a man to play the perfect Asian woman convincingly. Because she's not real—she's the object of male fantasy.

Right. *Think fantasy, Gemma, not reality.* I say my lines about going to the ends of the earth for Ryan, and this time, I pull it off better. Without gagging, at least.

Jake says his next lines. "This is my hotel. Come inside and we'll get out of these wet clothes." My face burns hot as he ogles me over the top of his paper. Even bored out of his skull, he manages to leer—I swear it's a reflex.

I've known men like Jake. And I understand their fantasies—ancient erotic secrets and shy giggles—sex and modesty all wrapped up in one impossible package. I had been wrong when I was sizing up the other women in the waiting room. Julie, Vivienne, me—none of us can be the woman they want. Because that woman isn't real. But I don't have to *be* that woman. All I have to do is *act* the part. And it's about damn time that I remember to be an actress. My voice goes high and breathy as I glance demurely at Jake through lowered lashes. "Careful, Ryan. You might be getting more than you bargained for." I allow just a spice of danger to leak through my voice.

He straightens up, interest sparking in his eyes as he reads his next lines.

Eilene gives me an approving smile and leans back in her chair.

I finish the scene, ignoring the directions that have me saying goodbye to Ryan with helpless longing. That's not how I would feel if an ex-boyfriend came on to me with scummy lines about "little butterfly" and always looking after me. Instead, I read the lines with a sassy "kick-my-ex-to-the-curb" vibe.

When I'm done, *both* Eilene and Jake seem to like the way I played the scene. They have me do it again, this time with the cameras rolling. Then we shoot another scene. By the time the two directors tell me that they'll be in touch, I've been in here for as long as Vivienne was. *That's a good sign, right?* As I walk out back into the waiting room, I'm feeling tentatively OK about the audition.

I wave goodbye to the receptionist, and as I'm about to leave I hear Jake's voice from the other side of those thin walls. "That went better than I expected." Hope swells in me for a brief, joyous moment until he adds, "But Vivienne is still the clear choice."

My stomach twists, and my shoulders slump. *Well, there goes another chance at making rent.* At least I got to meet Eilene Deng, if nothing else. But it would've been nice to meet my hero under different circumstances—when I'm not failing an audition, for instance.

CHAPTER FOUR

As I leave the audition building, my phone buzzes, right on cue. It's my mom—I guess her Spidey sense told her this would be a good time to call. I sigh and tap answer. "Hi, Ma."

"Gemma, this is your ma," my mother says. It's not that she doesn't understand how caller ID works. It's just that she thinks it's necessary to state who she is at the start of every phone call.

"I know, Ma."

We talk for a little bit and she tells me all about her friends' children who are at college, forging a path to success and apparently having the time of their lives while they're at it. *Subtle, Mom.*

"Mom, it's called a gap year. Plenty of people take a gap year before going to college. It's not a big deal to take a year off to get a start on my career!"

"Remember last summer? You said you didn't want to work at the museum anymore, so you said you'd get a different job, and you didn't."

"I worked for two summers at your museum and on weekends during the school year! I needed a break!" I'm pacing the sidewalk, and I have to force myself to stop because I'm drawing curious looks from people passing by. "Besides, I was in a play last summer."

She sniffs so loudly that I can hear it over the phone. "Rehearsals and showtimes were at night. You still could have gotten a job, but you were on the couch, watching that show all day."

Admittedly, *The Empress of China* miniseries, clocking in at ninety-six episodes, is quite the time commitment. "That show was a Chinese drama, which you love, and it starred Fan Bingbing, your favorite actress," I remind her stiffly. "I thought you'd *want* to watch it with me." Actually, I'd counted on it because my Chinese is so basic that I'd be lucky to understand half of what was going on without her. Mom *did* eventually agree to watch it with me—but only to criticize. Mom, Dad, and I used to binge on Chinese dramas when I was a kid. But that was before I decided to be a serious actress. Now anything that feeds my dream of being an actress is suddenly a waste of time.

"That show got nothing right about Empress Wu Zetian!" Mom's graduate art history degree and interest in Chinese culture gave her more Chinese historical knowledge than the average person, but since Wu Zetian lived thousands of years ago, it's not like Mom or anyone else could *actually* know what the real empress was like. Plus, historical inaccuracy never stopped Mom from enjoying Chinese dramas about flying monks and magical warrior maidens.

"I think the show did a pretty good job! At least it didn't portray Wu Zetian as a heartless court harlot who killed her own baby daughter to frame a rival." The woman passing me on the sidewalk gives me an alarmed look. I smile at her as if to say, *Really, I'm a totally normal person who just happens to be talking about court harlots and infanticide on a busy public street.* The woman scurries by without meeting my eyes. I lower my voice. "I thought you'd appreciate a portrayal of Wu Zetian as a mother grieving her daughter's murder rather than a bloodthirsty empress."

"Please," Mom says scornfully. "They made Wu Zetian a lovesick innocent who let everyone walk all over her! That girl couldn't have run a household, much less an entire country."

She has a point. Empress Wu didn't get to be the only female ruler of China by being the damsel in distress that *The Empress of*

China portrayed her as. Still, I know better than to concede a point to my mother in an argument. "Look, I'm just saying that Fan Bingbing gave us a portrayal of Wu Zetian that was better than the one that male court historians gave us."

"The show just changed one wrong detail for another wrong detail. That doesn't make it *better*." So, now my mother is pretending to know what happened back in the time of the Tang dynasty? That just goes to show how *stubborn* she can be. My mom's the most strong-willed, determined person I know. That's why she speaks nearly flawless English even though she came to the United States as an adult. "Besides, I don't like the ideas that show gave you."

"What you really mean is that you don't approve of *anything* that inspires me to be an actress! You want me to be a doctor or lawyer or something!" All right—this is a *totally* unfair accusation. My mom's never pressured me toward a specific career. Besides, her own education in art history isn't exactly a conventional path to success.

"You want to be an actress? Fine! Be an actress! Just be smart about it and go to college first! You think I got to be a museum director because I saw a painting and got 'inspired,' just like that?" She takes an audible breath. "But this isn't about your acting. I just don't like that show. Luan qi ba zao! Filling your head with nonsense. Kai wan xiao!"

Now I *know* she's not telling the truth. Mom just used her two most scathing insults. "Luan qi ba zao"—disordered, chaotic—used on occasion to refer to the state of my room. "Kai wan xiao"—you've got to be kidding—reserved for items priced too high. She's *never* used either phrase to describe anything artistic. You'd think Mom, being a museum director, would be snobby about art, but it's just the opposite. She doesn't like insulting any kind of art—much less her beloved Chinese dramas. That's how I know her problem really *is* with my acting. "The show isn't nonsense, and you know it! And neither is my acting!"

She ignores my outburst. "Do you have a job yet?"

I don't respond, which is its own answer, and Mom's voice turns soft. "We can give you qian for rent."

Money. In the heat of our worst fight ever, Mom swore that they wouldn't support me if I didn't go to college this fall. But I should have known she would walk back her threat eventually. It must not have been easy for Mom to swallow her pride like that, but I've got my own pride. "No thanks."

She sighs. "Your father grew up poor, you know."

I blink in surprise. My parents never talk about their pasts.

"He's very worried about you," Mom says. "Delun," she calls out, "get on the other line and tell our daughter how worried you are!" My parents are the only people I know who still have a landline in addition to their cell phones.

"Mom," I groan. The last thing I want is a conversation with Dad about how worried he is. Talking about feelings always makes Dad awkward.

In the background, I hear my dad say, "Lei, she doesn't need me to tell her that."

Mom ignores him and says to me, "He doesn't want you to worry the way he did about food and a place to live. Here's your ba ba now."

OK, this is happening.

Dad comes on the line. "How are you for money, Gemma?" That's Dad, right to the point. But in Dad-speak, "How are you for money?" pretty much means "I love you." Plus, unlike Mom, *he* doesn't have any rash threats to take back. Dad wasn't thrilled about me putting off college either, but he didn't threaten to cut me off from financial support.

"Fine," I lie.

"Hao."

"OK," I repeat.

Awkward silence ensues.

Mom jumps in, rescuing me. "She's not OK!" Well, sort of rescuing me.

"I'm fine, Mom. I really am. You and Dad don't have to worry about me." I pause. "I didn't know Dad grew up poor. Were you poor too, Mom?"

My dad makes a strangled noise, and I hear the click of the phone, indicating that he's hung up.

"No," Mom says, "but it was nothing compared to the riches I have now. You know why?" *Here it comes—because I worked hard. Because I went to college.* But Mom's too smart to be that obvious. "Because your father and I have each other. And we have you. I just want the best for our bao bei." She's pulling out the emotional big guns now. My mom used to call me Bao bei—treasure—when I was a kid. And in case that was too *subtle*, my dad used to call me "Gem" for short. I'm their treasure—got it. No pressure at all.

"You think you'll go to college after this 'gap' year," she says, "but I know what it's like to be young and impulsive. It's too easy to get distracted from what's important—and trust me, you don't want to have regrets for the rest of your life because you lose sight of what's really important." The woman is wasted as a museum director—she could give *me* drama lessons.

Raising my voice to be heard over the roar of traffic speeding by me, I say, "I know what's important to me—and it's acting! This isn't an impulsive decision or a distraction. It's my career!"

"I'm not telling you to give up acting. I'm telling you to go to college first so you have options! How many people actually earn a living through acting?"

Time to change tactics. "Sara Li took a gap year, and her mom didn't give her grief for it." That poor girl *needed* a gap year after enduring endless jokes about her name since elementary school. To this day, Sara Li can't look at a frozen dessert without shuddering.

For once, Mom remains unmoved by the mention of her best friend's daughter. "You don't need to be like Sara Li."

Seriously? All my life, I've heard Mom talk about the perfect Sara Li, and *now* my mom tells me that I don't need to be like her? (If Sara weren't my friend, I'd hate her guts.)

Then—giving into the sheer force of her Sara Li–worshipping habit—Mom says, "And Sara Li ended up going to Harvard." It's like Mom can't help herself.

I seize on this. "And I *am* going to college next fall, just like Sara did after her gap year. Would you be happier if I did what Sara did during her gap year?" *Oh no, don't go there, Gemma*—but my stupid mouth is faster than my brain. "Go to Beijing?"

Icy silence forms on the other end of the line, and my throat turns dry.

Over the years, I've spun a lot of wild theories about why my mother doesn't want me to go to Beijing. A spurned lover turned stalker. A criminal past. The Chinese mafia (if there's even such a thing) putting a hit out on her. Or maybe she just thinks the air is unhealthy. Every once in a while, I'll blurt out a theory, hoping to surprise her into letting something slip. But nothing has worked so far. Eventually, I learned to stop pushing. For a woman who loves to talk, my mom is eerily good at the silent treatment. She doesn't use it on me often. Just when I ask about Beijing. Or her family.

Sara Li has a sister, two sets of grandparents, and a whole passel of cousins, aunts, and uncles. Some are in the United States, some in Taiwan, and some in China, but the point is that Sara *has* them. Here's the thing—I've never been jealous of Sara's grades or awards. But I *am* jealous of her family, bursting at the seams with siblings and relatives. I have no one but Mom and Dad. That's why I suspect the reason I can't go to Beijing has nothing to do with stalkers, criminals, the mafia, or air pollution.

It has to do with Mom's family.

Dad, at least, talks about his family . . . or lack of family, anyway. He's an orphan. I've tried to ask my dad about why I can't go to Beijing, but that doesn't work either. Dad doesn't give me the silent treatment like Mom does. But he does give me a wide-eyed, panicked look and a garbled "Talk to your mother" as he *literally* runs from me.

Finally, Mom speaks. "Do what you want with your life," she says coldly. "Just don't step foot in Beijing. You have no idea what will happen if you do." She says the same thing again in slow, precise Chinese. Then she hangs up.

My stomach twists in knots. Here I am, standing all alone in the middle of Washington Boulevard, having just failed an audition. And now I feel even worse after talking to my mother. Anger sparks in me. Why is it so bad to bring up Beijing? It makes me even angrier when I think about her calling again in a week or so. It will be like nothing happened. Like Beijing never even came up. In no time at all, Mom will be back to telling me what I'm missing by not going to college. As if she knows everything about what's best for me.

But she doesn't understand a thing about me. The only reason she thinks I'm too impulsive is that every decision *she's* ever made is so logical. Even Sara Li has a streak of rebellion. But not my mom. She's never deviated from the conventional path to success. I'll bet she's never even made a rash choice in her life, and she wants me to be just like her. Except that I'm nothing at all like her.

Cars whiz by on the busy road, underscoring that I'm the only one with nowhere to go.

CHAPTER FIVE

The crowd around me is screaming in an airless concert venue while the scruffy lead singer of an indie band I've never heard of belts out a song at the top of his lungs. Ken, Glory, and Camille seem to be having fun. That's more than I can say for myself, but by now I'm resigned to my friends and new boyfriend dragging me to dark little clubs that require me to have a fake ID. At least the ID part was easy. Getting one was simply a matter of asking Sara Li to give me her old driver's license and get a new one; I reimbursed her for the replacement fee, and that was that. The fact that I look nothing like Sara doesn't matter—the doorman at the club tonight didn't even blink when he checked my ID.

Camille says I'm "lucky." But that's not how I see it. After all, it's not often that white people's cluelessness benefits me.

If seeing this band is a benefit, that is. The lead singer's screech tears through the stuffy interior of the club, and someone accidentally bumps me, dripping cold beer onto my arm. I wince and try to move away, but there's nowhere to move *to*. For once, I'd like to go someplace where I can move more than an inch without coming into contact with the sweaty chest of a stranger. And I wouldn't mind listening to a band with intelligible lyrics either.

"*Dai* earplugs if you go to a rock concert, Gemma. Be careful of your ears." Before I left home, Mom loaded me up with advice—as if I were a fragile plate that needed to be wrapped up in layers of care before being shipped off. Still, it's nice to know that getting cut off from financial support doesn't mean getting cut off from parental advice—even though I've ignored most of it, including the one about being careful of my ears. I'm not about to be the uncool girl wearing earplugs at a concert.

But if Mom had told me in *all* English to make sure I understood and repeated the exact same thing again in *all* Chinese to underscore her feelings? Then I'd be shoving orange squishy cones into my ears—no matter what anyone else thinks. Looking uncool is nothing compared to ignoring *that* kind of warning. Because that's DEFCON 1 for Mom. Life or death.

Glory and Camille are too into the music to notice that I'm being elbowed aside by a crowd of excited fans trying to get closer to the front, but Ken notices. He puts a protective arm around me, and his touch is so lovely and tingly that I don't complain about getting even hotter and stickier from his body heat.

The set ends at last, and the crowd starts to ease away from the floor and toward the bar. My ears are ringing, so I don't immediately register that the phone in my back pocket is buzzing. Who's calling me near midnight on a Saturday? I pull out my phone and glance at the screen. Then the world tilts and I stop breathing. It's my agent.

In slow motion, I answer the call. "Hi, Laura," I squeak.

Ken drops his arm from my shoulders, and Glory and Camille both turn away from the stage to stare at me. They don't know about my *Butterfly* audition. Why tell them about every long-shot audition—only to be disappointed? But that doesn't keep the hope from rising in my throat.

"Are you sitting down, Gemma?" Laura asks.

"Yes," I lie, calves and feet aching from dancing in place for hours on a hard, concrete floor. My breath is coming in hard pants now. This could be *it*. This really could.

"Good." Excitement sparks in her voice. "Because you, Gemma Huang, just got cast in the lead role of Sonia Li!"

My heart goes numb in my chest, and my knees weaken, making me wish I actually *were* sitting down. "Oh, wow," I whisper in hushed awe. Ken, Glory, and Camille all lean closer to listen in, and I take a step backward. "Did you just say *lead* role?" Thrilled disbelief jolts my heart, making it thud painfully. I thought Sonia was a minor role. The scene I read made her seem like the ex-girlfriend of the white male lead. "We're talking about *Butterfly*, the *M. Butterfly* update that I auditioned for, right?"

Camille gasps, clutching her chest dramatically, and Glory starts doing a little victory dance. But Ken doesn't react at all. A prickle of unease works its way down my spine, but *goddammit*, I'm finally being offered a role, so Ken should be the last thing I'm worrying about.

"Unless there's some other audition that I don't know about." Laura laughs. "Yes, *Butterfly*, and it's absolutely a lead role!" She pauses, and I hear the ruffling of paper, probably her notes. "The production company needs you to send a copy of your passport so they can get you an expedited visa. Shooting in China begins in two weeks."

The joy blazing through my body freezes suddenly, and cold dread stabs my stomach. China. Right. I was so sure I wouldn't get the role that I didn't pay much attention to where the film was being shot. "Um, do you know what city?" *Not Beijing. Not Beijing.* Mom's warning to stay out of Beijing doesn't even have a spot in my ranking system of motherly advice. It's off the charts. More than life or death.

"Beijing," Laura says.

My hands go hot and clammy, and I have to clutch the phone to keep it from sliding out of my grasp. Of course it's Beijing. It's the capital city, after all. "That's so amazing!" My voice sounds like it's coming from a long way off. *Wait!* Am I actually accepting the role?

Laura seems to think so. "Great! I'll send the contract along with a synopsis of the script."

I end the call and look up at my friends. "I just got the lead role in a film update of *M. Butterfly!*" I don't tell them about my mom forbidding me to go to Beijing because I'm still freaking out about that. And I don't want Camille to give me a knowing look and mentally file the information away in a "Gemma's tiger mom" file. I'm probably being unfair to her. Camille should get some credit for being the only white person in our little friend group.

"Awesome!" Glory's eyes shine. "I didn't even know you auditioned for it!"

Camille shrieks in joy. "I love that opera! But does that mean you have to sing?"

"Not *Madama Butterfly*, the opera by Puccini," I explain. "*M. Butterfly* is a gender-bending play and film by David Henry Hwang. Totally different."

"For one thing, an Asian woman doesn't kill herself over a white man," Glory says dryly. Glory and I both identify as Asian, but when a film does a casting call for an Asian actress, they don't have someone like Glory in mind. They're thinking of someone like me, small-framed with delicate features. That's the film industry's idea of Asian womanhood. Scarlett Johansson has a better chance of getting cast as an Asian woman in a film than Glory does. After all, when Scarlett Johansson was cast as the lead in the live-action remake of the Japanese anime film *Ghost in the Shell*, they added a whole convoluted plotline to explain why the character has a white woman's body. I mean, they could have just casted an Asian actress. It's seriously messed up. Glory says her only chance is with "ambiguous" roles—she means in terms of both gender and race. One time, she showed me a casting audition that literally called for an "ethnically ambiguous" actress. *That's me*, she said with a wry smile.

"But," Ken says, speaking at last, "there are no female lead roles in *M. Butterfly*."

I stiffen at his flat tone. "Like I said, it's an update." But Ken does have a point. I can't think of a female lead role in *M. Butterfly* either. It's why I originally thought I was trying out for a supporting role. I wonder if I'm being cast for the part played by B. D. Wong on Broadway and John Lone in the film version. And if so, how am I supposed to play a woman playing a man playing a woman?

"An update." Ken's face turns blank. There aren't a lot of roles for Asian men—and Song Liling, the male Chinese opera singer who seduces a white male diplomat by pretending to be a woman—is a role Ken would've killed to play.

My breath goes hot with indignation. There are as few roles for Asian women as there are for Asian men. Ken knows that, so it would be nice if he could be happy for me.

Glory groans. "Don't tell me they're straight-washing the whole thing!"

My stomach twists. Oh no. What if Glory's right? Casually, I slide my phone back out. Laura said that she would send me the synopsis. I've got to know what I'm getting myself into.

Camille is gazing in amazement at Glory, Ken, and me. "How do you all know so much about a film I've never even *heard* of?"

That's easy. We're all Asian actors. Of course we know every Asian actor who's ever made it and what roles they played. It's not like there are that many. Ken and Glory explain this to Camille while I check my emails. My pulse races when I see Laura's email in my inbox. I open the attachment with the synopsis and start reading.

Outspoken, vivacious Song (everyone calls her Sonia) Li's dream job negotiating overseas business contracts has just opened up! The problem? Ryan Glenn, her ex-boyfriend, will be her boss. And it's not like their breakup was amicable. How can she convince him to hire her . . . and keep dangerous sparks from flying again?

Damn. Glory *is* right.

Ken's eyes narrow. "I saw that casting call. They weren't casting Asian male roles." His face, normally so calm and easygoing, is pinched. "Just extras. I'll bet the romantic interest is a white man and all the Asian men in that film will be sexless and nerdy or chauvinistic and domineering."

And there's another hitch. Sonia's first contract will be for a deal in China, and Chinese businessmen won't take a female lawyer seriously. But Sonia has a plan to solve both problems. By becoming Song Li, unassuming, reserved . . . and male. The opposite of everything Sonia Li is.

Shit. Ken's right too.

I look up from my phone, a forced smile on my face. Everyone is looking at me, and a cold bead of perspiration slides down my neck. Ken has his arms crossed, and I wish he'd just give me a hug and say he's on my side.

But it's Glory who puts a hand on my arm and says, "You've got to go for this, Gemma. It's the chance of a lifetime, and you're going to be amazing."

"Of course you're doing it," Camille says. "It's a lead role. It's what we've all dreamed of!"

"Yeah." Ken's smile doesn't reach his eyes. "Congratulations, Gemma."

At least he's trying. Maybe he just needs time to come around. And maybe if I take the role, I can influence the direction of the script. *Right.* That's about as likely as my mom not caring that I'm taking a job in Beijing. But I need this role. Like Glory said, when will a chance like this come again? I'm just going to have to keep my mom from finding out where I'm going. My throat tightens as I brightly say, "Thanks, everyone. I think it's all going to work out."

CHAPTER SIX

I'm haphazardly throwing clothes into my suitcase, ticking off in my head everything I've done and still need to do before leaving for Beijing in two days. *Join Screen Actors Guild.* Check. *Meet Eilene Deng for dinner.* That's tomorrow night. *Get roommates to cover for me if my parents show up in LA unannounced.* Check—sort of. Glory agreed immediately, but Camille was more reluctant. Still, I *think* I can count on them both not to give me away. *Say goodbye to Ken and hope that he doesn't meet someone else while I'm six thousand miles away.* As soon as I think this, the doorbell rings.

I climb over my open suitcase and various pairs of shoes that I'm still deciding between to get to the door. Ken is standing at the entrance with a bouquet of bright flowers.

I fling my arms around him. "I love these! Thank you!" Maybe I'm being a touch too enthusiastic, but things have been a little strained since I was cast in the film, and the flowers give me hope that the weirdness is gone now.

"You're welcome. You better put them in water. They probably won't last long. Not that you'll be here to notice."

Nope. Weirdness definitely not gone yet.

Things are better when we leave the apartment. We talk a bit about the commercial and how it's an important stepping-stone in Ken's career. In the back of my mind, it registers that we're talking more about his toothpaste commercial than we've ever talked about *my* movie. But I shove away such thoughts as petty. He should get to enjoy his moment too.

Ken suggests a movie he's been wanting to see, and it sounds good, so I agree. I did kind of hope we'd go somewhere we could talk, maybe the beach again—but being at a movie with Ken turns out to be nice. We hold hands and share popcorn in the dark, and I realize that this is our first movie date. We're so new as a couple that I still get excited about our "firsts." When I point out that this is our first movie, Ken whispers back, "There's a reason I suggested a dark theater for a date." Then he nuzzles my neck, sending sparks through my body.

After the movie, Ken takes me back home, and both Camille and Glory are there, so all four of us hang out for a bit until my roommates simultaneously decide to "turn in early" and leave the living room/my bedroom to us. *I'm really going to miss those two.*

To my surprise, Ken gets to his feet when my roommates go to their rooms. "I have an early morning tomorrow, so I should go too."

I stand up, hiding my disappointment. "Oh. I guess this is good-bye, then, for two to three months."

He shuffles his feet uncomfortably. "Look, you're going to be gone for a while, and I think we should clear some things up before you go."

My body tenses. *Is Ken breaking up with me?* "OK . . ." The silence that follows is torturous.

"Maybe we shouldn't be exclusive while you're in China." Quickly, he adds, "I'm not saying that I actually *would* meet someone, and I definitely wouldn't get serious with anyone else, but we could . . . uh, keep our options open. Just for the three months you're gone."

That seems . . . not horrible. As long as it's not code for *I want to break up with you but am too much of a wimp to say so.* "Sure. That works for me." Because I'm a decent actress, it comes out sounding light and unconcerned.

Ken seems relieved by my reaction. "Hey, you're still my girl-friend, OK?"

"You bet." I bump his hip with mine. "Don't think you can go out and replace me." Inwardly, I wince. I was trying to sound totally blasé about the whole non-exclusive thing, but all I've done is remind Ken that he *could* meet someone.

He laughs. "Impossible. You're one of a kind, Gemma Huang." He pulls me in for a kiss.

Only after he leaves do I realize that neither of us considered the possibility that *I* might meet someone else.

I cannot believe this is happening. I'm actually sitting across the table from Eilene Deng at Nobu. Yes, Nobu is one of those hot-spot restaurants that makes me feel totally unhip and out of place, but it doesn't matter. Because I'm with *Eilene Deng*! She could take me to an organic vegan raw food restaurant where everything is served juiced or frothed in shot glasses, and I wouldn't even care.

Eilene does the ordering and starts with an order of Hamachi Kama Miso Salt. This isn't my first experience with sushi, but I have no idea what that is. *Since when is salt a meal?* She follows this up with the Toro Spicy Karashi Su Miso Caviar at market price (I gulp because the printed prices on the menu are already astronomical) and then rattles off a whole bunch of other dishes. I have to admit that the ingredients I do recognize sound delicious.

As the waiter rushes off to put in our order, Eilene leans back in her seat and takes a sip of her cocktail. "Tell me about yourself, Gemma. How did you get into acting?"

Once I get over my nervousness, I find Eilene easy to talk to. I even tell her about trying out for Snow White in fourth grade and getting cast as a bird instead, with a single line of "Tweet. Tweet." And how it didn't matter because just getting on the stage with everyone pulling together to make the magic happen was enough to infect me with the acting bug. Whenever I pause, self-conscious about talking so much, she draws me out with another deft question.

When Eilene asks me what roles I'd like to play, I say, "All kinds. I want to be like Awkwafina, who got to be a con artist in a female heist movie. The quirky best friend in a rom-com. A girl figuring out her Chinese American identity in an award-winning family dramedy. *Especially* that last one. *The Farewell* is one of my favorite movies ever." I went to see it by myself and was unprepared for how that movie would break my heart and put it back together again. I didn't even bring any tissues, which was stupid given that the trailer alone had reduced me to tears. Fortunately, two sympathetic older white women in the row in front of me had handed me some tissues before my sleeves got too soggy.

Eilene smiles. "*The Farewell* is one of my favorites too. Seeing that movie is one reason why I think I *can* be a director and make the movies I want to make."

Awkwafina is good in everything she does, but in *The Farewell*— as Billi, a young Chinese American woman who returns to China with her family to visit her dying grandmother—she's downright luminous. I'm pretty sure a big reason why Awkwafina was so good was because of Lulu Wang, the Chinese American filmmaker who wrote, directed, and fought a white Hollywood for her vision of the movie. Eilene says that's the kind of movie she wants to make. And that's the kind of movie I want to be in.

Then Eilene asks the one question that causes me to stumble. "Where's your family from? Mainland China? Taiwan? Somewhere else?"

I swallow my mineral water too fast and start coughing. She

waits patiently while I dab my lips with a cloth napkin. "Mainland China." Tension winds up my spine as I wait for Eilene to ask what provinces and what cities.

She shoots me a penetrating look and changes the subject. "Do you know why you were chosen to play Sonia?"

I shake my head. That's exactly what I've been wondering since I got the call from my agent, almost two weeks ago now. "I thought it would go to Vivienne." Jake Tyler had clearly wanted Vivienne for the role, and I can't imagine her turning it down.

Eilene's mouth turns up in a wry smile. "Audition waiting rooms are notorious for having thin walls."

"So if Jake wanted Vivienne, how did I end up getting cast as Sonia?"

"To answer that question, I need to first explain why *I* was brought into this project. The producers anticipated backlash when they hired both a white screenwriter and a white director for a remake of *M. Butterfly*—or rather, it was pointed out that they *should* anticipate a backlash." This time, her smile is sharply edged. "I was brought in to be the film's . . ." She pauses as if searching for a diplomatic phrasing.

"Token," I finish. "You were brought in to give the film authenticity." I make air quotes around the word "authenticity."

Her eyebrows rise. "Ah. You understand. Perhaps you also understand that I wanted a Chinese American actress for the role?"

I remember Jake asking Eilene, *What does it matter?* after Vivienne's audition, and Eilene saying, *Isn't that why I'm here—to tell you what matters?* Everything clicks into place. Vivienne is Vietnamese American, and Eilene must have told Jake that it is important for a Chinese American actress to play a Chinese American character. And of course Jake didn't get why it mattered. He probably thought all

Asians were the same. "Was I the only Chinese American actress who got a second callback?"

"No, as a matter of fact," Eilene says. "Of the other two actresses up for the role, one was Vietnamese and one was Chinese like you. But you're the one I wanted." She leans forward, fixing me with a steady gaze. "You understand Sonia as a character."

I shift uncomfortably in the plush leather booth. No way that I can confess what I *really* think of Sonia as a character. "Um, OK."

"And by understanding Sonia," she says, eyes never wavering from mine, "you understand why she needs to *change*."

The waiter arrives with a ceaseless procession of small plates. Gorgeous food is laid before us, but I can't even focus on the stunning array of dishes. I'm taking in what Eilene just said.

After the waiter departs, I ask, "So you want me to . . . do what exactly?"

Instead of answering, Eilene uses her chopsticks to slide jewel-red fish, beautifully garnished, onto my plate. "Asian actresses have it tough. Sometimes we have to make compromises to get roles." Her expression turns bitter. "It can make you feel like you're selling out." She takes a serving for herself. "And even then, once an actress—any actress, not just Asian—in Hollywood hits a certain age, roles get scarce."

"There have to be roles still for someone like you—someone with your talent!" Then I wince because that's *so* naive, and really, I know better.

Eilene waves away my protest. "It was time for me to move on anyway." She gestures for me to eat. "I've always wanted to direct, but the problem is that no one wanted to take a chance on me. Then this film came along, and they needed a Chinese co-director for . . . authenticity . . . as you so astutely put it." She sets down her chopsticks without taking a bite herself. "The problem is that *Butterfly* is complete drivel."

The sushi is smooth as butter, and it's a good thing too, or else I would have choked midswallow at Eilene's words. "Drivel?" I repeat weakly.

"Oh, don't pretend it isn't," she says with a smile. "But I understand why you're hesitant to speak your mind. I was a young actress like you once. It's not easy in this business to be true to yourself, especially as an Asian woman, but to truly be a great actress, that is what you have to do."

I nod, barely resisting the temptation to nerd out and take notes about what she's saying on my phone.

"I need this film to do well. And the way it's going right now, that's not going to happen," she says quietly. "So, back to what I want you to do? I want you to become a truly great actress."

Becoming a great actress is easier said than done. And also . . . *what does she even mean by that?*

She lifts her glass to me. "Together, we're going to take over this film."

Oh damn. I don't know what I was expecting, but it wasn't *this*. Eilene Deng is asking me to hijack *Butterfly* with her.

CHAPTER SEVEN

The second my plane touches down in Beijing, I take my phone off airplane mode, and then texts pop up. Ken, Glory, and Camille all wish me luck, but I don't have time to text back right now. Instead, I scroll through my emails. I see what I suspected. I've been on the plane for just thirteen hours, and my parents have already emailed me *three* times. The one from my dad is a link to an article about love and money—he sends me random articles, never with any context, clarifying message, or (thankfully) expectation of a response. Another one is from my mother. She and my dad want to fly out and visit me next week. Panic fogs my vision, and cold moisture films my forehead.

The passenger in the window seat, a white American woman, edges away from me. I don't bother pointing out that if I were going to be airsick, it would have been while we were in the air and not when we've finally landed. Come to think of it, I *am* feeling a little nauseous at the thought of my parents' visiting. Maybe the woman's right to worry about me puking on her pretty pastel blouse.

On the other side of me, the older Chinese man in the aisle seat smiles reassuringly. Most of the other passengers are American like me, but this man is Chinese and speaks only a smattering of English. My Chinese is better than his English, but I'm not what you would call fluent.

But despite the language barrier, we've still managed to have a conversation of sorts. Mostly, the man showed me about a hundred pictures of his granddaughter, and I exclaimed, "Zhen ke ai!" in my

American accent. "So cute!" is pretty much all I said the whole flight, but he still complimented me on my Chinese, saying it was pretty good for an "ABC" (American Born Chinese).

Now he releases a rapid torrent of Chinese, which comes to me in just a few understandable words and phrases. Dao—arrived. Fei ji—plane. And Mei shi—don't worry. Against all odds, tension uncurls from the tight muscles in my shoulders. It doesn't even matter that this man with kind crinkles around his eyes has no idea what I'm really worried about. There's just something soothing in hearing "mei shi"—the same thing my parents have murmured to me all my life, offering comfort for everything from a scraped knee to a fight with a friend.

"Xie xie. Wo mei shi." I thank him and tell him I'm OK.

I click on the next email from Mom, and all the tension shoots back into my shoulders. She wants to know why I haven't responded yet. She also sent a potential travel itinerary.

Now I'm hyperventilating, my breath coming in sharp, hard gasps. The nice man's forehead furrows, and it's a wonder he isn't shoving an emergency airplane bag into my hands. The words on the top of the itinerary make me grip the phone in white-knuckled dread. "Budget Economy Ticket." That means no refunds. Once my parents buy those tickets, it will take a small miracle to keep my parents from visiting, because there's no way they'll eat the price of two plane tickets. It's not that they can't afford the tickets—it's that they're too cheap.

This is bad. Very, very bad. My heart pounds jaggedly as I envision my mom saying to my dad, "Gemma didn't write back! We should buy the tickets now! Find out what's happening." If my parents find out that I've broken my mom's cardinal rule, they'll never believe in my decisions again—or in me. I'll have destroyed their trust for good. My chest tightens. I have to stop them from finding out I'm actually in Beijing. Gulping stale airplane air, I lose my head completely and tap frantically on my phone: *Don't come! I'm sick! Quarantined for months.*

Uh. No. Sending that would *guarantee* my parents booking the next flight to LA . . . and calling every Chinese doctor acquaintance they know. Which is a surprisingly large number. Sticky sweat pools in my armpits at the thought of every Chinese doctor within a twenty-mile radius descending upon my LA apartment. I delete the email. *Whew.* One nightmare scenario averted. But I still don't know how to dissuade my parents from coming to visit. The plane is pulling up to the gate at the Beijing airport, and it won't be long before I lose this window to email my parents.

Quickly, I type something about getting a job and long shoots. Could they come in the winter instead? I'd love to see them! The smiley face emoji is too much, but I don't have time to overthink it. People are moving down the aisle, and the Chinese man says goodbye to me. The woman by the window is sighing loudly and tapping one foot on the floor. Throat dry with nerves, I send the email and hope for the best.

I sling my messenger bag over my chest, grab my rolling suitcase from the overhead bin, and then join the flow of people disembarking the plane. Jet-lagged and shaking from the possible impending disaster of Mom finding out where I am, I go through customs in a daze, too bleary to attempt my elementary Chinese. Luckily, the customs officials understand and speak English just fine.

At last I get through customs and emerge onto an air-conditioned concourse with bright overhead lights in neat rows. It's packed with people, but I catch a glimpse of my friendly seatmate. He's crouching down on the polished pale gray floor, and his granddaughter is diving into his arms with a loud shriek of "Gong Gong!" Her mother watches with a fond smile.

Because the girl called him "Gong Gong," I know that he's her maternal grandfather. If she called him "Ye Ye," he would be her paternal grandfather. The correct Chinese terms of address for relatives is super confusing. But all around, there are people who look like me, being greeted in a way that indicates their precise relationship to each other. Everyone is speaking the language I'll always associate with family . . . no matter how poorly I speak it.

My eyes sting with tears. In all my anxiety about taking the role and figuring out a way to keep my parents from finding out, there was one very important thing I forgot. I am standing in my parents' homeland, my mother's birth city.

I forgot that I was coming home.

I hadn't even known that I wanted to. Of all the reasons I thought I had for coming to China, none of them were this.

Blinking away the hot prickliness in my eyes, I scan the crowd for a driver holding a placard with my name on it. Because there are no grandparents or relatives coming to meet me. No one knows me here in my homeland. But as soon as I think this, heads start turning. Conversations trail off, and people's eyes widen as they whisper to each other. They're looking at *me*. I didn't think my sudden wave of emotion was that obvious. Wiping a sleeve across my eyes, I glance down to make sure my shirt isn't unbuttoned or something embarrassing like that, but everything looks fine.

A group of young girls giggles excitedly as they raise their phones to my face. Flashes go off, and more and more people are staring at me. People are pointing now, and the whispers are loud enough that I can make out words. Shi ta! It's her! Then words I don't understand. More flashes go off, the blinding brightness making me flinch, and people are coming closer, elbowing each other in their haste to reach me, their voices growing louder and more excited.

What's going on?

CHAPTER EIGHT

A man in his thirties materializes by my elbow, making me jump. I relax when I see he's holding a placard with my name on it. This must be the driver the studio sent. "Miss Huang?"

"Yes!" I all but grab on to his arm. The mob is pressing closer, and in pure panic, I smile dazedly at them.

The voices rise to a fevered pitch. More flashes go off.

"Come with me," the driver says, having no problem with pushing through the crowd and forging a path for me to the exit. I drag my suitcase behind me and hurry along in his wake, but the crowd follows us all the way. A blast of humid heat hits me as soon as I step outside. My neck itches unbearably, and I pull at my shirt collar, but that's not the problem. The problem is that complete strangers are dogging my footsteps and calling out questions too fast for me to understand. I feel like I'm in a pressure cooker, about to explode from the heat and all the noise.

At last we reach the car, and the driver opens the back door for me. I can't scramble in fast enough. Immediately, I'm greeted with blessedly cool air. I'd normally be appalled that the driver had left the car running, but the air-conditioning is such a relief that I send a silent apology to the ozone layer and settle against the smooth tiles of the bamboo seat cover.

The driver puts my suitcase in the trunk (I've arranged for a delivery service to take the rest of my luggage to my hotel, thanks to a pro tip from Sara Li) and gets in the front seat. As soon as we pull away from the still-shouting crowd, I ask, "What was that all about? What did I do?" This is nuts. I've only been in Beijing for twenty minutes and I'm already being stalked by a rabid mob.

The driver glances at me in the rearview mirror. "You don't know?"

Obviously. "I have no idea what's going on." My shoulders are still tight from being hunched under the gaze of all those eyes. "Please tell me."

"You look exactly like Alyssa Chua." He says it as if I should know who she is. Then he lays on the horn and shoots around another car in a move that has me gripping the edge of my seat in white-knuckled terror.

"Who?" I ask weakly when I get my breath back.

The driver tries to lurch into the next lane and then returns to the original lane when no one lets him in, narrowly missing the car behind us. More honking all around. *What the hell?*

But my driver seems less focused on our near miss than my woeful ignorance. "You don't know who Alyssa Chua is?" His voice rises in disbelief. "Just look at Weibo."

Weibo is *the* social media platform in China, but since I don't have the app for it, I pull out my phone to try Instagram. Before I left the United States, my friend Sara Li suggested that I do two things: buy a local sim card online to avoid international roaming charges, and download a virtual private network app. Hopefully, the VPN I downloaded will get me past the Great Firewall of China. Without a VPN, Western social media sites like Instagram are blocked in China. I type Alyssa's name into Instagram and wait. Luckily, my VPN works great.

There she is—Alyssa Chua. A couple million followers (probably double that on Weibo) and a few hundred selfies (*at least* double that on Weibo) taken in places that make the restaurant that Eileen took me to in LA look like a small-town diner. Every single image looks as if it were shot in a professional studio, and in them, Alyssa is dressed in gorgeous clothes with flawless makeup and her expensively cut hair blowing artfully into her face or loose around her shoulders. Other than her high-fashion style, we look eerily alike.

"Oh," I mutter. So I have a doppelgänger. And she happens to have millions of followers and an insanely glamorous lifestyle. "So, Alyssa Chua is famous for . . . doing what, exactly?"

The driver shrugs. "She has a life everyone wants," he says simply.

Got it. Alyssa is famous for having more money than she knows what to do with and partying with a string of other teen celebrities. I look at the image of Alyssa again and think of my mother's warnings to stay out of Beijing and her refusal to talk about her family. Could Alyssa be related to me? Except that both my parents were only children. So how could I have a relative my age who looks so much like me? No, I'm sure it's just a coincidence.

But thanks to my accidental resemblance to Alyssa, I now have to worry about being mobbed by strangers wherever I go. *If I don't die first.* With a jerkiness that makes me worry about keeping my last meal down, my driver finally succeeds in getting ahead of the car in front of us. But the car in the lane next to us rolls down its window. My driver does too. We're going slowly enough that the two drivers are able to have a heated argument. Then traffic speeds up again, and my driver rolls his window back up like nothing happened.

"First time in Beijing?" he asks.

I swallow my heart back into my chest. "Yes. Um . . . the people seem nice." If I discount the fact that I was mobbed as soon as I set down in Beijing. And that everyone drives with a death wish.

"Oh yes," he replies. "You will enjoy your visit here."

To my ever-lasting relief, we make it to the hotel in one piece. I put on a large pair of dark sunglasses and don't take them off as I check in. The sunglasses, combined with my jeans and plain cotton top, are enough to get me to my room with no one mistaking me for Alyssa Chua.

My room, like every single interior space so far, is aggressively air-conditioned. Now that I'm not hot and panicked from being hunted down by a mob, my fingers start to numb from the unceasing blast of frigid air. The climate-control remote has a lot of confusing buttons all labeled in Chinese, and after a few half-hearted efforts, I give up trying to turn down the air-conditioning and put on a sweater. Other than the air-conditioner overkill, the room is fine. It's pretty basic with a double bed, desk, and a small bathroom, but everything seems clean and comfortable.

Well, this has been quite a day. My head droops, and my body aches from tiredness. All I want to do is climb into bed and sleep for about a hundred hours. But first things first. I set the alarm for 3:00 a.m. That will be around lunchtime in LA and I can pretend that I'm calling my parents during my lunch break on the movie set. Which is definitely not in Beijing.

The next morning, I'm gritty-eyed and woozy from lack of sleep when the studio car arrives to take me to the set of *Butterfly*. This time, the oversize sunglasses I'm wearing are as much to hide the ravages of jet lag and a late-night conversation with my mom—in which I managed to create a semi-fictional plot of *Butterfly* that does *not* involve the film being set in Beijing in any way, shape, or form. Needless to say, falling back to sleep after our phone call wasn't easy.

I decided to sacrifice washing my hair in favor of sleeping in a bit longer this morning, and that's why I have a hat jammed on my head. I figured it also couldn't hurt my plan to keep from being mistaken for Alyssa Chua again.

The car drops me off on the outskirts of Beijing where we're shooting on location on a blocked-off street guarded by security, who check my ID before letting me onto the set. My first impression is one of chaos. Dozens of grips and personal assistants are running around, setting up lighting, microphones, and props. There's a little group of people standing off to the side that seems to have nothing to do—the other actors, probably. I dodge around busy PAs to walk over to them, and they all introduce themselves. None of them have major roles, and when I tell them I'm playing Sonia Li, there's more than one look of surprise. A sudden attack of doubt hits me. It's clear that I'm the youngest actor by far. Are they wondering why I got the lead actress role?

Maybe that's a question *I* should be asking.

My gaze swivels to Jake and Eilene, who are at the epicenter of the set's bustle and action. *What if I got this role because I look like Alyssa Chua?* My whole body goes numb with cold. Murmuring an excuse to the other actors, I hurry over to Jake and Eilene.

Stomach knotted in dread, I hold up my phone to show them an image of Alyssa. "Is that why I got this role? Because I look like the rich social media queen of China?"

Jake shrugs, making my heart plummet. "Why else would I agree to hire an untried teen actress?" He points to the screen. "That girl has millions of social media followers—and she looks like you. You can't buy that kind of publicity."

I feel sick. *That's how Eilene convinced Jake to pick me over Vivienne.* Was all her talk about changing the movie a lie? Throat dry, I turn to Eilene. "Is this why you wanted me for the role?"

A wrinkle forms between Eilene's eyes. "It's true that I noticed the resemblance when you auditioned," she says, "but that's not why

I wanted you for the role, Gemma." She holds my gaze. "You're the right actress to play Sonia, and that has nothing to do with Alyssa Chua."

I want to believe her. I do. But with Jake still staring greedily at the picture of Alyssa, it's hard to know what the whole truth is. After all, Eilene neglected to mention my resemblance to Alyssa in her pitch for us to hijack the film together.

She seems to know what I'm thinking. "I'm sorry, Gemma. I should have told you."

"Told her what?" Jake snorts. "That I wouldn't agree to cast her for the part until you told me who Alyssa Chua was and how much Gemma looked like her? Please. You did her a favor, Eilene. Yeah, her audition wasn't bad, but she was still lucky to get this role fresh out of high school."

Eilene's mouth crimps. "That's enough. Like I said, Gemma is the right actress for the part, and *that's* why I fought for her to get the role."

My spirits lift at her words. "I appreciate this role." I *do* understand how lucky I am, but it still stings to find out that I hadn't gotten the part on my own. "But I'll earn my place here through my *acting*—not because of who I might look like."

"I absolutely believe that," Eilene says.

"Fine," Jake says. "Now, if you're done with your daily affirmation, can you please get to hair and makeup? We don't have all day."

Gritting my teeth, I do a slow spin because there are a dozen trailers set up, and I have no idea which one is hair and makeup. Taking pity on me, Eileen points me in the right direction. Jake tells me not to "take too long."

I hurry to the trailer Eileen pointed out, still irritated by Jake. It's going to suck if the director is holding a grudge against me for not being the actress he originally picked.

The woman in charge of my hair and makeup is American and introduces herself as Liz. She's an older white woman who clucks in distress at the dark circles under my eyes. The two women assisting Liz and doing general cleanup are Chinese, and neither introduces herself to me. They seem to be under the impression that I don't understand any Chinese because they talk freely about me. But like a lot of American-born Chinese, I understand a lot more Chinese than I can speak. Still, even if I *didn't* understand the language, their repeated mention of Alyssa Chua would've clued me in to the topic of their conversation—how much I look like the glamorous social media star. From their talk, I gather that Alyssa is the daughter of a socialite mother and a rich businessman father.

"Xie xie," I say, thanking them in Chinese, as one woman hands me a cup of tea and the other whisks the towel from my neck.

They dart anxious looks at each other and don't say another word to or about me. I would've liked to tell them that I don't mind them talking about me, but I'm too shy to say it in my stilted Chinese.

Then Liz swivels my chair to face the dressing room mirror, and my jaw goes slack at what I see. No wonder the two Chinese women couldn't stop talking about my resemblance to Alyssa Chua. With my hair arranged in impossibly chic layers and the professional makeup . . . I'm a dead ringer for her.

CHAPTER NINE

Jake is easier to deal with when I get back to the set. I mean, he's still an asshole, but at least he's an asshole who seems to know what he's doing. Fortunately, Aidan Keller, my co-star, is not only professional, but he actually seems like a decent human being. Eilene told me that he's a rarity in Hollywood—notoriously faithful to his wife. In fact, they had to throw an obscene amount of money his way to get him to take a role that required him to be so far from his family. As for me . . . I wouldn't call the amount they're paying me *obscene*—in fact, it's downright prudish. But it's still way more than I'd ever dreamed of being paid as an actress, so I'm not complaining.

When I told Eilene this, she said that might be true as I'm starting out, but that I shouldn't get too far into my career before I *do* complain. *Believe me*, she said darkly, *I'm no stranger to pay disparity.* Not for the first time, I wonder what Eilene's getting paid to be a co-director. Not enough and not nearly as much as Jake—that's for damn sure.

Jake is having Aidan and me rehearse a scene a few times before we start shooting. The scene we're shooting today is of Sonia out of male drag. Sonia is enjoying a solitary dinner at a restaurant and bumps into Ryan. This is the scene I did for my first audition, and I'm more eager than nervous to dive in. We start with the rehearsal of the scene, and it goes pretty well. For one thing, Aidan is a good actor, and he makes even the sappy lines work.

Eilene lets Jake take the lead and doesn't comment as Jake runs through a rapid-fire critique, starting with Aidan's performance. Aidan doesn't seem fazed in the least and takes in every direction with a nod of his head or an even-keeled "Got it." When it's my turn, I'm not nearly as chill, but I have to admit that everything Jake says makes sense, and the second rehearsal of the scene goes smoothly.

It requires a few takes before Jake is satisfied. The only direction Eilene gives through the rehearsal and shooting of the dinner scene is "Relax, Gemma," in a voice wound tight as a spool of thread. The weird thing is that I *was* relaxed. As relaxed as I could be on my first day on the set. But I'm not now. What's Eilene up to? She said that she wants me to help her change the direction of the movie, but how am I supposed to do that if she's not doing any directing?

When we take our first break, Jake suggests (oh so casually) that I take a walk near the barricade dividing the set from the rest of the street. There are a few curious onlookers that the security guards efficiently wave off, but it's clear as day that Jake is hoping to cash in on my famous look-alike.

I fold my arms across my chest. "No way," I respond. I might have to take Jake's directions when we're shooting scenes, but I'm not about to let him trot me out like a prize horse for the paparazzi.

In a dangerous voice, Eilene says, "Drop it, Jake."

To my surprise, he *does* drop it.

We wrap up the shoot before the end of the day, and Jake decides to have us rehearse the scene that follows—the scene I did for my second callback. In this scene, Ryan chases Sonia out into the rain after their argument at the restaurant.

It's in the middle of our rehearsal for this scene that Eilene makes her move. "This isn't working." She stands up from her director's chair next to Jake's.

I'm caught off guard, foolishly batting my eyes up at Aidan. But I straighten immediately, my gaze snapping over to Eilene. She's right. We're both trying our damnedest, but this scene just isn't coming together.

Aidan and I have enough on-screen chemistry, so that's not the problem. The problem is that we're saying the same lines I read during my callback two weeks ago—and they haven't gotten any less icky since then.

"Are you kidding me!" Jake throws his hands in the air. "How can you tell it's not working if they haven't even finished the scene?"

"Do *you* think it's working, Jake?" she asks reasonably.

"No," he admits sulkily. "But we can fix it."

"Fine." Eilene sits down and crosses her legs at the ankle. "Fix it, then."

Jake gives Aidan some blocking directions and positions him to "generate heat." To me, his directions boil down to "sex it up."

Great. If I sex up this scene any more, I'll be draped onto Aidan like plastic wrap with my tongue in his ear. Aidan and I exchange a *look*, but what can we do? Jake's the director.

We do the scene again, and if anything, it's worse.

My shoulders hunch up defensively as Jake yells, "Cut!"

I'm expecting Jake to blow his top, but instead, he turns to Eilene and says wryly, "Point taken." My mouth drops open. *The great Jake Tyler admitting that someone else might be right?* "Any ideas?" *And that someone else might have ideas?* Hell hath officially frozen over.

"I'd like to do a rewrite of the scene," Eilene says calmly. No unseemly gloating or smugness—just pure confidence. My admiration for her, already high, shoots into the stratosphere. "See if we can't get something Gemma and Aidan are more comfortable with."

Jake glances at Aidan. "What do you think?"

"I'll go along with whatever you decide," Aidan says easily.

Jake transfers his gaze to me. "What about you? Are *you* uncomfortable with this scene as is?"

"Well," I hedge, "I can get into the part where I tell Ryan to be careful, but there's an earlier part . . ."

"What part?" Jake asks.

To be truthful, *most* of the dialogue makes me want to crawl out of my skin. How do I pick just one thing? Behind Jake's back, Eilene gives me an encouraging nod, so I take a breath and say, "Like when Ryan calls me his little butterfly."

"The film *is* called *Butterfly*," Jake says sarcastically. "Or hadn't you noticed?"

Unexpectedly, Aidan speaks up. "You know, that line does make Ryan seem like a jerk."

I shoot Aidan a grateful look and wait for Jake to glare at Aidan or say something sarcastic, but he just shrugs. To Eilene, he says, "It looks like both our leads agree with you. Work with Henry and do a rewrite, but do it fast. We're on a tight schedule." He turns to Aidan and me. "As soon as Eilene and Henry get you the new lines for this scene, memorize it. We pick up rehearsals tomorrow." He picks up his megaphone and booms, "That's a wrap for today!"

As everyone scatters to shut down the set, Eilene pulls me aside. "Thank you for speaking your truth, Gemma," she murmurs.

I blush furiously. "It was nothing."

"It was something," she corrects me gently. "It's a chance to make something of this movie."

The next day, we rehearse Eilene's rewritten scene in the rain, and I'm so nervous about not messing it up that, of course, I do just that.

Jake does a lot of yelling, and my stomach curls tensely because I know he's right. I did play that scene with about as much emotion as a wet noodle.

But as bad as Jake's anger is, it's not as bad as when Eilene pulls me aside and tells me that she has faith in me. Like I didn't know that. Like my worry about letting her down wasn't the *exact* reason I effed it up.

For the second run-through, Jake reminds me to play Sonia as a "sex kitten in heels." Wow, Jake really is an ass. As if there was any doubt. To make matters worse, his words remind me of my aching arches and the pair of patent leather torture chambers currently squishing my toes.

Eilene adds, "Remember you're conflicted. You've never gotten over Ryan, but you're afraid of getting burned. It's a dangerous attraction that you just can't resist."

I fall upon her directions in relief. I can't play Sonia unless she comes alive for me. *Sex kitten in heels?* All that does is conjure up a distracting mental image of a wobbly kitten in stiletto heels and a corset. But . . . *Irresistible attraction? Playing with fire?* I'm into it.

The second rehearsal is better. And after a couple takes, I stop second-guessing myself and start getting into character. By the end of the day, I feel like I've nailed it.

Jake grunts his approval, and Aidan tells me I did a great job.

"Bu cuo," Eilene says to me with a smile.

My face heats in the glow of her praise. Like I said, there's nothing like a "not bad" in Chinese. And one from my idol? Even better.

Bu cuo, indeed.

CHAPTER TEN

Two days later, I'm totally wiped out by the time I get back to my hotel after a day of shooting. Jake was being extra finicky, so it was nearly ten at night before he called a wrap on today's shoot.

The first week on the set of *Butterfly* is almost over, and it's been a blur of exhaustion, but I've never been happier. Eilene's successful rewrite of the scene means that she now has oversight on the script. In practice, she's now not only the co-director but the co-screenwriter too. But it's still Jake's movie, and he doesn't let anyone forget it. *I've learned to pick my battles*, Eilene tells me dryly.

As for me making a suggestion of my own? Not going to happen. Still, I'm living my dream as a lead actress in a Hollywood movie, so I'm not going to let one bad-tempered director spoil things for me. In fact, there are only two things marring my happiness. One—I'm lying to my parents. Two—I haven't talked to Ken since I got to Beijing four days ago.

Between my movie and his commercial, Ken and I are already independently busy. Throw in a fifteen-hour time difference, and talking on the phone becomes nearly impossible. We're giving each other text updates, but it's not the same. *What if Ken's dating up a storm while I'm in Beijing?* Meanwhile, I haven't even met anyone my own *age* here.

Just then, my room's landline starts ringing. Wearily, I pick it up, remembering to answer with a "Wei?" instead of a "Hello?"

The polite female voice on the other end of the line replies in English. "Miss Huang, this is the hotel desk," she says. "You have a visitor. She's waiting for you in our private VIP room."

Eilene. She's probably here to debrief today's shoot. I would have thought that she'd first let me get a good night's sleep, but I guess sleep will have to wait.

When I get down to the main desk, a receptionist is waiting to escort me to Eilene. She leads me through the hotel bar to a mirrored door in a discreet corner, opens it, and then steps aside. It's not Eilene.

The girl sitting in a red leather booth in a sleeveless black silk dress with little clusters of diamonds flashing at her throat, ears, and wrist . . . is Alyssa Chua.

My jaw drops. Alyssa Chua—who's so famous that she causes *riots* with her mere presence—is at my hotel.

"Who *are* you?" My heart is pounding as I ask the question. Now that I'm seeing her up close and in person, the resemblance is startling. There are small differences like her cheekbones being higher and her chin being sharper, but we could still be twins. Visions of *The Parent Trap* dance in my head. Is Alyssa my twin sister? My stomach twists sickly. Did my mother have a secret daughter that she abandoned? Is that why she didn't want me to come to Beijing? *No. I'm overreacting.* Plenty of people who aren't related look alike. But seriously. This girl looks a *lot* like me.

Alyssa smiles, but her expression is wary. "I'm Alyssa Chua. And *you're* Gemma, an American actress shooting a film in Beijing." She speaks flawless English with the slightest of accents. Holding her phone out, she asks, "Is this you?"

Chills run down my spine. It's an image of me from the first day I was on set. Looking closer, I can make out a bunch of Chinese characters accompanying the picture, making it look like a social media site. Shakily, I slide into the seat opposite her. "What is my picture doing on . . . Is that Weibo?" I remember the curious onlookers hanging out during the shoot and wonder if one of them took this picture.

"It's a paparazzi site on Weibo dedicated to celebrity gossip," she says, radiating an intensity at odds with her carefree social media image. "In the last few days, the site has blown up with speculation that I've decided to start a career as an actress. Except I haven't. That's *you* in that picture." Her eyes narrow. "And as soon as I saw your picture, I knew who you were."

My mouth goes dry as I think of all my mom's cloak-and-dagger warnings about staying out of Beijing. This is no joke. Something seriously strange is happening. "And who do you think I am?"

"My mother has a twin sister who was cut off from the family thirty years ago," Alyssa says hesitantly. "I think there's a possibility that . . . you're her daughter."

Shock jolts through me. "My mother doesn't have a twin sister." *I need to sit down.* Except I'm already sitting down. Maybe if I put my head between my knees and take a few breaths, all this will seem normal. Maybe it will make perfect sense that I'm related to an über-rich family—*that my mother never told me about.* A rich family that cut my mother off. Nope. Calm breathing will *not* help.

"Eighteen years ago, my mother received an envelope with no return address." Nervousness leaks into Alyssa's voice. "Inside, there was a picture of a baby." *Whoa. My mom sent a baby picture of me to her twin sister? A twin sister I didn't even know she had?!* As if Alyssa is *trying* to make my head explode, she continues. "And written on the back of the picture, there was a message. It said, 'Do not forget.'"

Feeling like I'm drowning in a whirlpool, I ask faintly, "What does that even mean?"

"It could mean many things." Alyssa's eyes shift away from me.

She's hiding something. "But my mother took it to mean that my aunt wanted to remind her about *you*—who should inherit a part of our family fortune. Although my mother is the eldest by a few minutes, my grandparents intended for both daughters to inherit equally. Your mother knew that, and she has not forgotten or forgiven the family that drove her out."

My heart goes still in my chest. In all my wildest imaginings about my mother's past, heiress to a vast fortune has *never* even crossed my mind. "So, my mother was kicked out of the family." It would make sense for my mother to be bitter about that. But to send a baby picture of me, reminding her family of how they had wronged her? That doesn't seem like my mom. An ache blooms in my lungs, making it hard to breathe. "Why?"

"I don't know." She still won't meet my eyes. Under that cool silk and the hard glitter of diamonds, Alyssa Chua is lying—and I want to know why.

"Try again," I say, and the sudden, furious pulse in my throat startles me.

She studies her hands clenched in her lap. "All I've ever known is that I have an aunt who gave birth to a girl eighteen years ago. Given how much we look alike and that your Instagram feed says you're eighteen, I'm guessing you're my cousin."

"My mother never told me I had an aunt." My dizziness grows worse, and my voice sounds like it's coming from a long way away. "Or a cousin." But, of course, this must all be a mistake. My mother can't possibly come from an incredibly wealthy family. *I* can't possibly be related to a super-famous girl like Alyssa Chua.

Alyssa raises her gaze to mine. "I know your family name is Huang, but what was your mother's family name before she married?"

Heat floods my face. There's no way that I'm going to tell Alyssa that I have no idea.

Her expression softens. "My aunt's given name is Lei," she says. "That's your mother's name, isn't it?"

My heart starts banging against my rib cage like a feral beast. "Yes." It would be one too many coincidences for her lost aunt and my mother to share the same name. Alyssa is telling the truth—she *is* my cousin. "Oh my god." *Don't freak out, Gemma.* But it's no use—the room is already spinning, and I'm pretty much breathing into an imaginary paper bag at this point. *Well, at least my mother's not hiding a secret, abandoned daughter.* No, she's just hiding the fact that her high-society family kicked her out for some mysterious reason. Oh, and that I was supposed to inherit a fortune. There's that too. *Shit. All this soap opera stuff is actually true.*

"I know it's a lot to take in." Alyssa studies me. "You know, I've always wanted to meet you. When I was little, my mother told me that my aunt went to Hong Kong." She pauses. "One year—for my tenth birthday—I asked if we could take a trip to Hong Kong to find you."

A sudden pain hits my heart at her words. I thought I had gotten over that childish longing for a sister, a brother, a cousin—someone my own age to grow up with. Unlike Alyssa, I didn't grow up knowing I had a cousin. If I had—I would have wanted to find her too. Did Alyssa actually look for me? "You wouldn't have found me in Hong Kong." My voice doesn't betray the turmoil of my inner thoughts. *I could have met my cousin in time to grow up with her. If I had been in Hong Kong, that is.* "My parents did live there, but they moved to the U.S. before I was born."

"What year did your parents leave Hong Kong?"

My breath catches. "1997." I knew that my parents came to the United States the year Hong Kong reverted from British to Chinese control. I just never thought it might mean something.

"I see." Her expression doesn't change, so maybe there's nothing significant about the year my parents left Hong Kong. *Just another coincidence among too many other coincidences.*

I can't help but ask the question burning in my heart. "Did you . . . ever go to Hong Kong to look for us?" *For me. Your cousin.*

"No." Alyssa plays with the diamond-encrusted bangle on her wrist.

A sick feeling of hurt punches me in the gut. But why should it matter? I've only just met Alyssa. In fact, I've only just found out that I *have* a cousin. Still, my body is numb with loss as I ask, "Why not?" The air seems to thin out as I wait for her reply.

"Because of my po po. My grandmother."

"I know what po po means." *Even though I've never had reason to call anyone Po Po.* But what does her grandmother have to do with anything?

"Of course you do," Alyssa says politely. "Po Po is the reason your presence in Beijing needs to be a secret. You see, I made the mistake of asking to look for you in my grandmother's presence, and"—a pained expression comes into her eyes—"she fainted."

"Fainted?" My voice is skeptical. "Like turned pale, clutched her heart, and collapsed to the floor?" I've done that as a character in a scene, but *real* people don't faint from shock.

"Yes," she says tensely. "That's exactly what happened." *OK, apparently real people do faint from shock.* "It scared me so much that I never brought up looking for you again."

Disappointment clogs my throat. I guess Alyssa must not have wanted to find me that badly. I sit there, the red leather of the booth sticking to my thighs, and moisten my lips, but despite all the questions bubbling up inside me, I don't know what to say.

The silence stretches out between us until Alyssa leans so close that the light, spicy scent of her expensive perfume wafts into my face. "After the incident with Po Po, Gong Gong made me promise never to mention you or your mother again." *Gong Gong.* That was what the little girl at the airport called her grandfather. A mass of emotions squeezes my chest as she continues. "Gong Gong said that talking about your mother is too painful for Po Po to bear. So that's why Po Po can't find out that you're in Beijing." Her face pinches tight. "Po Po is old and has a bad heart. She pretty much lives in seclusion now. I just want to protect her from—"

"Me." My voice is dry as an old corpse gone to ashes. I would sympathize with Alyssa's concern for her grandmother—if *I* weren't the monstrous secret that her . . . *our* grandmother needed protecting from.

She flinches. "I don't have a right to ask, but could you be careful? I don't want Po Po to find out about you."

This is all too much. A cousin who's a famous social media star. A grandfather who bans talk of my mother. A grandmother who faints at the mention of my mother. Then a question penetrates the fog in my head. "If your grandmother is in seclusion, why do you think she'd find out about me?"

"Po Po follows me on Weibo," Alyssa explains, as if it's the most reasonable thing in the world for her elderly, reclusive grandmother to follow her on social media. "She might get suspicious if someone who looked like me were spotted where I wasn't supposed to be."

"Fine," I say tersely. My shock is fading, and I'm thinking more clearly now. There's more to my mother's past than Alyssa is telling me, and I need to know it all. Adrenaline speeds up my pulse. "I won't push myself onto your grandmother, but if you don't know what happened to drive my mother off, then I want to talk to someone who does. I want to talk to your mother. My aunt. Or our grandfather."

She taps her fingers on the black lacquered table between us. At last, she says, "I'm sorry, Gemma, but that's not possible."

"Why not?" My mouth sets. "At least tell your mother and grandfather that I'm in Beijing and want to see them."

"I already told my mother. And she doesn't want to see you." This time, Alyssa holds my gaze. *She's telling the truth.*

A dull ache spreads through my chest. This is worse than thinking that I had no family in China. Now I find out that I *do* have a family—but there's a catch. They don't want me.

Alyssa says, "Gong Gong doesn't know you're here, and you'd better hope that *he* doesn't find out."

"What are you talking about?" *Is she seriously saying I should be afraid of my own grandfather?*

"It's just that . . . Gong Gong won't like it." Dryly, she says, "Sung Shen Yi has made a name for himself as someone you don't want for an enemy."

"Is he my enemy, then?" Prickles of cold form between my shoulder blades.

"Of course not," she says. "All I'm saying is that it's better if no one else in my family finds out you're here."

The tension between us grows thick and palpable. If she thinks I'm going to just lie low and ignore this mystery about my family—then she doesn't know me at all. *Which, of course, is exactly the problem.* My cousin doesn't know me. And she doesn't want to know me.

"I can see how this seems unfair." Alyssa's eyes darken with a sympathy that I don't want. "After all, you have a right to . . . Well, let's just say you deserve some compensation."

"No. I don't want *anything* from you!" That's not true. But the only thing I want—that I've ever wanted—is the one thing I can't have. Family. A feeling of belonging to the country where my parents were born.

"Gemma," Alyssa says, sounding worried, "I'd still like to do something to make up for all this."

Fury races through me. Does she think I'm just some problem that will go away if she throws some money at me? Ignoring her outstretched hand, I stand, almost upending the table. "It's been a long night," I say coldly. "Good night."

As I stumble out of the private room, with its red leather and ebony tables, I can feel Alyssa's eyes following me.

CHAPTER ELEVEN

*O*h hell, I played that all wrong. That's the conclusion I come to the next day as I replay the conversation with Alyssa in my head. She knew more than she was letting on—I'm sure of it. But instead of pressing her about why my mom was kicked out of the family, I let my anger get the best of me and stormed out without any of the answers I desperately want. *If only I hadn't been so damned freaked out by finding out that I'm related to one of China's elite rich.*

A peal of laughter outside my trailer makes me sigh. I should go out and join my castmates for lunch and celebrate a successful first week of filming. But instead of joining them, I take out my phone.

I haven't been able to connect to my VPN recently, which my friend Sara Li warned could happen. The Chinese government constantly updates their security measures and cracks down on VPN access—so no more Twitter, Instagram, or Facebook for me. *Great Firewall of China strikes again.* Google still works—but I'm not about to google Alyssa Chua for the hundredth time. I already know that she's nineteen, just a year older than I am, and she has oodles of money and a killer fashion sense. What else do I need to know about her?

Instead, I search for "Alyssa Chua's grandmother." Nothing comes up. I try Alyssa's mother next, and some articles in Chinese come up. Luckily Google Translate works even without a VPN, so I skim a few articles. There are some mentions of Alyssa's socialite mother and her involvement in charities, but no images of her. It looks like Alyssa is the face of the family.

Then I search for Alyssa's grandfather. Again, no results. Then I remember what Alyssa said about him. *Sung Shen Yi has made a name for himself as someone you don't want for an enemy.* I type in my grandfather's name. At once, I get an error message. That's odd. I try again and get the same message. Then I google something random and have no problem getting access.

This is so weird. I've heard that searches for topics like the Dalai Lama or the Tiananmen Square massacre get blocked by the Great Firewall of China. But it's not like I'm searching for the kind of sensitive information that usually gets blocked. With my stomach knotting, I google *1989 Tiananmen Square massacre.* Immediately, I get the same error message that came up when I was searching for Alyssa's . . . my . . . grandfather. Chills run down my back. *Why would information on my grandfather be blocked?*

Thoroughly unsettled, I put away my phone. Our lunch break will be over soon, and I've frittered it away with Internet searches. Listlessly, I pick at my dry sandwich. It would be unappetizing at the best of times, but the discovery that my grandfather is some kind of shadowy, powerful figure makes the sandwich even less appealing. I'm not sure who's catering our meals, but they have some odd notions about what Americans want to eat.

Eilene comes by my trailer and smiles sympathetically as I set down the sandwich. "Not doing it for you?"

I make an effort to push away thoughts of my grandfather. "I have a list of food that I will *not* leave Beijing without eating." I've had all the food on my list before, but I'm *dying* to eat my favorite Chinese food in China.

She laughs.

"No, I mean a literal list, as in I wrote it down by hand." I give the sandwich a contemptuous flick. "And a sandwich with processed cheese and mystery meat is not on my list."

"Then it's a good thing tomorrow's your first day off."

Excitement wriggles through my body and distracts me from thoughts of Alyssa. "I. Cannot. Wait."

Eilene's eyes drift to the ever-present tablet in her hand. While I'm enjoying my day off, she'll probably use the time rewriting scenes with Henry, the screenwriter. There are new worry lines on her forehead, and she's been looking a bit pale lately. It can't be easy to be a co-director and now a co-writer in all but name. Just the thought of juggling those roles gives me a sympathetic headache. My own troubles with Jake and the pressure of not letting Eilene down seem minor in comparison. *But I bet Eilene doesn't have a long-lost cousin and a family secret to contend with.*

Eilene visibly tears her attention from her tablet and sets it on my dressing table. "Let's see this list of yours."

I pull a steno pad out of my bag, flip to the first page, and hand it over.

She takes it and starts reading. "Hand-shaven noodles, dumplings, radish cake, green onion pancake, egg tarts, hot pot . . . Why is hot pot crossed off?"

"Oh." I blush, not sure how to explain. "It was always a family thing." My dad, the cook in our family, would spend hours chopping vegetables to stew in the hot pot, and when the vegetables were finally done, we'd all sit down with a plate of thinly sliced raw meat and long chopsticks. I loved dropping the meat into the electric pot and watching it curl in the boiling stew, bobbing among cabbage and turnips. I'd want to pull my meat out too soon, but my mom would tell me to be patient, until I finally learned when it was the right time to pull the meat and vegetables out to be dipped in a little dish of soy sauce and sesame paste.

Just the memory is making me salivate, but it's not just the food

I'm missing. It's the warm, scented steam rising into my face as we talk, laugh, and mock fight over the "best" corner of the pot. But sometimes, through that steam, I'd catch a look on my mom's face as she looked around our small table. Like she was searching for faces that weren't there at the table with us. *Who the hell is my grandfather and why doesn't my mother want me in Beijing?*

A frown passes over Eilene's face. "It doesn't feel right to eat hot pot on your own, does it?"

She's seconds away from offering to take me out for hot pot, and that's time she can't spare, so I rush to say, "I'm looking forward to seeing Beijing on my own, eating at those little food stalls with no one to tell me to hurry and get into costume!"

"Well, you deserve it." Her smile is tinged with relief. "Have fun!"

When I get back to the hotel, one of the receptionists sees me and hurries over—completely abandoning the middle-aged couple she was checking in. They glare at me as if this is *my* fault.

But I'm just as confused. Is this another case of mistaken identity?

"Miss Huang," the receptionist says, shooting down my assumption that she's mistaken me for Alyssa. "I'm happy to tell you that your room has been upgraded. Please come with me so I may show you where you'll be staying."

Huh? "There must be some mistake," I say. "No one has told me about an upgrade."

"There's no mistake," she assures me.

Maybe the film studio is feeling generous. "Just let me pack my things."

"Your belongings have already been moved."

"Um, OK then." Wow, they really want to give me this upgrade. "Thanks."

The couple bursts into complaints as the receptionist turns to lead me to my room, and she answers them politely in Chinese. "I'm sorry, but this is an important guest." She clearly doesn't realize I understand Chinese.

My eyes widen. Important guest?

The couple is staring at me in speculation. "Shi ta," the woman says, her eyes glued on me. *It's her.*

Great. Questions can wait. My first priority is to get away from Alyssa's fans.

The receptionist takes me all the way to the top floor. Here, the halls are lined with metal sconces that look like art pieces, and my footsteps echo on richly veined granite floors. She wasn't kidding about an upgrade. The receptionist opens one of the doors and then hands me the card with a little bow.

The card almost falls from my nerveless hand. This isn't an upgrade. It's a superpowered boost into the stratosphere.

For one thing, it's not so much a room as it's a full-size apartment bigger than the one I shared with Glory and Camille in LA. A sitting area with white couches and pillows in muted golds greets me, and the polished wood floors are piled with soft white rugs that come up to my ankles when I walk inside. Next to the sitting area is a full kitchen with a stocked bar. Copper accents and warm wood make the whole space seem bright and lavish.

The receptionist says proudly, "This is our best suite, and I hope you will be comfortable here."

Comfortable is an understatement, I think dazedly. I blink in astonishment as each new shiny luxury is revealed. A game room with a state-of-the-art gaming system and huge projector screen. A balcony garden fragrant with flowers. I have to pinch myself to make sure I'm not dreaming.

Next the receptionist shows me the bedroom, which has a stunning view of the city skyline. As for the tall four-poster bed with a bronze-colored silk throw draped at its foot and fluffy pillows at its head . . . Well, that looks like it will give me the best sleep of my life.

Then she opens the bamboo sliding door to the bathroom. Everything is gorgeous, but the most arresting feature—displayed on a wooden platform with steps leading up to it—is a gigantic jetted soaking tub. That's when my brain snaps out of its luxury-drugged state. There's no way the studio would spring for this suite.

"I'm sorry, but I don't think this suite is supposed to be mine." I cast a longing glance at the bright hammered copper bowls set next to the tub. They're filled with bath salts of various colors and . . . Holy crap. Are those actual rose petals? Discreetly, I wipe the drool that no doubt must be oozing down my chin.

"Ah," the receptionist says. "Perhaps this will make things clearer." She takes me back to the sitting area and gestures to the heavy wooden coffee table, where a bottle of champagne rests inside a copper ice bucket.

Is she actually suggesting that alcohol will clear things up? The drinking age is eighteen in China, but still. Then I notice a pale pink envelope propped up against the ice bucket. My fingers itch to rip into it, but I glance at the receptionist. Maybe I should wait until I'm alone before reading the note.

"I leave you to enjoy your suite," she says tactfully. "Please call down to the front desk if you need anything. By the way, room service is included in your upgrade, so feel free to order anything you want. The bill will be taken care of." After dropping that earth-shattering information, she leaves.

I snatch up the envelope and register that it smells like Alyssa's expensive perfume. Inside is a brief note on pale pink paper that matches the envelope.

> **Dear Gemma,**
> **Sorry about how weird everything is. I know**
> **you don't want anything from me, but I**
> **wanted to give you a better welcome than**
> **the one you got from me last night.**
> **Xoxo,**
> **Alyssa**

Reading Alyssa's note makes me even more confused. Is this a bribe so I'll lie low and keep quiet? Or is this a goodwill gift? I know which one is more likely. A self-centered social media darling wouldn't think twice about buying me off with a hotel upgrade. But I want to believe that she's being sincere. I know it's naive, but I want to believe that Alyssa is genuinely trying to make things right between us.

With a sigh, I put the note down. I'm not going to solve the mystery of Alyssa anytime soon, so I might as well enjoy this unexpected luxury while I can. First order of business—a glass of champagne in a jetted tub. With rose petals.

CHAPTER TWELVE

The next day, I wake up disoriented as a rosy glow lights my room. It's coming from the round lamp on the nightstand. Blinking, I think about sitting up, but the soft nest of blankets and pillows is just too cozy. *Since when was my hotel bed this comfortable?*

That's when I remember setting the wake-up time on my natural-light lamp . . . and why I have such a thing as a natural-light lamp in the first place.

I bolt upright on the bed. Gold silk curtains. Matching silk chairs. A dressing table with a mirror framed in lacquered rosewood. A walk-in, lighted closet—that's where my small collection of clothes hangs on velvet hangers and flutters sadly in the cavernous depths.

So, this fairy-tale suite wasn't a dream after all. I don't even know how to reach Alyssa to thank her for this fantastic upgrade. I feel a little bad that I got so angry at her when we first met. But my chagrin doesn't stop me from ordering a big breakfast from room service as I plan out my day of sightseeing on one of the plush couches in the sitting room.

Even though it isn't on my food wish list, I order shi fan (soupy rice) in a fit of nostalgia. Dad makes shi fan, but plain, without the dizzying array of sides that are delivered to my hotel room. Diced pickled black turnips. Spicy cucumbers. Marinated tea eggs. Not at all like the shi fan Dad makes. He's the only one in the family who eats shi fan plain. He calls it his comfort food, but my mom teasingly calls it "peasant food." Whenever Mom says things like that, Dad smiles and fondly calls her "Gong zhu." Princess.

Suddenly, the food in my mouth loses its flavor. My mother must have grown up in the kind of luxury that surrounds me now. What Alyssa has given me is a small part of what my mother lost. Guilt stabs me. How can I order room service and soak in a jetted tub when all these expensive gifts come from a family that has rejected my mother? My stomach turns as I push away the shi fan.

Then Mom's dry voice comes into my head. "That's perfectly good food. Don't waste it!"

She's right. Mom is, if nothing else, practical. Although I don't enjoy it as much as I did a few minutes ago, I finish my breakfast.

Then I sit for a moment, looking at the empty plates and bowls. *Stop feeling sorry for yourself,* I tell myself sternly. So what if my life's a little complicated at the moment? I'm about to be all touristy and go sightseeing in a city teeming with culture and history.

Feeling a bit better, I find my steno pad and flip past the food wish list. Time to start a list of places I want to see in China. The Great Wall, of course. And equally important—Tiananmen Square.

A couple of months ago, my mother's museum had an exhibit to commemorate the thirtieth anniversary of the 1989 Tiananmen Square massacre—and the images still haunt me. A long line of tanks rolling into the square. Student protesters throwing stones at those tanks. Blood streaming from the faces of protesters as they're carried out by their frightened comrades. Dead bodies among the smoke and rubble.

I couldn't help but ask my parents if they had been there. June 4, 1989. They would have been around my age at the time. The age of the student protesters. Except that the thought of my middle-class, stodgy parents as youthful revolutionaries fighting against government control and censorship is laughable. There's no way they were at the Tiananmen Square protests.

My mom confirmed this when she replied, "It wasn't allowed." That would be enough for my pragmatic mom to stay away from Tiananmen Square.

My dad also responded as expected—with his political science professor hat on. He actually tried to give me a lecture about the political function of Tiananmen Square . . . beginning in the Qing dynasty of the seventeenth century.

Luckily, Mom shut him down before he could really get going. She usually lets him ramble, but this time was different. "That's enough, Delun," she said sharply, and he stopped at once. I guess she could see that I wanted to take in the images in the exhibit without Dad's professorial commentary.

But as much as I want to see Tiananmen Square in real time, I don't feel that it should be my first stop. It would set a grim tone for a day that's supposed to be fun and make me forget my worries. Luckily, Tiananmen Square is within walking distance of a place that would be a much better start to my day.

The Forbidden City.

It's called that because the walled, sprawling complex was the exclusive residence of royalty. A plebeian like myself (and the millions of tourists who visit it) would have been forbidden to enter in imperial times unless we were servants. Or performers. I smile and fantasize about being summoned to the Forbidden City for a performance.

Firmly, I jot down, "Forbidden City" in my steno pad. *It's decided, then.* First the Forbidden City. And then Tiananmen Square.

One of the perks of my job is the use of the studio car, so I get dropped off at Zhongshan Park. The southern gate is the only entrance to the Forbidden City, but there are several ways to get there. My driver suggests that I walk along the moat in the park to avoid the crowds approaching the southern gate through Tiananmen Square.

I'm happy to take his advice. Especially when the scent of roses and peonies hits my body with a jolt of pure sweetness, which is better than a sugar rush. The fragrance unfurls the tense muscles down my spine as I walk along the tree-lined, still waters of the moat. I guess I've been pretty tightly wound, between the pressures of the movie, lying to my parents, meeting Alyssa, and missing Ken. *Speaking of which . . .*

I check the time and run the time difference in my head—it's now seven on Friday night in LA. Maybe I'll get lucky and actually reach Ken this time. I try calling him, but he doesn't pick up. As I leave yet another voicemail, doubt zings through me. *Why isn't he answering his phone on a Friday night? Who's he out with?* And his emails have been pretty short. Maybe he's just not good at emails?

I have to remind myself that this kind of jealousy is exactly *why* being non-exclusive is a good idea. Ken has every right to see whoever he wants. And I have every right to enjoy myself too. I take a few relaxing breaths and let the beauty of the park work its magic.

Unfortunately, the green quiet of the park comes to an abrupt end when I arrive at the southern gate a little while later. I thought I was here pretty early at ten on a Saturday morning, but the crowd at the gate is already about fifty people. Uneasily, I stand in line and adjust my oversize sunglasses. Memories of the bright flashes of cameras and the excited babble of voices flood me. *So much for forgetting about Alyssa Chua today.* My neck tenses back up, and my stomach twists. *Relax, Gemma. No one's going to think you're Alyssa. Not in your off-the-rack capris and thrift-store tank top.*

Still, I'm glad that there are two lines—one for local Chinese who already bought their tickets online, and another for foreigners to buy tickets. There's less of a chance that other tourists or expats would even know who Alyssa is, so relief fills me as I join the latter in line. The line moves quickly, and no one spares a glance at me. There is one touchy moment when the ticket seller seems to stare at me a little longer than necessary, but I tell myself it's just because I ask for the ticket in my accented Chinese. In any case, she gives me the same canned instructions in English that she gave the group before me. This southern gate is the only entrance point, and the northern gate is the only exit point. One way in, and one way out.

Once inside the complex, I'm separated from the other foreigners and open to the speculative gazes of local Chinese tourists. The heat is beating down on my head, making my scalp itch, and I'm wishing I'd brought a hat for more than one reason. I scan the courtyard for a quiet, shady place, but all I see is an immense expanse of gray brick and imposing red buildings in every direction. My face heats in prickling discomfort as people press around me. Is that girl with her phone out taking a picture of *me*? No, of course not. She's taking a selfie. *Duh.* Because she's in the *Forbidden City.* And so am I. *So enjoy yourself!* I take a deep breath and force my pulse to slow. I'm not going to let my paranoia distract me from the fact that I'm walking toward an actual imperial palace.

Yes, there are hundreds of people walking with me, but it's still an *imperial palace.* Rising into the heavens with red pillars, a yellow curved roof, and broad stone stairs. A lump of awe and excitement congeals in my throat. I'm totally ready to bathe in thousands of years of culture—like the Forbidden City is some kind of renewal pool that will spit me out the northern gate somehow more authentically Chinese. Pretty corny—I know.

In modern times, the imperial palace houses a museum. My mom will probably never forgive me for coming to Beijing against her wishes . . . but she'll *really* never forgive me if I come to Beijing and neglect to go to the Palace Museum, one of the most famous museums in all of China.

I wander around the museum for about half an hour in geeked-out bliss before I strike gold. It's in a quiet room that whispers with green silk hangings, but unlike the other rooms full of calligraphy, jade ornaments, and other antiquities of the Qing dynasty, this is part of a temporary traveling exhibit of the Tang dynasty. The informational placard is in Chinese and English, so I can read the title of the exhibit: *Empress Wu Zetian*.

Excitement surges through me. Ever since I saw Fan Bingbing's *Empress of China*, I've been obsessed with Wu Zetian, and here's a chance to find out more. There isn't much actual art in this exhibit—just some copies of Empress Wu's poetry, modern-day imaginative renderings of her, and photographs of a large Buddha statue at the Longmen Grottoes in Henan Province that is said to be created in her image.

Mom would have said that the lack of art from Empress Wu's reign wasn't surprising—a lot of classical art and cultural artifacts were pillaged or destroyed during the Cultural Revolution. I can just picture Mom with her eyes lit up and her face flushed if she were here. She'd be even more excited by an exhibit about Wu Zetian than I am—and she *definitely* wouldn't dismiss this art exhibit the way she did the TV show. *Too bad I'll never get to tell her about it.*

The museum lighting is dim, so I push my sunglasses to the top of my head so I can more easily read the placard. The historical Wu Zetian—while probably just as fictionalized as she is in the show—is riveting. I already knew that she was rumored to have done many nefarious things. Like killing her own infant daughter to frame a court rival and creating a secret police force to terrorize her political enemies. What I didn't know was that Wu Zetian was also a well-educated woman credited with advancing women in the arts and the position of women in general.

No wonder Fan Bingbing was so determined to star in a series based on Empress Wu's life. My Chinese will never be good enough to star in a Chinese production, but if an English-language version of Wu Zetian's life gets made, I'd kill to play her. She was not only a woman of many names—Wu Hou, Wu Mei Niang, Mei-Niang, Wu Zhao—but of many roles—concubine, consort, mother, friend, lover . . . empress. So, I wouldn't play her as a scheming sadist or passive victim. I'd play her as a frustrated, intelligent woman who was *both* cruel and compassionate, as a woman must be to achieve the breathtaking transformations that Wu Zetian had in a world of men. I'd play Wu Zetian with the complexity and fullness she deserves.

The next item in the exhibit yields yet another piece of new information about Wu Zetian. It's a family tree, showing Wu Zetian's lineage and immediate descendants. She had four sons along with the daughter who was murdered as an infant—Princess Si of Anding. And one daughter who survived into adulthood—Princess Taiping. *The Empress of China* miniseries didn't include Princess Taiping in its narrative, so my curiosity is roused as I read the informational placard about her.

Princess Taiping was said to resemble her mother both in appearance and intellect. By all accounts, she had a close relationship with Wu Zetian, who taught her the art of statecraft. After Empress Wu's death, Princess Taiping tried to rule in her mother's place but was defeated by her male relatives.

Thoroughly fascinated now, I search the exhibit for an image of Princess Taiping. It would be too much to expect that a portrait of the princess had survived from the Tang dynasty, but I hope to find *something*—even if it's just a modern imagining of what the princess looked like. After making the rounds twice, I'm forced to conclude that there's nothing of Princess Taiping in the exhibit. And of course there wouldn't be anything of Princess Si of Anding, who didn't survive long enough to have her portrait painted.

Then the whispers of the people nearby start to register.

Uh-oh. Not again. Too late, I realize that I'd lost my disguise when I absentmindedly shoved the sunglasses to the top of my head.

A young couple is staring at me, and another group of teens is whispering excitedly to each other. They're staring at me too.

My forehead beads with sweat, and I slip the sunglasses back over my face. Instantly, I realize the mistake I've made. The whispers grow louder, and the teens start moving toward me. *Dumb move, Gemma.* Putting on sunglasses in the dark interior of the exhibit room has only made me more conspicuous.

My hands now clammy with nerves, I turn and try to saunter casually out of the exhibit room. The bright sun of the courtyard makes me blink, even with my eyes protected by sunglasses, and I feel way too exposed out here with no dark corners to hide. Now that I'm trailed by a gaggle of teens, glances are turning toward me. And they're not looking away. It's so sunny that there are no flashes this time, but everywhere I turn, I'm greeted by an upheld phone. The clicking of cameras crawls along my skin, and my breath quickens. *One way in, and one way out,* the ticket seller said.

The northern gate. That's my exit—but which way is north? I pivot in a panic, looking for the exit, and three girls my age come running up to me. They're all screeching something, and I know I should be able to understand what they're saying, but they're speaking too fast in Chinese, and I can't make out anything but *Alyssa Chua.*

"I'm not Alyssa Chua," I say desperately, but that just whips up the girls' frenzy. I take a step backward, and the girls press closer. They're not the only ones. Other people are jostling each other to get closer to me. It's the Beijing airport all over again. My lungs constrict as if all these people are sucking the air out of me. Even if I do get to the northern gate ahead of this stampede, there will probably be a long exit line. People in the courtyard are coming toward me to find out what all the excitement is about. Someone screams in my ear, making me wince.

"I'm not Alyssa Chua!" This time I shout it, but the swarm of people doesn't magically part for me. I try saying it in Chinese, hoping my American accent will convince them, but even that doesn't work. My heart pounding crazy fast, I try to edge my way through the crowd yelling "my" name, but the solid wall of shrieking fans won't budge. *Great. I'm about to be trampled by groupies in the Forbidden City.* And the worst thing? They're not even *my* groupies.

So far, no one tries to touch me on purpose, though I'm jostled plenty as people try to take selfies with me.

All that changes when a hand clamps down on my shoulder, sending a jolt of adrenaline racing through my body. My heart jumps about a mile as I instinctively twist away and chop down at the offending hand.

A young Chinese guy in a suit snatches his hand away and utters a swear word—at least I'm pretty sure it's a swear word since I don't know any profanity in Chinese. But it's a safe bet, given that he's rubbing his hand with an outraged scowl on his face. He switches to a light-Chinese-accented English. "What the hell, Alyssa!"

A rapid succession of thoughts run through my head. *He must know Alyssa. His English is good, but why isn't he speaking in Chinese? He's cute—clean-cut in a suit isn't usually my type, but damn if he doesn't make it work. And why am I checking out a strange guy in the middle of a mob?!*

"Sorry." Insincerity drips through my voice. After all, *he's* the one who came out of nowhere and grabbed my arm.

He sighs. "Come on. Let's get you out of here." He takes my arm more gingerly this time, but I pull back until another excited squeal from a fan makes my ears ring. Abandoning all dignity, I duck my head and let this bristly guy hustle me through the crowd.

Authoritatively, he pushes through the crowd, which is getting louder now that they sense their prey is escaping. He calls out in Chinese for people to move out of the way, and something in his tone makes people grumble and shift the few inches needed for us to move forward.

We're making good headway, but then I realize he's not steering us toward the northern gate. My steps falter. "We're going the wrong way."

"Keep moving," he grunts.

Who is this guy and why does he think he can boss me around? But he seems to have a plan, so I start walking again, because my only other option is to risk the mob at my back. He's steering us to one of the outer walls of the compound, and paranoid visions of being pinned to the wall by rabid fans dances through my head. "Where are we going?"

He doesn't answer, just propels me forward until we get to a small side exit. There's a guard there, and my mysterious escort slips a colorful bill to him, muttering something in Chinese that's too low for me to catch. The guard smiles broadly and opens the door for us while blocking the determined fans still trying to get to me.

Suddenly we're outside the Forbidden City. I gulp in deep breaths of relief . . . or I would be relieved if it weren't for the fact that I'm alone with a stranger. A stranger who's glaring at me as if my very existence were a personal affront to him.

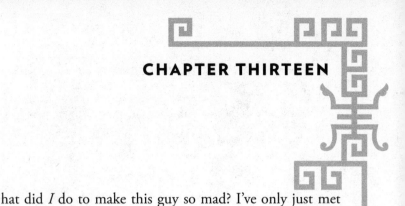

CHAPTER THIRTEEN

What did *I* do to make this guy so mad? I've only just met him, after all.

He drops my arm as if it were coated in scalding poison. "What were you thinking, playing tourist to incite a riot? That's a new low, even for you, Alyssa!"

Ah. The better question would be—what did *Alyssa* do to make this guy so mad? I remember that he called me by my cousin's name earlier. "I'm not Alyssa." I'm getting seriously tired of saying this.

He snorts. "Right. You just happen to look exactly like Alyssa Chua." *Well . . . yeah, actually.*

"Wo bu shi Alyssa," I repeat in Chinese, hoping my American accent will convince him, even if it didn't convince the crowd earlier.

"Unbelievable!" He shakes his head. "Your new insistence on only speaking and responding to English is bad enough." *Ah. So that's why he spoke to me in English.* "But now you're pretending to have an American accent?"

Honestly. There's no convincing this guy.

Then he frowns. "Say something else," he demands.

My blood pressure rises. "I'm not your trained monkey to perform on demand!"

He gives a long, low whistle. "You really *aren't* Alyssa!" He peers at me more closely. "You might look like her, but there are differences. Alyssa wouldn't be caught dead in that outfit or that hairstyle. And you sound totally different. It's not just the American accent. It's your voice. It's—"

"If you're done dissecting my clothes, hair, and voice," I say tartly, "I'll be going now."

"Wait!" he calls out. "If you're not Alyssa, then who the hell are you?" His expression is completely baffled. "I could swear you look just like her."

I don't bother to answer, but because *I*, unlike this guy, have manners, I add, "Thanks for getting me out of there" before spinning on my heel and stalking away. Unfortunately, I only get about two steps before I realize I have no idea where I am. There are willow trees and greenery everywhere, but no discernable landmarks other than the Forbidden City, and I'm not about to go back there. *No need to panic.* All I have to do is find the moat and follow it back to where I got dropped off. Then I can call a studio car, crawl into bed, and pretend this day never happened.

Mr. Cute-guy-in-a-suit strolls up to me. "Lost?"

"No." *Yes, dammit. Where the hell is the moat?! How could I have lost a frigging moat?!*

He grins like he doesn't believe me, and then he has the audacity to hold out his hand to me. "I'm Eric Liu."

"Gemma Huang." I ignore his proffered hand. So much for my manners, but I don't care. This guy rubs me the wrong way.

"And Gemma Huang is . . . ?" He trails off invitingly. Oh, so now he's being nice because he's curious about who I am? *Well, he can just go ahead and wonder.*

When I don't answer, he asks, "What's on the agenda for the next place to start a riot? The Great Wall?" His mouth quirks up.

Adjusting my glasses firmly over the bridge of my nose, I start walking in a random direction, hoping this will lead me back to the park entrance. "Where I'm going is not your business. And I can handle myself."

"Right." He follows me. "Maybe I should stay close in case you *do* start a riot."

I ignore him.

"Come on. Just tell me where you're going so I can point you in the right direction." He adds reluctantly, "Or I can take you to where you're going. My car's nearby."

"Ha." I stop and jab a finger at his chest. Which, admittedly, feels pretty solidly muscled for a guy in a suit. To cover the flush rising in my face, I say, "I'm not stupid enough to get into a car with you. For all I know, you're planning to kidnap me for ransom!"

Eric throws up his hands in mock surrender. "Not a kidnapper, I swear!" His smile is crooked, and his teeth aren't perfectly straight, so no one's going to cast him in a toothpaste commercial anytime soon. But when he smiles, he looks a bit like my dream boyfriend—Simu Liu's Jung in *Kim's Convenience*. Simu (in my head, we're obviously on a first-name basis) plays a Korean guy on the show, but in real life, he's Chinese like me. And like this annoying but cute Eric Liu.

"Yeah, well, that's exactly what a kidnapper *would* say." I don't care that this guy happens to have an adorable crooked smile—I'm not about to get into a car with a complete stranger.

"Listen, when I thought you were Alyssa . . . I might've been a little rude."

"A *little* rude?" My steps slow. "You accused me of starting a riot on purpose and wouldn't even listen when I told you that I'm not your Alyssa!"

Eric's eyes hood over. "She's not *my* Alyssa!"

"So, you two don't have a history together?" If he were a jealous ex-boyfriend, it might explain why he was being so rude. Though it would still make him a jerk.

"History?" His forehead wrinkles. His English is perfect, but it's clear he doesn't get my meaning.

"Like a *romantic* history," I clarify.

"No! Absolutely not." He actually sounds revolted by the idea. Which doesn't do a lot for my ego, considering how alike Alyssa and I look.

Now my curiosity is piqued. "Then what *is* your history with her?"

"Unless you want to walk right into Tiananmen Square," he comments, "you might want to turn around."

"Tiananmen Square *is* where I'm going next." Refusing to get sidetracked, I say, "You didn't answer my question. What's your deal with Alyssa?"

"We go way back," he admits with a grimace. "Every few months, the tabloid sites try to spin the angle of a forbidden romance because our families don't get along, but we've never actually been involved. In fact, it's safe to say that Alyssa dislikes me as much as I dislike her."

This hint of gossip about my cousin is way too juicy to ignore. "If that's true, then why did you go to the trouble of rescuing her from a mob?"

"I didn't. I was rescuing *you*, remember?"

I flush. "You know what I mean, and I didn't *need* rescuing. I would've managed just fine even if you hadn't decided to manhandle me out of there." No need for him to know about my admittedly shaky sense of direction. *Well, he's probably figured that out by now.*

"I happened to be nearby."

"Right." My tone is skeptical. "You just happened to be sightseeing on a Saturday in a suit." Eric can't be much older than me, but the tailored suit, shaved face, and short hair screams corporate guy who works all the time, even on weekends. So different from Ken's sexy scruffiness—which makes Ken *totally* my type. Unlike clean-cut Eric, who probably spends his days looking for tax loopholes or something.

"I had a lunch meeting nearby," he explains, "with a scientist whose work on sustainable energy has me pretty excited about its application to the fashion industry."

"Fashion industry?" That would explain his sleek, perfectly fitted suit. More doubtfully, I ask, "Sustainable energy in fashion?"

Eric smiles. "If you think about how cotton, silk, and other fibers get produced and how garments are transported, you'll see why the fashion industry needs to reduce its carbon footprint."

OK, maybe he doesn't spend his days looking for tax loopholes. "That still doesn't explain what you were doing in the Forbidden City."

"The scientist I was having lunch with follows Alyssa on Weibo, and he told me that Alyssa had been spotted in the Forbidden City. I . . . uh, had something I needed to talk to her about." His strides lengthen.

"Something to do with your family feud?" I ask, keeping pace with him. My irritation fades as my curiosity grows. "Come on, you can't blame me for wanting to know more about Alyssa! This is at least the third time I've been mistaken for her."

"You can read about the feud on gossip sites."

My face goes hot. "I can't read Chinese." And there are limits to translation programs. *Who would have thought I'd regret dropping out of Saturday Chinese school?*

Eric sighs and stops walking. "Look, it's going to sound silly. My grandmother snubbed Alyssa's grandmother by not inviting her to some society charity event, and in retaliation, Alyssa's mother didn't invite my grandmother to some other charity event." He runs a hand through his short, bristly hair. "My grandmother and Alyssa's mother have been at it ever since."

He's right—that does sound silly. "So," I say, trying to wrap my head around this, "your grandmother is fighting with Alyssa's mother over who gets invited to . . . charity functions?" I almost say that it doesn't seem very charitable, but I stop in time. *He does see the irony, doesn't he?*

"There's more to it." He pauses. "It was only in the last two decades that my father made his fortune and improved our family's social standing. Nai Nai, my grandmother, was finally admitted into the same circles as Alyssa's family. Maybe she shouldn't have snubbed Alyssa's family, but Nai Nai had her reasons." A muscle twitches in his jaw. "After all, Alyssa's family was responsible for—" He bites the words off.

Ah ha! I *knew* there was more than just snubs over charity events between the two families. "Responsible for what?" I prompt.

"Nothing." He starts walking again.

I start walking too. Obviously, it's not *nothing*. But I'm willing to let it go as long as I can get some answers about my cousin. "So, are you going to tell me at least why you wanted to talk to Alyssa so badly that you rushed from a lunch meeting when you heard she was spotted in the Forbidden City?"

"I guess I owe you some explanation."

"You do," I agree.

"I wanted to talk to Alyssa about my little sister, Mimi." He glances at me as if he's gauging my reaction.

"Go on." I'm not about to let him stop when he's finally opening up about Alyssa.

Eric blows out his breath. "Mimi used to think that Alyssa and her crowd were pretty shallow—just like I do—but last year, her attitude changed. She started talking about how we've misjudged Alyssa. I thought it was strange, but I was away at college in the U.S., so I didn't know what was *really* going on." *College in the United*

States—that's why his English is so good. "But when I got back from college a few weeks ago, I found out that Mimi's been partying with Alyssa for the past year like the feud between our families never existed. Even without the feud, I'd *still* be worried about Mimi hanging out with a thrill seeker like Alyssa. Mimi isn't exactly naive, but she's only nineteen."

I almost choke on that. "*Only* nineteen?" The way Eric was talking about his little sister, I thought she was like fifteen or sixteen and way younger than Alyssa—who, according to her Instagram, just turned nineteen as well. "I'm only eighteen! And if you just graduated from college, you must be about twenty-two. That's not much older."

"Twenty-one," he says. "I graduated from high school early."

"OK, then. You're just two years older than your sister and telling her that you don't approve of her friends. Got it."

"It's not just that," he protests. "Mimi has a promising future ahead of her, and Alyssa could ruin that. Mimi's young, but she's already starting a career as a fashion designer. A year ago, she had a chance to show her debut line at a fashion show here in Beijing. Alyssa was there. And she bought Mimi's entire collection. All of a sudden, Mimi's career took off." He doesn't sound happy about his sister's success. "Alyssa's a fashion influencer, and whatever she wears gets noticed. So, Mimi got noticed."

"So, that's a bad thing because . . . why exactly?"

"Because people like Alyssa don't have friends—they only keep around people they can use. Alyssa could easily exploit Mimi's talent, build up her career, and then pull the rug out from under her feet." He sounds agitated. "If that happened, it would completely destroy my sister's confidence."

My heart turns over as I remember how it felt when I realized that I got the *Butterfly* job because of my resemblance to Alyssa.

How much worse would it be for Mimi to think that her success was because of a nasty prank by her so-called friend? "OK, that would suck," I concede, "*if* that's what Alyssa is up to. But don't you think Mimi would know if that's what Alyssa plans to do?"

"The Mimi I knew would know better than to trust Alyssa Chua, but Mimi is so different these days." Eric is breathing hard, and I don't think it's from physical exertion, even though he's walking fast. "It's like Mimi thinks she needs Alyssa's help to succeed as a designer. And the worst thing is that she's lying to my parents and grandmother about it! They don't know she's become friends with Alyssa."

Guilt twinges in me. *Mimi's not the only one lying to her parents.* "Maybe Mimi doesn't think your family would understand." I think about my hotel upgrade. Bribe or gift? I still don't know, but there's a chance that Alyssa's motivations were sincere. "And maybe Alyssa bought Mimi's clothing line because she wanted to make up for whatever bad blood is between your families."

"No, that's not it." Eric's eyes are blazing and hard. "And even if that's what Alyssa intended, it's too late to fix what's between our families." *Yeah, there's definitely more going on than Eric's telling me.* "The reason I wanted to see Alyssa," he says coldly, "is to warn her to stay away from my sister."

To my horror, I burst into laughter. I can't help it. Not because it's funny, but because it's such a bizarre twist. "I'm sorry," I gasp, coming to a stop. "It's just that Alyssa came to see *me*. To warn me to stay away from her family!"

He stares at me in surprise and also stops walking. "Why would Alyssa want to keep you away from her family?"

"I'm Alyssa's long-lost cousin."

Eric pales, horror etched on his face.

My heart plummets. *Oh right.* Being related to Alyssa automatically makes me an enemy in Eric's eyes. "I never even knew Alyssa or her family existed until two days ago!" The alarm in his face recedes a bit, and I breathe easier. *Why do I even care what Eric thinks of me?* "And it's not like Alyssa laid out the welcome mat." A pang of conscience stings me as I think of the hotel upgrade. "She implied that her grandmother would die from shock if she found out about me."

"From what my grandmother has said, Sung Mei Tian isn't the type to die from shock." Eric eyes me speculatively. "So, you're Alyssa's cousin, huh?" It looks like he's recovered from the surprise of finding out I'm related to Alyssa.

I decide that I might as well lay out the whole truth. "My mom was cut off because of some scandal, so she's never mentioned her family in Beijing to me. Apparently, my mother is Alyssa's mother's twin sister." *I have to ask.* "Do you know what happened with my mother?"

"No," he admits. "I never even knew that Alyssa's mother had a twin sister." Then understanding dawns in his eyes. "No wonder Alyssa's scared! But she's not scared for her grandmother. It's her own interests that she's trying to protect. Alyssa stands to inherit an obscene fortune from her grandparents, and Alyssa—maybe her mother too—is afraid you're here to collect your share."

"That doesn't make sense," I protest. "Alyssa didn't seem like she was exactly hurting for money."

"You don't know how the super rich think. No matter how much they have—they always want more." His mouth twists. "And your grandparents' money is the kind most people can't even imagine. Trust me—Alyssa will do anything to keep that inheritance to herself."

That *would* explain Alyssa's efforts to soften me up with a hotel upgrade and expensive champagne. But that doesn't quite ring true to me. As an actress, I'm pretty good at reading people, and Alyssa really did seem afraid for her grandmother. "I need a moment." I sit down on a nearby park bench, trying to wrap my head around what I've just learned.

An inheritance most people can't imagine. Alyssa and my aunt trying to keep me from that inheritance. Oh, and a mysterious family feud involving one Eric Liu—let's not forget that. Whatever my mom's reasons are for keeping me out of Beijing—it's definitely *not* the poor air quality.

Eric sits down next to me. "You know, if you want that inheritance, I can help you."

"Because it would stick it to the family that *your* family hates?" I ask wryly. "Yeah—as much as I'd love to be a pawn in your feud—no thanks."

He nods like he knew I'd refuse. "How about this, then? Anyone who gets under Alyssa's skin is someone I want on my side. And I might be able to help you get the answers you want."

"How do you know what I want?"

"You could have walked away anytime, but here you still are, asking me questions." He gives me a sly glance. "I can't imagine it's because of my charming personality, so it must be that you want answers about your family."

I grimace. *Guilty as charged.* "It's definitely *not* your charming personality. If you remember, you insulted me as soon as we met."

"To be fair, I thought you were Alyssa." He sounds totally unrepentant.

I sigh. "You know, in America I'm mistaken for other Asian women all the time. I just thought that I'd avoid that in *China* of all places!"

"Did the women you were mistaken for look like you?" he asks curiously.

"Not in the slightest."

"Good. I'd hate to think there were more Alyssa clones around."

"Alyssa clone?" My voice goes dry. "I happen to have a name and an identity of my own."

"I'm sorry," Eric says. "I'm sorry, *Gemma*." He smiles. "See. I get that you're your own person. Totally different from . . . um . . . what's her name again?" He cocks his head to one side and squints as if he's trying hard to remember.

My irritation fades, and despite myself, I start to laugh. "OK, I forgive you. Just this once." Smug, know-it-all Eric is easily resistible. But this funny, charming Eric? That's the kind of *irresistible* that could get me into trouble. The problem is, I've never been one to shy away from trouble. "So," I say, "are you proposing an alliance across enemy lines?"

"Something like that." His imperfect smile spreads over his face.

My breath snags in my throat, and I tell myself sternly, *You. Have. A. Boyfriend.* Then a sly voice whispers, *Yeah, but Ken's not here. And you're both allowed to see other people, remember?* But even if Ken weren't in the equation, there are more than enough reasons to run as fast as I can from Eric Liu.

Slowly, I get to my feet. "Let's do it."

CHAPTER FOURTEEN

Tiananmen Square isn't what I expected. Of course, the square isn't crowded with protesters. But I just didn't expect it to seem so ordinary—especially since the thirtieth anniversary of the Tiananmen Square massacre was just two months ago. Today, everyone seems to be on their way to somewhere else, most of them barely glancing at the monuments all around them—not even the looming Gate of Heavenly Peace that Tiananmen Square is named for—a huge structure of red pillars, a gold roof, and hundreds of broad stone stairs. But grand as the Gate of Heavenly Peace is, even *it* doesn't distract me from thinking about what happened here thirty years ago. I expected Tiananmen Square to be a place weighted with history and revolution, maybe with bloodstains still on the ground. Instead, it's just a big square paved with gray stone. No blood in sight.

"Do you want me to take a picture of you?" Eric asks, having walked me here after we exchanged contact information. He doesn't seem to be in a hurry to leave.

It feels disrespectful to treat a place of revolution like a tourist attraction, but I don't know how to explain this. Stomach squirming, I let him take my picture. But I'm thinking of ghosts and tanks as he takes it.

Eric lowers his phone. "Something wrong?"

"It's just that . . ." I stop and try again. "Do people remember the Tiananmen Square massacre?"

"Some do—yes," he says slowly. "But it's not only a matter of remembering. The government censors all mention of the massacre. You won't find it in history books or online here."

"I see," I say, thinking of the error message when I tried to search for the 1989 Tiananmen Square massacre. "But wouldn't people alive back then still talk about it?"

"Not necessarily. Fewer people knew about it than you might think. Back then, unless you were in Beijing or knew someone in the protest, chances were that you didn't know what was happening. As for those who knew about it—well, some just want to forget or don't want to burden the younger generation with such a tragic history." His mouth sets. "Anyway, it's still a dangerous topic."

"Then how do you know so much about the Tiananmen Square protests and massacre?" I ask. "Were your parents in the protest?"

Eric shakes his head. "No, my parents didn't protest. My dad was a college student in Beijing, but he wasn't the revolutionary type, and my mom was still in high school in Shanghai at the time."

"I don't think my dad was in Beijing at the time either. He grew up in Anhui Province." Not that my dad would be waving around protest signs and shouting revolutionary slogans even if he *were* in Beijing.

"What about your mother?" Then he says, "Never mind. I forgot whose daughter she was. Your grandfather is a high-ranking Communist Party official. No daughter of *his* would have taken part in those protests."

Your grandfather is a high-ranking Communist Party official. That's not something you hear every day. My blood turns to ice. The officials of the Communist Party who were threatened by the protesters' demands for freedom from censorship and control . . . were the same ones who were responsible for the massacre. What if my grandfather was one of those officials? I think about the blocked search I tried to do on my grandfather. Is that why information on him is censored? Because he's so high up in the Communist Party? Then I remember what Alyssa said. *Gong Gong doesn't know you're here, and you'd better hope that he doesn't find out.* Just how dangerous is my grandfather?

Eric's expression is somber as he looks across the span of gray stone to the red gate. "My mother told me," he says abruptly, "about Tiananmen Square. She wasn't at the protests, but she lost a lot. Her older brother was killed in the massacre, and her best friend was later arrested as a counterrevolutionary."

I gasp. "That's terrible."

"Yes. Mom said hundreds—maybe a thousand—were killed. And thousands were arrested. My mother honors her brother's memory every year on the day of his death." He bends over his phone while I'm still reeling from what he's told me. I knew the estimate of how many had died in the massacre. But knowing that Eric lost an uncle before he was even born makes this history seem more . . . real. And sad.

What my own mother said about the Tiananmen Square protests pops into my head. *It wasn't allowed.* I thought she'd meant that in the general sense. But maybe she meant that *she*, as the daughter of a Communist Party official, wasn't allowed to protest. Of course she wouldn't have gone against her father in this. Not my mother. Except there must have been a time when she *hadn't* followed the rules and got herself banished from her family. *But what could my rule-following mother have done that would cause her to leave the country and break off all ties with her family?*

My phone dings. Eric has sent me the picture he took of me, unsmiling and solemn, with the red-and-gold gate in the background. I zoom in to look at a large placard on the gate. "What does the sign say?"

He says it in Chinese and then translates. "'Celebrate the togetherness of the people of the world.' Or something like that."

"That's a nice sentiment for a place that's seen so much violence, and it's kind of funny that Tiananmen means 'Gate of Heavenly Peace.'"

Eric smiles in ironic agreement. "Yeah." He pauses. "But Tiananmen Square isn't just a place where people died. It's a place where people came together to fight for their beliefs. People our age who believed in something bigger than themselves. So, in a way, the words on the gate are true."

I turn this over in my head. *Just when I think I have a read on Eric . . . he reveals another, even more interesting layer.*

He gestures toward the gate. "We talk about peace and unity like it's the absence of fighting, but that doesn't feel quite right to me—I don't think unity and peace are things that just happen. I believe they're something we have to fight *for*."

"Yes." My whole body thrums at his words. "I think that too." The pressure on my chest eases. I glance around at the people walking through Tiananmen Square, and the place doesn't seem quite so haunted anymore.

Eric is looking at me, his eyes hooded and intense. Unaccountably, my heart beats faster. *Time to lighten things up.* "Thanks for taking my first tourist pic," I say, zooming back out until the gate is normal-size and in the background of the picture, "if you don't count the hundreds of pictures taken of me in the Forbidden City by complete strangers."

The color suddenly drains from his face. He starts frantically scrolling through his phone.

"What's the matter?" I demand. *What now?*

He groans and looks up from his phone. "The gossip sites are going nuts," he explains. "Apparently, pictures of me escorting Alyssa away from a mob at the Forbidden City are popping up on Weibo. According to multiple sites, rumors of our forbidden romance have just been confirmed."

Laughter bubbles up in me—and then is cut off. "Oh hell, Alyssa's going to think I did this on purpose. She *did* tell me to be careful and lie low." I pat the sunglasses on my face to make sure they're still in place.

Eric, in contrast, looks more cheerful. "Alyssa's going to be furious," he predicts. "It's almost worth having my name linked with hers." He smiles at me. "So, what other tourist sites are you visiting today? Need any company?"

I put my hands on my hips. "Planning to push Alyssa's buttons by feeding the rumor mill, are we?"

"No, no," he says, holding up his hands. "I'm just saying that I do have a car, and if you had more sightseeing to do . . ." His eyes glitter with mischief.

Tempting. And not just to annoy Alyssa either. There are worse fates than sightseeing with a fun, cute guy . . . But I don't want to throw Alyssa into a tizzy. "I think I've had enough sightseeing and excitement for one day." I put my phone back in my bag, and my fingers brush against the food wish list. "Don't laugh, but the main thing I'm interested in anyway is food."

Eric, of course, laughs.

"Didn't I tell you," I demand, "not to laugh?"

"Sorry!" He holds up his hands in apology. "Now I know you're not Alyssa!"

"Doesn't Alyssa like food? How is that even possible? I personally don't trust anyone who doesn't like food." I might be trying a little too hard to distinguish myself from Alyssa, but it's true that I don't trust anyone with a "take it or leave it" attitude about food. I mean,

I don't need people to be as obsessed with food as I am, but a little enthusiasm for, say, a perfect chocolate chip cookie goes a long way to winning my heart.

"I love food," Eric says promptly. "Big fan of it." A tinge of red sweeps into his cheeks. "Big fan of people who love food too."

Um. What's going on here? He can't possibly be flirting, can he? *No*, I assure myself, *I'm imagining things.* He just wants to hang out with me to irritate Alyssa. Eric Liu is definitely *not* flirting with me. Almost definitely not. Probably not . . . *OK, face it, Gemma, the man is flirting with you.*

Stomach tightening, I blurt out, "My boyfriend laughed too." Ken *did* think my food wish list was hilarious. But that's not why I mentioned Ken. I brought up my boyfriend out of pure panicked instinct. Because I'm not ready for this sizzling, crackling *thing* between Eric and me.

"Boyfriend. I see." Eric looks away, and the redness in his face deepens.

My own face goes supernova hot in response. I'm tempted to tell him that Ken and I aren't exclusive, but what's the point? I'm leaving Beijing in a few short months. Then there's the not-so-minor detail of Eric hating my estranged relatives. All in all, it's probably better not to explain my exact relationship status with Ken. Besides, Eric's not my type. So, there must be some other perfectly logical explanation for why my heart is thudding out of control—except I know exactly why there's a percussion band in my chest. And he's standing right in front of me, blushing and waiting for me to say something.

Maybe a *tiny* bit of flirting wouldn't hurt. "Again, don't laugh." I hand Eric my list, my fingers brushing against his. *Whoa.* Suddenly, my skin is a tangle of heated nerves, making me snatch my hand away. Eric takes a step back, the list clutched in his hand.

Apparently, the line between a *little* flirting and total out-of-control, fiery attraction is nonexistent in this case. *OK—good to know.* "Uh, so that's my food wish list." I take a step back myself.

"Right." He snaps his mouth shut and tears his eyes from me, swallowing hard. *Guess I'm not the only one who felt that.* He smooths out the list in his hand, and his eyebrows skyrocket as he reads it.

My breathing evens out as I watch him read the list from a safe distance. "Too ambitious?"

"Not at all. I love everything on this list. In fact, I can tell you where to go for good egg tarts. But are you telling me that you came to Beijing for the food?"

"Of course not," I say with an injured air. "I came to Beijing to start riots at cultural sites, threaten a rich socialite's inheritance, form an alliance with my ancestral enemy, *and* eat food!"

Eric laughs again, revealing an adorable dimple in his cheek. "Sounds like a great vacation!"

"Actually, I'm not really on vacation." I tell him all about the movie, my hesitations about it—everything.

I may not have millions of social media followers or a rich, über-hip lifestyle, but Eric listens to every word with his complete, undivided attention. I'm not going to lie—it feels pretty awesome.

Did I make the right call in not revealing the whole truth about my relationship with Ken? But what could I have said? *Thanks for the tip about the egg tarts—by the way, did I mention that I'm free to see other people?* He'd assume I was interested in him. Which I'm definitely not. And he's not interested in me either. Except that maybe he is.

The old me would have been *thrilled* by this situation—a relationship with a gorgeous, cool boyfriend and a flirtation with an equally gorgeous, fascinating stranger. In fact, it wasn't that long ago that I was watching *To All the Boys I've Loved Before* for the millionth time and talking to my roommates about what it would be like to be Lara Jean Song Covey, with all those great guys interested in her.

Well, now I know. It's pure hell.

But it doesn't have to be. I could put the brakes on this little pseudo-flirtation before it goes any further. *In any case*, I tell myself sternly, *you're leaving in a couple of months and going back to your boyfriend. Remember him? Ken? Fun, sexy, and doesn't mistake you for his family's mortal enemy?*

While these thoughts are rushing through my head, Eric starts to hand back my notebook. A breeze flips up the page, and he glances down at it. "The Great Wall. Tiananmen Square. The Forbidden City. That's it? You're going to be here for two to three months, and that's all you've got on your list?"

"I didn't have time to plan more," I say with all the dignity I can muster.

"You should put the Summer Palace on your list."

"I was planning on it." My pulse picks up. *Is he going to offer to take me there?*

But he just hands me back my notebook. "Good. It's worth seeing."

Probably better that I'm not making fun tourist plans with Eric anyway. Let's keep this uncomplicated.

Good sense restored, I say, "I guess this is goodbye."

"We'll stay in touch," he promises.

"Sure." *See?* No need to get into a tizzy. Eric and I are parting in a perfectly platonic way . . . the way two people who just met each other would. Two people who are plotting against one of the richest families in China, that is.

CHAPTER FIFTEEN

After Eric and I part ways, I hit the food stalls, but I'm so freaked out by what I learned about my family that I don't enjoy the outing as much as I should. Plus, every time I think about Eric, it feels as if I'm charged up on a hundred fireflies. *Not good.*

When I get back to my fancy hotel room, the first thing I see is another pale pink envelope on the coffee table. This time, there's no expensive bottle of champagne accompanying the note.

> **Gemma,**
> **Stay away from Eric Liu! He's trouble!**
> **Alyssa**

No "Xoxo" this time. Alyssa must have seen the pics of Eric and me at the Forbidden City. Eric was right—the rumor that they're together *did* piss her off. But there has to be more than that. Everyone seems to be warning me about something. Alyssa warns me about Eric. Eric warns me about Alyssa. And my mother warns me to stay out of Beijing. *But no one seems to be telling the whole truth.*

I sink into the white plush couch, still clutching the note. Looking around at all the opulence surrounding me, I wonder where Alyssa's money comes from anyway. If her grandfather is so big in the Communist Party, why does her family have so much money? Isn't the Communist Party supposed to be about class equality and "*Down with the rich!*" ideals?

My dad would tell me that I was being naive. Except that he'd never put it that harshly. He'd give me some professor lecture about the complexity of communism in practice, and then he'd talk about how capitalism was also problematic. *Problematic* is my dad's favorite word, and by the time I was seven, I was saying things like "Not having enough peanut butter in this sandwich is just as problematic as not having enough jam." Dad was so proud. *Well, he wouldn't be proud of me now.* I'm living in the lap of luxury in the city Mom has forbidden me to be in.

I finger the tasseled silk of a gold pillow. Is this why Mom didn't want me to come here? Does she not want me to know about what I could have had? And is Alyssa really trying to keep me from my inheritance? Maybe if I had all *this* for real and not just on loan, I'd do anything to keep these riches to myself too.

But I don't think so. In spite of the luxury hotel suite, I'm not Alyssa Chua, fashionista superstar heiress. I'm Gemma Huang, recently graduated high school student and aspiring actress.

I need a little normalcy.

Dropping the pillow, I pick up my phone and try again to reach Ken. Instantly, I regret it. I'm not actually in the mood to talk to him right now.

Then, just when I think I've missed him again, his voice comes over the line. "Gemma! At last!"

Are you kidding me? This is when I finally connect with Ken? After getting a weird note from my cousin and after meeting a cute guy I can't get out of my head?

My "Hi!" in return sounds overly enthusiastic. Even over the phone, Ken can probably smell the guilt streaming from my pores. I try to take it down a notch. "I was just running lines and figured I might as well try to call again." *Argh! That sounded way too casual.* My whole body tightens as I pace my small hotel room. I hate lying.

Now I have to go over the script again so I won't technically be lying to Ken. The worst thing is that I'm not even sure *why* I'm lying.

"I'm glad you did." Ken's voice is warm. "I miss you."

He doesn't suspect a thing. But what am I trying to hide? Nothing happened with Eric, and even if something had, Ken and I have an agreement. To cover up my confusion, I ask about his commercial.

Ken's so happy talking about his commercial that I can *almost* ignore the little voice that's pointing out how Ken isn't asking a single question about my movie. It doesn't help that the same little voice is *also* pointing out how interested Eric was in hearing about my movie and how he asked questions. I shut down the voice with ruthless determination and focus hard on making the appropriate noises every time Ken pauses in his narrative.

Finally, he wraps up and asks me about the movie. "Busy but good." I want to tell him about my struggles with Jake, my fear about letting Eilene down, and my worry that Sonia is still too flat and one-dimensional. Except that Ken was so weird about me taking the role in the first place that I don't want to give him more ammunition to criticize the movie. *Butterfly* might be flawed, but it's still my break-out role.

"Have you gotten to see Beijing yet?" he asks.

Inwardly, I groan. That's an even *worse* topic of conversation. I stop pacing, flop down on the couch, and brace myself to leave out key details. "Just today. I saw the Forbidden City." I'm tempted to tell Ken about Alyssa, but that feels too wrapped up in meeting Eric to be a safe topic of conversation. You'd think that being an actress, I'd be a great liar. Unfortunately—that's not true at all. I'm a terrible liar.

Left with no other choice, I tell Ken a little about the movie. None of my concerns . . . just how great it is to work with Eilene. Which is completely true.

"That's awesome," Ken says.

My spirits lift. Just one supportive comment and I already feel better about us. "The food is amazing! I wish I could bring you back some egg tarts."

"I love those," he says, "but they probably won't keep. Can you even bring them through customs?"

"Maybe not. You'll have to settle for whatever touristy, nonperishable souvenir I pick up."

"I'll like anything you give me."

"Paper fan?" I tease. "Postcard with ancient poetry in calligraphy? Key chain that says 'I've been to the Great Wall'?"

"Anything," Ken says firmly.

"You have a seriously low bar for presents." I'm so relieved to be back in the rhythm of chatting and joking normally with him.

"But a high bar for a girlfriend," he says in a low, sexy voice.

Girlfriend. Warm fuzzies fill my whole body. *See? You were being totally paranoid about what Ken's doing on a Friday night without you.* So what if he's not great at staying in touch? What matters is how well we click when we *do* connect. "I suppose, then, that for my boyfriend, I can step up my gift-giving game. We're talking a miniature of the Great Wall here. Or maybe a pair of those little doorway guardian foo dogs." Foo dogs are "shi shi" in Chinese, which actually means stone lions. I have no idea why they're known as "foo dogs" in English.

"Now I'm going to be disappointed if I don't get a foo dog!" I can tell Ken's grinning even if I can't see it.

"I'll try not to disappoint you."

"You'd better not." He laughs. "Don't break my heart, Gemma."

Guilt floods the happiness away like icy water poured over my head. "I won't." My words and tone are too solemn for our banter, but Ken doesn't seem to notice.

Once we hang up, I fling my phone aside and roll over onto my back on the bed and stare up at the smooth white ceiling. What's the big deal? So I met a guy I can't stop thinking about. It's not like anything is going to happen . . . and even if something did, it wouldn't mean anything. *Ken is a long-term relationship. Eric is a temporary infatuation.*

Still, I could tell Glory and Camille about Eric. It would be nice to get some advice. I pick up my phone again and start a group thread to my roommates.

Hey! Had my first day off and went sightseeing. Finally.

Camille is the first to respond. **Ooh! What did you see? Pics plz!**

I send them a selfie at a food stall. My finger hovers over the unsmiling picture of me at Tiananmen Square, but I end up not sending it. That's way too hard to explain.

Glory chimes in. **Nice! Glad you got out! How's the film going?**

Awesome! I add heart emojis for emphasis. There isn't an emoji for "I love being an actress on a real movie set, but it's way harder than I thought, and I'm afraid of letting down my mentor and totally blowing it, plus the director doesn't like me." So I add a wow emoji instead.

Camille texts back. **Meet any interesting people yet?**

Perfect time to mention Eric. But what do I say? Met a cute guy. Enemy of my newly discovered family. We met when he thought I was my cousin. *She* warned me to stay away from her family and then paid for my hotel upgrade. So . . . yeah, some interesting people.

Miss Ken. I add a sad emoji to my text and send it off.

We all text a bit more about what Camille and Glory are up to, and then I sign off. It's getting late, and I've had an exhausting day. *Time for bed.*

Then my phone buzzes. It's my mom. For just a second, I consider letting it go to voicemail, but then she'll just call again. And again. I answer the phone. "Hi, Mom." My mouth clenches around a million questions threatening to spill out of me. *Why were you kicked out of your family? Why would you need to go all the way to the United States to get away from your family? Why won't you even talk about your family? Why did you forbid me to come to China? What the hell did you do?*

"Gemma, this is your ma."

"I know." Here we go—the familiar phone-answering ritual. My heart is beating so loudly that I'm afraid she can hear it.

"Why haven't I heard from you? No time to call your mom?"

"Sorry. I've been so busy with work." I like to stick as close to the truth as possible. Like I said, I'm a terrible liar. Though I seem to be getting plenty of practice lately. How did I become the kind of girl who lies to her parents *and* her boyfriend? *This isn't me.*

"You're acting at night? When I call you at night, you don't answer."

Crap. Nighttime for her in Illinois is daytime for me in Beijing. "I've been . . . out." Again, not technically lying.

"Oh?" Sly speculation slips into her voice. "Out with anyone special?"

How the hell does she do that?! Mother's intuition is a scary-real thing. "Um, maybe?"

"Zhong Guo Ren?" She's trying to sound casual, but I can hear the underlying hope as she asks me if this "special" person is Chinese.

I've never dated anyone Chinese before, so she'll be over the moon about a Chinese boyfriend. "Mom, don't make a big deal out of this—but yes."

There are muffled squeals on the other end of the line, and she's probably doing a happy dance right now. *So much for not making a big deal out of it.* "What's his name?" she demands when she's done squealing.

"Eric." Immediately horrified, I yell out, "No! That's not right! *Ken*. His name is Ken."

I tell myself that it means *nothing* that my overtired brain landed on the wrong name initially.

"What happened?" I hear my dad ask. "Is Gemma going to college?"

"No." Mom sounds like she's come back to earth a bit. "She's dating a Zhong Guo Ren. Someone named Ken. Or Eric."

"Ken," I say firmly.

"Hao," Dad says. Good. That's what he says to everything. Except for me not going to college. He probably wouldn't approve of me going against their express wishes to stay away from Beijing either.

"Is there an Eric?" Mom asks shrewdly.

"Oh, he's just a guy I met today." I hope my mom doesn't ask how I met Eric because I can't come up with a lie off the top of my head.

"As soon as I met your ba," she says mistily, "I knew he was the one."

My face heats up. It's embarrassing, but also endearing, that my parents are still head over heels in love with each other after decades of marriage. Dad murmurs something in Chinese to Mom so softly that I can't make it out. No doubt he's saying something revoltingly adorable.

OK, I have to try. "So, where did you and Dad meet again? Was it Hong Kong?" I take a deep breath. "Or Beijing?"

A vast silence greets me. The only thing I hear is my own shallow breathing. Just when I think I'm going to drown in the rivulets of sweat pouring from my forehead, Mom speaks at last. "I told you that we both went to college in Hong Kong," she says coldly.

"Yes, I know, but—"

"And why do you ask now?" Her voice is sharp and suspicious.

Shit. "No reason," I mumble. *How can I be so bad at this?* You'd think I've never done improv before. *Pull it together, dammit!* I've got to change the subject fast—otherwise, that scary Mom-intuition will kick in, and she'll somehow find out I'm in Beijing. But what will deflect her from her suspicions? "It's just . . ." Then a brainstorm hits. "You know how it is when you get to know another Chinese person? We end up talking about our families and where they're from." Luckily, this is true. Ken and I did have this conversation. *And nothing will distract Mom like the topic of my new Chinese boyfriend.*

"Oh." Mom pauses, and I hold my breath. "You and this Ken were talking about your families?"

"That's right." I let my breath out slowly so she doesn't hear the relief in my voice. "So, you knew Dad was the one, huh?"

Mom doesn't let herself get distracted. "Is this Eric Zhong Guo Ren too?"

"Yes," I admit. I don't add that Eric is Chinese, as in a *citizen of China.*

"Ah." The tone of maternal satisfaction in that one syllable makes me smile despite the earlier close call. It must be making my mom delirious with happiness that I have not only one but *two* Chinese romantic interests. It's a win-win for her. Then she says, "Even if this Eric is not Chinese, it doesn't matter. I can tell that he's the one for you."

What? This is mind-blowing on many levels. First, Mom is super practical and not at all romantic (except when it comes to my dad). This is the woman who's always told me that I should never let a boy get in the way of my education and that I should have a career so I'll never have to rely on a husband to support me (not that I disagree with her). Second, Mom hasn't ever said that she wants me to date someone Chinese. But it's kind of obvious. Paul, my boyfriend in high school, was white, and she never thought much of him. Then again, maybe she didn't like Paul because he was a bit of an ass, and not because he was white.

"How can you tell that I like Eric? Because I don't. Not in that way." *Another lie.* That damnable little voice is back.

"I know these things. Ken may be a nice boy, but you obviously forget him too easily. This Eric—you can't forget him. You want the one you can't forget. I know because you are just like me."

There are worse things than being just like my mom. After all, she's a smart, successful art director at a nationally famous museum, and she married a great guy. Still, I can't let her think she's right about Eric. "I haven't forgotten Ken. It was just a little slip of the tongue. Ken's wonderful—you'll see when you meet him."

"When will that be?" she asks, switching gears so fast it makes my head spin. "This is a good time for us to visit. Your dad's still on summer break from teaching at his college, and I have some vacation time I could use."

"Winter," I say resolutely. "You'll meet Ken when you visit during the winter holidays." Filming should be wrapped up by then, and I'll be back in LA with my parents none the wiser about where I've been.

"And will we meet Eric too?"

"He won't be in LA over the winter holidays." Well, that much is true. Eric will be in China, and I'll be thousands of miles away. I should keep that in mind. Ken is in LA. Eric isn't. "Besides," I say with a certainty I wish I felt, "there is absolutely nothing going on between Eric and me."

CHAPTER SIXTEEN

I t's been two weeks, and I've talked to Ken only once more after our first phone call. The second conversation was brief because he was off to a rehearsal and I was needed on set. The few emails and texts that I *have* gotten from him have been a little . . . lacking. Not cold exactly. Just not warm. But mine haven't been much better. Maybe we're both just busy. *Or maybe we both have something to hide.* The thought fills me with worry about what Ken *might* be hiding and guilt over what I *am* hiding.

In those two weeks, I also haven't heard from Eric. Given the whole "our families are enemies" situation, Eric's probably waiting for me to make the first move. But I don't. Part of the reason is the weirdness of it all, but the other part is the sixteen-hour days on the set of *Butterfly*. By the time the weekend rolls around, I'm totally wiped out. The other actors go out together on the weekends, and although I get along well with them, they don't invite me to join them. I have a feeling they think of me as their kid sister.

I did consider texting Eric last weekend, but decided against it. Instead, in a stroke of genius (if I do say so myself), I booked a tour to see the Great Wall. A tour for Americans. *No one* expects to see Alyssa Chua sightseeing with a group of American tourists. It was just as awe-inspiring and grand as I had imagined. But a little lonely to be seeing the Great Wall with a bunch of strangers.

The whole time I was there, I had a little daydream running through my head of Alyssa and me—racing each other up and down the steps of the Great Wall, strolling arm in arm, and catching up on the lives we led without each other. But I haven't heard anything from Alyssa since her pink note warning me about Eric.

I shove aside this silly fantasy of becoming friends with Alyssa. For tomorrow, I've booked a tour at the Summer Palace, like Eric suggested. I'll see it on my own, and I won't waste a single minute thinking of what it would be like with my cousin at my side.

But first . . . one more day on the set. We've mostly been shooting on location in the suburbs of the city, but today, we're back in the studio. My pulse races. I have to admit that I'm excited about today's shoot. Today is the first day I get to play Sonia in her Song male drag.

Beijing is hot in late August, and the air conditioner in my dressing room trailer is broken, so there are fans everywhere, blowing my hair into my face and melting my makeup. Liz is in despair, but at least I don't need as much makeup as usual today.

While Liz does my makeup, my mind turns to the original *M. Butterfly* play. I've been reading David Henry Hwang's script for inspiration. The play spans decades, but the most fascinating time period in it for me is the Chinese Cultural Revolution that started in 1966. It was a time when art was outlawed—except for revolutionary art approved by the Communist Party—because that art was seen as the trappings of the elite, ruling class and possessing any of it was considered proof of being a counterrevolutionary. Even owning classical art or Beijing opera recordings was a crime punishable by public humiliation, imprisonment, and . . . worse. But there wasn't much worse than actually *being* an artist.

There's a scene in the play that haunts me. Two dancers enter upstage to the sound of relentless percussion. They're dressed as revolutionary Red Guards who go from house to house—looting and burning cultural artifacts—in a mockery of a communist revolutionary performance. Then the dancers drag in Song Liling from the wings to be sentenced to hard labor in a commune. He is no longer Butterfly—the beautiful, elegant opera singer. But he is no less graceful in a Mao suit as he kneels before his comrade-turned-accuser. Then, with brutal suddenness, Song Liling is beaten and forced to confess his "crime" of being an actor and performing "perverted acts" with another man. It's a chilling scene that I can't imagine replicating in a rom-com. Fortunately, however, I don't have to.

The current *Butterfly* isn't set during the Cultural Revolution, so my only concern is doing justice to my character. The original Song Liling/Butterfly is strong in a time of terror, and although *Butterfly* is a modern-day story set in today's China—Sonia/Song should be just as strong. *That's how I'll play my character.*

Liz finishes my makeup and then stuffs my flyaway hair into a short wig. I sneak a peek at my reflection in the mirror. *Huh.* With this movie's budget, I'd think they could do better than straight, bowl-cut bangs. It's a cute haircut on a five-year-old, but it just looks silly on an adult. Maybe Liz is going to style it now. She always does wonders with my hair.

But Liz gives the wig a final pat and asks, "Ready for costuming?"

"Oh, OK." Should I say something about the wig? No. I shouldn't second-guess my hair-and-makeup person. Maybe the bowl cut is all the rage now, and I'm just an unsophisticated American who doesn't know any better. I stare in the mirror and silently tell my reflection, *You will rock this bowl cut.*

Liz wheels out the rack with a single garment bag hanging on it and leaves to give me privacy. I unzip the bag and perk up immediately at the sight of the neatly pressed black suit and white dress shirt. *Oh, this is going to be fun!* I put on the shirt first and button it up. Then I tuck the long tails into the pants and finally button the jacket over the pants. Anticipation bubbles up in me . . . and fizzles out again at the first glimpse of my reflection in the full-length mirror.

The jacket hangs loosely around my shoulders, and the hem of the pants is too long, as are the arms of the jacket. The shirt is made of some kind of stiff material that won't lie flat against my collarbone. The shirttails are so long and the pants so oversized that the material is bunching around my waist in weird little bulges. Dismay fills my throat. *This can't be right.* A tailor was brought in to take my measurements, so how is it possible that this suit fits so poorly? With the bowl haircut and misfitted suit, I look utterly ridiculous.

I sigh. Jake's probably going to fire whatever poor sod is responsible for this costume.

I'm reluctant to leave my trailer and face Jake's formidable wrath, even when it's not directed at me. But the heat in my trailer is heaving at me like a living thing, and today's shoot is taking place in an indoor set with a working air conditioner.

I walk the short distance to the studio, and as soon as I get inside, my makeup starts to solidify, and my scalp itches a little less under the wig. I exhale in relief as I approach the set, a sterile office with black leather chairs and lots of chrome. We're shooting the scene where Ryan hires Song as a lawyer for his company, not knowing it's really Sonia, his ex-girlfriend.

Jake, Eilene, and Aidan are already there.

The relief I feel at the cool interior fades as I wait for Jake to explode. Instead, he looks me over and says, "OK, you look the part of Song. Now you've got to act the part." My eyes widen when he doesn't say anything about my costume. But my surprise doesn't end there. Jake proceeds to tell me what "acting the part" of Song means. "Gemma, when you walk in, I want you to trip over your pant legs. Be awkward. Make it clear you're uncomfortable in menswear."

Wait a minute. . . . "But I'm not—" I protest.

Eilene straightens in her director's chair. "Not what?"

"I'm not uncomfortable in menswear." I gulp in a lungful of air because Jake's glaring at me, but I make myself go on. "Or at least I wouldn't be uncomfortable if this suit fit right."

Jake speaks very slowly and carefully, like he's talking to a small child. "This is a rom-com we're shooting. That means we need some laughs. Some physical humor. So you're playing someone who has trouble acting like a guy. Because you're really a girl. It's supposed to be *funny*. Got it?"

Oh, I get it all right. Ken's words pop into my head. *All the Asian men in that film will be sexless and nerdy.* The bowl haircut, the ill-fitting suit, Jake's directions—it all makes sense now. Whether Jake realizes it or not, he wants me to play Song as a comedic stereotype of an effeminate Asian man. Because, of course, it's hilarious to think that an Asian man could possibly be a *real* man. And how can he drive home that point? By having a woman play an Asian man in drag. A sick feeling worms into my stomach. No way can I be part of that. Before I know it, words are pouring out of my mouth. "What if I do this differently? What if I play my character in a way that's not so . . . um . . ." *stereotypical, offensive, racist.* I edit out all that on the fly. ". . . awkward?"

Jake sighs. "Eilene, explain it to her, please."

By the appalled look on Eilene's face, I can tell that she's just had the same realization I had. I expect her to step in the way she had before when she suggested a script rewrite, but instead, she says, "I'd like to hear more of what Gemma has to say."

My heart drops. I really wanted Eilene to say what I can't say. *Or am too afraid to say.*

Jake repeats what he said before, except even more slowly, enunciating each word.

Your character is strong, remember? It's not like I'm a criminal actor facing down the Red Guard. I'm just up against Jake—asshole director.

Desperately, I muster all my courage and try again. "How about if I play Song as, uh, hot?" Eilene nods at me encouragingly. "Ryan could be attracted to Sonia as Song." Quickly, I add, "But he's not freaked out! Because homophobia isn't funny, and that's not what we should go for." Jake is staring at me in disbelief, and I start talking way too fast, stumbling over my words. "But maybe Ryan's bi, and maybe Sonia never knew that Ryan was bi, and that makes Ryan seem less stiff and uptight than she thought he was, so then she's attracted to *him* again, plus she's really into the whole outside-the-gender-binary dynamic between them, but she can't act on it as Song without revealing who she really is, which is ironic because she dressed up as a man in the first place to *stop*, not *start,* sparks from flying again." I pause to take a breath and add weakly, "It's funny."

Jake is now looking at me as if I've lost my mind. "You can't be serious. It's just not believable for Ryan to be attracted to Song as a man." He waves a hand at Aidan. "Anyway, Aidan will never go for it."

"Actually," Aidan says, "I like it." *Thank you, Aidan.*

"I do too," Eileen says.

"Well, I don't," Jake says. "We're hoping to capture the Asian market as well as the U.S. market with this film, and the Asian market, especially a country as traditional as China, will never go for a film with such overt gay content." Then, almost gently, he says, "It's not a bad idea, Gemma. It just won't fly."

I glance pleadingly at Eilene. This is where she offers to rewrite the script again. But instead, she says, "Why don't we see what Gemma's vision looks like."

"It's a waste of time." Jake's mouth sets. "So, can we *please* get on with this scene now?"

Eilene looks at me calmly. "Well, Gemma? How are you going to play this?"

I let Eilene's double meaning sink in. That and the fact that she's not going to save me. The weight of this whole impossible situation settles into my back muscles, making them feel tense and tight. What does she expect me to do? What *can* I do? I'm just a newbie actress who badly needs to make a good impression. "Trip over my pants," I say dully. "Got it."

Eilene comes by my trailer after I've taken off the horrible suit and changed into a sundress. The air conditioner still hasn't been fixed, and my hair is plastered to my forehead with sticky moisture. I'm bad-tempered from the humidity and my failure to make a difference in the film. Jake seemed reasonably satisfied with today's shoot, but I'm filled with disgust by selling out and playing my character as a cheap racial caricature.

"Why didn't you show Jake your vision of the scene?" Eilene asks at once, shutting the door of my trailer behind her. Then she visibly recoils as the stifling heat hits her. "Are those fans doing anything but redistributing hot air?"

"No," I say sullenly, answering the second question and ignoring the first one.

Eilene perches on a spare stool and contemplates me for a moment. About a ton of sweat pools between my shoulder blades as the silence stretches out between us. Unfairly, Eilene looks as cool and collected as always.

Finally, she says, "Did you ever hear the story of what Michelle Yeoh did on the set of *Crazy Rich Asians*?"

I nod. Michelle Yeoh is right up there with Eilene as someone deserving my undying adoration. So I can guess where she's going with this. Michelle Yeoh famously refused to accept the role of Eleanor Young if she were written as an Asian tiger mom stereotype. As a result, Eleanor is one of my favorite characters—layered and multifaceted. The way I picture the scene in my head is like this:

Michelle Yeoh: *I'll take the role, but it has to change.*

Everyone involved with the film: *Yes, oh goddess! Whatever you want!*

But I'm not Michelle Yeoh. I'm a mere mortal. Worse than a mere mortal—a debut actress.

"You have a promising career ahead of you, Gemma," Eilene says. "You'll work with directors who might be a lot worse than Jake, and it's not always certain that there will be anyone on your side. Actors *do* have the power to change a movie for the better. But you'll never learn how if I swoop in every time you start to stand up for yourself."

I wipe furiously at the makeup on my face with a towel soaked in makeup remover. "So, you're saying that I'm on my own?" The makeup remover burns across my skin like a swarm of fire ants.

"I'll be there to back you up." Eilene stands. "But you're the actress. You've got to figure out who your character is. Then you've got to fight for her."

Who my character is? I don't even know who *I* am anymore. I'm lying to my parents, confused about my feelings for Ken, wondering just what's going on with Eric, worried about disappointing Eilene and pissing Jake off. Oh, and let's not forget that my cousin is a socialite celebrity running around Beijing with *my* face.

I toss my towel onto the dressing table. "You saw how Jake shut me down when I tried to suggest a change to Sonia's character today!"

"I didn't say it would be easy." Eilene smiles without humor. "We're actresses. We're supposed to play roles that other people create for us. But I call bullshit on that."

The shock of hearing profanity from Eilene makes me almost fall off my chair. I'm paying attention now.

"The people who've created characters like Sonia—and every character I've ever played—have no idea who we really are," Eilene says. "That's why you *have* to make Sonia your own. If you don't—then you're sunk." Heat smolders in her eyes. "You're not just fighting for your character—you're fighting for yourself."

I swallow hard. It's clear that Eilene is speaking from her own experience. And isn't this what I wanted—to learn from my idol's wisdom?

Yeah, but that was before her advice boiled down to: *Sink or swim. And if you sink, I won't save you.*

CHAPTER SEVENTEEN

My depression about the film seeps into the next day. I have the tour to the Summer Palace booked for this morning, but I don't have the heart to deal with people, so I end up canceling. Instead, I look over my sides for next week and start memorizing lines. *OK, this isn't so bad.* There aren't any more "Song" drag scenes coming up this week. Even better, we're going to be shooting on location in the city all week.

Maybe I should march down to the concierge and book a tour to the Summer Palace after lunch. But as soon as I decide this, a draft of the whole script is delivered to my hotel room. *Don't look at it, Gemma.* My inner voice gives good advice . . . but of course, I ignore it. In an exercise in masochism, I read through the whole thing, and when I'm done, I order room service and full-on *wallow*. If anything, the later Song scenes are *worse* than the one I did yesterday.

So, no Summer Palace.

Instead, I park my butt in front of the TV screen. My eyes are dry and burning, and I'm deep into a martial arts scene in a Wuxia drama when my phone lights up with a call from Ken.

For one long, breathless beat, I just stare at my buzzing phone. My first thought is totally instinctive. *I don't want to talk to him.* Then I give myself a mental shake. *Don't be silly. This is your boyfriend. Talk to him! You'll feel better.*

I tap the green answer icon. "Hi, Ken!"

"Hey, Gemma!" Ken says. "Man, it's good to hear your voice!"

"It's good to hear your voice too!" And it is. I'm glad that I picked up the phone. Maybe my attraction to Eric doesn't mean anything. And maybe Ken's disappointing emails and texts don't mean anything. After all, I'll be leaving Beijing—and Eric—and be back home in a month or two. "What's up?" I check the time. It's 5:00 p.m. here, which means it's two in the morning for him. *Chill, Gemma.* Ken staying out until the bars closed doesn't mean a thing. It definitely doesn't mean he was on a date.

"Well, I finally got paid for that commercial I did!"

I love this version of Ken—happy and upbeat. "Hey, that's great!"

"So," he says slyly, "guess what I'm going to do with the money I got for the commercial?"

"Clearly you're excited about it, so I'm guessing it's not rent or bills."

He laughs. "Well, that's part of it, but I'll have enough left over for something really special."

"A seventy-inch TV? A party to end all parties? All-you-can-eat buffets for a month?" I tease.

"No, no, and . . . tempting . . . but no," Ken replies. "Actually, you're not even close, so I might as well tell you. I'm going to buy a ticket to Beijing and visit you!"

My heart lodges in my throat. "Really?" Panic makes me sit up on the couch and clutch the phone hard. Is there a chance I could have misunderstood? "Did you just say you were going to come and visit me?"

"Yeah! Isn't that awesome?"

It *should* be awesome. So why am I all flustered at the idea of Ken's visit? In my head, I'm already envisioning myself dragging my exhausted ass back from the set to a boyfriend who's on vacation and wants to go out. And explaining this luxe hotel suite, Alyssa, my mom, and the family secrets that are driving me batty.

While I'm struggling with an answer, he says, "Oh, before I forget, I just wanted to say that picture of me doesn't mean anything." *What picture?* He's talking way too fast, and a clammy sense of foreboding crawls down my back as he says, "I mean, it's not like I couldn't have—"

"Ken," I interrupt, my insides all twisted up, "I haven't been able to get onto social media since my first week in China."

"Oh."

"So . . . what picture?" I'm not stupid. I can guess. All too clearly, an image of Ken with his tongue in another girl's mouth pops into my head. *Our agreement didn't extend to posting pictures on social media that I might see! I would never do that to Ken.*

"Just an embarrassing picture a friend took of me," he says. "I was pretty drunk and looked silly."

Well, I think uncharitably, *Ken does hate to look silly.* He might be telling the truth after all. But the sick feeling in my stomach worsens.

"Anyway, it's not important," he says quickly. "The important thing is that I'm coming to see you!"

"Yeah. About that." I know I'm making the right decision, but that doesn't make the heaviness in my chest go away. "I'm on the set all the time. The hours I'm working are crazy. I won't have any time to spend with you."

"Believe it or not," Ken says with a forced laugh, "I do have some experience with being on a set."

"Yes, but this is a movie set." *Oh crap.* Am I *trying* to sabotage this relationship? Maybe I'm overreacting about this picture of Ken with another girl that may or may not exist. And let's face it—Ken was honest with me about seeing other people while I was gone. My tongue trips all over itself. "I mean, of course you've been on set too. Lots of them. More than I have. So you *totally* know what it's like." I'm actually making this worse. If that's even possible.

"So do you want me to come or not?"

I get why Ken's upset. After all, he's just made this big gesture by wanting to spend his hard-earned money to visit me, and instead of squealing with joy like any other girl with a romantic bone in her body, I'm being all hesitant and cagey. *It's not too late. I could still turn this around.* I take a deep breath. But what comes out of my mouth is: "I don't think it's a good idea."

"I see." His voice is subarctic.

My heart spasms in response. "Ken, I *do* want to see you, but there's just so much going on right now." Maybe if I tell Ken what's at stake, he'll understand. "Eilene's counting on me to help her to turn this film around and make it something we can both be proud of." This is as close as I've ever come to admitting to him how badly the film is going, and part of me wants to cover up the truth. But the other part of me remembers how good it felt to talk to Eric about the film. If I can't talk to Ken about my problems, then what does that say about our relationship?

Still, my stomach curdles with anxiety as I take the plunge. "To tell you the truth, things aren't going well. Eilene's trying so hard to help me with my career, and I'm worried about letting her down. There's also a lot going on with my family that I need to tell you about. That's why it's not a good idea for you to visit, OK?"

There's a chilly silence before Ken replies. "Let's get real, Gemma," he says. "This is a fluffy rom-com we're talking about. It's not exactly serious filmmaking, is it? The chances of this being your big break are pretty much nil."

What? I finally spill my guts about how tough the last month has been, and *this* is how Ken reacts? He didn't even pay attention to what I'd said about my family! Maybe this will all blow over if I just tell him I want him to come after all.

But I can't.

Rage boils up in me and spills into my voice. "Are you even listening to me? Do you even hear *yourself*? This film might be nothing but a 'fluffy rom-com' to you, but it's important to me! And it would be nice if my *boyfriend* could be supportive of that!" I'm hissing fire, and my phone screen fogs up with the heat of my breath.

"Well, it would be nice if my *girlfriend* could show a little appreciation for the fact that I want to fly to China to see her." His usual chill is gone. "But no, you're too infatuated with the great Eilene Deng to see what's really going on!"

My anger goes cold and hard in the pit of my stomach. "What does that mean, Ken?" Taking potshots at my career is one thing. Going after Eilene, who's shed blood, sweat, and tears to blaze a trail for Asian actresses like me—that's a completely different thing. "And I'd think very carefully about what you say next if I were you."

"This film that means so much to you is nothing but a vanity project for Eilene. Face it—she's past her prime and can't get cast anymore," he says. "She weaseled her way into this film and has everything riding on it now, but I doubt anyone else sees this film as anything but a sop to Eilene's pride." *Oh no, he didn't.* Only the sheer fury clogging my throat keeps me from interrupting. "Eilene's using you to prop up her own career. She doesn't care about you or your career. And you're too blind to see it."

That checks my anger a bit. *Could Ken be right?* Eilene did hang me out to dry at the last shoot. She said she wanted me to learn to fight for myself, but what if she just didn't want to get her own hands dirty? What if she *is* just using me? "You don't know what you're talking about." But my voice comes out faint and frozen.

"I just don't want to see you get your hopes up for a doomed film. So, if I were you, I wouldn't count on the film or your role in it going anywhere." Then Ken hits the nail home. "But don't feel too bad. This movie is just the studio's token attempt to cash in on the Asian rom-com craze. And you knew that when you took the role."

This strikes a nerve. Doubt worms into unguarded chinks, splitting apart my certainty. "Are you calling me a sellout?" I demand. A chilly dread turns my skin moist and clammy. It's true that I took the role knowing what this movie was. I knew full well that it might reinforce every hideous, dangerous Asian caricature I've hated all my life. Doesn't that make me a sellout?

Ken hesitates for too long. "No."

The answer should have been immediate. And it should have been "*Hell* no!" Followed by a million abject apologies. There's no doubt that Ken said some jerky things. But that doesn't mean he's entirely wrong. And he's probably hurting from what he sees as my rejection of him. I'd probably be more sympathetic if not for the fact that he's bringing to light the ugly demons I've been pushing into dark corners for weeks. I may be acting small and petty—but I can't forgive him for that.

After a moment of fraught silence, Ken says, "Don't get defensive, Gemma. I'm not trying to be insulting. I'm just calling it as I see it."

"Are you done?" I ask with icy calm.

"Yes." He sounds tentative, like he realizes that maybe he's gone too far.

But it's too late.

"Good. Because so am I." A part of me is screaming, *You'll never find anyone this cool and sexy again!* But the other part of me is thinking of all the red flags I've ignored throughout our short relationship. My heart slams painfully into my ribs.

"What's that supposed to mean?" he demands.

It's pretty clear I liked the idea of Ken more than I liked Ken himself. And that's not fair to either of us. I swallow down the dryness in my throat. "I'm sorry, Ken, but I'm afraid this isn't working."

"Unbelievable! Are you really breaking up with me?"

Yeah, Gemma, are you really going to do this?! "I am. I'm sorry."

"Don't be too sorry," he says coldly. "It's not like I don't have other options."

"Like the girl in the picture with you?"

"Exactly." Then there's nothing but dead silence. Ken has just hung up on me.

Oh shit. I really did it. I just broke up with Ken.

CHAPTER EIGHTEEN

The next morning, I wake up to the soft glow of the natural-light lamp, and the mellow light is like a razor scraping across my nerves. *What have I done?* But the awful heaviness in my stomach isn't regret. I'm not sorry—exactly—that I broke up with Ken. I just wish it had worked out. Or that he'd been just a little less self-absorbed. The only thing I can't judge him for is dishonesty. Yes, he might have covered up that he was going full throttle on the "let's see other people" thing, but I've done much worse.

I'm actively lying to my parents.

It's the thought that keeps coming back to haunt me. Look at how awful I felt about Ken hanging out with another girl when he was actually pretty open about being non-exclusive. I can just imagine how my parents will feel if they find out about my *way* bigger deception.

I bury my head under a mound of pillows, but sleep eludes me. I pretty much went to bed after my breakup with Ken—which means that I've been sleeping for an obscenely long time.

Blearily, I drag myself out of bed and right to the soaking tub. I fill the tub, turn on the jets, and empty the entire bowl of rose petals into the water. Then *all* the bath salts that I've been carefully rationing. *I can get more. Alyssa included room service in her . . .* What is this, exactly? Bribe? Gift? *Who cares?* Whatever it is—I'm going to take full advantage of it. Apparently, all it takes is the world's worst breakup for me to become a full-on princess.

Argh. I need ice cream. And cue room service.

Hours later, I have an empty bowl of ice cream and am officially a prune from soaking in the jetted tub.

Unfortunately, I don't feel all that better. OK, maybe a smidge better. But I need more ice cream. My stomach gurgles in protest. Forget ice cream. I should order lunch. Did I eat breakfast? It's really bad when I skip a meal. I *never* skip meals.

Just as I'm telling myself that ice cream doesn't count as a meal and that I will *not* order more, my phone lights up. It's Eric. Great. Just great. I don't hear from him in two weeks, and *this* is when he texts me—when I'm a sad, wrecked ball of mopiness.

Hi Gemma. Can you meet me?

Nope. No way. I'm in no state to cozy up with Eric to discuss a scheme that might have me blackmailing my cousin or something equally dubious.

Another text from Eric pops up.

I have information about your mother.

What the hell? When I last talked to Eric, he didn't seem to know anything about my mother, and now he has information? My hands shake as I text back.

I can meet now.

Armed with oversize sunglasses and a wide-brimmed hat, I enter the East Palace Gate of the Summer Palace. My electronic guidebook says that it will take hours to see everything in this imperial pleasure garden and summer resort complex, but I'm not here to sightsee. I'm here to find out what Eric knows about my mother.

Eric suggested that we meet in the Garden of Virtue and Harmony, and when I arrive, he's already there. He's standing in front of a beautifully ornate three-tiered building in brilliant red, gold, and green. This time he's wearing jeans and a T-shirt instead of a suit.

"Hello, Gemma." His tone is unexpectedly formal. This isn't the funny and sweet Eric I last saw. It's not even the pissed-off Eric I first met. This Eric is somber and distant—and this version is the most unsettling of all. *It's because of what he knows about my mother.*

My heart careens to my feet. "What did you find out about my mother?"

He doesn't reply right away. Instead, he gestures to the building behind him. "Empress Dowager Cixi of the Qing dynasty had the Grand Theater built in the late nineteenth century for the Beijing opera performances that she loved."

Grand Theater. It's grand all right and *totally* deserves its name. Although I'm dying to know what Eric knows about my mother, I pause to take in the jade-green pillars, fancy scrollwork, and curved roofs climbing into the heavens. "It's beautiful." What wouldn't I give to perform in that theater? Except, as a woman in Empress Dowager Cixi's time, I would have been forbidden to perform in classical Beijing opera.

"When you told me that your movie *Butterfly* is based on *M. Butterfly*, a play about a Chinese opera singer, I thought you would be interested in seeing this."

"Wow. That's really thoughtful." I didn't realize *this* was why Eric suggested that I go to the Summer Palace. *M. Butterfly* is set during the Cultural Revolution when classical Beijing opera, usually performed for imperial rulers, was outlawed. Even the fictional opera singer Song Liling—who played the part of a woman to spy for the Communist Party—was punished for his art. Loyalty to the government was no protection in the time of the Cultural Revolution. "You're right that I'm interested." A pang hits me. If only Ken had been as supportive. *And if only Eric weren't keeping things from me.* "But stop stalling."

A wry smile softens his face, and for a moment, he looks like the Eric I'd met. "I wanted to ask for your help."

"My help?" My amazement quickly turns into suspicion. "Wait. Does that mean your information about my mother was just a way to lure me here?"

"No! Of course not," he says. Then his ears flush red. "I mean, I really do have information, but also, I hoped you could help me."

"I see." My voice is frosty. "So, this is a trade."

He shakes his head. "It wouldn't be a fair trade. You'd be doing me a favor if you agree to help me, but I'm not sure I would be doing you a favor by telling you about your mother."

My stomach churns, and it takes an effort to speak. "Tell me."

"After I met you," he says slowly, "I asked my grandmother if she had known your mother." He clears his throat. "She said that she had. She told me . . ."

"Just spit it out." My whole body tenses up as I wait to hear what he'll say.

"Your mother is a thief."

"Are you crazy?!" I'm so loud that other tourists turn to look at me; my chest is heaving and my face is hot with anger. I step away from Eric so abruptly that my heel catches on a jutting edge of stone and I almost trip.

Eric doesn't say anything, just looks at me with a face full of wariness.

The rage pounding through my body settles down enough for me to ask, "What, exactly, is she supposed to have stolen?"

"A painting."

"Ha! That shows you what you know. My mother is a director at a museum. She'd no more steal a painting than she'd burn down her own house!"

"My grandmother says it was priceless." Eric's face sets in grim lines. "A Tang dynasty painting believed to have been destroyed during the Cultural Revolution. Your mother stole it from our family."

No. It's not possible. "Your grandmother is a liar!"

"My grandmother isn't lying." Eric's face and shoulders are rigid. "I've seen the scars on my grandfather's knees from kneeling on broken glass and the scars on his back from being caned until he passed out. His back is twisted and bent from years of hard labor in a communist commune. Ye Ye was in constant pain until the day he died. And it was because of that painting." Those caught with contraband classical art during the Cultural Revolution were often punished the way Eric's grandfather was.

My body goes limp with horror. *This can't be real.* What Eric described is what happened to Song Liling in *M. Butterfly*. How could it have happened to actual people? Except of course it did. The Red Guard found it in Ye Ye's home, so he paid for that painting with his blood and bones. But why would my mother steal a painting that had caused Eric's family so much tragedy? The air presses down on me, and suddenly there are too many people around, and the heat beating down on me stifles my breath and makes my skin prickle.

Eric glances at me in concern, but then he stares at the brightly colored theater, and his voice is hard. "I haven't told you the whole truth about the feud between our families."

No shit. "So why don't you tell me now?"

His gaze returns to me. "Before the Cultural Revolution, our grandfathers were best friends—closer than brothers. But the revolution turned friend against friend. Anyone, even family, could betray you. It was a time when fear was stronger than friendship or family. Our grandfathers both joined the Red Guard—a militarized youth organization under Chairman Mao. That's when they became enemies—rivals for power in the ranks of the Communist Party."

With a jolt to my heart, I remember what Alyssa said about my grandfather. *Sung Shen Yi has made a name for himself as someone you don't want for an enemy.* A chill runs down my spine. That's my grandfather Eric's talking about. The same one whose very name is censored by the government. And, according to Alyssa, he won't like that I'm in Beijing.

"Your grandfather betrayed mine. He accused my ye ye of being a counterrevolutionary, an enemy of the people, and when his fellow Red Guard searched his home . . . they found the painting. Ye Ye swore that he didn't know how it got there, but you can see how it looked. A Red Guard caught with art from the Tang dynasty in his possession."

I can. All too well. Bile rises in my throat as scenes from *M. Butterfly* flood my mind. The elegant Butterfly singing in a theater like the one in front of me. Song Liling beaten for his art.

"I thought the painting had been destroyed by the Red Guard like so much other art, but Nai Nai said that Ye Ye kept it from being destroyed somehow. For years, he held on to that painting as compensation for his suffering—until your mother stole it."

"No," I whisper, my mind numb with shock.

Eric doesn't seem to hear me. "And it wasn't just any painting," he says bitterly. "It was a painting rumored to be from Empress Wu's art collection from the Tang dynasty. Of course, it meant Ye Ye's destruction."

"Sorry." My head goes woozy with lightness. "*Whose* art collection?"

He shoots me a strange look. "Wu Zetian. She's—"

"I know who she is." I shake my head to clear it, but that doesn't help. Too many questions buzz in my brain. *A painting believed to have been destroyed during the Cultural Revolution. A painting rumored to be from Empress Wu's art collection from the Tang dynasty. A painting kept from being destroyed somehow.* Nothing makes sense. Only one fact remains unchanged—and I cling to it in this sea of confusion. My mother wouldn't have stolen that painting. Her whole career has been to *give* people the experience of art.

"Eric, I'm so sorry about what happened to your grandfather. And I believe everything you told me about my grandfather. But my mother didn't steal that painting."

Eric's eyes go cold. "My grandmother says she did."

"What proof does your grandmother have?" I ask, trying to sound calm.

"Your mother disappeared without a trace right after the painting was stolen."

"*That's* your proof?" I'm almost giddy with relief. "Just because my mother left her family after the painting disappeared doesn't mean that she stole it!"

A muscle jumps in Eric's cheek. "If my grandmother says your mother stole the painting, then she did. My grandmother isn't a liar."

"And my mother isn't a thief!"

We glare at each other, the tension building up between us like invisible bricks. Then I think of my mother, year after year, warning me against ever stepping foot in Beijing. *What do I really know about my mother?* "My mother didn't steal that painting." Even to my own ears, the denial sounds weaker than it did before.

"My grandmother described the painting to me." His gaze never wavers from my face. "It's a painting of a lady wearing a red dress with a blue-green shawl and sash in the style of the court ladies of the Tang dynasty. She's sitting with a brush in one hand, writing calligraphy."

I've seen that painting.

Shivers cascade over my body like I've been dumped in freezing water. That's the painting hanging on the wall in my mom's office at home. *It's a copy. It has to be.* My breath crowds into my chest. Could this be the reason my mother doesn't want to come back to China? Is she a wanted criminal after all? Voice taut with fear, I ask, "Did your family ever press charges?"

"No. My grandmother didn't press charges," Eric says carefully. "It's not a good idea to admit that your family possessed a painting that was supposed to have been destroyed during the Cultural Revolution."

I don't say anything. The dizziness is making my head spin like a tornado. *You've never fainted in your whole life,* I tell myself sternly, but my watery legs and wobbling head don't seem to be paying attention. Is this what Alyssa meant when she said her grandmother collapsed from shock? I suddenly get how that can happen.

"Gemma?" Eric's voice seems distant and far away. "Are you OK?" Worry loosens the hardness of his face. "Listen, maybe I shouldn't have told you about your mother."

"I'm fine." I make myself stand straight, spine rigid. *If* my mother stole that painting—and it's a big if—then she had good reason. But what were those reasons? And would my mother tell me if I asked her? *Right.* I can just imagine how that conversation would go. *Do you know that Tang dynasty painting in your office that I always thought was a copy? Funny story—I happen to be in Beijing (against your express wishes), and this guy told me that it's the original. From Empress Wu's own collection. That you stole. From our family's sworn enemy. Thoughts? Anything you'd like to tell me?*

Never mind. Asking my mom isn't an option.

That means I have to find out another way. "I need to talk to Alyssa. Do you know where I can find her?"

"Funny." He smiles, but it doesn't quite reach his eyes. "That's actually the favor I was going to ask you. I know exactly where Alyssa will be tonight. And my sister will be with her. But I need you to impersonate Alyssa so I can get in to talk to Mimi."

"Then," I say, "it looks like we need each other to get what we want."

CHAPTER NINETEEN

Eric and I make plans to meet again tonight, and then he suggests that we explore the Grand Theater and the rest of the Garden of Virtue and Harmony. We go through the motions of sightseeing, and he shares some historical information while I nod without taking in anything he says. Neither one of us seems to be enjoying this.

Maybe I should just call it a day. Then I look at the blooming trees and the peaceful paths surrounding me. *No, dammit—I'm going to have fun even if it kills me.* "Let's go somewhere else," I say. "What's your favorite thing to do at the Summer Palace?"

"I have a lot of favorite things here." The grave expression on Eric's face lightens a bit. "What about a dragon boat ride on Kunming Lake?"

"Sounds good."

At first, our conversation is stilted as we walk to the dock for the dragon boat ride, but the pleasure gardens of the Summer Palace eventually work their magic, and we both start to relax. It's late afternoon and the place is relatively deserted of people, so we have the beautiful pagodas and lakeside paths mostly to ourselves.

"Wait." I stop in my tracks and point dramatically to the lake and the sleek boats with awnings and pointed prows. "What. Are. Those?"

He peers over to where I'm pointing and grins. "Looks like pedal boats. You know, in all the times I've been to the Summer Palace, I've never tried them. Want to do it?"

"Duh! Of course!" I'm bouncing up and down in excitement. I've been on little pedal boats, but these are bigger and way cooler.

I let Eric have the first crack at the steering wheel, but it turns out that a pedal boat of this size is harder to operate than it looks. "Steer right!" I yell as we careen toward the dock.

The boat rental employees on the dock are yelling the same thing in Chinese.

Eric cranks the wheel to the right as we both pedal madly, but it doesn't keep us from bumping the dock again. At least the next time, we actually clear the dock.

The people on the dock burst into applause, and Eric turns to me sheepishly. "There go my dreams of racing pedal boats."

"Don't give up on your dreams of pedal boat racing just yet." I lean back against my seat and adjust my hat over my eyes. "We rented the boat for an hour, so you have plenty of time to redeem yourself."

He pokes me good-naturedly. "Hey, you stopped pedaling!"

"You're the one with pedal boat racing ambitions." I grin at him. "Not me." He pretends to glare at me, and I say, "OK, OK! I'm pedaling!"

The boat gliding over the glass-smooth lake and the blood pumping through my veins are just what I need. My spirits lift and stay strong, even when Eric asks me about the film.

To my surprise, I end up telling him about Friday's shoot, the ugly suit, and Jake's dismissal of my suggestions for Sonia's character. The only thing I *don't* tell him about is breaking up with Ken yesterday. That still feels too raw.

"Wait a minute." Eric frowns. "Your director actually said the Chinese people were too 'traditional' to accept gay characters in this film?"

"Yeah. Why?"

"Well, it's just that pre-Westernized, ancient China accepted LGBTQ people just fine. Records of same-sex relations go as far back as ancient China. In the imperial court, in monasteries, in Buddhist nunneries and love poems between Daoist nuns—it was everywhere and just a part of life." *Love poems between Daoist nuns—how cool is that?* I'm still wrapping my head around that when Eric adds, "I'm not saying that there isn't homophobia and transphobia in China today—because there is." He snorts. "But modern Westernization is arguably more to blame for that than Chinese *traditional* values."

Averting my face from a group of tourists on a dragon boat with their phones out, I say, "I get that. I mean, there's still homophobia and transphobia in the U.S. too."

"I'll go as far as saying the modern Chinese government is more restrictive than yours when it comes to LGBTQ rights," Eric says somberly. "I mean, same-sex relations were only decriminalized in China about twenty years ago, and same-sex marriage isn't legal yet."

"The U.S. didn't legalize same-sex marriage until recently," I admit.

"See, that's my point." His feet churn the pedals harder. "When I was in the U.S. for college, I met Americans who think of the U.S. as a modern, progressive country and China as stuck in the past. Like China never left the time of the Cultural Revolution when being gay was criminalized and punished. But we're changing and growing like any other country. That's why I think your director doesn't have the whole story."

We pedal in silence past pagodas and stone bridges as I think about what he said. He's right that Jake doesn't know the China that Eric knows, but maybe I don't either. *I certainly didn't know about lesbian Buddhist and Daoist nuns in ancient China.* It's pretty cool that Eric knows all this history. Maybe that was his major in college. "By the way, where did you go to college?"

"Stanford."

My eyebrows rise. "Most guys I know would've led with that." And worked it into the conversation about a dozen times by now.

"I'm lucky that my parents could afford to send me there," Eric says. "It would've been cheaper for me to go to college in China, but Stanford has a good sustainability program."

"Is that what you majored in?"

"Hey, I think it's your turn to steer. Want to trade places?"

It's obvious that he's avoiding my question, but I decide to let it slide. "You bet."

He gets up at the same time I do, and the boat tilts dangerously. We both sit down again.

"Um," I say, "why don't you slide under and I'll go, uh, over?" My face burns. *Did I really just say that out loud?* It didn't sound quite so suggestive in my head.

Eric's face is bright red. "Good idea."

Gingerly, I stand and try to edge over to the driver's seat without actually touching him. At the same time, he tries to scoot under my crouched body to the passenger seat.

I can't explain how it happens, but suddenly I'm awkwardly perched over Eric, hands braced on either side of his body. My chest constricts in panic as he stares at me, wide-eyed, for a beat, his breath puffing hotly against my face. Then he abruptly ducks into the passenger seat, leaving me free to sink into the driver's seat.

My heart beats fast, and my face is a perspiring mess. Carefully, we avoid looking at each other. And that's when I remember Ken. *Shit.* How could I have broken up with my boyfriend just twenty-four hours ago and be all flustered and sweaty over another guy already? A guy who thinks my mom stole a painting from his family.

"Business," Eric says abruptly.

I look at him in surprise. "What?"

"You asked me before what I majored in," he clarifies, "and I majored in business, but I did take some classes on sustainability." Then he reddens. "To tell you the truth, Stanford's not even where I really wanted to go. That would be UCLA. I applied and got into their environment and sustainability graduate program, but I ended up deferring my admission and coming back home." He starts to pedal without looking at me. "I didn't even tell my parents that I'd applied or gotten in."

The funny thing is that I applied and got into UCLA too, for my undergraduate studies, and I also deferred my admission. Except my experience is just the opposite of Eric's. Lost in thought, I begin pedaling again. I'm pursuing my dreams against my parents' wishes. He's sacrificing his dreams to fulfill what he thinks his parents want. "I get it," I say. "Your parents wouldn't have approved, right?"

But he shakes his head. "No. That's not it. They would have supported my decision." He slows down his pedaling. "It's just that they sacrificed so much for me and invested in my education, you know? I feel I owe it to them to come back and help with the business. Plus, Mimi . . ."

"Mimi what?" I prompt.

Eric averts his eyes and mumbles something in Chinese. Then he says, "I messed up." He meets my eyes. "I told my parents that Mimi is hanging out with Alyssa. I shouldn't have said anything, but it just slipped out. Then Nai Nai found out."

I suck in my breath. "That does sound bad." I don't have the heart to say that tattling on Mimi wasn't cool. Besides, it's clear he knows that already.

"It gets worse," he says glumly. "Nai Nai flipped out and even threatened to disown Mimi. That's when my dad got into it with my grandmother. He said that it was his money in the first place, and he wasn't about to disown Mimi because of her choice in friends.

Mom tried to keep the peace, but it was too late." He winces as if it's a painful memory. "Dad said he regretted that his money got Nai Nai the social status to indulge in such a petty war with the Sung/Chua family. You would not believe the yelling after my father said *that* to my grandmother. My family usually gets along, but now it's a complete mess, and it's all my fault."

"Oh, wow, Eric! I'm so sorry."

"I tried to apologize to Mimi, but she won't take my calls. I just want to see her and explain. It's why I texted you."

Right. I'd almost forgotten the plan. Why we're here in the first place. Eric and I are nothing but collaborators. I yank on the steering wheel to turn us back toward the dock. "We should be getting back. I want to rest up before tonight."

He nods. "That's a good idea."

Anything I felt between us was just an illusion. My heart twists painfully. Eric wants me to impersonate Alyssa so he can talk to Mimi. *But that's OK*, I tell myself. I want Eric's help too. He knows where Alyssa will be tonight. And I need to talk to her.

CHAPTER TWENTY

Later that night, my driver drops me off at the northwest exit of the Tuanjiehu subway station, where I've arranged to meet Eric. He's there waiting for me, wearing another beautifully tailored suit that makes the one I had to wear on set look like a clown costume. Although I'll bet anything that Eric would've pulled off my suit somehow. The thought makes me grumpy.

"Ni hao," Eric greets me with the Chinese phrase that translates literally into "you good" but pretty much means "hi."

"Ni hao," I reply.

A man jostles me as he hurries by, causing me to clutch my wide-brimmed hat to my head. It's still not much of a disguise, but it's still less conspicuous than wearing sunglasses at night. Fortunately, the hat seems to do the trick, and the man barely looks at me.

"Come on," Eric says. "Let's get out of here."

As we walk down the street, I'm bathed in the heavy warmth of the night air. Eric hugs my arm closer to him, sending shivers of delight down my spine. It's such a natural gesture for him, and it's actually pretty nice.

But I wonder what it means. Chinese people my age seem comfortable with physical touch without it necessarily meaning anything romantic. In contrast, Americans like me are all or nothing. We either don't touch, or else there's a sexual implication. *Which, maybe, I wouldn't mind so much if he hadn't accused my mother of being a thief.*

About ten minutes later, we reach a trendy area of huge glass buildings and jumbotrons. Eric tells me that we're in the Sanlitun area, known for its shopping, food, and nightclubs. In awe, I take in the great swaths of light and colorful signs. Some of the shops are ones I recognize, but bigger and brighter than any I've ever seen, like they've been pumped up on steroids.

Eric comes to a stop at a tall, sleek building with no windows on the bottom floors, though the top floor is lit up like a sparkler. Two burly guys in suits are standing at the metal double doors of the building, and they're eyeing us skeptically. I don't blame them. This place looks über posh. Eric might fit in a place like this, but I certainly don't in my floral print sundress, sandals, and big hat. I wish I'd packed something more nightclub appropriate before I'd left LA, but I didn't know I'd be impersonating a rich socialite to get into a club.

Nerves jangling through my body, I walk up to the doormen with Eric. With clammy fingers, I take off my hat to reveal my face, and the guards straighten up immediately. "Chua xiao jie!" one of them exclaims. *Ms. Chua*. It worked. He thinks I'm Alyssa.

I'm about to launch into a convoluted tale about sneaking out the back and then changing clothes because, obviously, I'm wearing different clothes than what the real Alyssa would be wearing, when Eric nudges me none too subtly. Right. We agreed that I shouldn't say too much. Alyssa Chua doesn't need to explain. She just goes where she wants.

The inside is echoing marble floors and a large foyer with a bank of elevators. The interior of the elevator is mirrored, so I take my hat off and try to deal with the hat-head situation by combing my hair with my fingers before deciding it's useless and jamming the hat back on. Anyway, now that I got us into the club, I don't need to pretend to be Alyssa anymore.

"You look fine," Eric says.

I glower at him. "I definitely do *not* look fine for an exclusive nightclub!"

Unabashed, he grins and pushes the button for the top floor. "I owe you."

"No, you don't," I say. "I'm here for my own reasons, remember?" The only way to get to the bottom of the mystery of why my mom left Beijing is to start demanding answers from the people who might have them. Starting with Alyssa Chua.

As soon as the elevator door opens, I'm hit by a disorienting wave of noise and flashing disco lights. The music is low, so the bulk of the noise comes from the constant clink of ice cubes in cocktail glasses and laughter from the crowd of insanely beautiful people. I mean, they don't even look real. My stomach twinges with nerves as they give Eric and me only a cursory glance before turning back to their conversations and drinks. Every single person here is wearing haute couture, and I realize it wouldn't have mattered even if I'd packed something to wear to a club. Nothing I own remotely resembles anything this crowd is wearing.

My fingers dig into the cheap fibers of my sun hat. "You're sure Alyssa is here?" I ask Eric as I take off my hat.

"Yes." He points to a bank of windows where the crowd is the thickest. "There she is. Alyssa owns this club."

What? Alyssa is only nineteen and she owns her own club? My eyes adjust to the play of lights and shadows, and I see Alyssa. She's up on a platform, sitting on an ornate chair, and surrounded by admirers. As I watch, she laughingly throws her arms around two young men glowering at each other. I'm too far away to hear what she says to them or to see her clearly, but even from this distance, one thing is more certain than ever: Alyssa and I couldn't be less alike. I'm in an off-the-rack floral-print sundress, and she's wearing an impossibly chic white dress with clean, elegant lines and a gem-studded choker. I'm keeping Eric at a wary distance, and she's flirting with two guys at once. Yes, there might be some similarities in our features, but I'm willing to bet that's all we have in common. See-ing Alyssa holding court only makes me aware of how much I don't belong in her world.

"Are you going to talk to her now?" Eric asks me, but we're inter-rupted before I can answer.

"Eric!" A cute girl with a pixie haircut is storming over to us, anger sparking in her eyes. "What are you doing here? How did you even get in?"

"Hi, Mimi," Eric says with a sheepish smile. "I came to apologize actually."

But Mimi isn't looking at him anymore. She's looking at me with eyes wide in shock.

"Ah. Gemma, this is my little sister, Mimi," Eric says. "Mimi, this is Gemma."

Dazed, Mimi says, "She looks like—"

"Alyssa," he finishes with a slight grimace. "That's because Gemma is Alyssa's cousin."

"It's nice to meet you, Mimi," I say, wishing she'd do something other than stare at me in that glassy-eyed way.

Mimi glances over to where Alyssa is holding court, as if to con-firm that Alyssa's there and I'm here.

My eyes also flicker over to Alyssa, and as if pulled by the weight of my gaze, she looks in my direction. Immediately, Alyssa's ruby-red lips pucker into a pout. Then she turns her back to me in a clear snub, throwing back her head and letting out a peal of laughter in response to something one of her admirers whispers into her ear. *So much for cousinly affection.* The tone of her last pink note should have clued me in to the kind of welcome I'd get, but disappointment still pricks at my heart.

I look away, only to encounter Mimi's sour scrutiny. "You're Chi-nese?" she asks.

Why is she staring at me like I'm an American bumpkin who's just crashed her exclusive little party in my rustic clothes? "Yes. I'm Chinese." Self-consciously, I discard my hat on the nearest table.

"Wai guo ren," Mimi says in an aside to Eric.

"Mimi!" Eric's eyes narrow in warning. "That's enough."

My cheeks flush. I want to like Eric's sister, but hearing her call me a "foreigner" doesn't exactly endear her to me. "Wo shi zong guo ren." I try not to sound defensive as I tell Mimi that I'm Chinese, but from the worried look Eric shoots me, I'm not sure I succeed.

"Chinese *American*," she retorts.

"But still Chinese," Eric says firmly, and my heart lifts.

Mimi ignores him. "Does Nai Nai know about her? She gave me enough grief about hanging out with Alyssa, thanks to you and your big mouth! I can only imagine what she said about you two! You've got some nerve warning me about Alyssa when you're with *her*!"

"Nothing is going on between us!" Eric flushes. "There's nothing to tell Nai Nai or anyone else. Gemma came here to see Alyssa, and I came here to see you."

"That's right," I confirm.

Mimi rakes me with a scornful glare and then flounces away.

As soon as she leaves, Eric heaves out a sigh. "Wow. Sorry about that. I've never seen Mimi so . . ."

"Snobby?" I say before I think. Oops. Maybe that was a little tactless.

He winces, but doesn't contradict me. "It's not like her," he says helplessly. "I don't know what to do. Coming here has just made things worse." He attempts a wry smile. "Still want to talk to Alyssa?"

"Speaking of making things worse . . ." My eyes drift to where Alyssa is planting a kiss on the cheek of one of the guys vying for her attention. Mimi, who's close to Alyssa now, bends down to her ear and whispers something. Alyssa isn't looking at me, but there's a frown on her face that leaves no doubt that I'm the topic of their conversation. "Yeah, I still want to talk to her." And this time, I'm not leaving until I get answers about my mom.

"Do you want me to come with you?"

I eye Mimi, her face screwed tight with anger. "It's probably not a good idea."

I make my way across the room, feeling Alyssa's eyes on me the whole time. At last, I reach the foot of Alyssa's platform. The crowd surrounding her falls silent as they catch sight of me. Alyssa herself rises from her throne-like chair, her lips pressed together in a harsh line. Heart beating fast, I climb the steps up to her.

Then we're face-to-face.

"Come with me," Alyssa says tightly, leaving Mimi and her other admirers staring after us as she leads me to a black door behind her chair. It seems Alyssa doesn't want an audience for this little chat. Which suits me just fine.

She flings open the door and practically slams it shut after we step inside. The room is hung with bright orange silk tapestry, and round, embroidered pillows are strewn all over the floor around low, black lacquered tables. It's a place designed for lounging, but Alyssa doesn't sit down. Instead, she whirls to face me. "What do you think you're doing?" she demands. "I warned you not to trust Eric Liu!"

"Why?" I ask, watching her face closely. "Because our grandfather betrayed his grandfather during the Cultural Revolution? Or because our grandfather's betrayal led the Red Guard to find a Tang dynasty painting from Wu Zetian's collection? Or is it that the painting almost cost Eric's grandfather his life?"

Her face drains of color.

She knows about the painting. The painting my mother supposedly stole. My pulse runs a jagged course from my heart to my throat.

"You know more about why my mother was cut off from the family than you'll admit."

Face still pale, Alyssa says, "And you don't know what you're talking about."

"Did my mother steal that painting?" All the air seems to rush away from my lungs as I wait for her answer.

She flings a word at me like a throwing knife to my chest. "Yes."

And just like that, all I thought I knew is gone. "Is that why she was banished? Why? What could that painting possibly mean to you all?"

The color rushes back into her face all at once. "You know *nothing*! You don't even know what it means that your mother stole that painting, do you?"

"Then tell me!" I clench my hands, my mind writhing in denial. *Why would my mother steal that painting?* "Tell me what it means that my mother took that painting, because I sure as hell don't know!"

"Think! Your mother stole a painting that destroyed her father's rival! A painting too dangerous to have in your possession. Don't you understand what she did? The danger she put our family in?"

"D-dangerous?" I stammer. "But I thought it was only dangerous to have classical art during the Cultural Revolution."

"Typical American," she says scathingly. "You have so *little* understanding of history." She raises her eyes skyward in exasperation. "That painting isn't just classical art. It's a priceless original from the Tang dynasty. A painting said to have been commissioned by Empress Wu, the woman who dared to be a ruler! You have no idea how dangerous owning that painting would be. That kind of wealth and cultural history would be sure to draw the attention of the government."

I struggle to understand, feeling like I'm groping for pieces of a puzzle in the dark. "But *you're* rich, and you don't seem to be in danger."

Alyssa purses her lips. "Again, your ignorance is unbelievable!"

"Why don't you enlighten me, then," I say sarcastically.

"My grandfather made his money in the eighties under the market reform policies of the Communist Party! It's one thing to make money in that kind of economy, but if anyone thought that—" She stops abruptly. *She was about to tell me something more.* She starts again, speaking more slowly and carefully. "Inherited wealth through many generations of rich landowners is different. It's considered elitist. Money made on the backs of the people. That kind of wealth is frowned upon."

"Especially for a high-ranking Communist Party official like your grandfather, I imagine." My voice is dry.

"Like I said, my grandfather made his money under party-approved economic policies, so we had nothing to worry about." Her face closes tight. "Not until your mother decided to steal that painting out of greed and selfishness. My grandfather had no choice but to banish your mother. What she did threatened us all." A strange emotion flickers in her eyes. "Just like Gong Gong had no choice but to report Mimi's grandfather. Gong Gong did what he did to protect our family."

That doesn't make sense at all. How would reporting Eric and Mimi's grandfather to the Red Guard as a counterrevolutionary protect our family? And why am I just standing here, accepting whatever she says without protest? Why should I believe these horrible things about my mother just because Alyssa says that they're true? "I don't believe you," I say clearly. "My mother would never put her family in danger. And nothing excuses what our grandfather did to Eric and Mimi's grandfather."

"You don't understand." Alyssa's voice is as hard as the diamonds in her choker.

"You're the one who doesn't understand," I shoot back. "You're so ready to believe whatever your grandfather tells you that you can't see that it doesn't add up. Why keep my grandmother in the dark about me? Why inform on a friend, starting a generational war with Eric and Mimi's family? Why kick my mom out of the family if she took that painting—no one even pressed charges, so how would anyone know she had it?"

Alyssa's body tenses, and I think she's going to scream at me. Instead, she walks to the black door and opens it. Music, laughter, and talk rushes in, jarring me to the bone.

A few of her friends, including Mimi, float to her side, and Alyssa smiles widely, as if our intense exchange never happened. "Stay and drink if you want, Gemma," she says airily. "The band is coming on soon."

I'm tempted to throw a fit in front of all these beautiful people. *I bet they would just love that.* I can just imagine the headlines on the gossip sites—*Heiress Throwdown with Long-Lost Twin.* Tossing my hair over my shoulder, I stalk to the door, head held high. But before I sweep past Alyssa, I murmur, "Maybe you don't know the whole truth either. If I were you, I'd ask your grandfather."

Alyssa rears back as if I'd slapped her, and Mimi, standing next to her, gives me a troubled look.

I begin to push through the crowd, but it eventually parts; the people let me pass even as they look after me curiously. I don't blame them. My skin is burning, and my scalp prickles with sweat. *What the hell just happened?* Heart thumping erratically, I rush down the stairs.

At the bottom, someone puts a hand on my shoulder to steady me. "Gemma, what's wrong?" It's Eric.

"We should go."

"OK." He starts to lead me toward the elevator and then stops midway across the room. "Do you want to tell me what Alyssa said about your mother?"

"Nothing that different from what you told me." It's true. Eric told me my mother had stolen Wu Zetian's painting, and Alyssa told me the same thing. But the part about my mother selfishly putting her family in danger? I just can't believe it. And there's something else. Or someone else. The person responsible for what happened to Eric's grandfather and my mother. *My grandfather.* I shudder.

Eric's forehead wrinkles in worry. "You're all pale and shaky. At least eat something before we go." He snags a plate of green onion pancakes from a server passing by. "I think these are on your food wish list."

I manage a wobbly smile. "I'm not hungry." But I take one of the pancakes anyway and dip it into a small dish of spicy soy sauce. As I bite into the pancake, the crunchy outer layer gives way to the soft underlayers of dough studded with green onions, and an amazing burst of salt and spice fills my mouth. "Oh wow. Is this what they serve at all the rich, exclusive parties?" *When was the last time I ate? Have I actually eaten anything but post-breakup ice cream today?*

Eric laughs. "Feeling better?"

"I am actually." It's true. I don't know if it's because of the best cong you bing I've ever eaten or Eric's kindness, but the shakiness after my encounter with Alyssa is fading.

In reply, he hands me the whole plate.

"Are you sure?" I ask. "Because I don't think I can do the whole polite Chinese thing where we go round and round, insisting that the other person takes the food. That can last *forever*, and these cong you bing are just too good to resist!"

"No, please!" he insists. "I eat these a lot of the time, so they're all yours."

I eye him suspiciously. "See, that's what you're *supposed* to say. And I'm supposed to say something about not being hungry. Even if I am."

"You're right—this can take forever. How about this? You go ahead and eat it all," Eric says with a glint in his eye, "and I'll stand here, silently judging you."

A grin tugs at my mouth. Eric's dry sense of humor is my favorite kind of pick-me-up. "Well," I say, pretending to think it over, "I suppose the only thing more Chinese than outpoliting someone else is . . ."

In unison, we say, "Silent judgment!"

Despite Eric's protests, I share the pancakes with him, and while we're polishing off the plate, he leads me farther into the room until we're standing close to a small stage. Unlike Alyssa's raised platform in the opposite corner, this one is empty of everything but sound equipment.

I turn to Eric. "Shouldn't we get out of here before we're kicked out?"

"Not just yet. There's something you should see. I think it will cheer you up."

I glance toward Alyssa, who's sitting again on her own stage, as if she were a queen commanding a special performance. Except that Alyssa's unwavering gaze isn't on the performance that's about to start. Her attention is directed at *me*, and it makes me feel like I have a target painted on my back. "I don't have a burning need to see a band."

"I think you're going to want to see *this* band." Eric's eyes are lit up with secrets. The fun kind, not the criminal-in-the-family kind of secret.

Then the lights suddenly dim and the music in the background cuts off. Eric opens up a hand toward the stage. "I present to you Gen XX!"

"Gen . . . what?"

Four young Asian guys saunter onto the stage, and all around me, guests are bursting into cheers and rushing the stage, which pushes Eric and me closer to the front.

What did I say to Eric to make him think I'm a Chinese boy band groupie? "So, Gen XX is a boy band?" Gritting my teeth, I refuse to budge as a mass of girls press against me, screaming their undying love for various members of Gen XX. The girls simply eddy around me—an unstoppable, shrieking wave of haute couture and high heels. At least they're not after me this time.

Eric anchors me to him with a light hand at my elbow, and all my senses zoom to that tiny square of skin where he's touching me, making my nerve endings go completely haywire. The crowd, the noise—everything fades away.

"Look again," he says.

Oh, I'm looking all right. It takes me a moment to understand that he's talking about the band. My face heats up, and I turn quickly to the stage to hide my confusion. The four band members are blowing kisses and thanking their hysterical fans. They all have slim, graceful builds, cool haircuts, and the poreless faces of angels. In other words, they look like a boy band.

The only thing that distinguishes them from other Asian boy bands is that they're all wearing suits, but not matching ones. One has a pin-striped suit with a red bow tie. Two of them wear their suits more casually, with their jackets rolled to the elbow and open over T-shirts. The last one is wearing an all-black suit, the top buttoned up over a black silk shirt and black tie. "Um, beautiful suits?"

Gen XX starts singing and dancing, and the crowd goes wild. Their voices are as angelic as their faces, and their dance moves are spectacular, but boy bands have never been my thing.

Eric leans in to make himself heard. "Mimi will be glad to hear that. She's the one who designed that particular line of clothing for the family business." It's impossible to miss the note of pride in his voice.

I bring my mouth to his ear and yell, "Your sister is very talented." And the thought of unfriendly Mimi takes the edge off the odd feeling threatening to burst through my skin at Eric's nearness.

"Thanks, but I didn't want to stay for the band to show off the clothes Mimi designed!" The crowd cheers as the lead singer does a split in midair, and it's a moment before the cheering fades enough for Eric to continue. "When you told me what your director said about China and our so-called traditional views, I wanted to show you a different China. Show you that China *isn't* just a repressive country with rigid views on gender and sexuality."

Gen XX executes a series of moves that involves weaving in and out in a synchronized pattern, all while singing about unrequited love—I don't really know what they're singing since my Chinese isn't good enough to make out the lyrics. But from the soulful way they're gazing out at the audience and the panting, shrieking response of that audience—I'd say my guess is a pretty good one.

The song ends, and I have to wait until the applause dies down before I can resume my conversation with Eric. "And this boy band proves my director wrong?" I gaze at Gen XX doubtfully. I guess there's a sexiness the band has without being hypermasculine. "That's cool." But I'm still confused. Gen XX doesn't seem different from any other Asian boy band I could've watched on YouTube, so I don't get why Eric felt it was important that I see them live.

Eric grins. "And even cooler that the band members are all girls."

"What? You're kidding!" My attention snaps back to the stage, where Gen XX is launching into another pop song with high-octane dancing. As a boy band, they do nothing for me, but a band of girls? That's hot.

Apparently, I'm not the only one who feels that way. Girls all around me are screaming and shoving past me to get closer to the front. As much as I'm loving Gen XX, I am *not* into the ear-piercing enthusiasm of the audience. If only Jake could see and hear this.

Eric bends his head to mine. "Had enough?"

"Yes," I say gratefully. "Gen XX is awesome, but . . ."

"Say no more," he replies promptly. "Let's get out of here."

Smoothly, Eric extricates us from the crowd, and I'm reminded of when we first met, at the Forbidden City. We were escaping a crowd that day too. But unlike then, no one—except Alyssa—is watching us leave this time. I grab my hat from the table near the elevator where I'd left it on our way into the club.

Even as we step into the elevator, I can still feel Alyssa's eyes on me, and I turn back for one last glimpse. Alyssa's face is unreadable as she stares back at me. Then Mimi, sitting next to Alyssa, says something in her ear. Alyssa's reaction is . . . surprising. The impassive expression on her face melts into something that looks a lot like fear.

CHAPTER TWENTY-ONE

The elevator door slides shut, and I breathe a sigh of relief to have escaped.

"How are you doing?" Eric asks.

"I'm fine." I'm not about to tell him that something his sister had said to Alyssa seemed to have struck fear in Alyssa's heart. Shaking off the unsettling image, I ask, "How was Alyssa able to get Gen XX to play at her private club?"

"Money. How else?" Eric says sardonically. "Alyssa, or her family, has more money than they know how to spend. The huge amount of money it must've taken to get a wildly popular band like Gen XX is nothing to Alyssa."

"Do their fans know that Gen XX is made up of all girls?" It's hard to reconcile everything I've heard about a conservative China with the popularity of a gender-nonconforming band of girls.

"Of course," Eric replies. "Girls talk openly about their crushes on the group members. Gen XX is as popular and gets as much fan mail as any other boy band." As I take that in, he adds, "You have to understand that there's the Chinese government's stance and policy, and then there are the actual Chinese people's views and practices—it would be a mistake to think the two are the same."

The elevator slides noiselessly down the many floors, and I look out the glass walls of the elevator at the space-age Beijing skyline, all spires and lights. "My parents are from China, but I don't know a thing about this country. Not what you call 'actual Chinese people's views and practices.' What your sister said about me—it's what

I feel I am sometimes. Wai guo ren. Foreigner. Because I'm not just Chinese. I'm Chinese *American*." I laugh hollowly. "I sometimes feel like a foreigner in the U.S. too. But there I'm *Chinese* American." No matter where I am, one part of who I am marks me as different.

"Hey, don't listen to my sister," Eric says, taking one of my hands in his own. "You're not a foreigner. It doesn't matter that you haven't been to China before now. Or that you were born in America. None of that matters. You are Zhong Guo Ren. Chinese."

Something squeezes at my heart. When I first came to Beijing, I wasn't thinking about what I wanted or what I was looking for, other than my success as an actress. But now I know. I want to belong. And Eric is speaking as if that's already true—that I already belong. "But if your grandmother and Alyssa are right, then my mother gave up her family and homeland because she's a criminal." The elevator stops smoothly on the ground floor, and we step out into the marble hallway.

I shoot Eric a covert glance, but he doesn't reply until we're back out into the still-warm night full of people. "After the Summer Palace," he says at last, "I called my father and asked about the painting. I asked if your mother had stolen it like my nai nai said."

"What did he say?" My hands grow damp with anxiety.

"He said to forget the painting. That it's better for everyone that it's gone."

"What? You said that painting was priceless! That it may have come from Empress Wu's own art collection."

"Yes," he agrees, "but my father didn't seem to blame your mother for stealing it. He wouldn't even say that she *had*. In any case, as you pointed out, my family never pressed charges." He stops a little distance from the guards flanking the doors to the club. "Listen, neither of us knows the whole story of that painting or what happened to make your mother leave. Until we do . . . or *even* if we do . . . can we call a truce? Be friends?"

Eric's father believes it's better that the painting is gone. Except that it isn't gone, and I know exactly where it is. On a wall in my mother's office. *The lady with the red dress and calligraphy brush.* But Eric is right that we don't know the whole story.

"OK, let's call a truce," I say. "And as a friend, can I give you some advice?"

He looks at me warily. "Sure."

"If you can give my mother the benefit of the doubt, then maybe you can do the same for Alyssa."

His eyes widen in startlement. "Why would I do that? Why would you even *want* me to give her the benefit of the doubt?" he asks. "After ten minutes with Alyssa, you came out of that room looking like you'd seen a ghost!"

It's a good question, and I don't have an answer ready. I think of Alyssa's unexpected acts of kindness and the shocked look on her face when I suggested that she didn't know the whole truth. Maybe there's more to Alyssa than meets the eye. Plus, I've never had a sibling, but it seems silly for Eric and Mimi to be fighting over who Mimi gets to be friends with. "Your sister did have a point—you and I are friends. Why can't Mimi and Alyssa be friends too?"

"That's not the same!" Eric argues. "You and Alyssa are nothing alike. I just don't understand why Mimi would want to be friends with someone as superficial as Alyssa, and I don't like the way she acts around Alyssa. Mimi is smart, talented, and kind. But ever since she became friends with Alyssa, Mimi's been . . . different. Guarded and even rude."

Yeah, I got a dose of that head-on. But no matter how rude Mimi was to me, she's still important to Eric. "Look, maybe it would help if you gave Mimi some space. Show her that you're not trying to control her life or her choice in friends."

He nods reluctantly. "You're probably right. Mimi has a good head on her shoulders. I should trust her to take care of herself."

My stomach chooses this moment to let out a loud rumble. Mortified, I clap my hand to my stomach. "Sorry! I didn't have dinner."

"No, I'm the one who's sorry!" Eric says. "One small shared plate of green onion pancakes is definitely not enough food." He glances around at the jumbotrons and big-name stores surrounding us. "Let's go somewhere else."

Eric hails a taxi and takes me to Wangfujing Street, promising that I'll be able to knock off everything I have left on my food wish list and then some.

We end up at the Wangfujing night market, which is lined with red lanterns and crowded with people. Our first stop is a food stall wafting out clouds of fragrant steam from big bamboo steamers.

"This place makes the best hum bao," Eric boasts.

Hungrily, I eye the pillowy white hum bao being lifted out of the steamers. "Let me pay," I insist, reaching into my purse.

Eric, no stranger to the rules of this game, throws himself bodily in my way. "No way!"

I try to duck under his arm, but he's too quick and hands the amused vendor some bills before I even get my wallet out.

Round one of "let me pay" goes to Eric.

I win round two when I run to a stall selling turnip cakes while Eric is still getting the hum bao from the first food stall. Round three, four, and five are a jumble of laughter and good-natured pushing and blocking. At last, we have to call a truce so we can actually eat the food we've competed to buy.

We set our well-earned gains down at a table outside a noodle shop with red lanterns casting their glow over us. Sneakily, Eric buys us a plate of hand-shaven noodles to share.

"Not cool, Eric," I say. "I'm going to have to make up for that, you know."

Eric laughs and tells me a story about being out with his cousin and winning the fight to buy lunch. "The next day, my cousin had a meal delivered to my office from the same restaurant where we had lunch the day before!"

I shake my head in disbelief. "I don't have a story to beat that." In fact, I don't have any stories at all. I've seen my parents do the "let me pay" fight with Chinese friends and acquaintances, but this interaction with Eric is the first time I've done it myself. In fact, I've always been embarrassed when my parents did it, especially in a public place with all those judgmental eyes on us. I knew what everyone was thinking—*crazy Asians.*

This time, I'm not worried about what people will think. Part of the reason is that we're in China, where everyone is supposed to act this way. But part of it is Eric. He's just so at ease with being himself, and doesn't care what anyone else thinks. And that makes it easy to be myself with him.

Eric already knows about my dreams as an actress, but I tell him more. "Eilene Deng is my hero. She's changing the face of Hollywood and fighting for fuller representations of Asians. That's what I want to do too."

"That's awesome!" His face lights up with admiration, but then a shadow crosses over it. "I wish I had your passion."

"What do you mean? You're passionate about sustainable fashion! How cool is that?"

He smiles. "I *am* fighting to make the fashion industry more sustainable, and I'm lucky to have my parents' support. I'm also proud that our business has environmentally sound practices and pays equitable wages, but . . ."

"What?" I lean forward. "Still thinking about that graduate sustainability program at UCLA?"

"Yeah," he says wistfully. "There's still so much for me to learn. And so much more to do, especially in my family's international branches." He gets so animated that he doesn't notice the sprinkle of crumbs on his lips from a bite of you tiao, which is basically a long tail of fried dough.

The desire to brush the crumbs away is so strong that I bite my own lip to stop from reaching over the table.

When we've cleaned our plates and can't eat another bite, Eric suggests that we go shopping. I'm glad he made the suggestion because I can't bear for the night to end yet.

We stroll along stalls selling everything from touristy souvenirs to knockoff purses. A pang hits me when we pass a stall selling foo dogs. It reminds me of my conversation with Ken about a foo dog souvenir. This is the first time all night I've thought about yesterday's breakup with Ken.

"What's wrong?" Eric asks.

"Nothing," I say quickly. "It's just a bit crowded here, and I don't want to be mistaken for Alyssa. Is there somewhere we can go with fewer people?" It's not completely a lie. I really don't want to be mobbed by Alyssa's fans again. I also don't want to be reminded of my ex-boyfriend when I'm with Eric.

"I know just the place." Eric takes my arm to steer me around a large clump of people, but he doesn't let go of it, even as we leave the night market and make our way to a quieter part of the pedestrian street lined with shops.

Eric stops in front of a small boutique with floor-to-ceiling display windows and a sign with large red Chinese characters.

"What are we doing here?" I ask. "It looks closed."

"It is," Eric replies, "but this is one of my family's stores, so we can go in." He punches in a code on the number pad and opens the door for me.

I raise an eyebrow, but the temptation to see one of Eric's stores is too great to resist, so I step inside.

Eric flips the lights on, and I see sparse racks and an expanse of pale hardwood floor. It looks like the kind of upscale place that sells "pieces" rather than clothes. I'm already backing away from the racks when something catches my eye. A mannequin is wearing a near replica of the black suit with satin lapels that one of the band members of Gen XX was wearing.

"That's Mimi's line of 'menswear' for women." Eric walks over to a rack and pulls off the black satin suit. "This one should be close to your size. You can try it on if you want."

I do want to. So much that my hand trembles as I reach out to take it. "I've never worn anything so beautiful in my life."

He grins and nabs a black silk button-down shirt and silk tie as well. "Black on black is very in right now, so you might as well go all out."

Arms full of silk and satin, I head to the dressing room Eric points out to me.

He settles himself on a bench near the three-way mirror and says, "Go ahead. I want to see you in that suit."

The shirt goes on like a silk whisper. The jacket lays smoothly over my shoulders and chest without a single bulge or wrinkle. It's clearly cut for a woman's body. The pants fit like a glove without being too tight or restrictive and are made of soft cotton without exposed seams or itchiness. I have no idea how to knot a tie but do my best. There isn't a mirror in the dressing room, so I don't know how I look, but I *feel* great.

But that's nothing compared to how I feel when I walk out of the dressing room and see Eric's eyes darken and a muscle in his jaw jump.

He swallows hard. "Wow," he says reverently. "Gemma, you look . . . amazing."

I blush and tug on the silk tie. "I didn't do the tie right."

Eric stands up. "Let me help with that."

He's standing just inches away from me, and I can see the convulsive movement of his Adam's apple. My breath goes short, and my body fires up like an avalanche of lava is pouring through my veins. Here we are, both in impeccably tailored suits, and he's reaching out to loosen my tie. Eric's fingers are shaking as he pulls the black silk away from my skin. My chest heaves as I release a quivering breath, and his hands freeze in midair. Neither of us meets each other's eyes as he starts folding and pulling the ends of the tie through complicated loops. The back of his knuckles brush the skin of my neck, sending shock waves through my nervous system.

I can't stand this anymore.

And just as I'm about to break us apart to escape the heat between us, Eric steps away. "You look good." His tone is casual, and I might think he was unaffected—if it wasn't for the glazed, heavy-lidded look in his eyes.

No one's ever looked at me like that before. And it's not just lust. Eric's looking at me like he knows me down to my deepest truths . . . and wants to know even more.

"Come here, Gemma," he says hoarsely.

Slowly, I walk toward Eric, my heart stuttering wildly in anticipation. But when I reach him, he doesn't pull me into his arms as I half dread/half hope he'll do. Instead, he spins me to face the three-way mirror. "Take a look."

My jaw drops, and my reflection in the mirror also looks stunned.

And, if I do say so myself—*hot*. The suit fits like it was made for me. The clean, crisp lines skim the shape of my body, and instead of hiding my curves under bulky material, the suit hints at curves but never quite reveals them. The layers of differently textured black material create a mysterious suave cool that I would have never associated with myself. "Oh wow," I breathe reverently. "The suit *does* make me look good."

"*You* make the suit look good," he says. "I won't even have to do many alterations to make it fit perfectly. Just take the pant legs in an inch, I think."

I'm so lost in the vision of Eric kneeling at my feet to pin up the pant legs that it takes a moment for his meaning to sink in. "Alterations?" Does he think I'm going to buy the suit? I break out in a cold sweat and then worry about staining this beautiful suit that costs more than my entire existing wardrobe. "Eric, I can't afford this suit!"

"Of course you can't," he says calmly. "That's why I'm going to comp you the suit."

"Listen, this isn't the same as buying me some noodles. This suit probably costs a fortune!" My hands fiddle with the buttons on the jacket. "I can't possibly accept."

Eric places his hands over mine to stop me from unbuttoning the jacket. "We do this all the time! Do you think Gen XX paid for their suits? Our company gets the exposure of a famous person wearing our clothes, and you get a free suit. It's a win-win."

I set my jaw. "I'm not famous."

"Gemma, you've got to stop underestimating yourself. You're an up-and-coming actress at the start of a promising career!"

I take one last longing look in the mirror before turning resolutely to Eric. "Thank you, but I still can't accept it."

He smiles wryly. "I'm not going to press anything on you that you don't want, but can I ask a question?"

Warily, I nod. I *do* want the suit. Badly. But not the strings that come with it.

"Are you rejecting the suit because you don't think you'll make it as an actress? Or because you can't take a suit from me since you have a boyfriend back home?"

"That's two questions," I say, not meeting his eyes.

"And that's still not an answer."

I take a deep breath. "I broke up with my boyfriend yesterday."

Eric looks like he's stopped breathing, his face is so still and watchful. "You broke up with your boyfriend?" His eyes bore into mine. "Why?"

Because I could never be myself with Ken and it never felt quite right—not the way it feels with . . . But I don't need to finish that thought or say any of that out loud. "He . . . I don't know. It just wasn't working." The silence that follows my statement makes my stomach tense up. "But I still can't accept the suit."

A muscle twitches in Eric's face. "Fair enough," he says at last. He takes a breath. "But if you're refusing the suit because you don't think you'll make it as an actress or because you don't think you deserve it . . . Well, that's bullshit."

"You met me two weeks ago, and you think you know me? Well, you don't!" But what scares me is that he does know me. All the way down to the tender insecurities I'm hiding.

Eric holds up his hands. "I just want you to know that I believe in you—in your strength and talent and willingness to fight for what you believe in." He gestures toward the suit. "It just kills me that you think you don't deserve something that's not half as beautiful as you are and not worth even a fraction of everything that's wonderful about you."

My anger drains away. "Eric, you're the one who's wonderful." I swallow past a lump in my throat and smooth down the lapels of the suit, finding comfort in the cool satin. "But I still can't accept it." I don't need any more expectations that I can't live up to.

His mouth quirks up. "It's the feud between our families, right?" It's an attempt at humor, but it falls a little flat.

My mother may have stolen valuable ancient art from his family. My grandfather betrayed his grandfather during the Cultural Revolution. And if I keep digging, I might find out even *more*.

"Our families," I say with a smile, but my tongue is heavy with the weight of those two words.

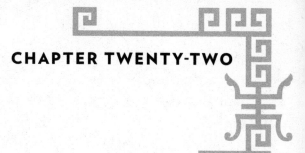

CHAPTER TWENTY-TWO

After my epic confrontation with Alyssa at her night-club, I kept expecting to hear from her. But there's been nothing—not even a pink note. Eilene asked about my weekend the following Monday, but what could I tell her? *Broke up with my boyfriend, found out my grandfather is a shady character who did some really horrible things during the Cultural Revolution, and also that my mom might be a thief.* Instead, I told Eilene that I visited the Summer Palace.

Now it's been two weeks. Still no word from Alyssa. Eric and I have been texting each other regularly since the night he tried to give me the suit, but neither of us has been brave enough to suggest hanging out in person.

"Gemma, you're up!" Jake shouts. Startled, I jump to my feet, almost knocking over my folding chair.

Sarah, another actress waiting for her turn to be in a scene, gives me a sympathetic smile. "Don't let it bother you. Jake's just edgy because of today's shoot."

"Yeah, I can understand." I hurry over to Jake, Eilene, Adrian, and a handful of extras standing in front of a stone bridge over a lake.

Before today, we had been shooting on set or out in a suburb of Beijing, but today's scene takes place in Beihai Park, where Sonia and Ryan meet up and spend a romantic day among the pagodas, lake pavilions, and gardens. It's a gorgeous location. It's also, according to Jake, "a logistical nightmare." The studio was only able to get permits to shoot for one day in Beihai Park, which means we're under intense pressure to get this scene in the can. To make matters worse, the park is such an open space that we don't have nearly enough security to keep curious gawkers from practically wandering directly onto the set.

All this means that Jake is a powder keg of frustrated nerves.

The only one who hasn't lost her cool is Eilene. "Gemma, why don't you and Aidan—"

A high-pitched squeal interrupts her.

Oh shit. Slow dread fills me as I turn around, and sure enough, there they are. *Fans.* Dozens of them, faces bright with Alyssa-worship. They're pressing against the flimsy sawhorse barricades, and the five security guards with outstretched arms and panicked looks on their faces don't seem to be enough to contain the crowd.

"What the hell is going on here?" Jake demands, his face red in outrage. For once, I don't feel like he's overreacting.

"Alyssa!" a teenager screams, and the others take up the by-now-familiar chant of Alyssa's name. My whole body freezes.

Eilene turns to me. "I guess it was only a matter of time," she says wryly.

"This is insane!" Jake throws his hands up in the air. "How are we supposed to shoot a film with a crazed mob who thinks you're Alyssa Chua hanging around?"

Yeah, right. Like Jake wasn't the one who had to be convinced by my resemblance to Alyssa to hire me in the first place.

"Gemma, do we need to get you away?" Eilene's face is puckered with worry.

"No!" Jake shouts. "We can't do this scene without Gemma!"

Aidan looks over at the crowd, which seems to be multiplying by the second. "I don't think getting Gemma away is an option anymore."

The overpowering scent of flowers and underlying acrid smog presses on me, thick and cloying, making me feel light-headed. *Maybe I can distract the crowd by pushing Jake into the lake as I flee.*

Sudden authoritative shouts in Chinese interrupt this tempting vision and cut through the fans screaming Alyssa's name. My mouth drops as a dozen men in tan uniforms march up to the set and efficiently clear the crowd away. Alyssa's fans grumble a bit, but they're not going to argue with a bunch of hard-faced, official-looking security guards.

"That's more like it," Jake says in satisfaction. "It looks like the studio has sent more security."

Eilene doesn't look so certain. "They don't look like the security guards our studio would hire."

I'd trust Eilene's assessment over Jake's any day. Besides, my gut tells me that she's right. Something is off. For one thing, none of the new security guards even speak to Jake, Eilene, or any of the crew. They just form a loose perimeter around our set and turn their backs to us. It makes no sense.

Unfortunately, there's no chance to get to the bottom of the mystery. Jake is too determined to finish the shoot to look a gift horse in the mouth. I can understand. Why would he waste time questioning the appearance of extremely efficient security?

By the time Jake finally calls it a wrap, I'm exhausted. "Was it really necessary to film a daytime *and* nighttime scene?" I grumble to Aidan, who grins in return.

The security guards escort us all to our cars. But then I see a new car parked with ours. A sleek black limousine. A driver gets out and opens the back door.

My eyes widen when I see that it's Alyssa in the back seat. "Need a ride?" she calls out.

Well, that solves the mystery of who sent the security guards. The only question is why Alyssa keeps playing fairy godmother.

It doesn't occur to me to refuse. I'm way too curious about what Alyssa wants from me.

Ignoring everyone's questions—including Jake's excited one of whether I know Alyssa—I slide into the back seat, and she quickly makes room for me.

"Thanks for sending the guards." I sink into the buttery soft leather of the seat. "And the hotel upgrade." Have I really never thanked her for the hotel room? "So, what are you doing here? Thought of a few insults that you couldn't fit on a pink note?"

She bites her lip. "I keep screwing up. I'm sorry."

Just like that, my irritation disappears. I don't actually *want* to be fighting with my own cousin. And I'm relieved that she doesn't want to either. "It's OK, but just to clarify, what are you sorry for this time?"

Alyssa laughs. "For starters, how about calling you an ignorant American?"

I can't help but smile. "That's a good starting point." Then my smile fades as I think about everything she's told me. "But you weren't totally wrong. There's a lot I don't know about Chinese history."

She opens a compartment in front of her, takes out two tumblers, puts ice cubes in each one, and then pours a rich amber liquid into them out of a cut-crystal decanter. "To be fair, with censorship in China, there's a lot of history that the people *here* don't know either."

"Like the Tiananmen Square massacre," I say, accepting a tumbler from her. Tentatively, I take a sip, thinking it will be scotch or brandy, but it's just iced tea with hints of fruit and flowers. Actually, this is delicious. Not surprising, since it came from Alyssa.

I half-expect that she won't know about Tiananmen Square, but Alyssa says, "Yes, like that. I only found out about the massacre a few years ago when I went abroad for a fashion show. It shocked me." She takes a sip of her own tea and stares down into the tumbler. "In fact, I asked my grandfather about it."

My heart skips a beat. "What did he say?"

Her mouth twists. "He said that it was a lie. Western propaganda. According to him, a few rioters were arrested in Tiananmen Square, and that was it."

I stare at her in shock. "*Hundreds* died. And *thousands* were arrested."

"Yes, I know." Alyssa looks up at me, her gaze steady. "It's things like my grandfather's lie about Tiananmen Square that makes me wonder if you were right. Maybe I don't know the whole truth either."

That's quite the admission. My fingers numb with cold as I grip the chilly tumbler in my hands. Afraid I'm going to break the glass, I set the tumbler in a cup holder. "Ready to tell me the real reason your family kicked my mom out?"

"I told you the real reason." I'm about to protest when she adds, "But you're right that there's more to it." *I knew it.* "I want to tell you. You deserve to know, but—" Conflicted feelings sweep over her face. "Let me talk to my mother. I can't make this decision by myself. After I talk to her, I'll get in touch with you."

"When?" I don't want to wait another agonizing two weeks wondering when or even *if* my cousin is going to contact me.

"Soon," she promises. "By Zhong Qiu Jie. Mid-Autumn Festival."

Mid-Autumn Festival. An ache spreads through my chest. Mid-Autumn Festival is a time for family and reconnection. Except that this will be the first one I'll spend without my parents. And I had forgotten all about it. "Mid-Autumn Festival is in a week. That's hardly soon. Why will it take you that long to talk to your mother?"

A cagey look comes into her eyes. "I have some other . . . complicated things going on. But I'll talk to my mother as soon as I can. Let's say Mid-Autumn Festival at the latest, but probably before then."

"Fine," I say tightly. "But if I don't hear from you by Mid-Autumn Festival, I'll come looking for you."

"I don't doubt it," Alyssa says wryly. She downs the rest of her iced tea in one swallow, and the diamonds at her throat glitter as coldly as the ice in her glass. "But it won't be necessary."

It had better not be.

Alyssa drops me off at my hotel, and when I get to my suite, I find another surprise. A pink envelope on the coffee table—tucked under a yellow silk bag embroidered with a phoenix. I read the note first.

> **This belonged to your mother. It's yours**
> **now. I want you to have something of your**
> **inheritance.**
> **Xoxo, Alyssa**

With shaking fingers, I pull the silk cords to open the bag. An oval green jade pendant hung from a gold chain spills into my palm with a Chinese character I don't recognize carved into the jade.

For a long time, I sit on the luxurious white rug, holding the pendant in my hand as if it's hiding all the answers I want in its luminous green depths.

The jade grows warm and heavy in my hand. But it gives me no answers.

CHAPTER TWENTY-THREE

For the rest of the week, gifts start arriving like it's the Twelve Days of Christmas. But it didn't start with a partridge in a pear tree. It started with a green jade pendant in a yellow silk bag.

On Tuesday, the second day, a Hermès shoulder bag and matching clutch showed up in my hotel room. Both bag and clutch were in soft, supple leather that baby calves gave their lives for, and each was adorned with a gold-plated clasp. The accompanying pink note said, *One for everyday use and one for special evenings! Xoxo, Alyssa.*

On the third day, a pair of Jimmy Choo strappy heels in my exact size arrived. They had chunky platform heels and looked like they had been dipped in glittering gold fairy dust. That time, the note said, *So your every step will shine! Xoxo, Alyssa.*

On the fourth day, a ticket for that night's performance of a modern Beijing opera appeared, propped up against another bottle of Moët. The show was at the National Centre for the Performing Arts—a glass-and-metal-plated dome structure surrounded by an artificial lake in the heart of Beijing and accessible only via a long underwater corridor. Tickets, of course, were superexpensive. The note simply said, *Enjoy! Xoxo, Alyssa.*

It's now Friday morning, and I'm lying in bed with the natural-light lamp glowing bright. But it didn't wake me up because I wasn't asleep. I'm lying here, wondering why I'm getting presents and pink notes instead of answers from Alyssa. Of course, I'm bowled over by her generosity, but Alyssa's deadline is almost up. Mid-Autumn Festival is on Monday.

Ugh. My head feels like it's been stuffed with sludge. It can't be because of the single glass of champagne I'd drank last night after the Beijing opera.

No, it's the endless questions running in a loop through my head. *Did my mother steal that painting? If not, then what's the real reason my mother was kicked out of the family? Does Alyssa really have more information about my mother? Will Alyssa actually tell me? Will her mother let her?* Those thoughts kept me up last night, and I'd be surprised if I got more than a few hours of sleep.

My phone buzzes at that moment, and I roll over in bed to grab it off my nightstand. It's Eric.

Hey! How are you doing on the food wish list?

Blinking the crustiness out of my eyes, I text him back.

Nothing left. Glad to hear from you!

I hesitate. Does that last part about being glad to hear from Eric sound too eager? We've been texting regularly for three weeks, so you'd think I'd be better at this by now.

Argh! I delete the second sentence. But now the text sounds too abrupt. *Why is this so hard?* Because there might be some people who are good at flirt-texting, but I, Gemma Huang, am not. I retype the sentence I just deleted. Then I send off my text and spend a small eternity hyperventilating and staring at the three pulsing dots—proof that Eric is texting back his reply.

His text finally pops up on my screen.

Want to go out Sunday night? It's Mid-Autumn Festival eve. Fun things are happening that night.

Like I need a reminder that Mid-Autumn Festival is approaching fast with no word from Alyssa. As usual, I don't have plans. But that doesn't mean it's a good idea to go out with Eric.

I'd like to say that I hesitate or spare more than a passing thought of all the excellent reasons to turn Eric down. But the truth is that my thumbs fly so fast that autocorrect is challenged to translate my text into an intelligible response. In the end, I delete everything and respond with just one word.

Sure!

We text a bit more and agree to meet at my hotel on Sunday.

Then I drag myself out of bed and into the shower. The reflection in the bathroom mirror makes me grimace. My hair is in tangled knots, and the bags under my eyes are big enough to pack my luggage into. *Maybe*, I think morosely, *Jake will actually like this look for Song.* We're shooting more of Song's scenes today, and it would be an understatement to say I'm not looking forward to it. Groaning out loud, I turn the taps on and yelp when the icy water hits me. Hastily, I turn the taps to warm.

Apparently, I don't even have enough mental energy to take a shower. How am I going to play Song on set today? Especially since I still haven't figured out how to follow Eilene's advice to stand up for myself.

No brilliant ideas come to me as I throw on clean clothes, run a comb through my hair, and walk to the hotel lobby to take a car to the studio.

The driver is the same man who picked me up from the airport over a month ago. By this time, I know his name is Wei, and we've become fairly friendly. Enough so that he looks at me in concern as I climb into the back seat.

"You OK?" he asks.

"Never better." I smile wanly. "Right as rain."

Wei is silent, probably running my comment through a mental translation.

I try again. "Wo hao." Saying I'm good is a total lie, but Wei brightens anyhow. Maybe he just likes that I'm speaking Chinese.

"Na hao," he says. *That's good.* It seems that he's taking my assurances at face value.

The time passes in silence as Wei drives. By now, I've almost gotten used to the fact that driving in Beijing is a competitive sport. Everyone—pedestrians, bicyclists, other drivers—is vying for the same narrow slice of road. And everyone goes at top speed. I've hardly ever seen Wei take his hand off the horn when he's driving.

Traffic slows a bit, and Wei scans the left lane for an opening. I brace myself when our car starts inching to the left. To my cowardly American eye, there isn't an opening, but Wei's been known to force a space out of nothing. The window on the car next to us slides down. Uh-oh. Here we go again. More car-to-car angry shouting. Wei seems to anticipate the same thing because he rolls down his window too.

But the two young women in the car aren't even looking at Wei. And they're not yelling. At least not in anger.

They're looking right at me. "Alyssa Chua!" the girl in the passenger seat screams. The rest of it is in Chinese and turns into a dull roar in my panicked brain. I didn't get nearly enough sleep to deal with this.

Way too late, I scramble for my hat and sunglasses, but what's the use? I've been made. My hands drop limply into my lap. "Roll up the window please," I tell Wei tightly.

He does so, but it barely cuts down on the noise. "They think you're Alyssa Chua."

"Yeah, I figured that out somehow." Then I feel bad. Wei's been nothing but nice to me and doesn't deserve my sarcasm. "Sorry." Wincing, I press my fingers into my temples. The fans' shrieking is bringing on a killer headache. And the incessant flash of the camera isn't helping either. Shielding my face, I say, "I guess the noise and lights are getting to me."

"No problem," he says cheerfully. "Let me get you away."

For once, I'm grateful for Wei's death-defying driving skills. Again I brace myself and lock my legs as Wei lays on the horn and swerves to the right, slotting us into the next lane. Everyone honks, which doesn't bode well for my headache. But even worse is that the driver of the car to our left seems to be as much of a risk-taking demon at the wheel as Wei—based on how quickly she slips into the spot we just vacated. That means my fans are next to us again, with their window still rolled down and shouting Alyssa's name.

In disbelief, I stare at the other car as both girls wave at me in wild elation. "They are batshit crazy."

"What is this 'batshit' and who is crazy?" Wei asks.

He loves to ask me about American slang, but now is not the time for a lesson. "They are." I point to the fans still waving at me.

Wei looks to the left. "That driver is good, but I'm better," he says confidently. "We will lose them." He steps on it, only to slam on the brakes when traffic slows again.

My seat belt cuts into my stomach as I'm thrown forward. "Maybe," I gasp, "we should just wait until traffic lets up a bit."

"It's OK," Wei assures me. "They are bothering you, yes?" As if to underscore his point, the girl in the passenger seat starts taking pictures of me again.

Resigned, I sink back into my seat, prepared to let Wei do his worst.

Wei shoots ahead when our lane picks up the pace and angles our car toward the left lane. The driver of the car ahead of Alyssa's fans is a burly man around forty. He glares at us and speeds up to close the gap Wei is nosing toward.

"Wei," I say nervously, "I don't think this is a good idea."

Wei doesn't answer me. I'm not even sure if he hears me. His mouth is set, and he's pressing on the horn with stubborn determination as he eases the bumper over the line. The other driver is honking like crazy and not slowing down. *Great. My life is in the hands of two grown men playing chicken.*

"Wei!" I shriek. But it's too late.

In slow motion, our car barrels into the other car. Again, my seat belt knives across my stomach as my body is slammed forward. All I can smell is burned rubber, and all I can hear is the squeal of brakes. There's a sickening crunch of metal and glass, and then all is quiet.

"Huang xiao jie, ni hao ma?" Wei cries. "Miss Huang, are you OK?" He's twisting back to peer at me in worry, and his eyes are round, pupils dark and dilated.

I put my hand to my aching head, half-afraid it will be sticky with blood, but there's nothing. No bones seem to be broken either, and when I turn my neck, it's a little stiff but not painful. "I'm OK," I say weakly. "Are you OK?"

"Yes." He sighs. "I think everyone else is too."

The driver of the other car has gotten out of his vehicle and is yelling at us in Chinese. Given that I don't understand most of what he's saying, I'm guessing that he's swearing at us. My parents never use profanity, so that's a big gap in my Chinese vocabulary.

Even worse is that Alyssa's fans are getting out of their own car. Leaving it in the middle of the road for cars to go around, the two girls are making their way to us, phones out ahead of them as if they're scanning for alien life-forms. The air is now filled with honking as the other cars have to make their way around three cars at a standstill.

Alyssa might regularly cause stampedes and car accidents with her presence, but this is brand-new territory for me. I'm not a crier, but tears of sheer frustration bubble at the corners of my eyes. Not only did I get zero sleep last night, now I have to deal with a car accident and two fangirls who are posting this on social media. To top it all off, I'm going to be late to work.

And Alyssa still hasn't told me if she can reveal the big secret about my mom. I don't care how many expensive gifts with cheery pink notes she's giving me—right now, I really hate Alyssa Chua.

CHAPTER TWENTY-FOUR

My bowl-cut wig sticks to my scalp, and the cheap synthetic material of my suit rubs against my skin in slithery discomfort. We're on the office set again, shooting another scene between Song and Ryan. And nothing is going right.

Everyone had to wait around until I got to the set almost an hour late, and that didn't exactly do wonders for Jake's less-than-sunny disposition. Eilene, Aidan, and everyone else were super nice about my lateness and kept saying they were glad that I didn't get hurt from the car accident. Jake made some obligatory remark along the same lines and then hustled us into the shoot to make up for lost time. He was even relatively patient when I flubbed my lines during the first take. But he was less patient when I did it again in the second take. In the third take, I managed to deliver all my lines correctly, but my performance could only be described as wooden. Or, as Jake called it, "a travesty."

To make matters worse, my headache hasn't gotten any better. My neck feels like a tightly coiled spring radiating pain into my skull. The only comfort I can take is that the headache came on before the accident, so it's probably not a concussion. Although, a concussion might explain why I'm such a wreck. Is it bad that I'm hoping I have a concussion to excuse how awful my acting is?

Throughout this ordeal, Eilene's expression is perfectly composed, and her directions are given calmly, but I'm sure that speaks to how good *her* acting skills are, rather than any confidence in *mine*.

Jake huffs out a long-suffering sigh. "Let's try that again. Aidan, just do what you did last time. *You* are playing Ryan exactly right."

"Thanks." Tactfully, Aidan looks away when my face flames up.

"Gemma . . ." Here Jake seems to grope for his last fragments of patience. "At the risk of repeating myself, this is a comedy."

Eilene says to me, "Your sense of humor is one reason we wanted you for the role of Sonia." *Nope. My resemblance to Alyssa is the reason they wanted me for the role.*

Jake looks like he's about to dispute what she said, and I wonder which part he disagrees with. The part where I have a sense of humor or the part where they both wanted me for the role? "Right. Gemma, let's get you into character."

I take a deep breath, willing myself to ignore the pounding pain in my head and pay attention. "OK."

"You come into the office," Jake says. "You see Ryan wearing a tie that you, Sonia, gave him. For a moment, you forget that you're dressed as Song. Your eyes soften with emotion, and you walk right up to him, touching his tie. Ryan reacts with confusion and recoils from you. In horror, you realize that you've just hit on your ex-boyfriend, who thinks that you're a man."

Recoil. Horror. Yeah, that's what I'm feeling now. A sick feeling spreads through my stomach. I blame my lack of sleep on why I didn't understand what had been happening in those last three takes. All the humor of this scene is based on that old comedic standby— homophobia. Ryan recoils because he thinks a man is interested in him. And Sonia reacts with horror because Ryan thinks she's gay. It's not funny at all—it's offensive.

Jake wraps up his directions. "You and Ryan both get real macho, real fast. Got it?"

I get it all right. And it sharpens my headache into a wincing rain of sparks at the edges of my vision.

"Gemma, are you OK?" Eilene's face is pinched in concern.

My gaze snaps to her. Doesn't Eilene get it? Can't she see what this scene is about? It's bad enough that I have to play Song as some effeminate Asian male stereotype, but now I have to play this scene for cheap, homophobic laughs. "This scene . . ." I trail off, remembering what happened the last time I tried to speak up. Jake shut me down. And Eilene didn't step in.

"What about this scene?" Eilene asks.

Aidan watches me in confusion.

"Yeah," Jake says with a belligerent undertone. "What *about* this scene?" He's ready for a fight.

But I'm not ready. Not without Eileen. And not with a headache making the backs of my eyeballs throb in agony. "Nothing." Eileen doesn't get it and wouldn't support me even if she did.

"Are you sure?" Eilene asks. "Is there something you want changed?"

She's giving me an opening now, and I can't help but remember what she'd said after the last shoot. *I'll be there to back you up. But you're the actress. You've got to figure out who your character is. Then you've got to fight for her.* Maybe Eilene *will* support me if I can just explain what's wrong with the scene.

But when I open my mouth to speak, my thoughts get jumbled and confused. I'm an unknown actress on a big-film set. It would be stupid to make waves. Eilene should know that. If she were really looking out for me, she'd tell me to keep my head down and just do my job.

Ken's sneering voice pops into my head. *Eilene's using you to prop up her own career. She doesn't care about you or your career. And you're too blind to see it.*

"The scene's fine," I say, mouth dry as sand. I can't take the risk of pissing off the director on the chance that Eilene will stand by me.

But my gut feels all hollowed out when Eilene shoots me another worried look. Her face goes tight, like she knows what I'm thinking.

"OK, then," Jake says. "Take your positions." Ryan perches on the edge of the desk, and I also go back to my starting position. "Take four."

I walk onto the set with the exaggerated, bowlegged stride that is my character's approximation of masculinity. *I look ridiculous.* In my peripheral vision, I see Jake nod in approval. So far, I'm following Jake's directions perfectly. Now I'm supposed to greet Ryan in a fake-deep voice—again, a parody of a man. One that falls hilariously short. "Good morning, Ryan." *I sound like someone died.* Shit. That's not right at all.

"Cut!" Jake yells. He doesn't even bother to tell me what I did wrong because it's obvious that my character's not supposed to sound as if she's in deep mourning for her soul. Even though that's exactly how I feel.

Jake tells us to take our positions. We try again.

And again.

When dinnertime rolls around, we've done so many takes that they've all blurred together. All the takes have one thing in common. Me. Screwing up big-time. Jake calls over a PA, and I know what's going to happen. Jake's going to have the caterers deliver dinner. Then we'll keep shooting as long as necessary—probably up to midnight at this rate—until Jake says those three magic words to set us free: *That's a wrap.* Long shoots are part of a Hollywood film and nothing new, but this time it's all because of me. I'm the one keeping everyone here.

Instead, Jake tells the PA, "We're done for today. Prep for a reshoot."

My stomach twists. *A reshoot?* Is this normal?

Aidan curses under his breath. No. Definitely not normal if easygoing Aidan is taken aback.

"We're not going to keep shooting today?" Eilene's eyebrows arch up.

"What's the point?" Jake's gaze swivels to me, and nerves prickle at the back of my neck. "Thanks to Gemma, today's a wash."

Aidan makes a noise in his throat, but it doesn't become an actual protest. What could he say in my defense? Jake's right. This is my fault.

Heat rises into my face. I can feel the rest of the cast and the crew staring at me, but I avoid meeting anyone's eyes. *Can't everyone just go away?* But no one's budging. I can't say I blame them—this little scene between Jake and me has as much drama as the *Butterfly* scenes.

Jake sighs in disgust. "We'll start again Monday."

"Monday's a holiday, remember?" Eilene reminds Jake. When he looks at her in disbelief, she adds, "To celebrate the moon. It's Mid-Autumn Festival."

At home, Mom will be making celebratory mooncakes to send to me. Mooncakes are the one thing not on my list of food to eat in Beijing. Because there isn't a mooncake in the world that can compare to my mom's. A lump of longing congeals in my throat.

The mention of Mid-Autumn Festival has a different effect on Jake. "Dammit! Who the hell has a national holiday to celebrate the moon?"

Roughly twenty percent of the world's population, for starters. But this isn't the time to get snarky.

Placatingly, Eilene says, "Maybe it's a good idea for us all to have a day off and start fresh after Mid-Autumn Festival. I'm sure we'll be able to get a good scene in the can after a day's rest."

"We'd better. Gemma just cost the studio a boatload of money on today's wasted shoot." Jake glares at me. "I don't know where your head is at, but you'd better get your priorities straight. If it weren't so expensive to replace you at this point, I'd do it in a heartbeat!"

Icy shame fills my body. *Jake wants to fire me.* No one will want to hire me after this. All my hopes and dreams will go up in smoke.

Eilene glances at me and then back at Jake. "Gemma was in a car accident today—"

Jake interrupts her. "Were you hurt?" he demands of me.

"No." My voice is a tiny whisper.

"Then you have no excuse for your performance today."

Jake didn't say it like it was a question, but I answer him anyway. "You're right. There's no excuse." I shouldn't have listened to Eilene and all her talk about changing the film together.

Eilene slides off her director's chair to face Jake. "This isn't Gemma's fault, Jake. Everyone has an off day sometimes." She doesn't flinch as Jake stares at her, and my heart rises to have Eilene's support.

"Always standing up for her, aren't you?" Jake says. "I told you we shouldn't have cast Gemma, even if she does look like some famous Chinese social media star, but you insisted. Said she was a talented actress, if I recall. Still think so?"

"Absolutely." She doesn't miss a beat.

Jake doesn't bother to reply. He rises from his own chair and stalks away from Eilene. "Why are you all just standing around?" he yells at the crew. "I said to prep for a reshoot!"

As the cast scatters and the crew hurries to carry out Jake's orders, Eilene comes to my side. Anxiety steals over me in a cold film of perspiration. In spite of what she said in my defense, I'm still worried about what she thinks of me.

Eilene places a cool, dry hand on my hot, sweaty shoulder. "Gemma, listen to me," she says. "This isn't your fault. You're not the one doing anything wrong."

My relief that Eilene's still on Team Gemma is weaker than it should be. "How can you say that?" Tears spring to my eyes. "Didn't you hear what Jake said?"

"I'll talk him down," she promises. "He's hotheaded, but he'll listen to reason. I'll get him to see this isn't your fault."

"How isn't this my fault? Because of me, we have to do a reshoot!"

"That's because the scene is wrong. Not you!" Eilene says urgently. "I've been there so many times. You have to trust your gut on this. I don't know what's wrong, but you do. So let's fix it together."

I want to believe her. And maybe Eilene's not using me the way Ken thinks she is, but it doesn't mean she's right. Eilene is an established actress. I'm not. I can't afford to take the stand she wants me to take. It was stupid to think the film industry could change or that I could do anything to change it. The only thing that matters is not blowing my big chance.

Shaking off her hand, I walk over to Jake. "Jake," I say, ignoring Eilene's sharp intake of breath, "I'll play Song exactly the way you want."

CHAPTER TWENTY-FIVE

I can feel Eilene's concerned gaze on me as I flee to my trailer, but she doesn't follow me. Liz is already there, ready to help me with my wig and makeup removal, but she takes one look at my face and quietly slips out to leave me in peace.

I collapse into my chair, put my head on the dressing table, and cry until I'm a sniveling mess. What just happened? I just flubbed a whole shoot. And to top it all off, I've disappointed Eilene. I'm not the strong, outspoken actress she thought I was when she took a chance on me. I've given up on my character and all my ideals. Ken's right. I'm a sellout.

My lungs aching from heaving out one breathless sob after another, I finally lift my head. As Song, I don't wear as much makeup as in the scenes when I'm Sonia, but black mascara streaks all down my flushed face, and my eyes are red and swollen. I look as awful as I feel.

I should go to Eilene, talk to her, tell her what I'm feeling. But I can't. I'm too ashamed. She gave me chance after chance, offered her support, and I let fear for my own skin stop me from listening to her. I really blew it.

Hands shaking, I pull out my phone. I need to talk to someone who might understand. *Please pick up. Please don't be asleep.* My head is too muddled to do the time zone calculations, but I know it's way late in LA. Or maybe way early.

A moment later, Glory's face pops up on my screen, and she doesn't look groggy. Good. She wasn't asleep. Maybe she just finished a late-night shift at work. "Hi, Gemma." Her face wrinkles in worry. "God, you look terrible. What happened?"

"I screwed up. Badly." My hands are still shaking, but already I feel a little better seeing Glory's face and hearing her voice. Even though I'm afraid of what she'll think of me, I tell her what happened.

She gives a low whistle when I'm done. "That sounds like a shit-show all right."

I laugh weakly. "Listen, you can tell me the truth. I know I shouldn't have caved in without even trying to explain how horrible that scene was."

"So, you want me to tell you that you've betrayed your values, are a terrible person, and all that?"

Well, not *exactly* like that. Hurt steals over me, even though Glory's just putting into words the thoughts I had been thinking about myself.

"Tough," Glory says. "Because I don't think any of that. That's not how this works."

Relief floods me. "Not how what works?"

"*This*," she replies promptly. "You know, one Asian actress supporting another. And our friendship. Let's not forget that."

"I love you, Glory," I say devoutly.

"I love you too." Her gaze sharpens. "So, now that we've established that we love each other and I'm not going to rip you to shreds for every mistake you might have made . . . how are you going to fix this mess?"

My stomach tightens. I still don't know the answer to that.

But before I can reply, Camille's face squeezes into the screen next to Glory's. "Hi, Gemma!"

"How are you both up at . . ." I'm finally able to calculate the time difference. "Two a.m.?"

"I just got home from a waitressing shift," Camille explains. "That's why I didn't have a chance to call you earlier. I was going to text you, but it really seemed like a phone call thing and not a text thing, you know?"

Wait. Huh? "What are you talking about, Camille?" I glance at Glory, but she looks as confused as I am.

"I'm talking about your parents showing up at our apartment."

Oh shit. I have to clear my throat before I can squeak out, "My parents? In LA? Today?" I realize I just repeated what Camille said as a series of fragmented questions, but my head is going all woozy. "Why didn't they text or call me?" At least that one was a complete question. Then my brain disgorges a *much* more relevant question. "And what did you tell them?" My voice rises in panic.

"I think they wanted to surprise you. They told me not to tell you that they're here, but obviously, I had to tell you."

"Camille." I fight to stay calm. "What. Did. You. Tell. Them?"

Her eyes widen. "I couldn't lie to your parents." My stomach drops, but then she says, "So I told them you were at work. Which you were."

My body puddles in relief. "Oh. *Thank you!*"

"But I can't keep covering for you." Camille pins me with her gaze. "You're going to have to come clean to your parents."

Glory squishes her face close to Camille's so she's firmly in my screen too. "I'm going to have to side with Camille. It was one thing when your parents were still in Illinois, but now that they're in LA, your parents are going to figure out you're not here."

"Not if I email them, saying that the location of my shoot has moved," I improvise desperately. After all that's happened today, the last thing I need is to disappoint anyone else. Especially if that "anyone else" happens to be my parents. "Maybe Nevada."

"Nevada." Glory's disbelieving voice makes it clear what she thinks of my idea.

Camille is more direct. "Gemma! How long are you going to keep lying to your parents?"

Her question cuts me to the bone, and it's hard not to sound defensive. "Look, I know it's not ideal, but you don't understand why it's so important to keep my parents from finding out that I'm in Beijing."

Glory sighs. "They're your parents, and you know them best. I think it's a bad idea to tell them that you're in Nevada, but what do I know?"

As far as support goes, Glory's is pretty lukewarm, but it's still better than Camille's. Her face set in a mutinous scowl, Camille says, "I'm not going to lie for you."

"I'm not asking you to." Panic rises in my throat, making my voice stiff and tight. "But can you just . . . not say anything that will give me away?" Maybe I'd consider taking my roommates' advice to tell my parents the truth if it didn't seem like *everything* in my life is falling apart. It's bad enough that I broke up with Ken and now can't stop thinking about Eric, a guy who's all wrong for me. And now there's my epic failure with this film and failing everyone who trusted me to succeed. I just can't face losing my parents' trust too.

Camille rolls her eyes, but in the end, she agrees to keep covering for me as long as she doesn't have to say anything that's a direct lie. Glory says she doesn't have a problem with covering for me, exactly. It's more that she thinks my deception will catch up with me and that it's better to get in front of it.

I can't help but think she's right.

After I end the call, I go right to my email. Taking a deep breath, I type a note letting my parents know that my shoot was unexpectedly relocated to . . . Here, I pause. What's to keep them from following me to Nevada? After some thought, I put Vancouver, Canada, in my email. Maybe saying I'm in another country will dissuade them.

It's only after I send the note that it occurs to me to wonder why my parents showed up in LA in the first place. I scroll through my emails until I find the last ones from my parents. The one from Dad is a forwarded article about "The Five Best Workouts." As always, it has no subject or context. The one from Mom is all about the museum, the obligatory question about when I'm going to college, and how well her dahlias are doing. Nothing in it gives me a clue to her motivation for the visit. Until I get to the end.

Mid-Autumn Festival is almost here. Family should be together.

Maybe the answer is simple. Maybe she just misses me.

I can almost hear her voice warm with love, saying those words. Hot tears scald my cheeks. I should have guessed my parents would come to LA to see me. After all, we've never been apart on Mid-Autumn Festival. Even though it was never a big celebration with just the three of us, Mom would always make her famous mooncakes, and we would go to our favorite Chinese restaurant for dinner. Suddenly, all I want is my mother's comfort, her arms around my shaking body. I want her to tell me it will all be OK. I want to believe her because she is my mother who will love me no matter how badly I've messed up. And I wish I could say the same thing to her—that no matter what she did, even if she stole a whole museum's worth of paintings—I wouldn't care, because I know that she wouldn't do anything without a good reason.

I just wish I knew what that reason was.

CHAPTER TWENTY-SIX

The train wreck of a week doesn't improve over the weekend. For one thing, I get an email back from my mom. She's disappointed that they missed me in LA. I can't tell if she bought my excuse of filming in Vancouver. She might find it fishy that I didn't tell them about the filming relocation earlier. I can only hope that she won't look up the film online. Fortunately, her resounding lack of interest means that she hasn't asked me any questions about the film. So, it's unlikely that Mom has enough details about *Butterfly* to find out where it's being shot. But when she doesn't follow up her email with a phone call, I know she suspects something. My gut feels all hollow. I'll call my parents on Monday—Mid-Autumn Festival—a holiday we've always spent together. It would be suspicious if I didn't call them, but more than that, I just miss them.

And that's the other thing. Alyssa was supposed to contact me by Mid-Autumn Festival, so it's looking more and more likely that she's broken her promise.

Although the gifts and pink notes still keep coming.

On Friday, it was a pair of diamond chandelier earrings—*A little bling, just for fun! Xoxo, Alyssa.* On Saturday, it was an exquisite ebony jewelry box set with carved jade—*A treasure box for your treasures! Xoxo, Alyssa.* And today, Sunday—it's a Gucci poppy-print silk scarf—*Every girl needs some glamour! Xoxo, Alyssa.*

It's Mid-Autumn Festival eve, and I've got all the pink notes laid out in a row on my dressing table, hoping they'll reveal some kind of coded message. But of course, they don't.

The muscles in my neck and shoulders seize up into a vise of tension, and in a fit of temper I sweep the notes into a drawer. I don't know what to do about my cousin, and I'm too exhausted to figure it out.

It's not that late, only about seven in the evening, but all I want is a nice long bath and then bed. I still haven't figured out how to fix the mess with the film, my parents, or Alyssa, but I'm not going to figure it out right now. Especially since I'm completely wrecked after my pity party weekend of ice cream and late-night TV in the lonely splendor of my room.

In the bathroom, I see myself in the mirror and grimace. My eyes are swollen from crying, and my face is all blotchy and red with strands of hair sticking to my sweaty forehead. Good thing that my only plans tonight are with my jetted tub and my bed.

Just as I'm pouring the bath salts in, I hear a knock at the door. Am I so depressed that I ordered room service and forgot? Then I remember. *Oh crap.* I'm supposed to go out with Eric tonight.

Quickly, I turn off the jets and run to the door. At least I'm fully clothed—in sweats, but still better than a bathrobe. I'm just going to have to apologize and explain that I'm in no mood to hang out.

But when I open the door, Eric is standing there, pale and wild-eyed.

"Eric! What's wrong?" Worried, I pull him into my hotel suite.

His eyes sharpen on me. "I could ask you the same thing. What happened to you?"

Right. My tearstained face is a dead giveaway to my state of mind. "You first."

Eric leads me to the couch and sits down with me. "I'm not going to barge into your hotel room and launch into my troubles. Not when you've clearly got troubles of your own," he says. "Now, tell me what happened." Then his gaze shifts beyond me and wanders over the lavish suite.

"You're wondering if Alyssa is responsible for this suite. Well, she is." My stomach tenses as I wait for his reaction.

"I figured that out when the hotel receptionist directed me to the penthouse suite," he says calmly. "Gemma, you don't owe me an explanation. But something has clearly happened to upset you, and I can listen if you want."

The urge to unburden my troubles to Eric is too much to resist. I find myself telling him about the disastrous shoot. Guilt about lying to my parents. Even what Ken said about Eilene.

Through it all, Eric listens with his head craned forward as if he wants to catch every word. His eyes stay on me the whole time, and he doesn't interrupt.

When I'm done, he shakes his head in disbelief. "How are you still upright? I'd be facedown in bed right now."

I smile weakly and don't tell him about the rose-scented water slowly cooling in the jetted tub. "If you'd gotten here a little later, that's where I'd be." My smile gets a little steadier. "But since you're here now, do you happen to have any words of wisdom for me?"

"I do," Eric says firmly. "First, your ex-boyfriend is an asshole, so ignore everything he said. Second, your director is *also* an asshole, so ignore everything he said too." I laugh, and he continues. "The people you might want to listen to are Eilene and your roommates. Eilene is right. What happened at the shoot isn't your fault."

I start to protest, but Eric says, "Nope. Not your fault. Nothing you say can convince me otherwise. And I would guess that Eilene feels the same way."

I sigh. "That was before I totally blew it."

Eric reaches out to grip my hand. "You're way too hard on yourself."

In a shaky voice, I confess, "I told Jake I'd play my character however he wants me to."

"Listen to me, Gemma, everyone makes mistakes. But you're a smart, talented, strong woman. Eilene told you to trust in yourself, and I think that's good advice."

Against all odds, I'm starting to feel better. Like maybe I *can* fix my mistakes. Then I remember my other problem. "You said I might want to listen to my roommates too. Does that mean you think they're right? That I should tell my parents I'm in Beijing?"

"That's up to you. But your family might worry if they think you're keeping secrets from them." Eric's eyes get a distant expression, and I get the feeling that he's not talking about me and my family anymore.

He came here tonight for a reason, and it wasn't to listen to my problems. "What's wrong?" I ask. "Mimi?"

Eric nods miserably. "No one in our family has seen or talked to her in nearly a week."

Anxiety flickers in me. "I take it that she didn't return your phone call—"

"Calls," he corrects me. "And I wouldn't be so worried if that were the only thing, but it's not." His face creases into a frown. "One of our store managers called me today. Mimi was supposed to come in to do a special fitting of a custom-designed dress. And she never showed. Never called. Nothing. If there's one thing Mimi takes seriously, it's her job as a fashion designer. She wouldn't just not show up with no word unless something's wrong."

My heart drops at his words. If Mimi's job matters as much to her as mine does to me, then Eric is right. Something's wrong.

I don't want to ask this question, but I do anyway. "Did you call hospitals?"

Eric stands up and starts to pace. "Every hospital in the city. She's not there. Thankfully."

"Good." My breathing eases a little.

"And here's another thing I'm worried about." He comes to a stop in front of my chair. "Alyssa was the client that Mimi was supposed to do a fitting for. And Alyssa didn't show up either."

"Did you call Alyssa? Maybe she knows where Mimi is."

"I don't have Alyssa's phone number." Eric's shoulders tense up before my eyes.

It would have been nice if Alyssa had put her phone number on one of those pink notes, I think glumly. "Is there anyone else you can call? Anyone who knows Alyssa?"

"*Everyone* knows Alyssa." Eric pulls out his phone. "And no one *really* knows her."

Unexpectedly, a twinge of sympathy for Alyssa hits me—it would be hard to be so famous and so unknown at the same time.

"Mimi is one of the few people who actually has Alyssa's phone number," Eric says. "Everyone else just follows her on Weibo. Which is what I did to try to find her. Alyssa leaves a trail on Weibo of all the hot spots she goes to." He opens up an app on his phone and hands it to me. "She posted two different pictures today, and I spent all day trying to track her based on those photos."

Of course Weibo is in Chinese, but the pictures of Alyssa don't need any text. In one photo, she's sipping bubble tea on an outdoor patio. In the other, she's taking a stroll in a garden, arm in arm with an attractive guy. "Did you figure out where these were taken?"

"I spent all damn day going to every bubble tea shop in the city. I even tried to figure out which one of her many admirers the guy in the second picture is." He rakes a hand through his hair. "It wasn't until about an hour ago that I realized the truth."

"Truth?" The way Eric is talking ratchets up my worry.

Eric takes his phone from me and scrolls back for a long time. When he hands the phone to me again, I see the same picture of Alyssa sipping pale green bubble tea in a red flared dress that matches her lipstick. It's an arresting image and unmistakably the same photo as the one Eric showed me before.

"When was this one posted?" I ask with an anticipatory catch in my voice.

"About a year ago," he says tersely. "The one with the guy was also first posted around a year ago." He scrolls through Alyssa's posts. "Alyssa hasn't posted a recent picture on Weibo in a week."

Since the night she gave me a ride to my hotel in her limo. Ice forms at the base of my spine. "Why would Alyssa repost old photos of herself?"

"She wouldn't," Eric says. "But someone *else* might be reposting Alyssa's pictures. Someone who doesn't want people to suspect that Alyssa's missing."

"What are you saying?"

"I'm saying that Alyssa is the type of person who could get mixed up in something dangerous. Like I said, she's always chasing the new big thrill. Drugs or gambling—who knows what Alyssa could be involved in? And whatever it is," Eric says, his face pale and tense, "she's dragged my little sister into the thick of it."

It's a struggle to keep my expression neutral in the face of this wild accusation, but I know better than to suggest that Eric's over-reacting, so I manage to make my voice even. "You think Alyssa is involved in drugs or gambling? And that, ah, she's gone on the run?"

Luckily, hearing his own theory repeated back to him seems to bring Eric to his senses. He gives me a rueful look. "Maybe not. But I just can't imagine why both Mimi and Alyssa would disappear."

"I have an idea about that." *Except that it's even wilder than Eric's drugs and gambling theory.* It feels like something is squeezing the air out of my lungs.

"What is it?" he asks.

"I think Alyssa is hiding from *me*."

CHAPTER TWENTY-SEVEN

Y ou?" Eric stares at me. "Why?"

I fill him in on the limo ride with Alyssa. "Alyssa said that she had to talk to her mother before she could tell me more about why my mom was cut off. She's supposed to get back to me by Mid-Autumn Festival."

"But that's tomorrow!"

"I know. Clearly, Alyssa has changed her mind about telling me the truth about my mom." My jaw sets. "I told her I'd come looking for her if I don't hear from her, and that's exactly what I'm going to do."

"That's the problem, isn't it?" Eric asks gently. "You don't know where to find her, and neither do I."

"We would if you could get ahold of Mimi," I say unthinkingly, and then my eyes widen. "Do you think that's why Mimi is with her? So we can't find out from Mimi where she is?"

Eric stands up and starts pacing. "It makes as much sense as anything else." *Which means not at all.* But just as I'm questioning my own theory, Eric is going full steam ahead. "By now, Alyssa knows that you and I are friends," he says. "Maybe she's convinced Mimi to go into hiding with her."

Except . . . why would Alyssa promise to tell me the secret of my mother only to blow me off? And why would she go to the extreme of going into hiding just to avoid me? She could just tell me that she can't reveal the reason my mom was banished. And how could she have convinced Mimi to go into hiding too? I rise from the couch.

Eric pauses in his pacing. "What is it?"

Maybe I shouldn't poke holes into this theory of Alyssa and Mimi hiding from me. It's a lot less worrisome than the alternatives Eric's spinning in that brain of his. "Never mind. What were you saying?" After all, I don't want Eric to go back to his drug and gambling suspicions.

"My parents are worried," he says helplessly, "and if Mimi doesn't show up for the family Mid-Autumn Festival dinner tomorrow, they'll *really* freak out."

I sink back onto the couch, a plan taking shape in my head. I may not know why Alyssa has disappeared, but I *do* know that I want to find her. And talk to her. "I have an idea."

Eric sits down next to me. "Yes?"

"Alyssa's wanted one thing from the start. To keep her grandmother from finding out about me. And you were right about her being furious about the gossip sites linking you two. What do you think would happen if 'Alyssa' showed up at one of her favorite spots tonight—with you?"

"I see," he says, his expression lightening. Then his face falls. "It's one thing to impersonate Alyssa to get into a club, but to get the kind of attention you're talking about so Alyssa notices will take . . . more effort."

"What kind of effort?"

"For this to work, we'd have to hit Beijing hot spots. Light up Weibo with our presence. You'd have to *really* pretend to be Alyssa. If Alyssa is reposting old pictures of her checking into one place while you're impersonating her somewhere else, the inconsistencies will start to show up." His eyes brighten. "We'll get Alyssa's attention all right."

I jump to my feet. "Let me just change into something more glamorous than sweats." I walk over to my closet and fling it open to reveal a neat row of cotton sundresses, capri pants, and comfortable T-shirts.

Eric follows me to my closet and peers over my shoulder. "Um, no offense, Gemma, but . . ."

"Nothing in my closet comes close to what Alyssa would wear?" I ask, saving him the embarrassment of saying it himself.

"Yeah." He fingers the hem of one of the sundresses. "Don't get me wrong, Gemma. I love your style, but if you're going to pass for Alyssa, we're going to have to get you some haute couture. Which, fortunately, just happens to be my line of work."

"For the better good," I say gravely, "I will subject myself to a glamorous makeover."

Eric leaves to get the clothes, and while I'm waiting for him to get back, I style my hair and put on makeup, applying an extra coating of mascara. Thankfully, Liz, my makeup artist, gave me a tube of glossy red lipstick that wasn't right for my character of Sonia, but is perfect for playing Alyssa.

Half an hour later, there's a knock at my door, and Eric wheels in a portable clothes rack loaded with about a dozen black garment bags. But his face looks grimmer than ever, and there's a tense set to his shoulders.

"Spit it out," I say. "What's wrong now?"

"I just got off the phone with my parents. After my dad told Nai Nai that he's done funding her 'high-society charity events' war against the Sung/Chua family, Nai Nai decided to take the war to a new battlefield. She talked to a reporter from one of the Weibo gossip sites." *That can't possibly be a good thing.* "Nai Nai says she won't do it again, and I think she already regrets it, but the damage is done."

My stomach drops. "What did she say?"

"Stuff about how Alyssa dresses, showing too much skin and flirting too much." Eric winces. "Nai Nai actually called Alyssa a . . . Well, I don't know the English translation, but trust me, it's not good."

Indignation sparks in me. *Did Eric's grandmother really just slut shame Alyssa?* "That's awful!"

"I know! Nai Nai has no idea what she's gotten herself into." His face hardens. "Alyssa is the queen of Weibo with millions of followers. She's going to destroy my grandmother on social media and maybe even take Mimi down."

"You've got to be kidding!" Heat rises up my neck. "*That's* what you're worried about? Some bogus retaliation plot by Alyssa that you're spinning in your head? Your grandmother used a gossip site to attack my cousin!" Only then do I realize that I'm yelling. And that this might be the first time I've referred to Alyssa as my cousin out loud.

"Your *cousin*?" Eric narrows his eyes at me. "I didn't realize you thought of Alyssa like that."

"She is family." Confused, I stop. Why am I defending Alyssa? *This isn't even my war.*

He looks around again at the lavish furnishings and gold silk accents of my suite. "I see."

Oh hell. Now he's going to make some jerky comment about how Alyssa has succeeded in buying my loyalties. And he doesn't even know about the haute couture accessories she's lavished on me. But it's not really about the expensive things Alyssa has given me. *Somehow, I've developed a fondness for my cousin—who happens to be a high-society fashionista social media star.* And if Eric wants to tear into me for that . . . then I guess our truce is over.

But Eric just sighs. "I don't want to fight with you, Gemma." He rubs his face. "Maybe I *am* jumping to conclusions about how Alyssa is going to react. I'm just worried about what she's going to do to my nai nai. And to Mimi."

I take a breath to calm down. "I don't want to fight with you either," I say, "but at some point you've got to realize that your grandmother and Mimi both made choices. Good ones or bad ones—they're not your choices to fix."

"That's fair." Eric smiles weakly. "So, do we still have an alliance? Because I have some outfits to show you if we're still on."

Relieved that he's not going to be a jerk, I smile back at him. "I'm game if you are."

Then I gape in amazement as Eric unzips each garment bag to reveal elegant jumpsuits, daring cocktail dresses, and gorgeous floor-length gowns. If I wasn't about to embark on a plan to find my missing cousin and Eric's missing sister, I'd be thrilled by this opportunity to try on designer clothing. The last bag he unzips only halfway before zipping it back up again. But I catch a glimpse of what's inside. It looks like Eric has sneaked in the black suit I'd coveted previously.

"See anything you like?" Eric asks.

"All of it," I say promptly, but I'm pointing toward a champagne-colored minidress beaded in sparkling rhinestones. "Too much?"

"Never." Eric takes the dress off the rack and hands it to me. "Go try it on."

I take the dress into the bedroom and shimmy into it. It takes a few tugs before I'm able to zip it up, but when I look in the mirror, I see an incredibly glamorous woman looking back at me. It's not just that I look like Alyssa. It's that I don't even look like myself anymore.

"How's it going?" Eric calls out.

"Just a minute!" I put on the diamond chandelier earrings that Alyssa gave me and then touch the jade necklace I'm wearing indecisively. Its brilliant green doesn't go with the outfit, but I'm reluctant to take it off. It's the only thing I have of my mother's inheritance. I compromise by turning the pendant around so the unknown Chinese character is hidden. There. Now there's just a smooth jade oval visible.

Taking a deep breath, I open the bedroom door. "What do you think?"

Eric's eyes don't light up the way they did the other night when I came out of the dressing room wearing the suit. Instead, he looks me over critically. "You'll pass for Alyssa easily."

What did I expect? This isn't the time to flirt or score points for my appearance. This is about finding Alyssa and solving the mystery of my mother's past.

I fasten the Jimmy Choo gold heels onto my feet, taking a couple of experimental steps. I'm not about to go hiking in these heels, but they're not as uncomfortable as I'd feared.

"OK," I tell Eric as I pick up my Hermès clutch and sail through the door in my glittering three-inch heels. "Let's go."

CHAPTER TWENTY-EIGHT

I thought we'd go to the nightclub Alyssa owns first, but Eric thinks it's a bit too exclusive for our purpose. Plus, the clientele at her nightclub know Alyssa *and* know of my existence. They'll be harder to fool. That's why Eric is driving us to Songbird Nightclub instead. It's one of Alyssa's favorite haunts, and more importantly, it's where she goes to be in the public eye.

I'm obsessively watching videos of Alyssa on Eric's phone, which has the Weibo app. Worrying my lip in concentration, I analyze her walk, her smile, her every little mannerism. "Hello, everyone!" I repeat over and over again. It's not just a matter of making my voice higher and breathier. Alyssa's accent when she's speaking English is subtle and hard to nail, so I have to practice saying the *l* in "hello" with a light *r* the way Alyssa does.

Eric doesn't interrupt me as I practice speaking like Alyssa.

At last, I feel I've gotten it. I scroll through Weibo again to study her facial expressions. I can't help but notice how many of the pictures posted have a certain pixie-haired girl in the background. Mimi.

Silently, I put Eric's phone back onto its stand.

Now that I'm not actively preparing for a role, my body grows jittery, and my fingers twist compulsively in my lap. This was my idea, but I'm getting more nervous the closer we get to Songbird Nightclub. What if Alyssa doesn't take the bait? Or what if baiting her like this makes her angry and drives her farther underground? Then I'll never get any answers about my mother. *Not true.* It just means that I'll have to get answers about my mother *from* my mother. Except hell will freeze over before *that* will happen.

"Hey," Eric says, "you've gotten quiet over there. Are you having second thoughts?"

"No." I bite my lower lip. "I just hope this works."

"So do I." He takes one hand off the wheel and places it briefly on my knee.

I stare out the window as the car pulls up to the curb in front of a sleekly dark building. Unlike Alyssa's selective nightclub, this one has a long line of people snaking out along the sidewalk. I can see why Eric thought we'd have a better chance here leaking the scandalous news that Alyssa is out and about with Eric. And with any luck, Alyssa will take notice.

A valet in a smart uniform comes out to greet us, and Eric hands the keys to him.

Then Eric comes around to open the door for me. "Ready?"

"Give me just a minute." Taking a deep breath, I give myself a little talk. *You are a glamorous celebrity. Those people out there are your fans. You live for their attention. This is who you are.* "OK. I'm as ready as I'll ever be."

I take the hand Eric offers me to help me out of the car, and as I pivot around to face the crowd in line, I flash the widest, most dazzling smile I can imagine and wave Alyssa's patented little two-fingered wave. "Hello, everyone!"

Heads swivel, and the all-too-familiar phrase of "Shi ta!"—"It's her!"—spreads like wildfire among the crowd.

"If I didn't know better," Eric whispers, "I'd think you were Alyssa."

"Convincing?" I murmur coyly, lowering my eyes the way Alyssa would.

He swallows. "Unnerving."

Blinding light hits my eyes as flashes go off everywhere, accompanied by the snapping of cameras. Through it all, I keep waving as Eric leads me to the head of the line. I smile as I see at least a couple of people pause to upload their pictures. In a matter of seconds, Weibo will light up with an Alyssa and Eric sighting. If that doesn't set the bait, I don't know what will. At the door, the two bodyguards don't even check a list. They greet me as Chua xiao jie, which would be "Miss Chua" in English, and let us in at once. Inside, the nightclub is much more crowded, less swanky, and hipper than Alyssa's nightclub. There are colored lights overhead, making it seem like we're inside some huge laser tag arena. But the people are holding cocktails instead of laser blasters and wearing Chanel and Gucci instead of brightly colored vests.

Two of those designer clothes–clad people start to approach me, their eyes lit up with the familiar excitement of an Alyssa-fan, but Eric shakes his head at them. To my surprise, they back off. I guess the nightclub clientele is too hip and cool to accost me the way other fans have. Then Eric puts his arm around my shoulders, and his body is so warm and solid by my side that I forget that I'm supposed to be Alyssa and melt into him.

But the heads turning in our direction snap me out of the intoxicating haze of Eric's nearness. No one takes pictures of us, but a few people cast excited glances in our direction and start texting furiously. We retreat into the shadowed corner with a table for two.

In my normal voice, I say, "I guess it doesn't take much to start a relationship rumor."

"Yup. Everyone will think that I've become one of Alyssa's many lovesick admirers." Except Eric's too worried about Mimi to look at all lovesick. "Good thing my nai nai isn't on Weibo." He looks even more worried at *that* thought.

"Keep up the act," I remind him. "You're supposed to be out for a fun night on the town with Alyssa Chua. You're not supposed to look like you're about to murder someone."

"This *is* how I'd look if I were out with Alyssa."

"Then pretend you're out with me," I say daringly.

Eric gazes at me somberly. "Out with Gemma Huang, who's leaving in a month?"

A charged silence stretches out between us. "Since we're pretending," I say, breath catching in my throat, "let's pretend away that I'm leaving. Pretend away our family secrets and histories."

"No secret pasts," he agrees, his face softening. "And no leaving the country soon."

Before I can respond, a waiter appears at our table with a bottle of Moët and two champagne flutes.

Eric talks to the waiter in Chinese, casually eliciting the information that this is Alyssa's standing order. I keep quiet, not wanting to blow my cover with my atrocious Chinese.

With a bow to me, the waiter sets the bottle and flutes down on the table with a flourish and whisks himself away.

"Being Alyssa has some advantages," Eric remarks, holding up the bottle to peer at the gold label.

I already have an almost-full bottle of Moët from Alyssa in my hotel suite, so without thinking, I put my hand on his wrist to stop him from popping the bottle open.

He goes still as soon as I touch him. Fire flickers in his eyes. "I can put it on my bill." His words seem to be spoken distractedly, and the sudden hammer of his pulse shudders through my own body.

Hardly paying attention to what I'm saying, I ask, "Won't it be expensive?"

"It's a special occasion."

"Then I suppose I'd better have some champagne to stay in character." My words sound hoarse as I push them through my constricted throat. "But what are we celebrating?" My gaze shifts downward to my fingers, which are still wrapped around Eric's wrist. *I should let go.* But I can't seem to break the contact that is heating my skin to an almost painful intensity.

Eric slowly puts the bottle back down. Then he takes my free hand, sliding his thumb over the sensitive skin on the inside of my wrist.

"Eric." My voice is breathless with the effort of holding back all the promises I shouldn't make.

Eric is leaning forward, his eyes locked on mine. All my nerves are stretched razor sharp and tight.

Then a harsh voice beside me says in English, "Miss Huang. Come with me."

I jump about a mile in pure surprise. A large man with black bushy eyebrows is staring down at me. It's not Alyssa's limousine driver, but there's no doubt who sent him. *Well, that was fast.* My pulse races for a completely different reason than it had just a minute before. This is what we wanted. For Alyssa to take the bait. I just hadn't thought that meant that she would send someone to *literally* take the bait—as in taking *me.*

For a breathless moment, I gape up at the man. Then I notice that the waiter and a busser are nearby. I still need to impersonate Alyssa convincingly in case they're listening—make them forget that they heard the driver call me "Miss Huang" instead of "Miss Chua." *I'm not an American tourist totally out of her element. I'm a rich pampered socialite, and I chew up and spit out men like this every night.* Alyssa's carefree laugh trills out of me. "Loving the whole intense, mysterious summons," I purr, "but slow down a little, won't you?"

Eric drops my hand and turns all his laser-like attention to the man. In Chinese, he demands to know what the man wants with me.

The man ignores Eric and says to me, "Please come with me." His flat, unfriendly voice is in sharp contrast to the politeness of his request.

Eric stays where he is and turns to me. "What do you want to do?" He gives me a searching look as if he's trying to tell me that we don't have to go with this scary, mysterious man.

Leaving the relative safety of Songbird Nightclub was never part of the plan, so I get why Eric has cold feet.

But there's no question in my mind of passing up this chance to find Alyssa and Mimi. With a flippancy that would have done Alyssa proud, I smile ruefully at Eric. "I guess we won't be having that champagne after all."

As the strange man leads us out of the club, Eric takes the opportunity to whisper in my ear, "You don't have to do this!"

"Of course I do," I whisper back with a certainty I'm far from feeling. "It's the only way to get the answers we both need."

Outside the club, the line of people is as long as ever. Since the trap has already been sprung, I don't wave or call out to draw attention this time. Still, some people turn to look at me. After all, being accompanied by a big dude with a ferocious grimace on his face doesn't exactly make me inconspicuous.

Our escort ignores the people yelling Alyssa's name and leads Eric and me to a long black car with dark windows parked at the curb. A valet waits at attention by the car and hands the man the keys immediately. The driver opens the back door, and I duck into the leather upholstered back seat. Eric is quick to slide in after me. Our driver slams the door shut with a loud finality that makes me start, and then gets into the front seat.

I can see the crowd in line at the nightclub wave and call out to me, but I can't hear anything. All I can see are their mouths moving and the fanatic gleam in their eyes as the cameras go off. Along with having darkened windows, the car is apparently also soundproof. There's clear glass between the front and back seats. Since I can't hear the driver's movements, I'm sure it's soundproofed too.

"So, we're doing this?" Eric speaks at a normal volume, so he must have come to the same conclusion about the soundproof barrier. The worry lines in his face are more pronounced than ever.

The driver pulls away from the curb, and the excited crowd recedes into the distance. It's not a good sign when I actually miss the protection that a hundred camera-happy fans might provide us. But I don't let anxiety leak into my voice. "We're doing this."

Eric doesn't reply, but he takes my hand in his. This time, no sparks ignite between us. We're each too focused on the unknown destination we're hurtling toward. And the confrontation that waits for each of us. Still, the heavy warmth of his hand enveloping mine helps slow the erratic beat of my heart.

We maintain our tense silence as the car exits the highway half an hour later.

My hands grow cold and damp as we barrel along dimly lit streets somewhere in the suburbs of Beijing. After another half an hour or so, the car turns onto a street lined with trees and manicured hedges. I crane my neck forward, and Eric's doing the same thing. It looks like we're in a wealthy suburban neighborhood.

The car slows as we approach a gated mansion of warm terracotta and blazing lights in the windows. As we get closer, an actual frigging peacock saunters up to the black wrought-iron gate. The driver pulls up to an intercom by the gate and has a conversation with someone that we can't hear.

This is it. If I have to, this time I'll literally sit on Alyssa until she coughs up the answers I need.

The gate slowly swings open.

We pass through the gate and go up the driveway until the car comes to a stop right at the bottom step of the mansion. The driver gets out and opens the back door.

With mounting anticipation, I climb out of the car, and Eric follows. Without a word, the big man leads the way up the stairs to a dark wooden door. He unlocks and opens the door, holding it ajar and ushering us inside.

I find myself in a foyer lined by carved rosewood benches with black silk cushions embroidered with golden dragons. Graceful urns of bamboo flank the doors, and the floor is pure white marble.

My heart is pounding so hard that my rib cage hurts. Our driver tells us to wait in the echoing marble foyer and disappears down a dark hall.

"Now what?" I ask.

Eric's face is tight with tension. "I'm not sure."

After that, there doesn't seem to be much left to say. In a silence so taut that it seems like it will shatter any second, we wait.

In actuality, the silence doesn't shatter so much as it's punctured. By the quick staccato of heeled footsteps. Angry footsteps.

In a silk bathrobe and fluffy, heeled mules, Alyssa Chua bursts into the foyer.

CHAPTER TWENTY-NINE

Why is the ever-chic Alyssa greeting us in a robe and slippers? Granted, her loungewear is fancier than my typical street clothes, but still . . . She *was* expecting us.

Except that Alyssa's face is rigid with shock. "Gemma!"

I don't know how she forgot that she sent a car for me, but *I* haven't forgotten why I'm here. "You promised me answers about my mom, remember?"

"Right." The surprise slowly melts from her face. "We just needed—"

"WE?" Eric demands. "Where's Mimi?"

Alyssa aims a death glare at him.

More footsteps echo in the dark hallway. "Eric? Do I hear your voice?" Then Mimi, wearing a silk robe that matches Alyssa's, appears in the foyer.

"Mimi!" Eric's face goes slack with relief. "Are you OK?"

"Why wouldn't I be?" Mimi walks over to Alyssa and puts an arm around her.

Oh no. We haven't stumbled into a love nest, have we? Then I remember Alyssa's odd surprise at our presence. Are we *intruding* on a love nest? My face flames up in mortification. That would be seriously awkward.

"I had no idea what had happened to you!" Eric says. "Do you know how worried I've been? You wouldn't even answer my calls or my texts!"

"It was my fault," Alyssa says, and when Mimi turns to her, Alyssa's voice softens. "Mimi, you know you would never have given me that ultimatum if I weren't behaving like an idiot."

"What ultimatum?" Eric asks.

I step forward and whisper into his ear, "Just listen." I'm still confused about the *how* part, but we've obviously just crashed Mimi and Alyssa's romantic retreat. There's no way to spin *that* as a good thing. So the least we can do is shut up and listen.

Mimi speaks up, answering Eric's question. "I told Alyssa that she had to stop pretending that she's someone she's not."

Alyssa lays her head on Mimi's shoulder, and images of Alyssa and Mimi at the club flash through my brain. Alyssa flirting with two men, and Mimi's tense face. And the fear that appeared on Alyssa's face when Mimi whispered something into her ear. *The ultimatum.*

Mimi gently strokes Alyssa's hair. "I told her that we're over if she can't make space for me. For once, I wanted it just to be the two of us. I wanted time away from her entourage and Weibo posts." She addresses Alyssa then. "It was wearing you out—playing the part of a celebrity party girl."

"*Playing* the part of a celebrity party girl?" Eric echoes in a dumbfounded way.

They both ignore him. "You also didn't love how I flirted with every guy in sight," Alyssa mumbles into Mimi's shoulder.

Mimi's lips tighten. "You're right. I didn't."

"But why didn't you tell me, Mimi?" Eric bursts out, the hurt evident in his voice. "You used to tell me everything!"

Mimi stiffens. "Why would I tell you anything? It was clear that you didn't like Alyssa. And you kept going on about how our families have been enemies forever."

"I was just worried about you!"

Maybe it's time I interrupt before he says something he regrets. "Eric," I say, "Mimi doesn't need your protection."

He swivels to stare at me.

I think of every time Eric's been there for me, paying attention to whatever I have to say. He'll listen to me now. "Remember when you told me how proud you are of everything that Mimi has done? That's what she needs to hear now." *Don't blow this, Eric.*

Eric's eyes dart between Mimi and me. "You're absolutely right."

Relief pierces me. I should've had more faith. Eric's not the kind of guy who blusters and gets defensive when he's in the wrong. He's the kind of guy who will do anything for the people he cares about.

He steps forward and envelops Mimi in a hug. "I'm so sorry. Ever since I came home, I've been trying to save you, when you never needed saving at all. You're doing amazing things with your life, and I'm so in awe of you. For everything you are."

Mimi sniffles and hugs Eric back. Alyssa glances away uncomfortably and backs off a bit, giving the siblings some room.

I feel like I'm intruding all over again. A hot emotion stings the backs of my eyes. As an only child, I can't imagine the kind of closeness Eric and Mimi have. Alyssa and I exchange glances, and she has an odd expression on her face—a mixture of confusion and wistfulness. She's an only child too.

Sheepishly, Eric says, "I know I made assumptions about Alyssa. It should have been enough for me that you liked her."

"More than like," Mimi says, though it's clear she's softening toward her brother. "Love."

Without hesitation, Eric says, "Then I'll learn to love her too." He turns to Alyssa. "I'm sorry about misjudging you. My sister loves you, and that's enough for me."

Alyssa's eyes go round with surprise, and she has to get a nudge in the side from Mimi before she says, "Apology accepted."

"Good," Mimi says. "Glad that's settled."

Eric clears his throat. "Uh, I hate to be a downer, but we need to think about our families. Mom has never been a part of this feud between our families, and she'll get Dad to accept Alyssa. But there's nothing Mom or anyone else can say to convince Nai Nai to accept Alyssa."

"I won't tell Nai Nai if you won't," Mimi mutters.

"The point is that it's not *our* family I'm worried about." Eric turns to Alyssa. "It's *your* family. Your grandfather."

"That's not your problem," Alyssa says icily, but there's fear in her eyes, and Mimi pulls away from Eric to take her hand.

My throat goes dry as I remember what Eric had said on the pedal boat—*the time of the Cultural Revolution when being gay was criminalized and brutally punished.* Our grandfather already proved his loyalty to the ideas of the Cultural Revolution when he betrayed Eric's grandfather fifty years ago. And he kicked my mother out of the family thirty years ago. Would he now cut Alyssa off for loving Mimi? I can only imagine how terrible it would be for Alyssa to lose her family like my mother did.

"Alyssa," I say, "even if your grandfather doesn't approve, your parents and grandmother will stand by you, won't they?"

Alyssa swallows visibly. "I don't think my mother and Po Po stood up for your mother."

A coldness spreads through my heart. Thirty years ago, my mother was banished from her family. And now Alyssa is afraid the same thing will happen to her.

"Gemma, you deserve to know more about why your mother was kicked out of the family." Determination sparks in Alyssa's eyes. "With everything going on, I haven't talked to my mother yet, and I'm sorry about that. Tomorrow, at our Mid-Autumn Festival dinner, I'll talk to her. You'll get an answer."

"Thank you," I breathe. My heart beats fast at the thought of *finally* finding out about my mother's past.

"Don't thank me," she says. "What happened to your mother was wrong, and I'm sorry I didn't see that before."

"Speaking of that," Mimi says, and my stomach tightens, "I owe you an apology too."

My eyes widen. "Me?" I'd thought Mimi was going to ream me up one side and down the other for butting in on her private affairs.

"Yes, I'm sorry about how rude I was to you when we met, Gemma."

Frankly, it's yet another surprise that Mimi even remembered my name. "It's OK."

"It's no excuse," Mimi continues, "but that night at the club was the last straw for me. I mean, my brother shows up with a woman who looks like Alyssa—my girlfriend—who happened to be draped all over some guy at the time. I guess I was jealous that you two could be so openly together when Alyssa and I couldn't."

"Ah, your brother and I aren't actually . . ." I glance at Eric in mute appeal.

Gallant as ever, he leaps into the breach. "We're not together."

Mimi narrows her eyes at us both. "Why not?"

That's our cue to leave. "Now that you and Eric have made up," I say quickly, "and Alyssa has promised to talk to her mother tomorrow, Eric and I should get going."

"Yes," Eric says. "We'll just . . . ah . . . get out of your way then. Can your driver give us a ride back?"

"He's not *my* driver!" Alyssa throws her hands up. "Wang works for my po po!"

"What?" Confusion makes my head spin. "Didn't you want to keep me away from your grandmother? So, why would you send her driver for me?"

"That's what I'm trying to tell you!" Alyssa's voice thins. "I didn't send anyone for you!"

Footsteps echo along the hall again, and in a minute, Wang appears in the foyer. "Ms. Chua," he says, "your grandmother asked me to give you this after you saw Ms. Huang." He hands Alyssa an envelope and then retreats back down the hallway.

I'd completely forgotten about the existence of the mysterious grandmother, but now I remember what Alyssa told me at our first meeting. *She follows me on Weibo. . . . She might get suspicious if someone who looked like me were spotted where I wasn't supposed to be.* Shock cascades over me in sheets of ice. *No.* It couldn't possibly have been the elusive grandmother who sent the car for us. How could she have known where Alyssa would be? And why would she send me to Alyssa anyway? The impossibilities multiply dizzily in my head.

Eyebrows knitted together, Alyssa takes out a thick sheet of cream-colored paper from the envelope.

The silence stretches out as she reads it. No one even exchanges glances—we're all breathlessly watching Alyssa read the letter from her grandmother.

At last, Alyssa looks up from the letter, her face troubled as she stares at me. "I was wrong about Po Po. She says that you . . ." Alyssa trails off and starts over again. "She wants you to be welcomed into the family. She wants you at the family's Mid-Autumn dinner that my mother is hosting tomorrow. Po Po promises to be there. With my gong gong." She swallows hard.

I stare at her, my pulse racing. "Do you mean it really was your grandmother who brought me here—to you?"

"Yes. Po Po says she knew who you were as soon as she saw your picture at Songbird. She knew it wasn't me because she could tell I had been reposting old Weibo pictures. She knows I've been gone for the past week and she hoped I'd be at this house. It was always my favorite." Alyssa's eyes fill with tears. "Po Po sent you here so her wai sun nu can be together. So we can both bring each other back. That's what she said in her letter."

Wai sun nu. Granddaughters. Jagged pain fills my lungs, and it's suddenly hard to breathe. "Back?" I ask through a throat thickened with emotion. "She wants us to go to her?"

Alyssa shakes her head. "Po Po is requesting that I take you to see my mother."

"Why your mother?" I ask. "Why not your grandmother?"

"Because my mother has the answers you want." She slides the letter back into the envelope. "Gemma, it's time we find out the truth." She glances at Mimi, and her chin lifts. "Maybe it's time for *all* the secrets to come out. Let's not wait until tomorrow. Let's all go see my mother now."

I guess Alyssa and I are more alike than I thought. "You know, I was thinking the same thing."

CHAPTER THIRTY

Alyssa and Mimi eventually return, looking like they stepped out of a fashion shoot. Alyssa is wearing a gray skirt with a fringed black overlay and a fitted crop top. Mimi is wearing a belted white jumpsuit.

"You both look gorgeous," I say. If I wasn't wearing the borrowed cocktail dress, I'd feel frumpy in their presence.

"Thanks!" Alyssa says breezily. "You look gorgeous too, if I do say so myself." She looks me over. "I like that dress on you. I think it's the one I was supposed to be fitted for today."

Mimi squeals, "It is! That's the dress I designed! You look great in it, Gemma!"

I blush and glance down at the dress, remembering the ridiculous lengths I went to in order to impersonate Alyssa. Apparently, I've not only stolen Alyssa's identity, but her dress as well. "Sorry." It comes out as an embarrassed whisper. "I'll get it dry-cleaned and return it as soon as I can."

Alyssa waves this aside. "I've already said it looks smashing on you. Go ahead and keep it!"

I gape at her. "I can't possibly keep the dress! It was commissioned for you!"

"Look," Alyssa says, her face grave in a way I've never seen in the many images of her on social media. "I've never had a sister I could give presents to or share clothes with. Let me get a tiny taste of what I never had." She ends her little speech with a pout, which, on the other hand, could've been lifted from any number of social media images. "Please?" she wheedles.

"You might as well just give in gracefully, Gemma," Mimi says. "Alyssa is *very* persuasive."

"Remember how you wouldn't sell me your clothes at that fashion show because of the feud between our families?" A reminiscent glint comes into Alyssa's eyes. "I had to wine and dine you to change your mind."

"Oh, was that what you were after?" Mimi says teasingly. "My clothes?"

Alyssa casts her a sultry look. "Well—"

"OK, that's enough," Eric says hastily. "I don't need to hear about my sister's love life." Then he smiles at me. "I think you look great in everything you wear, Gemma, but that dress does look amazing on you."

Alyssa smirks at Eric. "You and your sister have good taste in women."

Eric just gapes at her, speechless. It's clear that Mimi had told Alyssa to make up with him. I just wish that Alyssa didn't have to do it by teasing Eric about *me*.

Heat flares into my face. "Thank you, Alyssa. And you too, Mimi. It's a beautiful dress, and I accept." My hand goes to the jade pendant nestled between my collarbones. "But you've already given me so much. How can I thank you?"

Alyssa waves off my thanks. "It's my pleasure." Then her eyes go to the pendant. "Is that the one I gave you?"

Blushing, I turn the pendant around. "Yes. I don't know what the character means, and I didn't want to have it showing in case it actually said something inappropriate."

She laughs. "Oh, I wish!" Then her face grows serious. "No, the character is 'mei.' It means younger sister. Like I said, it was your mother's, and she is my mother's younger sister by just a few minutes." Alyssa pulls a similar jade pendant from under her crop top. "I inherited this from my mother." She shows me the character, which is different from mine. "This is 'jie.' It means older sister."

I try to smile, but it's hard to do when my throat is blocked with tears. "It's like those Chinese dramas when two girls discover they each have a half of the same pendant—"

Alyssa interrupts. "Because they're sisters separated at birth!" *She must have watched the same dramas.* She walks over to me and holds up her jade pendant next to mine. "Together, the two characters form another word. 'Jiemei.'"

Together, we look at the glowing green jade ovals, side by side. And the new word formed by the joining of the two characters. Jiemei. *Sisters.*

Outside the mansion, the black car's engine is purring gently, and Wang, the driver, holds open the back door for us. He doesn't seem nearly as imposing as he did earlier. In fact, when he sees us all approach, his face cracks into a smile.

Alyssa returns the smile and asks Wang to take us all to downtown Beijing. To her parents' place.

My heart thuds in excitement threaded with nervousness. I'm about to find out about my mother's past.

Mimi clambers in first, followed by Alyssa, then me, and finally, Eric. The luxurious back seat is so long that we all fit comfortably.

The driver gets into the front seat, and the car noses back into the night. Eric's hand briefly closes on mine. No matter what I discover, Eric will be by my side to help me deal with it.

"So, Gemma," Alyssa says cheerfully, "how were you able to

impersonate me so well? Wang, Po Po's driver, said you sounded so much like me when he picked you up that he started to doubt his sanity!"

The actress in me can't help but feel flattered. "I watched the videos you posted on Weibo. It helped that you speak in English. By the way, your English is excellent." In fact, I'm relieved that Alyssa, Mimi, and Eric have all been speaking English the whole time because I wouldn't have been able to keep up with the intricacies of the conversation if it had been in Chinese.

"Oh that." Alyssa makes a small moue of distaste. "My father thought it would be good to speak only in English. I'm supposed to do more Instagramming. He'd love for my social media presence to expand to the West. It's good for business. He's a . . . What do you call it in English? He invests in things?"

"Venture capitalist?" I guess, not having much notion of what a venture capitalist actually does.

"Yes, that's it." Her expression smooths over. "I actually don't mind. It's a way to be part of my family's business."

Eric gives a tiny exhale of surprise. It seems he wasn't expecting yet another connection in their shared sense of duty toward family.

"But enough of that!" Alyssa exclaims. "I want to see your impression of me!"

Strangely reluctant, I wave off her request. "Oh, it's nothing! I was only able to convince people because we look so much alike."

Mistaking my refusal for false modesty, Alyssa insists, "Wang doesn't exaggerate. If he said he almost believed that you were me, then you must be good!"

"Gemma is an excellent actress," Eric says.

Mimi shakes her head with a small smile and teasingly murmurs something about how she thought her brother would've gone for an environmental activist. Or at least that's what I think she said because she spoke in Chinese, and "environmental activist" is beyond the bounds of my vocabulary.

Although there's nothing mean-spirited in Mimi's whispered aside, Eric glances at me and says to his sister, "Let's speak in English."

"Mei guang xi. No problem," I reply. If Alyssa is practicing her English, then I can practice my Chinese, although they all speak much better English than I speak Chinese.

"Enough stalling!" Alyssa says with a toss of her hair. "Please do your impersonation of me."

"Fine." I sigh and then toss my hair exactly as she just did. "If I must be Alyssa Chua, then I'll do it with my signature style!" It's not easy to do an impersonation with the original sitting right there, but I muster up an insouciant grin. "After all, there's no one quite like me. I'm unique. Original. And unforgettable." A strange uneasiness snakes through me as I finish—I'm not feeling the sense of satisfaction I usually get when I nail a performance.

Alyssa claps her hands in delight. "Oh, well done!"

Mimi makes a noise of protest. "Except it wasn't really you."

My throat constricts because Mimi is giving voice to my disquiet.

"What are you talking about?" Alyssa demands. "Gemma did an amazing job!"

"I'm sure Gemma's a good actress," Mimi says, but her eyes turn steely as she looks at me. "I just don't think that was anything like the real Alyssa."

Under Mimi's gimlet gaze, I squirm, stomach churning with discomfort. And I begin to understand how I'd failed. "Mimi's right. I played the woman I saw on social media, but that's only part of you, Alyssa. Yes, you're as much of a confident fashionista as your online persona. But the real Alyssa is also fiercely loyal, savvy, and generous."

"Yes." Mimi grips Alyssa's hand in hers. "*That's* my Alyssa." The two of them gaze into each other's eyes and seem to forget our presence.

Uncomfortable to be intruding yet again, I look away and find myself staring into Eric's dark eyes. *I might be getting my own tender moment.*

Wang, the driver, lowers the glass partition and announces, "We're here!"

I jump, having lost track of time and where we were. It's dark outside, but there are enough streetlights to see that we've arrived at a tall modern building. A garage door opens noiselessly, and Wang pulls into a garage with a dark, shiny, mirror-smooth floor. He parks in a spot right next to an elegant chrome-and-glass elevator.

We all spill out of the back seat, but my steps falter as I take in the grandeur of the garage. I mean, it's just a frigging *parking garage*, and it's still more posh than most places I've ever been. The people who live in this building are so filthy rich that in spite of my borrowed dress and glamorous makeup, I feel positively provincial.

Alyssa detaches from Mimi to thread her arm through mine. "I grew up here, but I moved into my own apartment in Beijing as soon as I could," she confesses. "There were never other kids my age here. I wish I'd known I had a cousin. I would have liked growing up together."

Alyssa's kindness is just what I needed. "Me too," I say, letting her guide me into the elevator. Inside, there are only three buttons, even though there must be at least twenty floors in a building this tall. *Don't tell me that they have a dedicated elevator.* Of course they do. Just look at Alyssa, swathed in wealth and privilege. But I can't manage any heartfelt scorn. She's just too—*nice.* It's not the first quality one would associate with Alyssa. But when I really think about all I've learned about her tonight—willing to give up everything for Mimi, forgive Eric for his interference, and make me feel like I belong—I have to conclude that Alyssa Chua is a decent, good person.

The elevator glides up and up, giving me plenty of time to get all sweaty with nerves. Alyssa, with her surprising generosity of spirit, may have embraced me with open arms, but the rest of the family might not. Especially Alyssa's mother, who never talks about her sister. It's easy to guess what her reaction will be when she finds out that the prodigal child has returned to threaten her inheritance. She won't want to share all this luxurious expanse of glass and metal with me or my mother. Trying desperately to delay the inevitable, I ask, "Isn't it a little late to visit your parents? Maybe we should wait until tomorrow."

"My mother stays up late," Alyssa replies, "and my father's away on a business trip."

I nod and wipe my damp palms on my dress. The doors of the elevator swoosh open—not into a hallway but into the actual foyer of the penthouse suite. *Yup. Dedicated elevator.*

Unlike the formal opulence of the foyer in the suburban mansion, this foyer is all modern, sleek glass and white and black contrasts. Impractical sheets of framed, clear glass are actually hanging from the ceiling and serve no purpose that I can tell. *Except perhaps to strike terror into the heart of a parent of a small child.* But it's impossible to imagine a child growing up in this coldly beautiful place. No wonder Alyssa never liked it here.

Alyssa sashays into the foyer and beams with delight when an older woman pads into view.

This must be Alyssa's mother. I straighten up and fumble in my head for the right honorific to address her, but I don't really know.

My parents' lessons on polite ways to address my elders never covered the sticky situation of what I'm supposed to call a woman who has renounced her own sister.

It turns out to be a good thing that I don't try out an address since the woman isn't Alyssa's mother after all. Alyssa introduces the woman as the housekeeper. Of course Alyssa's family has servants. It shouldn't come as a surprise, but it does. Alyssa's world of servants and luxury penthouses is so outside my experience.

The housekeeper waves off apologies at how late it is and says only how happy she is to see Alyssa. She seems sincere in her delight over Alyssa's visit, and I get the feeling that she doesn't often make an appearance at her parents' home.

The woman offers to get her mother, and that's when hesitancy creeps into Alyssa's eyes. Is she having second thoughts? Maybe it's occurring to her that her mother might not want to see me.

Then Alyssa glances at me, and her face turns resolute. "Yes. I want my mother to meet Gemma. Please ask her to join us in the living room."

The housekeeper disappears up a spiral staircase, and Alyssa leads the rest of us into the living room, where white leather couches await and floor-to-ceiling windows provide a stunning view of the glittering city.

Alyssa sits on a love seat, and after a beat of hesitation, Mimi sits on the long couch facing the love seat. I sit next to Mimi, and Eric sits next to me.

None of us speak as we choose our seats. It's as if we're in a play, taking our positions based on inaudible, invisible cues.

And we all wait tensely for the next act to begin.

CHAPTER THIRTY-ONE

When a beautiful older woman with soft, sweet features finally wafts down the spiral staircase, all my breath leaves my body in a dizzy rush. *Wow. Oh wow. She looks like my mom!* Except my mom would have been wearing old sweats for lounging around in her own home. This woman is wearing a flowing silk tunic over wide-legged pants. But it's not just the older woman's style that's similar to Alyssa's. She looks as much like Alyssa as I look like my own mother. There's no mistaking this woman for anyone but Alyssa's mom. My aunt.

"Alyssa," my aunt begins, her eyes on her daughter. "What are you doing here?" Then her gaze flickers over to me and stays locked on my face. She comes to a dead stop a few steps away from the bottom of the staircase and clutches the railing as if she suddenly needs its support.

My throat works convulsively around a dry dustiness, but no words, in Chinese or English, emerge.

"Ni shi shui?" she whispers, her face ashen with shock. *Who are you?*

It shouldn't be a hard question to answer, but it takes several tries and a reassuring squeeze of my arm from Eric to find my voice again. "Gemma. Gemma Huang."

"Huang." My aunt slowly descends the last few steps. "I don't know that last name." She sinks next to Alyssa on the love seat. But her eyes don't leave my face. "'Gemma' sounds American, and Alyssa told me that you live in America. Is that true?"

I nod, not trusting my voice. Emotion dams up my throat.

229

"I didn't know Lei went to America," she murmurs, as if she's speaking to herself. Then, with shocking suddenness, she drops her face into her hands and bursts into tears, deep, shuddering sobs racking her body.

Visibly startled, Alyssa puts a comforting hand on her mother's shoulder. After a tense beat, Alyssa says, "I promised Gemma that I would talk to you about . . . about our inheritance." Her voice grows stronger. "Then I decided that I wanted Gemma to know. No matter what."

Inheritance? Alyssa didn't promised to talk to her mother about my inheritance. She promised to try to get answers about my mother. *What's this all about?*

My aunt raises her head. "Alyssa . . . are you sure?"

"I'm sure. Po Po wanted me to bring Gemma here. I think this is why."

My aunt pales in response.

I'm gripping my hands together now, my fingers cramping and my heart frozen in suspense. Mimi and Eric look away uncomfortably, but I lean forward, my whole body wired with tension. "Did my mother steal Wu Zetian's painting? Is that why she was cut off from the family?"

My aunt's eyes are still swimming with tears. "Yes. Your mother did steal that painting." My heart plummets like a bird shot from the sky. Then she says, "But that's not why my sister was cut off from the family."

Alyssa starts. "But, Ma, you told me . . ." Her words trail off at the stricken look on her mother's face. Alyssa's eyes meet mine. "You were right, Gemma. I didn't know the whole truth."

My aunt drops her gaze to her lap. "The biggest regret of my life was losing my mei mei. I should have fought for her. But I was weak." Her mouth trembles as she looks up at Alyssa. "And then I was weak again when you told me that Lei's daughter was in Beijing. All my feelings of shame came back to me. I didn't want you to know what I had done. So I let you believe the lies your grandfather has told you—that Lei was dangerous. That she was banished from the family because she stole a painting. But that was never the real reason. My mei mei never betrayed us. I betrayed her."

The sharp intake of Alyssa's breath barely registers. My own shock spirals through my chest. "Why, then? Why was my mother cut off from the family?"

My aunt looks at me. "That's not my story to tell." *I was this close to finally getting the last pieces of my mother's past!* Angry protest is about to burst from me when she adds, "It's Lei's story. And Delun's too."

Delun. A dull roar fills my ears. "But," I sputter, "Delun is my *father's* name." I've always thought Mom was the reason for the dire warnings to never step foot in China. It hadn't occurred to me that my dad could be part of it.

She nods. "Your father's family name wasn't Huang back then—it was Chuang. Your parents must have changed their name. You see, when your mother met your father, it was the beginning of their love story. But it was also the beginning of a tragedy."

I stare at her. *Tragic love story?* And even my name is a lie? Maybe I don't know my parents at all. And maybe . . .

Maybe my aunt is right. Maybe it *is* my mother's story to tell, after all. In the entire month and a half that I've been in China, I've been chasing down one wild rumor after another, looking for the truth about my mother. All because I was sure my mother would never tell me herself. And I keep hitting dead ends. *I mean, look at me!* I put on diamond earrings, gold heels, and a sparkly minidress just to get here. Now I'm face-to-face with the aunt I've never known, hounding her for a truth she can't give me. Alyssa. Eric. My aunt. Everyone's told me that they don't know the whole story. The only person who does know is Mom. It's time I asked her. Tomorrow, on the Mid-Autumn Festival holiday, I'll tell my mother everything. And I'll ask her for the same. For her story.

My aunt is watching me apprehensively. "Does . . . your mother ever mention me?" Alyssa wraps an arm around her mother's shoulders but stays silent.

"I'm sorry." My hands twist in my lap. "No. She didn't mention you." With a hot lump in my throat, I say, "I don't even know your name. What do I call you?" It's hardly my most pressing question, but it feels weird that I don't even know what to call my aunt. Chinese terms of address for relatives are ridiculously complicated, often based on maternal and paternal lines, birth order, degrees of separation, or all of the above.

"My name is Jun." My aunt smiles through her tears. "Call me Yi Ma."

"Yi Ma," I say tentatively, and my aunt's smile grows broader. I turn to Alyssa. The terms of address for cousins are easier, and I already know the term for older female cousin. "Biao Jie."

Alyssa blinks back tears as she looks at me. "Call me Jie Jie."

Alyssa asking me to call her "older sister" instead of "older cousin" makes me sniffle. My aunt gives Alyssa a side hug, and their closeness makes me miss my own mother. The hot knot in my chest tightens.

Then Alyssa says, "And you're Mei Mei to me. My little sister."

That does it. *Jiemei. Sisters.* My hand goes to the jade pendant at my throat that has the character for "mei" on it, and my sniffle turns into a torrent of jagged crying. Eric squeezes my shoulder. Mimi is looking lost in all this, probably wishing she could go to Alyssa, so I clasp Mimi's hand. That's all Mimi needs to tear up and grip my hand back.

My aunt's eyes dart from my pendant to Alyssa's pendant. "I'm glad that Alyssa gave you your mother's pendant, Gemma." She smiles wistfully. "When we were young, your mother and I made a promise to each other that we would pass our pendants on to our daughters. It was silly, really. How could we know we'd have daughters or that mine would be the eldest and hers the youngest? But our wish came true." Her smile fades. "When your mother sent me that picture of you eighteen years ago, I wanted to send her that pendant to pass on to you, but . . . I knew Lei wouldn't want to hear from me." Moisture tracks down her cheeks. "You have no idea how much I've missed my mei mei."

"My mother misses you too. She *will* want to hear from you." My heart clenches around a tide of emotion.

My aunt's face shutters down. "Lei won't want to talk to me. She hasn't forgotten the past. Or forgiven me."

"That's not true," I say with certainty. "You said that 'Gemma' is an American-sounding name, and I suppose it is. My father gave me the name. He calls me his 'gem.'" I blush, but my dad's embarrassing nickname for me isn't important right now. "My mother gave me my Chinese name. She named me 'Jun.'"

My aunt puts her hand to her mouth and sags like a crumpled paper doll. "She gave you my name? Why?"

"She must have missed her jie jie if she named me after you."

"I was not a good jie jie." My aunt averts her eyes. "I let her down," she whispers. "I failed my mei mei. I was weak."

My heart twists with sympathy, and I stand without conscious thought. "Yi Ma," I say, "my mother told me that Jun means 'king.' A leader." I walk over to her and crouch down. "She told me that the strongest person she ever knew was named Jun. She said that she wanted me to have the strength of kings. The strength of my namesake. Whatever you did or didn't do, my mother forgave you a long time ago."

"Jun." She touches my cheek with a butterfly brush of her finger. "My mei mei named you well. *You* are the strong one. You lead us all out of the pain of the past. To hope." Then my aunt gathers me into her arms. It's different from being held by my own mother.

But it's still like coming home.

At last, my aunt pulls away from me and turns to Alyssa. "You said you wanted Gemma to know about her inheritance. I think you're right."

Alyssa stands. "Gemma, I have something to show you. It's why my po po wanted me to bring you here."

Confusion mixed with electric anticipation makes my body thrum. What does Alyssa want to show me, and what does it have to do with my inheritance?

My aunt nods. "Go ahead. I'll stay here." Her face looks suddenly weary.

Alyssa turns to Mimi and Eric. "Er, do you two want to maybe look at the view from the rooftop patio?" It's a blatant ploy to *not* leave her mother and girlfriend alone in the same room together.

"I'll show you up," my aunt says to them politely, but her attention is still on me. Thankfully, she isn't really registering Mimi and Eric's presence. But if she did, would she even recognize them? Mimi and Eric aren't as high profile as Alyssa. Maybe they've flown under my aunt's radar. *As the grandchildren of the woman who regularly snubs my aunt in society charity circles and recently said nasty things about Alyssa to a gossip site reporter?* Yeah, fat chance. It's only a matter of time before my aunt realizes who Mimi and Eric are.

Mimi leaps to her feet so fast that several pillows fall from the couch. "No need," she says breathlessly. "We can find our way." Red in the face, she puts the pillows back on the couch and scurries to the staircase. Clearly, she doesn't want to be left with my aunt either. Especially since there's a strong possibility that my aunt could recognize them.

Slightly bemused, my aunt says, "Well, all right then."

Eric squeezes my hand and murmurs to me under his breath. "Gemma, this is a lot. Do you want me to go with you?"

Warmth spreads through me at his words of support. "No, I'm OK." Whatever I'm about to find out, it's clearly meant to be between family. But I grip his hand hard, and when I let go, it's with a sharp pang. "Thank you."

Eric leaves with Mimi, and Alyssa leads me away. Glancing over my shoulder, I catch a glimpse of my aunt looking spent as she leans back into the couch.

Alyssa takes me into the elevator, and puzzled, I ask, "Are we leaving, then?"

"No." She opens a small compartment below the three silver buttons to reveal what looks like a fingerprint scanner. Then she presses her forefinger onto the pad, and it lights up all green. The elevator glides smoothly down the floors. "We're going to a sublevel that no one outside the family even knows about. My mother had it included in the architectural plans—we own the building, you know."

This is getting seriously intense. A dedicated elevator is one thing, but a fingerprint scanner to access a secret sublevel in a building they own? That's not just some private convenience for the rich—that's a whole new order of paranoia.

Why all this secrecy? What is Alyssa about to show me?

The elevator stops, and the doors glide open. Alyssa steps out first. Moistening my lips, I follow her out.

"Lights," she calls out, and a warm, soft white glow comes on.

I can't believe what I'm seeing.

CHAPTER THIRTY-TWO

Ink paintings of lush landscapes. Scrolls of calligraphy. Marble lions. Horses carved out of green jade. Stone Buddhas. Glazed and painted vases. I could be in one of the galleries of my mother's museum.

I swallow my awe and try to speak. "What . . ." I have to clear my throat before I can continue. "What is all this?"

"Tang dynasty art." Alyssa's expression is unreadable.

I walk forward in a daze, my footsteps echoing on the marble floors, and then I stop still in front of a stone Buddha. Resting on a white marble pedestal, it's about three feet tall. And it looks familiar. All the hairs on my arm rise as my skin prickles. "I've seen this before. In a picture at an exhibit in the Forbidden City's Imperial Palace Museum." My head swivels to Alyssa, who comes to stand next to me. "The informational placard said the picture was of a gigantic Buddha carved into a limestone cave at the Longmen Grottoes in Henan Province."

"Yes. That's the Grand Vairocana Buddha. She's also called the Eastern Mona Lisa or Eastern Venus." Alyssa watches me closely. "More importantly, the statue was commissioned by and said to be carved in the likeness of Empress Wu Zetian."

"Is this"—I gesture to the smaller statue—"a copy then?"

"No." Alyssa contemplates the statue in front of us. "It would be more accurate to say that the statue at the Longmen Grottoes is a copy of this one. This is the template for the larger one."

All my breath packs tightly into my lungs. "What are you saying?" I choke out in disbelief.

She turns to me, her face solemn. "You're standing in the middle of Wu Zetian's personal art collection. The art of the women the empress supported. All thought to be lost or destroyed."

My breath whooshes out of me. That would be a collection beyond price. I remember standing in the sparse exhibit on Wu Zetian in the Palace Museum and thinking of how much art was lost during the Cultural Revolution. Shit. An imperial art collection from the Tang dynasty has been sitting like a ticking time bomb in their basement for who knows how long. Questions buzz in my head. How long have they had this collection? How could such a collection of art from the Tang dynasty survive intact when so little else did? I manage to push one of these questions past numb lips. "How did you get all this?"

"Gemma," Alyssa says gently, "it's time I told you who you are."

Alyssa's words strike me to the core and resonate deep inside me. "Who am I?" I whisper.

"A direct descendant of Empress Wu Zetian."

Lightness overtakes my body. Empress Wu Zetian. The only female ruler of China. My ancestress. "Are you joking? Because it's not funny."

Her face cracks into a small smile. "It's true. This is Wu Zetian's art passed down to her descendants from daughter to daughter. You, me, your mother, my mother, our grandmother, her mother before her, and all through the generations—in a single unbroken line. This is our inheritance, Gemma."

Alyssa's words from the nightclub rush into my head. *You don't even know what it means that your mother stole that painting . . . A painting said to have been commissioned by Empress Wu, the woman who dared to be a ruler! You have no idea how dangerous owning that painting would be.*

And then I know.

"This is where the painting originally came from. The one Eric and Mimi's grandfather had." My stomach clenches in anger because everyone wanted me to believe that my mother was a thief. "Here from the secret art collection of Wu Zetian! My mother's inheritance. My mother didn't steal anything. She was taking back what was hers."

Alyssa drops her eyes. "Yes. And I knew that all along. I'm sorry."

My knees go wobbly. My mother isn't a thief. But relief doesn't make the hardness in my stomach go away. "But why did you let me believe that my mother had no right to that painting? That she stole it?"

"Because . . ." Alyssa pauses and takes a shaky breath. "Ever since I can remember, I was told that your mother took that painting for selfish reasons. That she had no consideration for what it would mean to the family if anyone found out what we inherited from Wu Zetian. And I never questioned it." She flushes. "Not until you came to Beijing, pushing me to find out the truth. Now I'm questioning everything. Especially what my gong gong told me."

My blood runs cold. "It's our grandfather who has the most to lose if anyone finds out about Empress Wu's art collection, isn't it? You said that inherited wealth like this art could jeopardize his standing in the Communist Party."

"Exactly," she says. "Come look at this." She takes my arm and leads me past a row of landscapes to a blank wall. There are two spotlights hanging above, spaced far enough apart to account for two paintings. Two paintings that aren't there. "When my mother had this gallery built, she left this wall blank for the two paintings that were lost."

"Two? I thought it was just one painting that my mother took."

"Your mother got one of the paintings back, but there were two paintings that went missing during the time of the Cultural Revolution. These were my po po's favorites, and she described them to me. They were paintings of two different court ladies. One was a lady wearing an embroidered yellow dress playing a zither. The other—"

"A lady wearing a red dress with a blue-green shawl and matching sash, writing calligraphy."

"Oh, you've seen it, then!" She sounds almost envious.

"Yeah, I've seen it." There's no longer any doubt that the painting in my mother's office is the original Tang dynasty painting from Empress Wu's art collection. The same painting that my mother took back from Eric's family. "My mom has it in our house."

"I'm glad your mother has it," Alyssa says quietly. "I . . . I hope to see it someday."

"But what happened to the other painting?"

"Probably destroyed."

"You mean," I say in a taut voice, "destroyed when our grandfather accused Eric and Mimi's grandfather of being a counterrevolutionary and set the Red Guard on him?"

Alyssa stares at the two blank spots on the wall. "Gong Gong always told me that Mimi's ye ye stole those paintings from us." She touches the empty wall. "But after I talked to you in my limo, I went to see Gong Gong. I asked him if that was the truth."

"You confronted your grandfather because of me?" I stare at her incredulously.

"Not just you," she says. "Mimi heard what you said to me at my nightclub."

My own words come back to me. *Maybe you don't know the whole truth either. If I were you, I'd ask your grandfather.*

Alyssa's hand trails down the empty wall. "So, I asked Gong Gong if he had done it. Framed Mimi's ye ye by planting those two paintings in his home."

I shiver with revulsion. What a terrible thing to have done to anyone. And Eric and Mimi's grandfather had been his best friend. "What did our grandfather say?"

"He denied it, of course. Then he demanded to know why I was suddenly asking these questions. I panicked." Alyssa turns to me, her eyes shadowed. "I was afraid that he'd find out about Mimi. Maybe even cut me off from the family. And then I realized it didn't matter. I love Mimi. That's when I ran off with her."

"I see," I breathe. That's why Alyssa didn't get back to me. She wasn't just escaping with her girlfriend to a romantic retreat—she was reeling from an epic showdown with our grandfather. "Do you think our grandfather did it?"

"I don't know." Alyssa meets my eyes steadily. "But I told Mimi everything. About all this too." She gestures at the art around us. "I'm lucky that she's still with me."

Reminded of Mimi's presence, we both stare up, as if we can see past the many floors to where Mimi and Eric, out on the rooftop patio, are waiting for our return. "We should get back," I say.

She nods, pats the blank wall, and turns to leave. Casually, she says, "I've always wondered who the two ladies in the paintings are. I think one of them must be Princess Taiping. It would make sense for Wu Zetian to commission a portrait of her only surviving daughter."

At this point, there's no point in picking my jaw off the floor. Not with Alyssa casually dropping little tidbits about our royal ancestors like she's discussing what she had for breakfast.

I take one last look at the two blank spaces. I'm descended from a long line of daughters going back to Wu Zetian. It still doesn't seem real.

Arm in arm with my cousin, we walk past the dangerous riches of our inheritance. As we step into the elevator, a thought occurs to me. If one of the paintings was of Princess Taiping . . .

Then who is the other lady?

CHAPTER THIRTY-THREE

My aunt is sitting straight and stiff on the couch in the living room when Alyssa and I return. Alyssa goes upstairs to fetch Mimi and Eric, leaving me alone with my aunt.

"You know now?" she asks, her eyes searching mine anxiously.

I nod mutely. Then I think of my mother walking away from that art downstairs—her ancestral inheritance. All the muscles in my body tighten painfully. For her, that would have been like having a limb torn off.

As if she can read my thoughts, my aunt says, "It was Lei who was supposed to inherit the guardianship of Wu Zetian's legacy. It was never supposed to be me. I am the eldest, but my mei mei—she loved art."

"She still does." I sit down next to her. "She's a museum director now."

My aunt's face brightens, and she takes my hand in hers. "Tell me all about my mei mei. Please."

I'm in the middle of answering my aunt's questions about my mother's life in America when Alyssa, Mimi, and Eric return downstairs. My aunt reluctantly lets go of my hand as I scoot back to the long couch to let Alyssa resume her place on the love seat.

My aunt tears her attention from me with a visible effort. "Gemma, are these your friends?" She smiles distractedly at Mimi and Eric, who sit down again on either side of me on the long couch. "I'm so sorry I've neglected my guests. Would you like anything to drink? Eat?"

They both decline politely.

After an awkward pause, I say, "This is Eric and Mimi. They're brother and sister." There's a lot I left out of that introduction, and my aunt still looks puzzled. But what can I say? *Eric is my not-yet-but-maybe boyfriend, and Mimi is your daughter's definitely-yes-but-secret girlfriend. And, oh yeah, they're both part of the family that have been our family's enemy since the Cultural Revolution.*

An even more awkward silence descends as everyone evades my aunt's eyes. Apparently, no one else wants to explain the situation either.

Then my aunt's gaze sharpens on Eric and Mimi, and she gasps. "I know who you are. Eric and Mimi *Liu*."

I tense up, and Alyssa looks like she's been frozen in place. *I guess it would've been too much to hope that she'd continue to not recognize them.* Eric and Mimi exchange glances and turn back to my aunt, wary and silent.

My aunt studies them intently for a moment. "You both have the look of your father. I knew him from a long time ago—before this silly feud with your grandmother started." She doesn't bring up the larger feud—the one that started with my grandfather. But she *does* glance meaningfully at Alyssa. *Oh crap. She knows about the gossip site report.* "At least it *was* silly before your grandmother attacked my daughter. Now it's serious."

Alyssa asks, "What happened? What did I miss?" *Poor Alyssa. She's in for a nasty shock.*

Eric swallows and tells my aunt, "My nai nai promises to stop talking to reporters."

Mimi closes her eyes in resignation, muttering something too low to catch.

"She had better stop," my aunt says grimly. Then, to my utter surprise, she smiles. It's a bit strained, but it's still a smile. "But that has nothing to do with you two. I'm glad that you both came here with my niece."

Alyssa takes a deep breath. "Mimi's not with Gemma. She's with me."

"Your friend?" My aunt glances at Mimi.

Mimi stiffens. I touch her hand, and it's ice-cold.

Alyssa stands, and in an unconscious echo, I do too. Eric starts to scoot next to Mimi, but I stop him with a quick shake of my head. Understanding crosses his face, and he removes himself to an armchair. Alyssa and I exchange seats, with her next to Mimi and me next to my aunt. We're taking our places again, this time for a new scene.

"You gave me an ultimatum," Alyssa says to Mimi, clasping her hands in hers. "Get serious or get out, you said. If I do this, will your conditions be met? Will you believe I'm serious?"

"Are you sure?" Mimi asks in a low voice. "You don't have to do this."

My aunt, who's been tracking this exchange, grows still by my side.

"I've never been more sure of anything," Alyssa says. "Or anyone."

Mimi smiles tremulously. "In that case, my conditions are met."

Alyssa turns to her mother and says, "Mimi's my girlfriend." *Of course, my aunt would have to be a fool not to have figured that out already.* "I love her and need to know that my family will accept her."

I hold my breath in anticipation. I so desperately want a happy ending for Alyssa and Mimi that I can hardly stand the suspense of waiting for my aunt's response.

My aunt finally speaks. "Many years ago, I listened as my sister told our father something very similar about the young man she loved."

Mom . . . and Dad? I *have* to get that story out of them. With an effort, I bring my attention back to what's happening now.

My aunt's words are slow and cracked with emotion. "I did nothing all those years ago to prevent what happened afterward." Then her eyes go steely with resolve. "But this time, there *is* something I can do."

The room practically crackles with tension as we all wait to hear her verdict.

Very simply, my aunt says, "Welcome to our family, Mimi."

Before we leave, my aunt invites me to the Mid-Autumn Festival dinner tomorrow (well, *today*, technically, since it's about two in the morning by the time we leave my aunt's place). I'm nervous as all hell about meeting my grandfather, but I want to meet my grandmother. And honestly? I actually *do* want to meet my grandfather. His secrecy and lies have caused so much heartbreak—it's about time someone called him on it.

As soon as the black car pulls out of the parking garage with the four of us in the back seat, Alyssa checks out the gossip sites. Then she bursts into sudden laughter. "Mimi, I had no idea your grandmother had it in her!" Her reaction is not what I expected, but pretty on point for Alyssa. Wiping tears of mirth from her eyes, Alyssa adjusts her midriff-baring top and takes a selfie of all four of us in the back of the car. Then she posts it to Weibo. "Wait until she sees *that*."

"Nai Nai isn't on Weibo," Mimi says regretfully.

"Then we'll just have to make sure she sees it, won't we?" Eric says with a spice of mischief that makes me puddle into absolute goo.

Wang takes Alyssa and Mimi back to their mansion hideout before taking Eric and me back to my hotel. After Wang drops us off, we stand outside the hotel, staring at each other awkwardly. My heart beats hummingbird fast now that I'm finally alone with him.

Of course, now that the moment has come, I don't know what to say. "Where did you park your car?" I groan inwardly. *Really?* Is that all I can think of to say to him?

"In the hotel garage."

"Oh. OK." Apparently, I now have the conversational skills of a toddler when it comes to talking to Eric.

Eric shifts from foot to foot. "It seemed like a good place to park." *Wow, he's just as bad at this.* But *why* are we both so bad at this? I mean, it's *talking*—something we used to do easily.

I look him right in the eye. "Is our truce still good?" I'm thinking of what he said to me as we were leaving Alyssa's nightclub. *Listen, neither of us know the whole story of the painting or what happened to make your mother leave. Until we do . . . or even if we do . . . can we call a truce? Be friends?* I still don't know what happened to make my mother leave. But I now know more about what happened to Eric's grandfather. One day, I'll face the same decision Alyssa faced with Mimi. Whether or not to tell Eric that my grandfather might have framed his grandfather to hide the secret of Wu Zetian's legacy. But that's not a decision I need to make now.

Taking my hands in his, Eric says, "If Mimi and Alyssa are going to have a chance together, this rift between our families has to be mended. That means I'm done with the war between our families. You and I don't need a truce. Not when there isn't a war anymore."

A heaviness lifts from my chest. No matter what my family has done to his—it's not our responsibility to continue their fight.

Then I straighten my shoulders. *No more hiding from the truth.* The truth is that I like Eric Liu. He put aside any differences he had with Alyssa to support Mimi, and he was there for me tonight too. He's a wonderful, kind guy who might not be the height of coolness like Ken was, but it doesn't matter that Eric's not my "type." What matters is that he's the guy I want. And maybe it's a bad idea because I'm leaving Beijing in a month. But I'll kick myself forever if I don't try to find out if he feels the same way I do.

Now that I've made up my mind, I'm desperate to act. If only I knew how. "It must be pretty late." *Dammit!* Now Eric will think I'm hinting that he should leave.

Sure enough, he checks his phone and says, "Yeah, it's three in the morning. I should get going."

I swallow, and all the blood in my body rushes to my face, making it erupt with heat. "No."

He turns startled eyes toward me. "No? No, what?"

A glib evasion is already on my tongue. *Sorry! Just thinking out loud about something else!* It takes every ounce of bravery to say instead, "Don't go."

His pupils darken. "Gemma," he says, brushing his thumb against my cheek and making my breath stutter.

I cup the back of Eric's head and pull him toward me. His body melts into mine, and as soon as his lips touch mine, I forget everything except for the lick of fire in my belly and the storm of electricity raging over my skin. *I was completely nuts to wait this long for this.*

Eric lowers his head to trace my jaw with a line of kisses, and my knees turn into goo. I dig my fingers into his back.

"Eric," I gasp, and he drags his mouth back up to mine and kisses me, urgent and hard.

When we break apart at last, we're both panting, the mingled steam of our breath rising into the night air. I nestle against Eric's chest, fighting for control over the wayward beat of my heart.

"I've been wanting to kiss you since I saw you in that suit," Eric says, his breath still ragged and his heart pounding as fast as mine. "When you came out of the dressing room . . ."

I knew I looked good. "By the way, I'm having second thoughts about that suit," I say casually.

"The suit's yours." Eric smiles at me. "It's now official. The war between our families is over, and there's nothing about this night I regret. Not when I'm finally where I've wanted to be."

"What? Outside my hotel room at three in the morning?" I quip.

"Here, with you, Gemma Huang." He draws me into his arms. "This is where I want to be—anywhere, anytime. As long as it's with you."

"Eric Liu," I say, putting my cheek against his and savoring the slight rasp of stubble against my skin, "I feel the exact same way."

CHAPTER THIRTY-FOUR

Mid-Autumn Festival dinner with my new family comes too quickly.

I'm a nervous mess. After all, I will be coming face-to-face with my grandmother, who has masterminded this family reunion. And then there's my grandfather—who knows I'm coming but might not even want me there.

My palms grow itchy with sweat as the housekeeper leads me upstairs to the rooftop patio. We emerge into a glassed-off sunroom filled with ceramic urns and lounge chairs. Blinking in wonder, I look out to the rooftop patio. *Patio* is definitely not the right word. There are stone fountains in the shape of lions with water pouring out of their mouths, flowering potted trees, miniature pagodas, and stone bridges. *It's like the Summer Palace up here.*

Alyssa is running toward me from one of the manicured paths. She flings open the French doors. "Gemma! Come on—we're having dinner on the east patio so we can see the moon rise from the east."

"Your patio has a patio?" I tease her. "That's a whole new level of fancy."

"Joke all you want, but wait until you see the view of the city."

We step onto the stone path between potted trees, and I see what she means. Tall skyscrapers soar into the evening sky, and a twinkling lightscape sweeps the horizon. "Wow!" I breathe in awe.

"See?" she says smugly.

She tucks her arm into the crook of mine and leads me along the path. "Gong Gong knows you're here. He's under strict orders from my po po and mother to behave. It will all be OK."

The tinkle of water from stone fountains and the city below us almost distracted me from what awaits me, but my nervousness comes back at Alyssa's words. I'd believe her more if her arm weren't trembling. "As long as I don't bring up my mother, right?" Guilt worms into me even though I'm planning to call my parents when they wake up in a few hours. It will be the morning of Mid-Autumn Festival for them. Meanwhile, here I am on the night of Mid-Autumn Festival—about to meet Mom's estranged family without her.

"That's up to you," Alyssa surprises me by saying. "I'm done trying to tiptoe around my gong gong."

My eyebrows rise. "Does that mean you're going to tell him about Mimi?"

"No." Her mouth twists. "Mom won't let him kick me out of the family, but Gong Gong will be . . . unpleasant. He's all about his standing in the government, and there's still that whole feud with Mimi's family." She pauses to reflect. "Maybe I'll tell Po Po about Mimi. I already told my dad on WeChat."

"How did that go?"

"My dad told me to be discreet," she says dryly, "and I promised not to post pictures on Weibo of Mimi and me making out, so I guess we're cool. He says we'll talk more when he gets back from his business trip."

I don't get to ask more questions because we've crossed a stone bridge and reached the east patio.

There's still a little time before moonrise, but red lanterns have been hung all around the raised wooden patio. Their glow provides all the light I need to see three people sitting around a rectangular teak table on yellow silk-cushioned chairs.

My aunt sits facing us. An older elegant woman in a long black dress who must be my grandmother sits across from her. An elderly man with white bushy eyebrows sits at the head of the table. *My grandfather.* The one who disowned my mother and betrayed Eric and Mimi's grandfather. Nausea sweeps over me.

Then my grandmother turns around and smiles gently at me. "Wai sun nu, ni hui jia la."

Her words hit me right in the heart. *Granddaughter, you've come home.* "What do I call you?" I ask, but her forehead wrinkles. Maybe she doesn't speak English. I repeat the question in Chinese.

Confusion fades from her face, and she responds in Chinese. "Jiao wo Po Po." Her smile wobbles.

Call me Po Po. A hot core of emotion wells up in me.

My grandfather slowly gets to his feet. "Welcome," he says in accented English.

It's a mild night in mid-September, so there's no reason for the goose bumps rising coldly on my skin. My whole time in Beijing, I've pushed my way through obstacles, searching for answers about my past. I've finally reached the man who has been responsible for every dead end, every blocked question. But now that I'm here, I have just one question. "Is my mother welcome here too? Because I can't stay if she's not welcome."

A tense silence falls over the patio. Alyssa gives my arm a heartfelt squeeze of support.

"Lao Gong, ni da ying wo," my po po says. *Husband, you promised me.*

My aunt raises blazing eyes to her father. "Yes, you promised us both that Lei could come home."

My grandfather's bushy eyebrows draw down over his sharp eyes as he peers at us all. "Fine," he says at last. "It's been long enough."

A little half-assed, but I'll take it. My exasperation at my grandfather is mixed with relief. I would never claim a home that didn't welcome my mother.

"Will you join us, Gemma?" my aunt asks.

Not trusting my voice, I nod and sit next to my po po. This is my family now. And soon, I'll call my mother and tell her that it is hers again as well.

Alyssa sits beside me and grabs my hand. She's bouncing up and down, squeezing my hand so hard that it's cutting off my circulation, but I can't fault her for her enthusiasm.

A servant brings out a tray of rolled-up towels and uses tongs to give me one. It's warm and scented with roses. I accept with thanks but am confused about what to do with it. I peek at Alyssa to see her wiping her hands with the towel.

She winks at me. "You're going to make some joke about how fancy this is, aren't you?"

"No," I say dryly, "because then you'll send a box of these rose-scented towels to my hotel room tomorrow. But seriously, thank you for everything. I just wish there was something I could do for *you.*"

Alyssa looks at me in surprise. "You don't need to thank me for anything! This is as much yours as it is mine, remember? You're my family."

Fondness for my cousin swells up in me. "I can't believe I'm leaving in a month. I'll miss you." I never thought I'd be so sad at the thought of leaving Alyssa. It seems like just yesterday that I was being mobbed by her fans and cursing her name.

Her face falls. "I don't know how I'll be able to face another family dinner without anyone my age to talk to."

Maybe there *is* something I can do for her. After all, this whole

Romeo and Juliet thing must be getting old for Alyssa and Mimi. Patting her on the shoulder, I say, "I hear you." Then I turn to the adults. "I was wondering if I could ask for a favor."

My aunt translates for my po po, and once Po Po understands my question, she agrees at once before asking what the favor is.

My grandfather is more cautious. "What favor?"

My heart beats faster. "I met some friends in the city, and I was wondering if we could invite them and their parents over for dinner sometime."

Alyssa kicks me under the table. Hard.

Don't worry, I try to telecommunicate to her. *I've got this.* After a second, she gives me a slow nod. Alyssa's putting her trust in me. *I'd better not blow this.*

My aunt's mouth falls open and then snaps shut. She knows what I'm up to. Her gaze swivels to Alyssa and then back to me. My palms grow wet. According to Eric, it's my aunt and his grandmother who've continued the feud through their high-society snubs. Accepting Mimi is one thing—but will my aunt accept the whole family? At last she says, "That's an excellent idea."

My grandfather shrugs. "Shi ni de jia," he says to my aunt. *It's your house.*

"Great." Mentally, I crack my knuckles. *Time to put those acting chops to good use.* As innocently as I can manage, I say, "Their names are Eric and Mimi Liu. When should I invite them?"

My grandfather pins me with a glare. "The *Liu* family?!"

I pretend I don't notice his outraged reaction. "I met Eric when I was sightseeing at the Forbidden City. He thought I was Alyssa!" I laugh. "Isn't that funny? Anyway, we hit it off." *My request will make more sense if my grandfather thinks Eric and I are romantically involved. . . . Wait, that's actually true.* Well, I'm a better actor when I'm not outright lying. "I'd love to invite him and his sister over.

I guess Eric already knows our family?" I lean back and watch my grandfather squirm.

My aunt leaps into the breach. "I would love to have your friends and their family over to *my* house." She holds my grandfather's gaze as she stresses the part about it being her house.

Way to go, Yi Ma!

Po Po asks for a translation, and my aunt starts catching her up.

Alyssa's eyes are bright with hope and a dash of mischief. "Gemma won't be in Beijing for much longer. The least we could do is invite her friends over before she leaves."

My grandfather has had enough. He bursts into Chinese. The gist of it is: "*Over my dead body! You're all ganging up against me! What kind of trick is this?*"

Well, it was worth a shot. My heart drops, but what did I think was going to happen? One dinner invitation wasn't going to mend a decades-long feud anyway.

Alyssa leans over and whispers, "Thanks for trying."

My aunt's face is grim as she finishes her translation of the conversation for Po Po. Hopefully, she'll say something to support us.

Then Po Po bangs her hand on the table and glares at my grandfather. "Gou la!" *Enough.* She starts speaking rapid Chinese—too fast for me to follow, so Alyssa translates for me. "This feud has gone on long enough. We were all friends once, and Peng is dead now. I will not continue the war with his children or grandchildren. That war is in the past, and I will not allow it to damage our granddaughter's happiness." Po Po's gaze shifts to Alyssa when she says the last part. Alyssa falters and barely manages to finish translating.

I remember then what Alyssa had said about her grandmother. *Po Po follows me on Weibo.* The images of Mimi in the background of Alyssa's Weibo posts. Holy shit. My grandmother knows about Mimi.

"Jing tian wan shang, wo men qing Liu jia," Po Po says. It's a good thing that I know enough Chinese to understand that Po Po said that she will invite the Liu family over tonight. Because Alyssa is apparently too shocked to translate it for me.

My grandfather gapes at my grandmother, but he doesn't argue with her.

"It's settled then," my aunt says. "We will welcome Gemma's friends to our home tonight. After all, this is Zhong Qiu Jie— Mid-Autumn Festival. A time for reconnection and—" Suddenly, all the air seems to whoosh right out of her. "Family," she finishes weakly, her gaze frozen on something in the distance over my shoulder. Everyone turns to look.

It's *my mother.*

CHAPTER THIRTY-FIVE

'm in such deep shit. But my feet don't seem to register how much trouble I'm in. Because I'm running as hard as I can to where my mother is standing at the foot of a stone bridge. When I reach her, I burrow right into her warmth. "How did you know I was here?" My mouth is as dry as dust.

"I know my daughter. I knew something was wrong." Mom sounds mad as all hell, but her arms come around me to hold me tightly, and that's all I care about. "And your agent finally coughed up the information that you were in Beijing for a movie." She takes a deep breath. "Daughter, you lied to me." Then she bites out each word again in Chinese. "Nu er, ni pian wo." All in English and then repeated in Chinese.

No doubt about it. Mom is *definitely* at DEFCON 1.

"I'm sorry, Ma." My chest rises and falls with a deep, fortifying breath. "I'm sorry I lied to you."

"But why?" she asks. "Why did you lie? Was it really because of the movie?"

"At first, it was the movie," I admit. "But then it was because I was finding out so many confusing things. And I still don't know what it was that you did. Why you had to leave your family and China."

"We'll talk about it later." Her body tense as a wire, she's already turning away from me and toward her estranged family. They're too far away for me to see their expressions, but they must be freaking out about my mom's sudden appearance.

From force of habit, I'm about to let my mom evade my questions yet again. But then resolve crystallizes like ice in my stomach. I've fought too hard to know her past to wait any longer. I need to know why my mother was banished from her homeland—which was my banishment too, though I never realized it. No matter how painful it is, my family's past is my inheritance. "Ma, tell me what happened. Please. Tell me your story."

My mom turns back to me. Gently, she cups my face in her hand. "My past is so painful, and I made so many mistakes. I don't want to burden you with it."

"Ma, all my life I've wanted to come here—to China. To know where I come from and feel like I belong somewhere. But that's not what happened when I first came here. Not until I met my relatives." The rest of the family is still watching us from a distance, but I ignore them. This moment should be just for me and my mother a while longer. "Even then, there was something missing. Not knowing my past makes me feel . . . nanguo." "Nanguo" is a Chinese word that means sad and uncomfortable all at once—like your skin is bursting from grief—and it's exactly how I feel. "I won't know where I come from and where I belong until I know your past."

"I see." Tears sparkle in my mother's eyes. "You have to understand—I grew up rich and spoiled in a place like this." Her hand drops from my face, and she makes a sweeping gesture that encompasses the rooftop pleasure garden. "I never thought of anyone but myself. The Tiananmen Square protests changed all that."

My body seizes up with astonishment. "You . . . you were there in Tiananmen Square? During the massacre too?"

Her face empties of emotion. "Yes. I lost friends that day." The thought of my mother fleeing from bullets and tanks in that bloody massacre sends chills through my body. Somberly, she says, "I was afraid I would lose your father that day."

"Dad?" My voice goes thready. "He was there *too?*"

"It was how I met him—at the Tiananmen Square protests."

My mother being a revolutionary is one thing. But my kind, gentle father? There's only one explanation. I'm dreaming all this, and any minute now I'll wake up in a cold sweat in my hotel room bed. Surreptitiously, I pinch myself. *Any minute now.* "But," I say as I fail to wake up, "you told me you weren't there!"

"I never said that."

No, what she'd said was that *it was forbidden.* Forbidden by my grandfather. And like an idiot, I assumed that meant she hadn't been there. I remember what Eric told me. *Your grandfather is a high-ranking Communist Party official. No daughter of his would have taken part in those protests.* "Is that why you were kicked out of the family—because my grandfather didn't want you at the protests?"

"That was only part of it." Her gaze narrows on the patio, where my grandfather watches us, and her voice drops, even though he can't hear us at this distance. "My father—your grandfather—was a proud, powerful man, and Delun was nobody, a poor student."

"My grandfather didn't approve of my father?" Anger sparks in me, even though my aunt had already told me this. But how could anyone *not* approve of my father?

"It was worse than that." My mom grips her hands tightly together. "Thousands were arrested after the massacre, and your dad was one of them. Your grandfather had him sent to a labor camp." *Just a moment—my dad in prison?!* "Then your grandfather lied and told me that he'd had Delun executed as a counterrevolutionary. All to keep your father away from me."

Horror chokes my breath. Even after all I've learned about him, I still can't believe that my grandfather would do something so awful. My stomach sickens sourly at the thought of my father in a labor camp—and my mother thinking he was dead. It makes sense now.

My aunt's refusal to see me when I first came to Beijing. My po po fainting from shock when Alyssa asked to go look for me.

But it wasn't because of what my mother had done. It was their own guilt. "My aunt and grandmother knew. They knew Dad was still alive in a labor camp. And they let you believe he was dead."

"Yes." Just one terrible word. But it explains everything.

Oh, my heart. My mother wasn't cut off from her family. She'd left them. Because they'd betrayed her.

"I got Delun out," Mom says grimly. *How in the world did my upright, law-abiding mother spring my father from prison?* "But your grandfather had already sentenced him as an enemy of the people— so we fled to Hong Kong. Then we had to leave Hong Kong for the U.S. before it reverted back to China's control in 1997. If we hadn't, your father would have been arrested and imprisoned again."

Again, the thought of my father in prison makes me ill. *Dad could have ended up like Eric's grandfather, with his bent bones and ill health.* But that's not what happened to my dad. My mother saved him, and she lost her family and home because of it. "Ma," I say, "it's time to come home."

"They don't want me." Her voice is cold.

"They do—at least Yi Ma and Po Po do. They'll be on your side this time. But it's your fight." That was what Eilene had been trying to tell me—that she would be on my side, but it was my fight.

Surprise flashes in my mother's eyes. "What do you mean, Gemma?"

I look at the small, distant figures on the patio. Po Po. Yi Ma. Alyssa. My aunt and grandmother stood up for Alyssa. *They'll stand up for my mother now.* Eilene might have been right about me, but that doesn't mean she was *entirely* right. It's not always about learning to stand up for yourself. Sometimes, it's not just one person's fight. Sometimes, it's sisters and mothers and daughters together.

Thousands of students facing down a tank in the shadow of the red Gate of Heavenly Peace.

"I guess it's my fight too, Mom. I came to Beijing against your wishes. The least I can do is fight for you to reclaim it as your home. Our home." *It's my home too—lost before I was even born.* "Thirty years ago, you lost your home. Don't let my grandfather take it from you again."

My mom's face opens in wonder. "When did you get so wise? So strong?"

"That's easy—I have you as a mom," I say. "Now, are we going to kick ass or what?"

My mother straightens her shoulders, and there's a light in her eyes I've never seen before. *I can totally see her as a revolutionary activist.* "Yes, let's go."

Together, we walk to the table, where the others wait for us.

My aunt, ghost pale, rises from her chair at our approach. "Mei Mei."

Alyssa clasps her hand to her mouth.

My grandmother stands too, like she's in a trance. "Nu er, ni hui lai la." *Daughter, you've returned.*

My grandfather stays seated, his face emotionless.

My mother stops in front of the family she hasn't seen in thirty years. Her body is trembling at my side. "Ma, Jie Jie." She swallows. "Ni men zhi dao." *You both knew.* That my father was alive. "Ni pian wo." *You lied to me.* Because they'd let her believe my father was dead.

Pale as death, Po Po sinks to her chair, and Alyssa casts a worried look in her direction. I remember what my cousin said about our Po Po's bad heart, and anxiety worms into my stomach. Then Po Po stands up again. Tears pour down her wrinkled cheeks without her seeming to notice. "Nu er, wo dui bu qi ni." *Daughter, I've wronged you.* "Qing ni hui jia." *Please come home.*

Now Mom is the one who seems like she's about to collapse. Though I'm trembling with emotion myself, I hold her steady, my arm around her shoulders. "Ma, wo hui jia la," she says shakily. *Ma, I've come home.*

As if to herself, Po Po whispers, "Wo de nu er hui jia la." *My daughter has come home.*

Blinking away tears, my mother looks at my aunt, who gazes fearfully back at her. "Jie Jie." My mom's voice breaks. "Did you even try to find me?"

"Mei Mei," my aunt says in a voice so full of desperate love that my chest knots painfully, "please forgive me. I was so ashamed—that's why I didn't try to find you. But I always hoped you would come home. I've never forgotten you."

Heart weighted with pain, I touch the jade pendant at my throat. The pendant my aunt wanted to send to me at my birth—to honor a long-ago promise between two sisters. *Do not forget.* That was what my mother wrote on the back of the photograph she sent to my aunt. If only my aunt had looked for us then. If only she had found us. But she didn't because she thought my mother would never forgive her. The jade burns like a coal against my clammy skin.

A sob shudders through my mother's body. "There's nothing to forgive, Jie Jie." *All this time, my mother meant that she didn't want to be forgotten.* A single burning tear blazes down my cheek.

Then my mother turns to my grandfather, and my lungs collapse with dread. Will he welcome her back as he promised? And will she forgive him the way she forgave my po po and yi ma? But he's done so much worse. *He threw my dad into a labor camp.*

My grandfather looks up at his daughter, saying nothing, his mouth set into a stubborn line.

My mother's anger emanates from her in a palpable wave of scorching heat. "Ba, thirty years ago, you branded Delun an enemy of the state and imprisoned him to keep him from me. You failed. And now I am back—here with my granddaughter to demand justice."

My grandfather's knuckles whiten as he grips the arms of his chair. "I did what I had to do to protect my family. And that includes *you*. I lived through the Cultural Revolution. I know how dangerous young fanatics are. Delun was the same kind of revolutionary. The same kind of danger."

"I married him anyway," she says defiantly, and for a dizzying moment, I can see the rebellious teenager my mother once was. "I told him our family secret, and I've never had reason to regret it. Delun is faithful, kind . . . and a better father than you ever were."

At this, my grandfather hunches over as if she had hit him in the gut. It surprises me that he even cares about my mother's opinion of him.

It seems to surprise Mom too. Her breath catches before she continues. "In fact, he almost risked arrest to come with me to Beijing. He was that worried about our daughter—your granddaughter. That's the man you think is such a danger to our family." My chest tightens. It would have been my fault if Dad were arrested because he came to Beijing out of worry for me.

My grandfather's mouth loosens, and a shadow crosses his face.

More doubt about my grandfather creeps into my heart. In the time I've been in Beijing, rumors about my dangerous grandfather have swirled around me like a poisonous fog. His power. His ruthlessness. *I've been afraid of him.* But now I've seen him back down under pressure from his family. I've seen him pained by my mother's accusation that he wasn't a good father.

Maybe he's not the monster I've built up in my head. Maybe he's just a man with deep regrets. A man who doesn't know how to come back from his mistakes. "You can fix this," I say to my grandfather, the palms of my hands moist with nerves. "You can get my dad a pardon."

Everyone turns to me in surprise.

My grandfather barks a laugh out, but it sounds forced. "What makes you think I have that power?"

"Searches for your name are blocked by the Great Firewall of China. That tells me you're pretty high up in the Communist Party." When he doesn't react, I take a deep breath. "I know about the things you've done." *Eric's grandfather. My father.* "But this is a chance to do something good with your power. Pardon my dad."

He's silent at that.

"Lao Gong, ni da ying wo," my po po says. That's what she said before. *Husband, you promised me.* I thought she had been referring to a promise made recently. But maybe I was mistaken. Maybe it was a promise he made thirty years ago. And maybe what he promised was that my mother could come home. My heart rises in hope.

"Ba," my aunt says, "thirty years ago, you told me that if Lei didn't give up Delun and her revolutionary activism, it would get her killed. You said she would quit the revolutionary cause only if she believed that Delun was dead. So I let you lie to her. I was wrong. We were wrong. Give Delun the pardon. It is the only way Mei Mei will come home." Her face is tense, but her voice is strong. "And you promised us that she could come home."

He gazes at my po po, aunt, and mother for a long moment. "Wo da ying ni." *I promise you.*

My mother turns to her mother and sister, her face crumpling in tears. My own eyes sting as I step back to make room for my aunt and grandmother to embrace my mother. They huddle together, speaking rapid Chinese, making plans. *My dad will get his pardon. The women in my family will make sure of it.*

My grandfather looks on with his craggy eyebrows furrowed over watery eyes. He looks defeated but oddly . . . not angry. *Maybe I was right. Maybe he's relieved to have a chance to fix his mistakes.*

Alyssa comes over to me and hugs me. "Hey, are you OK?"

Reminded that I've found my own jie jie, I brush the tears from my cheeks and hug her back. "Yes, I'm OK."

It will all be OK now. We all get to come home.

CHAPTER THIRTY-SIX

At the patio table, conversations in Chinese are happening around me, too fast for me to join in easily, but I don't mind. It's enough to be here. My family and Eric and Mimi's family are having a late Mid-Autumn Festival dinner together. The Lius accepted my aunt's invitation and came over after their own family's celebration ended. Po Po, beaming at us all, sits at the head of the table with the adults to the right of her and the younger generation to the left of her. *It's almost too good to be true.* Yes, my grandfather left before the Liu family arrived, and Eric and Mimi's grandmother refused to come. But at least Eric and Mimi's parents are here.

It takes me about five seconds to fall in love with the elder Lius. They seem relieved that the feud is finally over, although there was one weird moment when they came face-to-face with my aunt. "Anwen," my aunt said to Eric's mother, "Yanlin is lucky to have married you." To him, my aunt said, "Yanlin, it's good to see you so happy." Abashed smiles all around.

There has *got* to be a story there.

I thought Alyssa would have been a nervous wreck meeting Mimi's parents, but in true Alyssa fashion, she takes the opportunity to announce that she wants to use her social media popularity to start a nonprofit supporting women in the arts the way Wu Zetian did all the way back in the Tang dynasty. Alyssa holds Mimi's hand while she makes the announcement, and no one even blinks. It looks like Alyssa and Mimi are on their way to getting their happily ever after. As am I.

I take a slice of raw meat from the platter in front of me with my cooking chopsticks and plop it in the boiling stew of the hot pot, nudging Eric's meat out of the way as I do so.

"Hey!" He's sitting next to me, all adorable and mock-indignant. "No fair! I already staked my claim on that spot!"

"I was just trying to save you from overcooked meat." His meat is tangled in bean threads and cabbage now and barely visible, but I lean forward and pretend to scrutinize it. "I think your meat is done."

"It needs five more seconds to be the perfect amount of done-ness," he says with lofty superiority, even checking his watch like he'd actually timed it. "I've done a study of this."

I grin at him. "Oh, is that what your fancy Stanford business degree is good for?"

He doesn't miss a beat. "There was a course on cooking meat in my second year."

"I stand corrected, then," I say gravely, "and bow to your superior knowledge on the subject. After all, it makes total sense to go to America to learn how to cook Chinese hot pot."

With fake ostentatiousness, Eric uses his chopsticks to lift out his meat, which, admittedly, looks perfect. "See, my college degree in America was *totally* worth it."

His father, sitting across from Eric, breaks off his conversation with his wife and my aunt and turns to his son. "Speaking of that, Eric," he says, switching to English out of courtesy to me, "what do you think of going to business school in America to get your graduate degree? Stanford has a good program."

It's not my place to say anything, but I want so badly to blurt out that Eric actually wants to do a graduate environment and sustainability program at UCLA. Instead, I kick him under the table. Hard.

Eric grimaces, but it's difficult to tell whether it's in response to my kick or his father's question. "That can wait, Ba," he says. "You need my help with the family business."

His father snorts. "Between your mother, Mimi, and me, I think we've got it covered. The question is, what do *you* need? Mimi's always been into fashion, but I've always felt your interests were different." There's a twinkle in his eye as he glances at me. "And maybe there's even more of a reason for you to go to America now."

Eric's mother, who's sitting next to her husband, looks over at us, her attention caught. "What's this about Eric going to America? You know, this could be good timing. Your ba and I were talking about opening a store in LA, and we'll need someone to oversee that." She speaks in English, and she's looking at me with bright inquisitiveness.

Now Eric's looking at me too, and my face feels all hot. I'm giddy at the thought of Eric actually moving to LA. But I don't want him to move for me. Or to think that the only way to get his parents' approval is to follow their plans for him. Eric's so used to living up to what he assumes his family's expectations are that he hasn't really stood up for what *he* wants. In spite of his über-supportive parents, he seems to think his own desires don't matter. Maybe I could stand to absorb some of his dedication to the collective good of his family, but maybe Eric could also stand to be a tiny bit selfish for once.

Instead of kicking Eric again, I place my hand on his knee under the table and squeeze. "Tell them," I whisper into his ear. "Tell them what *you* want to do."

His eyes darken as he stares at me, and for a moment, I worry that I'm pushing him too hard. Then he says, "From the moment I met you, you've never let me be less than what I can be."

My heart does frenzied somersaults and leaps in my chest. How is it that we just kissed for the first time fewer than twenty-four hours ago? "Same," I manage to say.

Eric tears this gaze away from me and turns toward his parents. "Actually, there's something else I'd like to do." He takes a deep breath. "I got into the environment and sustainability graduate program at UCLA. I know it's not a business degree, but I feel it would help us take our business to the cutting edge of sustainable fashion. If it's OK with you, I'd like to go there."

"Hao bon!" his mother exclaims, slipping into Chinese to say "Very good!"

"It's OK with us," his father says, confident and beaming. "It will make us very proud and happy to support you in this."

At this point, Mimi figures out what's going on and gets in on the family lovefest, and I'm just bursting with pride in Eric. And, of course, giddy with joy that he's coming to LA.

"Reconsidering college this year, Gemma?" asks my mother hopefully. She's drifted over from the other end of the table and arrived in time to hear Eric's plans for grad school.

I shake my head. "Next year," I say firmly, "just like I planned."

My mom sighs, and then her gaze narrows on Eric. "So, your name is 'Eric,' is it?" *Uh-oh. I don't suppose Mom forgot that accidental slip of the tongue when I called Ken by Eric's name?* Not a chance. Mom has a memory like a steel trap. Especially when it involves me and a romantic possibility.

"Um, yeah. I mean, yes, that's my name." He turns to me with a questioning look. *Nope. Not about to explain to him why my mom knows his name.*

Too bad my mom's not playing along. "So, Eric, are you Gemma's—"

"Mom!" I interrupt desperately.

Eric leaps to his feet. "Mrs. Huang, it looks like you and Gemma have a lot to talk about. Please, take my seat."

"Thank you, Eric!" She beams and sits down next to me. "Now Gemma and I can talk about her plans for the future."

"*Traitor*," I whisper to Eric, but he just grins and goes to sit between my aunt and Po Po at the other end of the table. No doubt he'll be completely charming, and I'll have *them* asking me questions about him too.

Mom fixes me with a determined look, and it looks like we're about to go round one hundred on the topic of college and my impractical acting career. But, to be fair, *I* have never run away from my family, participated in a protest that ended in a massacre, sprung a political prisoner from a labor camp, or gone on the run with said political prisoner (aka Dad). Remembering my mom's exploits, I say, "Mom, how *did* you rescue Dad? And how did you get that painting back?"

She doesn't shut me out the way she used to. She just smiles mysteriously. "A woman should get to keep some secrets to herself." Her expression turns stern. "Now, about your plans . . . I haven't heard much about this movie you're shooting in Beijing."

I'm so taken aback that I just gape at her. *The movie.* I haven't given a second thought to the movie in the past twenty-four hours, but now my fear of failure comes crashing down on me.

Mom studies me closely. "Tell me about it."

It all comes tumbling out of me. I tell her how I didn't fight for my vision of my character, that I didn't trust Eilene or stand up to Jake or do anything that I should have done. And that I don't know how to fix my mistakes.

She listens intently, and when I'm done, she puts a hand on my shoulder. "It sounds to me like you know exactly what to do, Gemma."

"I do?" Then in wonder, I realize that I do. "Tomorrow, I'll fight for my vision. I'll take back the movie."

"That's my daughter," my mother says approvingly, and pats my shoulder.

Dinner wraps up without any other life-altering decisions being made. It's time for the main event. At any other dinner, dessert would be an afterthought, but tonight, at the Mid-Autumn Festival dinner, the mooncakes have a starring role.

I break apart the round pastry, glazed with egg yolk to give it the ellow sheen of the moon, and pop a piece in my mouth. The flaky crust and smooth sweet date filling burst pleasurably against my tongue.

It's good—but not as good as my mom's. All my friends rave about Mom's mooncakes, which she makes for every special occasion, not just for Mid-Autumn Festival. My friends demand to know what my mom puts in her mooncakes to make them so good, and I always tell them what my mom always told me to say. That it's an ancient Chinese secret.

Mom would kill me if I ever revealed what her secret ingredient *really* is. Cream cheese in the crust. "Let people think my cooking is magic," she says.

I always respond in the same way. "You *are* magic, Ma."

She is. She really is. And thanks to her magic, I feel strong enough to take on—not just Jake—but the entire film industry. The entire world. Anything that makes me feel less than what I am.

My mother checks the time on her watch. "I promised to call your father," she says as she stands up. "He should be up now." In an aside, she mumbles, "If he slept at all, that is."

Guilt pricks me as I stand up from the table too. "Is Dad angry at me for lying? Um, did I mention how sorry I am?"

She presses her lips together. "You mentioned it, yes. Say it again to your dad. He's not mad—just worried about you." Her mouth softens. "I told him there's no reason to be worried. I told your dad that we raised a daughter who might not make choices we agree with." *Ah, college again.* "But that you have a good heart and would make your choices from the heart . . . as we did when we were your age." She smiles. "I don't suppose we can ask for more than that." *Maybe Mom understands me better than I thought she did.*

"Let's call Dad," I say, my throat suddenly thick.

We move away from the table to a nook shadowed by tall rose-bushes, and I put in a video call to my dad.

He picks up at once, and his anxious face fills the screen. "Gemma, are you OK?"

My mom scrunches up her face next to mine. "We're both fine, Delun!"

"Dad," I say, "I'm so sorry about everything—going against your wishes and then lying about it. I'm sorry you were worried, but I'm fine. I really am."

His face relaxes. "Hao." *OK.*

I'm not really going to be let off the hook that easily, am I? But that *is* pretty on brand for my dad. The muscles in my shoulders loosen.

Apparently, my mom has come to the same conclusion. With an exasperated sigh, she commandeers my phone. "Delun, you'll never guess what has happened!"

As she starts recounting tonight's events in Chinese, I back away. Until I bump into a solid, muscled chest. Eric's. I turn around. "Don't tell my mom I said this, but I think I got off easier than I deserve."

He leans against the iron railing of the patio with a grin. "How so?"

I tilt my head, considering the whole vision of cuteness that is Eric. "Well, for one thing, Mom's so caught up in all this family reunion stuff—that she hasn't asked a million not-so-subtle questions about *you*."

"Hey, listen," Eric says to me, "earlier, when your mom was about to ask if I was your boyfriend . . ."

I guess it was too much to hope that he hadn't caught that. "Yes?" my voice cracks.

"I didn't answer because we haven't talked about it, but I just wanted to let you know that if *you* wanted to, then I totally want to . . . to be your boyfriend." Red in the face, he shakes his head. "Sorry. Too soon, I know. Just pretend I didn't say anything."

A thrill pulses through my body. "By the way, I love that suit," I say casually.

Eric frowns in confusion. "Um, good?"

I smile. "And I love that it's a gift from my nan peng you."

He searches my eyes. "Gemma, I don't know if you realize it, but you just called me your—"

"Nan peng you," I say. "Boyfriend. My Chinese isn't so bad that I didn't realize what I just said."

"Are you sure?" Eric smooths a strand of my hair away from my face. "If I tell Mimi that you're my nu peng you, she's not going to let us get out of it."

Girlfriend. I could get used to hearing that. "I'm sure."

"Did I hear my name?" Mimi asks. She and Alyssa stroll over arm in arm to join us by the railing. "What are you two talking about?"

"Just talking about my mom," I say hastily, "and how she's thankfully not asking too many questions about us."

"You're lucky!" Alyssa says. "My mom has asked a bunch of questions about Mimi!" But she looks delighted by this turn of events.

Mimi grumbles, "You don't seem shy about telling your mom all about me. Just be glad I haven't told *my* parents everything about *you*."

Eric and I glance at each other and hide our grins. Because Mimi looks just as delighted as Alyssa.

"By the way," Alyssa asks, peering at us, "just what *is* going on between you two?"

I smile and turn to peer over the railing to where the first firecrackers are starting to burst into red and gold, lighting up the heavens. "A girl should get to keep some secrets to herself."

Together, on this Mid-Autumn Festival, we join arms and look up to the night sky, where the yellow moon rises among a splash of fiery lights—round as a new beginning.

CHAPTER THIRTY-SEVEN

L iz is visibly startled when I stroll into my trailer early the next morning with a garment bag slung over my shoulder.

"Good morning, Liz!" I call out before pushing Song's ugly suit aside on the rolling clothes rack to make room for the garment bag that I brought. "Could you do me a favor?"

Interest sparks in her eyes. "Sure. What is it?"

"First of all, how many of those"—I point to the bowl-cut wigs—"do we have?"

"Too many," she says, and then clasps her hand over her mouth as she realizes that she's inadvertently given her uncensored opinion about those awful wigs.

"Good," I say cheerfully, "then it won't matter if we modify one."

The interest in her eyes turns into a maniacal gleam. "What do you have in mind?"

I pull out my phone to show her images of Eric's short, urban-chic hairstyle. The fact that he patiently let me take as many pictures as I wanted from all conceivable angles last night speaks volumes about how much he likes me. I'm lucky to be with Eric for many reasons, the least of which is his awesome hair—but the hair certainly doesn't hurt. *Is it weird that I want to copy my boyfriend's hair?* Mentally, I shrug. If it's weird to want to look as hot as Eric, then call me weird. "Can you do something like this with one of the wigs?"

"Oh yes," she breathes in reverence. "It will be my pleasure."

I smile. Roping Liz into my plans didn't turn out to be all that hard.

Twenty minutes later, Liz puts her shears away, works some mousse into the wig, and blow-dries the last strand into place. "What do you think?" she asks, gesturing to the wig still on its mannequin head.

I look with admiration at the cool layers and texture she's added. "It doesn't look at all like the original!"

"I'll take that as the highest of compliments."

"Liz, you are a miracle worker! Thank you!"

"You're welcome," she replies modestly. "Let me do your makeup first, and then you can try on the wig."

She does my makeup quickly and then places the wig on my head, carefully tucking in the stray strands of my hair. Then she stands back to take in the whole effect.

Sitting in the makeup chair, I stare in awe at my reflection in the mirror. "Wow." For a moment, I forget that the sexy, handsome face staring back at me is *mine*.

Liz smiles in satisfaction. "I'll leave you to get dressed, then. But I sincerely hope you brought another suit with you because it would be a travesty to wear my masterpiece with that horrible suit."

I grin. "Don't worry. I'm in complete agreement with you."

As soon as she leaves, I unzip the garment bag to reveal the clean, sharp lines and quality fabric of *the* suit. The one I coveted and finally let Eric give me. Nothing at all inappropriate in accepting a gift from my boyfriend, I think with smug satisfaction. Besides, he's right. I'm an aspiring actress who'll be good for Eric's business once I totally *rock* this suit on film.

I'm going to take back Song's character, my role, and this film in general. If my mother can stand up to her family for her beliefs, then I can fight for *my* beliefs—and change *Butterfly* while I'm at it. My mouth firms. After all, the women in my family are descended from royalty. So maybe it's time for me to *rule*.

The suit feels just as good as I remembered. This time, I've practiced knotting a tie with Eric. *After some pleasurable detours.* Who knew that putting a tie on (and taking it off) with one's boyfriend could be so *hot?*

After I'm dressed in shimmering black silk and soft cotton, I put on a pair of shiny black loafers that Eric gave me as well. Only after I'm completely dressed does my stomach go wobbly with nerves. *I guess I'm ready to face the music.* I pick up my phone. Would it be too much to put on "Sail" by Awolnation, the song that played when Keanu Reeves walked into the restaurant to such great effect in *Always Be My Maybe?* Yes, I decide, and put the phone back down on the dressing table. *Quit stalling, Gemma. This is your moment.*

Channeling a confidence I don't quite feel, I leave my trailer and walk toward the studio, where we're doing the reshoot. My hand freezes on the handle that will open the studio door. My ancestress might have been an empress, but I'm just a newbie actress terrified about blowing my big chance. *No,* I tell myself sternly. *I'm not alone in this.*

The thought of Eileen on my side is what decides me. Not only do I have a legacy of powerful women in my lineage, I have one powerful woman in the film industry at my back. The doubts that Ken stirred up about Eilene are gone. Eilene will fight with me.

All I have to do is begin the fight and not give up. *I'm Sonia Li, badass lawyer. I'm sexy as all hell, oozing hot Asian masculinity, and I'm about to effing kill this role as Song, my bisexual ex-boyfriend's new crush.*

I press down on the handle with numb fingers and push the door open. My body burning with compressed energy, I swagger into the studio. One by one, each cast and crew member stops what they're doing to stare at me.

I come in just as Aidan, as Ryan, is speaking his lines to Eilene, who seems to be standing in for me. "Yeah, this is the tie that my ex-girlfriend bought. . . ." Aidan's words trail off, and his eyes widen as he catches sight of me.

Now everyone is looking at me. But instead of nerves, a surge of excitement runs up and down my spine as I stroll up to Aidan.

"What's this?" Jake mutters. "*That* sure as hell isn't Song's costume!"

Eilene, on the other hand, steps aside for me at once, a joyous look of understanding dawning on her face. She sits down in the director's chair next to Jake and puts out a hand when he makes a motion to stand up and stop the scene.

My body tingling with adrenaline, I touch the intricate folds in the taut knot of Aidan's tie. "Your ex-girlfriend has good taste." My voice is low and growly, the way I've been practicing. "I like this tie on you."

I'm close enough to see his Adam's apple bob as he swallows. "Line," Aidan calls faintly.

His line is about beer and football. Same as my next line. I recall Jake's direction from last time—for Aidan as Ryan to recoil from a man hitting on him and for us both to "get real macho, real fast" at this moment in the scene. Frantically, I try to improvise a different line in my head, but it will be hard to play off Aidan if he's following Jake's vision of the scene.

Jake begins to give Aidan his line. "How about those Patriots—"

Eilene cuts him off. "Let's play this Gemma's way." My heart explodes with gratitude as she continues. "Aidan, you're attracted to Song, thinking he's a man, and you're into it. Gemma, you're conflicted about starting up things again, but you're into Ryan being attracted to you as Song. Use the same lines for now with the different direction, or improvise." She smiles at me. "This is your vision now, Gemma. Let's see what happens."

Too choked up to speak, I just nod. *I was right to trust Eilene.* She wanted me to take the lead, to fight for my vision, but she'll be here to back me up.

"That's not what we agreed on!" Jake says.

"If I recall correctly, Jake," Eilene says coolly, "your objection had something to do with how it wasn't plausible for Ryan to be attracted to Sonia in drag as Song." She turns to Aidan. "Can you play Ryan as attracted to Song?"

Aidan clears his throat. "If Gemma plays the character like she just did? Not a problem."

Jake looks me over, but for once, it's not with a leer. In fact, I could swear there's a glimmer of respect in his eyes. "It could work," he admits grudgingly. "Let's take the scene from the top, but this time with the cameras rolling."

We do the scene, and I play Song with an edge of cockiness, but also with vulnerability and sweetness—just the way I like my men. And women too, now that I think of it. When the dialogue about football comes up, I go for broke. After all, if Jake didn't want me to make sly innuendos about balls and padding, then he shouldn't have handed me a topic so ripe with possibilities.

"A bunch of sweaty, muscular guys tussling over big balls, trying to score," I say archly, leaning toward Aidan like I can't help myself. "What's there not to love?"

Aidan also leans in. "There's more to the game than that!" His improvised line and delivery are both perfect. The stiff way he's playing Ryan is irresistible. It would tempt Song to mess with him, rattle that adorable proper facade and tease out his clear attraction to my character.

"Right." I wink at Aidan. "There's also padding to make the players look bigger." Slowly, my eyes lower—but not demurely like when I was playing Sonia. This time I'm all flirtatious mischief. Aidan's gaze follows, and then freezes. On where I'm packing. I may have overdone the padding, but as Jake keeps reminding me—this is a comedy.

Aidan is staring at my bulge and heroically struggling to keep a straight face. "How about those Patriots?" he chokes out. And that's all I'm going to get out of him. Because Aidan has now crammed his shirtsleeve into his mouth to keep himself from breaking character. *Yup. Overdid it on the padding.*

It's time for Song to pull back on the risqué humor and get a little vulnerable. "The Patriots? You used to love—" Pretending to correct myself, I say hastily, "I mean, I knew someone who loved . . . the game." I give him a small, bittersweet smile. "As for me, I never liked it when the players got hurt."

Aidan manages to sober up and get back into character. "Getting hurt is part of the game." He's looking at me like he's *really* into this game we're playing. Like he'd pay the price of getting hurt if he had to.

I clear my throat. *Song would pivot now, put a lid on those feelings for Ryan.* I grin at Aidan. "So, padding! Do you use padding when you have a . . . uh, scramble? Fromage? What's it called?"

"Scrimmage," Aidan gasps through stifled laughter, losing it again.

"Well, whatever it's called—real men use padding." To underscore the point, I widen my stance, emphasizing my own padding.

When we finish, I know we'll have to do the scene again—not because I messed up—but because my improvised lines kept making Aidan crack up. *I was right. This is hilarious.* And it doesn't have to be homophobic to be funny.

Jake seems to agree. "I actually like that," he says grudgingly before asking Eilene, "What do you think?"

Eilene's opinion is the one I really care about, so my breath freezes in my lungs as I wait for her reply.

"I have some suggestions, but what we've got to work with here is pretty amazing." Then Eilene looks at me. "Bu cuo."

Ah. I breathe again. There it is. The "not bad" in Chinese that I was hoping for. This time, I reply in Chinese, "Ni ye bu cuo." *You're also not bad.*

Eilene's eyebrows rise. "I don't think I've ever heard you speak Chinese."

"I've been practicing. Wo shi zhong guo ren. I'm Chinese after all."

"Yes, that you are." A small smile hovers over her lips.

Jake makes an impatient noise. "Can we get on with this, please?"

Eilene makes her suggestions, we talk over the scene a bit, and then we do the next take.

It's not an easy shoot, but at the end of ten grueling hours, Jake finally says, "That's a wrap! Gemma, good job today."

It's not as meaningful as Eilene's "bu cuo." But I'll take it.

CHAPTER THIRTY-EIGHT

A little over a month later, Eilene is sitting on the sofa in my hotel suite while I try to find space in my luggage for all the new clothes Alyssa and Mimi have pressed upon me. Not that I fought too hard against it. After all, Mimi *did* totally design an entire line of clothing catering to my tastes. It would be downright ungrateful to refuse the clothes.

I tried to offer payment (although I couldn't have afforded even a fraction of the cost), but Mimi refused, and Alyssa ended up footing the bill. *And* she bought me a whole bunch of accessories.

"I can't let my mei mei leave China without a new wardrobe!" Alyssa insisted.

I have to admit that I love the new clothes, like the black cigarette pants and white silk blouse I'm currently wearing.

Pressing down hard on my rolling suitcase, I finally manage to get it zipped. "Thanks for coming to say goodbye before I leave tomorrow," I tell Eilene. We'd put the film in the can a few days ago, but I can hardly believe it's actually time to leave China. Mom had stayed to make sure Dad got his pardon, and then when Dad *did* get his pardon, he came to spend a week with us in China. My parents went back to the United States nearly a month ago. Now it's my turn to go home.

"Actually, I'm not here just to say goodbye," Eilene says.

I glance up from my packing. "You're not?"

"I'm so thrilled with your work on *Butterfly*. Because of you, the film will be a success." As I bask in the warm glow of her praise,

Eilene says, "So, the reason I came by is to discuss a project I have lined up. I have you in mind for a role."

"*Seriously?* That would be so awesome!"

"And that's just the beginning." A mischievous grin lights up her face. "I couldn't help but talk you up to a well-known director friend of mine, and he wants to bring you in to audition for another part."

"Which one?" I demand breathlessly. Working with Eilene again is a no-brainer, but I don't know about another director. *And will it be a role I can live with?* "Sorry, Eilene! I didn't even thank you for hooking me up for roles or for saying such nice things about my work on *Butterfly!*"

She waves my apology aside. "Don't worry! This is an exciting time for you, Gemma."

"It is. So many things are happening." I hesitate and then say, "But I'm worried about the other role. What if it's one I don't want to do?"

"What if it's another *Butterfly*, you mean?" she asks shrewdly.

It seems risky to be picky about roles so early in my career, and it's not that I regret taking the *Butterfly* role and making it my own, but . . . "I'm not sure if I want to do *that* again anytime soon."

Instead of trying to talk me out of my decision, Eilene says, "Good for you, Gemma." I blink in surprise as she continues. "You have a brilliant career ahead of you, but it can be on your own terms. Do the audition and then decide whether you want the role or not." Decisively, she says, "Let's see what happens."

I smile. "You know, that's exactly what you said before. 'Let's see what happens.' You said it right before we shot the first take of that scene in *Butterfly*. The one where Song in drag flirts with Ryan? The one we hijacked."

"We saw what happened, didn't we? It's my favorite scene in the whole movie."

"Mine too." I'm tempted to make some kind of butterfly pun about metamorphosis and cocoons, but that's a bit too cheesy, even for me. "It's the scene where I finally figured out who I am." I don't mean my character, Sonia Li. I mean *me*, Gemma Huang.

Eilene nods. "That's worth fighting for. So stick to your guns and . . ."

"Let's see what happens?" I guess.

"Exactly."

It feels scary. To trust that the journey to myself is worth every risk. But Eilene is right.

I'm worth fighting for.

The next morning, Eric takes me to the airport, and we're both pretty somber as I check in my bags. I have to keep reminding myself that we're only saying goodbye temporarily. I'll see him in two months when he moves to LA for grad school at the start of winter quarter.

Still, we get to the security gate way too soon. The movie studio is paying for me to fly back first class, and there's not even a line at the gate for the first-class passengers. I sigh and turn to Eric. "I guess this is goodbye."

"For now," he says firmly.

Standing on tiptoe, I pull Eric to me. "For now," I agree. Our kiss is hard, tinged with desperation. It's also, as always, toe-curling and hot. Dimly, I register the flashes of lights of camera phones and rising whispers. *Not again.*

But there's something different this time. As the crowd calls, "Alyssa! Alyssa!" and people hold their phones in the air, desperate to get a picture of me, I can imagine something else.

One day, it will be *my* name the crowd is yelling.

I pull away from my lip-lock with Eric. "I guess that's my cue to leave."

He glances over at the multiplying crowd pressing closer. "You'd better get out of here before I'm tempted to whisk you away." The look on his face is tender. "Like the first time."

"You mean when you thought I was Alyssa and wanted to warn me to stay away from your little sister?"

"Well, when you put it like that, I guess I'm luckier than I thought to be your boyfriend in the end." He takes both of my hands in his.

"We both got lucky." I give him a final kiss that's way too brief to satisfy the ache of missing him already. But even this fleeting kiss whips up the frenzy of camera flashes.

"You'd better go," Eric says reluctantly, releasing my hands.

I nod and go through the security checkpoint. But with Eric's kiss on my lips and dreams of my own name being shouted someday, I can't help but smile.

After I go through security, I blow a last kiss to Eric. My fans think I'm blowing them a kiss and go nuts. My last glimpse of Eric is of him shrugging wryly and blowing a kiss back at me before dozens of people push in front of him and he's lost to my sight.

It's a lot quieter on this side of the security gate, and I'm able to text Glory and Camille in peace as I walk to my gate.

At the airport. Can't wait to see you in LA!

Glory's reply comes back first.

You'd better not be jet-lagged.

Before I can text a confused-face emoji, Camille's text pops up.

Epic welcome-home party in the works!

Could my life get any better? My thumbs fly on my phone.

You two are the absolute best!

I don't get a chance to read their response to my text because I'm being paged over the airport intercom. *What's going on?* Then I realize that I'm being asked to go to a different gate, than the one where my plane is leaving from. This is getting stranger and stranger.

Confused, I follow the directions to the gate, where I'm met by an airport employee. "This way please, Ms. Huang, to our VIP airline lounge." She gestures to a sliding glass door.

Wow. I knew that the movie studio upgraded my ticket to first class, but this is ridiculous. Still, who am I to refuse a cushy exclusive-lounge experience?

The sliding glass door opens at my approach, and the lounge is as posh as I expected, with black leather couches and little bottles of champagne and bowls of oranges on tables. And the lounge is occupied. By two of my favorite people on the planet. Who also happen to be related to me.

My cousin and my aunt. Jie Jie and Yi Ma. "Surprise!" Alyssa calls out from one of the leather couches, next to her mother. She raises a toast to me with a flute of champagne.

My whole body lights up with joy. "What are you doing here?"

"We go every year to Paris," my aunt explains.

"For the couture shows," Alyssa chimes in, "and we thought we'd take our flight at the same time you leave for LA so we could see you off in style!"

"You've already done that," I say, smoothing my dress down. "Just look at all these clothes you gave me!" For my last day in China, I'm wearing another of Mimi's designs—a yellow silk shift dress.

Alyssa and her mother both study me—my aunt with reserved satisfaction and Alyssa with smug pride. They are both gorgeously attired themselves. My aunt is wearing a tailored navy pantsuit with a silk water-colored scarf, and Alyssa is wearing a red lace midi dress.

"Oh, the clothes! That's nothing," Alyssa says airily. "You're descended from Wu Zetian, remember? A descendant of an empress who once ruled China should have nice clothes."

The clothes Alyssa gave me are leaps and bounds over the category of *nice*, but I don't quibble with her. It feels too good to be spoiled by my cousin.

"Besides," Alyssa says, "you're an heiress. You should get to dress the part."

"Your mother refuses to take the money that should be rightfully hers," my aunt explains, "but she did agree to let you inherit her share. Your grandparents have changed their will to reflect this."

"That's not necessary," I mumble.

"Entirely necessary," my aunt says firmly.

I turn to my cousin. "Are you OK with this?"

"Of course!" she declares. "We want you to know you're part of the family. We wouldn't want you to forget us!"

"Never." I sit across from them on another leather couch. "And not because of the clothes or the money. You're my family. I couldn't forget you."

"You'd better not!" Alyssa says, scooting over to me and having my aunt take a picture of us. Then she retrieves her phone from my aunt and plunks down next to me again. Together, we look at the picture of the two of us—alike in more than our faces. Alike in our joy in each other.

Alyssa laughs. "Look! You in a yellow dress and me in a red one. We look like the two court ladies in those paintings Empress Wu commissioned."

"Maybe they were cousins too." *Wouldn't that be cool?*

"We're *sisters*, remember?" Alyssa corrects me with a smile. "Jiemei."

"Jiemei"—the word that our two pendants form. "Yes, jiemei. Sisters." My heart melts in gratitude for Alyssa. It makes me shudder to think of never coming to Beijing and never knowing her. Never knowing *all* my family.

"We'll stay in touch." My aunt's face glows brightly. "Alyssa and I will be in Chicago next summer. Your mother has a surprise planned. Will you be there?"

"Absolutely!" I say. "What's the surprise?"

"You'll see," she says, and no amount of cajoling from me or Alyssa gets anything more out of her.

My aunt reaches over and covers my hands with hers. "I'm so happy to find my sister again, but that's not all. It's finding you too. We love you so much, Gemma."

"Don't make me cry!" Alyssa warns. "I don't want to smudge my makeup." But it's too late. Tears are already forming in her eyes.

Just like they're forming, hot and thick, in my own eyes. "I love you both."

"And I love you too, Gemma," Alyssa says, giving up on the battle to save her makeup and sniffling into a silk handkerchief.

It's the perfect way to leave China, seen off by my cousin and my aunt. But all too soon, it's time to say goodbye and depart for my gate. Alyssa hugs me hard, crying so much that I fear her makeup is a lost cause. Yi Ma kisses me on both cheeks and whispers her hope of seeing me soon.

At last I board my plane and sink into the luxurious first-class seat. This time I'm not squished between two other passengers. I have the row to myself and can stretch out. Smiling, I think of my arrival three months ago, when I had been frantically emailing my parents to keep them from finding out that I was in Beijing and then unexpectedly envious of the Chinese grandfather who was returning home to his family in China.

The plane taxis down the runway, and as it rises into the air, I see the Beijing skyline glittering and bright in the slowly darkening sky.

When I first came here, I had no family to meet me in China, and I was lying to the only family I had. Now my family in China sent me off with love and promises to meet again. And my parents and I understand each other in a way I never thought possible.

Don't get me wrong—designer clothes and money are nice, but their value for me is that they're gifts from people who love me and whom I love. That is the *real* inheritance that Wu Zetian has left me.

My family.

EPILOGUE

There she is—surrounded by a large expanse of white wall. Under the muted museum lighting, the colors of the painting are lush and rich—the dark gold background, the saturated red of her dress embroidered at the hem with pink peonies, the blue-jade shawl loose around her shoulders with a sash around her waist in a matching color, and her glossy black hair piled on top of her head with jeweled hair ornaments. The lady herself has a look of concentration as she touches her calligraphy brush to a blank scroll. The placard next to the painting reads "Court Lady of the Tang Dynasty Writing Calligraphy." The lady has certainly gained new grandeur on the wall of a Chicago museum as part of the exclusive international exhibit of Empress Wu's art collection.

But I still like to think of her gracing the wall of my mother's office.

It's opening night of the exhibit on loan by "an anonymous donor," and the doors of the museum will open to the public soon. As we wait, I turn to my mother. "Who do you think she is?"

Alyssa and my aunt stroll over in time to hear my question.

"Wu Zetian herself?" Alyssa guesses.

My mother is shaking her head. "Wu Zetian was considered a great beauty of her time. Look at this lady. Slight figure and delicate features. She wouldn't have been considered a beauty the way Wu Zetian was with her sturdy figure and strong features."

"A lady of the court then?" my aunt asks.

"Maybe." Mom, the art historian, sounds doubtful. "Except that Empress Wu was not known for favoring court ladies. If this painting is in Wu Zetian's collection, she must have commissioned it. I just can't imagine any court lady so high in Empress Wu's esteem that she would commission a painting of her."

I remember Alyssa's theory that one of the two lost paintings was of Princess Taiping, Wu Zetian's daughter. "Princess Taiping?"

"I don't think so. Your po po said that the lady in the other painting was wearing a yellow dress—the imperial color. It's likely that she was Princess Taiping. And Princess Taiping was supposed to have resembled her mother—unlike this lady."

My heart twangs in pain at the thought of that other, destroyed painting. Of the only painting of Princess Taiping engulfed in flames during the Cultural Revolution. But . . .

If this isn't Wu Zetian, a court lady, or Princess Taiping, then who is it? We all turn to look at the painting again. As a child, I spent hours staring at this painting, admiring the lady's dress and wondering what it was that she was going to write on the blank parchment.

"I actually have a theory about who she is," my mom says casually.

"Who?" I ask.

"Tell us," Alyssa demands.

"Of course you have a theory," my aunt says with exasperated fondness. "Let's hear it."

Mom waves off all our questions. "It's just a hunch. I have no proof." She contemplates the painting, and for a moment, the look on Mom's face and the lady's look as she studies the parchment are eerily alike. "I suppose we'll never know for sure who the lady in the painting really is."

Mom wants to keep one more secret to herself. Not for the first time since Beijing, I realize that I have yet to learn all of her story. I put my arm around Mom's waist so we're hip to hip, looking at a portrait commissioned by our ancestress of an unknown woman. I'll never know who this mysterious lady was. But I still have a chance to get to know my mother.

To know her story.

AUTHOR'S NOTE

Dear Reader,

Growing up, I wanted to read about Asian American teens who get to have adventure and romance. But books like that weren't around back then. Gemma's story isn't my story. But her story is the one I wanted to read as a kid searching for myself in books.

When I went to China for the first time as a young adult, I thought I'd feel an instant sense of belonging to the country where my parents and grandparents were born. I built up this visit as a *magical* homecoming. That's how much I needed a place where I belonged.

As you might imagine, it wasn't that simple. In *Heiress Apparently*, I wanted to write a story about a Chinese American girl who goes to China and gets that homecoming. While I was writing the book, I thought a lot about belonging. Asian Americans' right to belong in the United States has always been challenged. As I write this, we are in the midst of the COVID-19 pandemic when anti-Asian racism, harassment, and violence have been increasing at an alarming rate. It is harder and harder to feel like I belong in the country where I was born.

But when I wrote the last scene of *Heiress Apparently*—I felt it. A hope humming in my blood. I thought of you, reader, and I hoped you would recognize some part of yourself in Gemma—a Chinese American girl who gets to be the star of her own story. And that felt a lot like belonging.

In Chinese, the character for "jia" means both family and home. I hope you find both family and home in Gemma's story.

Warmly,

Diana Ma

ACKNOWLEDGMENTS

I have so many people to thank for getting Gemma's story into the world! Thank you to my agent, the fantastic Christa Heschke. Thank you also to the fabulous Daniele Hunter. I'm honored to work with the two of you. Christa and Daniele, you're both so brilliant and lovely, and your faith and support mean everything to me.

Thank you to my editor, Anne Heltzel, whose incredible vision and wisdom guided this story. You were a dream to work with! Thank you also to Jessica Gotz, Amy Vreeland, and Hana Nakamura. I'm sorry if I've missed anyone, but please know I'm grateful to everyone who worked on this book and for the entire Amulet/Abrams team. This was the perfect home for *Heiress Apparently*.

I'm so grateful to my amazing beta readers—Terri Chung and Melissa Grinley. I couldn't have asked for better readers or friends. Terri, you read scenes with zero notice and stayed up unreasonably late to finish a read so you could give me just the feedback I needed. Thank you for the many treats—I'm so lucky that food is your love language. Melissa, you worked through so many sticky scenes with me when we probably should have been grading or prepping for our class. Thank you for your confidence in me and always encouraging me to speak my truth. I appreciate and love you both so much!

I also want to thank Terri, Melissa, Dani Blackman, Cat Cabral, JC Clapp, Ann Culligan, Laura McCracken, Christy Scheuer, and Karen Stuhldreher for gifting me with a weekend writing retreat so I could finish my first draft. Your support and love kept me afloat! Christy, thank you for your willingness to follow me down rabbit holes—and for always pulling me out. Cat, your keen insight has saved me more times than you know. Jane Harradine, thank you for introducing me to *M. Butterfly* all those years ago. Cam Huynh, thank you for your friendship. Thank you to all my students and colleagues at North Seattle College—I've learned so much from you. Thank you to We Need Diverse Books for your mentorship program and all the wonderful things you do. Swati Avasthi, thank you for being the best mentor I could ask for.

This is a book about family, so no acknowledgment would be complete without thanking my family. First, I want to thank my parents for supporting my dreams of being a writer. David, my little brother, thank you for reading my very first stories—and not making fun of them. Thank you to all my cousins, especially Xiao-lan, who inspired a crucial scene in the book by calling me "Jie Jie"—sister—instead of "Biao Jie," cousin.

Joel, thank you for understanding every time I gazed steadfastly at the computer, mumbling, "Let me just get this scene down before it's gone forever." Often, a hug from you was just what I needed to keep going.

Liam, thank you for all the times you've patted me sympathetically on the shoulder and asked, "How's the book going?" Thank you for only occasionally asking, "Done with the book yet?" Kieran, thank you for inspiring me with your own wonderful books. Your drawings are funny and whimsical, and I adore your six-year-old phonetic spelling with no spaces between the words. I love you both, my beautiful children.

Finally, thank *you*, dear reader! I loved writing *Heiress Apparently*, and I'm grateful to you for joining Gemma on her journey.